MY SISTER'S HAND IN MINE

My Sister's Hand in Mine

AN EXPANDED EDITION OF

THE COLLECTED WORKS OF

JANE BOWLES

With an Introduction by Truman Capote

THE ECCO PRESS

NEW YORK

Published in 1978 by The Ecco Press. Published simultaneously in
Canada by Penguin Books Canada Limited.

The Ecco Press logo by Ahmed Yacoubi.

Library of Congress Cataloging in Publication Data
Bowles, Jane Auer, 1917-1973.
    My sister's hand in mine.
    (Neglected books of the twentieth century; 2)
    Contents: Two serious ladies.—In the summer house.—Plain
pleasures: Plain pleasures. Everything is nice. A Guatemalan idyll.
Camp Cataract. [etc.]
    I. Title. II. Series.
PS3503.O837M9 1977   818'.5'209   77-71329
ISBN 0-912-94644-X

Printed in U.S.A.

· Introduction

It must be seven or eight years since I last saw that modern legend named Jane Bowles; nor have I heard from her, at least not directly. Yet I am sure she is unchanged; indeed, I am told by recent travelers to North Africa who have seen or sat with her in some dim casbah café that this is true, and that Jane, with her dahlia-head of cropped curly hair, her tilted nose and mischief-shiny, just a trifle mad eyes, her very original voice (a husky soprano), her boyish clothes and schoolgirl's figure and slightly limping walk, is more or less the same as when I first knew her more than twenty years ago: even then she had seemed the eternal urchin, appealing as the most appealing of non-adults, yet with some substance cooler than blood invading her veins, and with a wit, an eccentric wisdom no child, not the strangest wunderkind, ever possessed.

When I first met Mrs. Bowles (1944? 1945?) she was already, within certain worlds, a celebrated figure: though only in her

twenties, she had published a most individual and much remarked novel, *Two Serious Ladies;* she had married the gifted
composer and writer Paul Bowles and was, together with her
husband, a tenant in a glamorous boardinghouse established
on Brooklyn Heights by the late George Davis. Among the
Bowles' fellow boarders were Richard and Ellen Wright, W. H.
Auden, Benjamin Britten, Oliver Smith, Carson McCullers,
Gypsy Rose Lee, and (I *seem* to remember) a trainer of chim-
panzees who lived there with one of his star performers. Anyway, it was one hell of a household. But even amid such a
forceful assembly, Mrs. Bowles, by virtue of her talent and the
strange visions it enclosed, and because of her personality's
startling blend of playful-puppy candor and feline sophistica-
tion, remained an imposing, stage-front presence.

Jane Bowles is an authoritative linguist; she speaks, with the
greatest precision, French and Spanish and Arabic—perhaps
this is why the dialogue of her stories sounds, or sounds to me,
as though it has been translated into English from some delightful combination of other tongues. Moreover, these lan-
guages are self-learned, the product of Mrs. Bowles' nomadic
nature: from New York she wandered on to and all over
Europe, traveled away from there and the impending war to
Central America and Mexico, then alighted awhile in the his-
toric ménage on Brooklyn Heights. Since 1947 she has been
almost continuously resident abroad; in Paris or Ceylon, but
largely in Tangiers—in fact, both Jane and Paul Bowles may
now safely be described as permanent Tangerinos, so total has
their adherence become to that steep, shadowy-white seaport.
Tangiers is composed of two mismatching parts, one of them a
dull modern area stuffed with office buildings and tall gloomy
dwellings, and the other a casbah descending through a medie-
val puzzlement of alleys and alcoves and kef-odored, mint-
scented piazzas down to the crawling with sailors, shiphorn-
hollering port. The Bowles have established themselves in both
sectors—have a sterilized, *tout confort* apartment in the newer

quarter, and also a refuge hidden away in the darker Arab neighborhood: a native house that must be one of the city's tiniest habitations—ceilings so low that one has almost literally to move on hands and knees from room to room; but the rooms themselves are like a charming series of postcard-sized Vuillards—Moorish cushions spilling over Moorish-patterned carpets, all cozy as a raspberry tart and illuminated by intricate lanterns and windows that allow the light of sea skies and views that encompass minarets and ships and the blue-washed rooftops of native tenements receding like a ghostly staircase to the clamorous shoreline. Or that is how *I* remember it on the occasion of a single visit made at sunset on an evening, oh, fifteen years ago.

A line from Edith Sitwell: *Jane, Jane, the morning light creaks down again—*. This from a poem I've always liked, without, as so often with the particular author, altogether understanding it. Unless "morning light" is an image signifying memory (?). My own most satisfying memories of Jane Bowles revolve around a month spent in side-by-side rooms in a pleasantly shabby hotel on the rue du Bac during an icy Paris winter—January, 1951. Many a cold evening was spent in Jane's snug room (fat with books and papers and foodstuffs and a snappy white Pekingese puppy bought from a Spanish sailor); long evenings spent listening to a phonograph and drinking warm applejack while Jane built sloppy, marvelous stews atop an electric burner: she is a good cook, yessir, and kind of a glutton, as one might suspect from her stories, which abound in accounts of eating and its artifacts. Cooking is but one of her extracurricular gifts; she is also a spookily accurate mimic and can re-create with nostalgic admiration the voices of certain singers—Helen Morgan, for example, and her close friend Libby Holman. Years afterward I wrote a story called *Among the Paths to Eden,* in which, without realizing it, I attributed to the heroine several of Jane Bowles' characteristics: the stiff-legged limp, her spectacles, her brilliant and poignant abilities as a mimic ("She waited, as though listening for music to cue her; then, *'Don't ever leave me, now that you're here! Here is where you belong. Everything seems so right when you're near, When you're away it's all wrong.'* And Mr. Belli was shocked, for what he was hearing was exactly Helen Morgan's voice, and the voice, with its vulnerable sweetness, refinement, its tender quaver toppling high notes, seemed not to be borrowed, but Mary O'Meaghan's own, a natural expression of some secluded identity"). I did not have Mrs. Bowles in mind when I invented Mary O'Meaghan —a character she in no essential way resembles; but it is a measure of the potent impression Jane has always made on me that some fragment of her should emerge in this manner.

During that winter Jane was working on *In the Summer House,* the play that was later so sensitively produced in New York. I'm not all that keen on the theater: cannot sit through most plays once; nevertheless, I saw *In the Summer House* three times, and not out of loyalty to the author, but because it had a thorny wit, the flavor of a newly tasted, refreshingly bitter beverage—the same qualities that had initially attracted me to Mrs. Bowles' novel, *Two Serious Ladies.*

My only complaint against Mrs. Bowles is not that her work lacks quality, merely quantity. The volume in hand constitutes her entire shelf, so to say. And grateful as we are to have it, one could wish that there was more. Once, while discussing a colleague, someone more facile than either of us, Jane said: "But it's so easy for him. He has only to turn his hand. Just *turn* his hand." Actually, writing is never easy: in case anyone doesn't know, it's the hardest work around; and for Jane I think it is difficult to the point of true pain. And why not?—when both her language and her themes are sought after along tortured paths and in stony quarries: the never-realized relationships between her people, the mental and physical discomforts with which she surrounds and saturates them—every room an atrocity, every urban landscape a crea·

tion of neon-dourness. And yet, though the tragic view is central to her vision, Jane Bowles is a very funny writer, a humorist of sorts—but *not,* by the way, of the Black School. Black Comedy, as its perpetrators label it, is, when successful, all lovely artifice and lacking any hint of compassion. "Camp Cataract," to my mind the most complete of Mrs. Bowles' stories and the one most representative of her work, is a rending sample of controlled compassion: a comic tale of doom that has at its heart, and *as* its heart, the subtlest comprehension of eccentricity and human apartness. This story alone would require that we accord Jane Bowles high esteem.

TRUMAN CAPOTE

July 1966

· Contents

❧ Two Serious Ladies

TO PAUL, MOTHER, AND HELVETIA

Christina Goering's father was an American industrialist of German parentage and her mother was a New York lady of a very distinguished family. Christina spent the first half of her life in a very beautiful house (not more than an hour from the city) which she had inherited from her mother. It was in this house that she had been brought up as a child with her sister Sophie.

As a child Christina had been very much disliked by other children. She had never suffered particularly because of this, having led, even at a very early age, an active inner life that curtailed her observation of whatever went on around her, to such a degree that she never picked up the mannerisms then in vogue, and at the age of ten was called old-fashioned by other little girls. Even then she wore the look of certain fanatics who think of themselves as leaders without once having gained the respect of a single human being.

Christina was troubled horribly by ideas which never would have occurred to her companions, and at the same time took for granted a position in society which any other child would have found unbearable. Every now and then a schoolmate would take pity on her and try to spend some time with her, but far from being grateful for this, Christina would instead try her best to convert her new friend to the cult of whatever she believed in at the time.

Her sister Sophie, on the other hand, was very much admired by everyone in the school. She showed a marked talent for writing poetry and spent all her time with a quiet little girl called Mary, who was two years younger.

When Christina was thirteen years old her hair was very red (when she grew up it remained almost as red), her cheeks were sloppy and pink, and her nose showed traces of nobility.

That year Sophie brought Mary home with her nearly every day for luncheon. After they had finished eating she would take Mary for a walk through the woods, having provided a basket for each of them in which to carry back flowers. Christina was not permitted by Sophie to come along on these walks.

"You must find something of your own to do," Sophie would say to her. But it was hard for Christina to think of anything to do by herself that she enjoyed. She was in the habit of going through many mental struggles—generally of a religious nature—and she preferred to be with other people and organize games. These games, as a rule, were very moral, and often involved God. However, no one else enjoyed them and she was obliged to spend a great part of the day alone. She tried going to the woods once or twice by herself and bringing back flowers, in imitation of Mary and Sophie, but each time, fearing that she would not return with enough flowers to make a beautiful bouquet, she so encumbered herself with baskets that the walk seemed more of a hardship than a pleasure.

It was Christina's desire to have Mary to herself of an afternoon. One very sunny afternoon Sophie went inside for her piano lesson, and Mary remained seated on the grass. Christina, who had seen this from not far away, ran into the house, her heart beating with excitement. She took off her shoes and stockings and remained in a short white underslip. This was not a very pleasant sight to behold, because Christina at this time was very heavy and her legs were quite fat. (It was impossible to foresee that she would turn out to be a tall and elegant lady.) She ran out on the lawn and told Mary to watch her dance.

"Now don't take your eyes off me," she said. "I'm going to do a dance of worship to the sun. Then I'm going to show that I'd rather have God and no sun than the sun and no God. Do you understand?"

"Yes," said Mary. "Are you going to do it now?"

"Yes, I'm going to do it right here." She began the dance abruptly. It was a clumsy dance and her gestures were all undecided. When Sophie came out of the house, Christina was in the act of running backwards and forwards with her hands joined in prayer.

"What is she doing?" Sophie asked Mary.

"A dance to the sun, I think," Mary said. "She told me to sit here and watch her."

Sophie walked over to where Christina was now twirling around and around and shaking her hands weakly in the air.

"Sneak!" she said and suddenly she pushed Christina down on the grass.

For a long time after that, Christina kept away from Sophie, and consequently from Mary. She had one more occasion to be with Mary, however, and this happened because Sophie developed a terrible toothache one morning, and her governess was obliged to take her to the dentist immediately. Mary, not having heard of this, came over in the afternoon, expecting to find Sophie at home. Christina was in the tower in which the children often gathered, and saw her coming up the walk.

"Mary," she screamed, "come on up here." When Mary arrived in the tower, Christina asked her if she would not like to play a very special game with her. "It's called 'I forgive you for all your sins,' " said Christina. "You'll have to take your dress off."

"Is it fun?" Mary asked.

"It's not for fun that we play it, but because it's necessary to play it."

"All right," said Mary, "I'll play with you." She took her dress off and Christina pulled an old burlap sack over Mary's head. She cut two holes in the burlap for Mary to see through and then she tied a cord around her waist.

"Come," said Christina, "and you will be absolved for your sins. Keep repeating to yourself: 'May the Lord forgive me for my sins.' "

She hurried down the stairs with Mary and then out across the lawn towards the woods. Christina wasn't yet sure what she was going to do, but she was very much excited. They came to a stream that skirted the woods. The banks of the stream were soft and muddy.

"Come to the water," said Christina; "I think that's how we'll wash away your sins. You'll have to stand in the mud."

"Near the mud?"

"*In* the mud. Does your sin taste bitter in your mouth? It must."

"Yes," said Mary hesitantly.

"Then you want to be clean and pure as a flower is, don't you?"

Mary did not answer.

"If you don't lie down in the mud and let me pack the mud over you and then wash you in the stream, you'll be forever condemned. Do you want to be forever condemned? This is your moment to decide."

Mary stood beneath her black hood without saying a word.

Christina pushed her down on the ground and started to pack the burlap with mud.

"The mud's cold," said Mary.

"The hell fires are hot," said Christina. "If you let me do this, you won't go to hell."

"Don't take too long," said Mary.

Christina was very much agitated. Her eyes were shining. She packed more and more mud on Mary and then she said to her:

"Now you're ready to be purified in the stream."

"Oh, please no, not the water—I hate to go into the water. I'm afraid of the water."

"Forget what you are afraid of. God's watching you now and He has no sympathy for you yet."

She lifted Mary from the ground and walked into the stream, carrying her. She had forgotten to take off her own shoes and stockings. Her dress was completely covered with mud. Then she submerged Mary's body in the water. Mary was looking at her through the holes in the burlap. It did not occur to her to struggle.

"Three minutes will be enough," said Christina. "I'm going to say a little prayer for you."

"Oh, don't do that," Mary pleaded.

"Of course," said Christina, lifting her eyes to the sky.

"Dear God," she said, "make this girl Mary pure as Jesus Your Son. Wash her sins away as the water is now washing the mud away. This black burlap proves to you that she thinks she is a sinner."

"Oh, stop," whispered Mary. "He can hear you even if you just say it to yourself. You're shouting so."

"The three minutes are over, I believe," said Christina. "Come darling, now you can stand up."

"Let's run to the house," said Mary. "I'm freezing to death."

They ran to the house and up the back stairway that led to

the tower. It was hot in the tower room because all the windows had been shut. Christina suddenly felt very ill.

"Go," she said to Mary, "go into the bath and clean yourself off. I'm going to draw." She was deeply troubled. "It's over," she said to herself, "the game is over. I'll tell Mary to go home after she's dried off. I'll give her some colored pencils to take home with her."

Mary returned from the bath wrapped in a towel. She was still shivering. Her hair was wet and straight. Her face looked smaller than it did ordinarily.

Christina looked away from her. "The game is over," she said, "it took only a few minutes—you should be dried off— I'm going out." She walked out of the room leaving Mary behind, pulling the towel closer around her shoulders.

•

As a grown woman Miss Goering was no better liked than she had been as a child. She was now living in her home outside New York, with her companion, Miss Gamelon.

Three months ago Miss Goering had been sitting in the parlor, looking out at the leafless trees, when her maid announced a caller.

"Is it a gentleman or a lady?" Miss Goering asked.

"A lady."

"Show her in immediately," said Miss Goering.

The maid returned followed by the caller. Miss Goering rose from her seat. "How do you do?" she said. "I don't believe I've ever laid eyes on you before this moment, but please sit down."

The lady visitor was small and stocky and appeared to be in her late thirties or early forties. She wore dark, unfashionable clothing and, but for her large gray eyes, her face might on all occasions have passed unnoticed.

"I'm your governess's cousin," she said to Miss Goering. "She was with you for many years. Do you remember her?"

"I do," said Miss Goering.

"Well, my name is Lucie Gamelon. My cousin used to talk about you and about your sister Sophie all the time. I've been meaning to call on you for years now, but one thing and another always got in the way. But then, we never know it to fail."

Miss Gamelon reddened. She had not yet been relieved of her hat and coat.

"You have a lovely home," she said. "I guess you know it and appreciate it a lot."

By this time Miss Goering was filled with curiosity concerning Miss Gamelon. "What's your business in life?" she asked her.

"Not very much, I'm afraid. I've been typing manuscripts for famous authors all my life, but there doesn't seem to be much demand for authors any more unless maybe they are doing their own typing."

Miss Goering, who was busy thinking, said nothing.

Miss Gamelon looked around helplessly.

"Do you stay here the greater portion of the time or do you travel mostly?" she asked Miss Goering unexpectedly.

"I never thought of traveling," said Miss Goering. "I don't require travel."

"Coming from the family you come from," said Miss Gamelon, "I guess you were born full of knowledge about everything. You wouldn't need to travel. I had opportunity to travel two or three times with my authors. They were willing to pay all my expenses and my full salary besides, but I never did go except once, and that was to Canada."

"You don't like to travel," said Miss Goering, staring at her.

"It doesn't agree with me. I tried it that once. My stomach was upset and I had nervous headaches all the time. That was enough. I had my warning."

"I understand perfectly," said Miss Goering.

"I always believe," continued Miss Gamelon, "that you get

your warning. Some people don't heed their warnings. That's when they come into conflict. I think that anything you feel strange or nervous about, you weren't cut out to do."

"Go on," said Miss Goering.

"Well, I know, for instance, that I wasn't cut out to be an aviator. I've always had dreams of crashing down to the earth. There are quite a few things that I won't do, even if I am thought of as a stubborn mule. I won't cross a big body of water, for instance. I could have everything I wanted if I would just cross the ocean and go over to England, but I never will."

"Well," said Miss Goering, "let's have some tea and some sandwiches."

Miss Gamelon ate voraciously and complimented Miss Goering on her good food.

"I like good things to eat," she said; "I don't have so much good food any more. I did when I was working for the authors."

When they had finished tea, Miss Gamelon took leave of her hostess.

"I've had a very sociable time," she said. "I would like to stay longer, but tonight I have promised a niece of mine that I would watch over her children for her. She is going to attend a ball."

"You must be very depressed with the idea," said Miss Goering.

"Yes, you're right," Miss Gamelon replied.

"Do return soon," said Miss Goering.

The following afternoon the maid announced to Miss Goering that she had a caller. "It's the same lady that called here yesterday," said the maid.

"Well, well," thought Miss Goering, "that's good."

"How are you feeling today?" Miss Gamelon asked her, coming into the room. She spoke very naturally, not appearing to find it strange that she was returning so soon after her first visit. "I was thinking about you all last night," she said. "It's a funny thing. I always thought I should meet you. My cousin used to tell me how queer you were. I think, though, that you can make friends more quickly with queer people. Or else you don't make friends with them at all—one way or the other. Many of my authors were very queer. In that way I've had an advantage of association that most people don't have. I know something about what I call real honest-to-God maniacs, too."

Miss Goering invited Miss Gamelon to dine with her. She found her soothing and agreeable to be with. Miss Gamelon was very much impressed with the fact that Miss Goering was so nervous. Just as they were about to sit down, Miss Goering said that she couldn't face eating in the dining-room and she asked the servant to lay the table in the parlor instead. She spent a great deal of time switching the lights off and on.

"I know how you feel," Miss Gamelon said to her.

"I don't particularly enjoy it," said Miss Goering, "but I expect in the future to be under control."

Over wine at dinner Miss Gamelon told Miss Goering that it was only correct that she should be thus. "What do you expect, dear," she said, "coming from the kind of family you come from? You're all tuned high, all of you. You've got to allow yourself things that other people haven't any right to allow themselves."

Miss Goering began to feel a little tipsy. She looked dreamily at Miss Gamelon, who was eating her second helping of chicken cooked in wine. There was a little spot of grease in the corner of her mouth.

"I love to drink," said Miss Gamelon, "but there isn't much point to it when you have to work. It's fine enough when you have plenty of leisure time. I have a lot of leisure time now."

"Have you a guardian angel?" asked Miss Goering.

"Well, I have a dead aunt, maybe that's what you mean; she might be watching over me."

"That is not what I mean—I mean something quite different."

"Well, of course . . ." said Miss Gamelon.

"A guardian angel comes when you are very young, and gives you special dispensation."

"From what?"

"From the world. Yours might be luck; mine is money. Most people have a guardian angel; that's why they move slowly."

"That's an imaginative way of talking about guardian angels. I guess my guardian angel is what I told you about heeding my warnings. I think maybe she could warn me about both of us. In that way I could keep you out of trouble. Of course, with your consent," she added, looking a little confused.

Miss Goering had a definite feeling at that moment that Miss Gamelon was not in the least a nice woman, but she refused to face this because she got too much enjoyment from the sensation of being nursed and pampered. She told herself that it would do no harm for a little while.

"Miss Gamelon," said Miss Goering, "I think it would be a very fine idea if you were to make this your home—for the time being, at least. I don't think you have any pressing business that would oblige you to remain elsewhere, have you?"

"No, I haven't any business," said Miss Gamelon. "I don't see why I couldn't stay here—I'd have to get my things at my sister's house. Outside of that I don't know of anything else."

"What things?" asked Miss Goering impatiently. "Don't go back at all. We can get things at the stores." She got up and walked quickly up and down the room.

"Well," said Miss Gamelon, "I think I had better get my things."

"But not tonight," said Miss Goering, "tomorrow—tomorrow in the car."

"Tomorrow in the car," repeated Miss Gamelon after her.

Miss Goering made arrangements to give Miss Gamelon a

room near her own, to which she led her shortly after dinner
was over.

"This room," said Miss Goering, "has one of the finest views
in the entire house." She drew the curtains apart. "You've got
your moon and your stars tonight, Miss Gamelon, and a very
nice silhouette of trees against the sky."

Miss Gamelon was standing in semi-darkness near the dress-
ing-table. She was fingering the brooch on her blouse. She
wished that Miss Goering would leave so that she could think
about the house and Miss Goering's offer, in her own way.

There was a sudden scrambling in the bushes below the
window. Miss Goering jumped.

"What's that?" Her face was very white and she put her
hand to her forehead. "My heart hurts so for such a long time
afterwards whenever I'm frightened," she said in a small voice.

"I think I'd better go to bed now and go to sleep," said Miss
Gamelon. She was suddenly overcome by all the wine that she
had drunk. Miss Goering took her leave reluctantly. She had
been prepared to talk half the night. The following morning
Miss Gamelon went home to collect her things and give her
sister her new address.

Three months later Miss Goering knew little more about
Miss Gamelon's ideas than she had on the first night that they
had dined together. She had learned quite a lot about Miss
Gamelon's personal characteristics, however, through careful
observation. When Miss Gamelon had first arrived she had
spoken a great deal about her love of luxury and beautiful
objects, but Miss Goering had since then taken her on innu-
merable shopping trips; and she had never seemed interested
in anything more than the simplest necessities.

She was quiet, even a little sullen, but she seemed to be
fairly contented. She enjoyed dining out at large, expensive
restaurants, particularly if dinner music accompanied the
meal. She did not seem to like the theater. Very often Miss

Goering would buy tickets for a play, and at the last moment Miss Gamelon would decline to go.

"I feel so lazy," she would say, "that bed seems to be the most beautiful thing in the world at this moment."

When she did go to the theater, she was easily bored. Whenever the action of the play was not swift, Miss Goering would catch her looking down into her lap and playing with her fingers.

She seemed now to feel more violently about Miss Goering's activities than she did about her own, although she did not listen so sympathetically to Miss Goering's explanations of herself as she had in the beginning.

On Wednesday afternoon Miss Gamelon and Miss Goering were sitting underneath the trees in front of the house. Miss Goering was drinking whisky and Miss Gamelon was reading. The maid came out and announced to Miss Goering that she was wanted on the telephone.

The call was from Miss Goering's old friend Anna, who invited her to a party the following night. Miss Goering came back out on the lawn, very excited.

"I'm going to a party tomorrow night," she said, "but I don't see how I can wait until then—I look forward to going to parties so much and I am invited to so few that I scarcely know how to behave about them. What will we do to make the hours pass until then?" She took both Miss Gamelon's hands in her own.

It was getting a little chilly. Miss Goering shivered and smiled. "Do you enjoy our little life?" she asked Miss Gamelon.

"I'm always content," said Miss Gamelon, "because I know what to take and what to leave, but you are always at the mercy."

Miss Goering arrived at Anna's looking flushed and a little overdressed. She was wearing velvet and Miss Gamelon had fastened some flowers in her hair.

The men, most of whom were middle-aged, were standing

together in one corner of the room, smoking and listening to each other attentively. The ladies, freshly powdered, were seated around the room, talking very little. Anna seemed to be a little tense, although she was smiling. She wore a hostess gown adapted from a central European peasant costume.

"You will have drinks in a minute," she announced to her guests, and then, seeing Miss Goering, she went over to her and led her to a chair next to Mrs. Copperfield's without saying a word.

Mrs. Copperfield had a sharp little face and very dark hair. She was unusually small and thin. She was nervously rubbing her bare arms and looking around the room when Miss Goering seated herself in the chair beside her. They had met for many years at Anna's parties and they occasionally had tea with each other.

"Oh! Christina Goering," cried Mrs. Copperfield, startled to see her friend suddenly seated beside her, "I'm going away!"

"Do you mean," said Miss Goering, "that you are leaving this party?"

"No, I am going on a trip. Wait until I tell you about it. It's terrible."

Miss Goering noticed that Mrs. Copperfield's eyes were brighter than usual. "What is wrong, little Mrs. Copperfield?" she asked, rising from her seat and looking around the room with a bright smile on her face.

"Oh, I'm sure," said Mrs. Copperfield, "that you wouldn't want to hear about it. You can't possibly have any respect for me, but that doesn't make any difference because I have the utmost respect for you. I heard my husband say that you had a religious nature one day, and we almost had a very bad fight. Of course he is crazy to say that. You are gloriously unpredictable and you are afraid of no one but yourself. I hate religion in other people."

Miss Goering neglected to answer Mrs. Copperfield because for the last second or two she had been staring at a stout dark-haired man who was walking heavily across the room in their direction. As he came nearer, she saw that he had a pleasant face with wide jowls that protruded on either side but did not hang down as they do on most obese persons. He was dressed in a blue business suit.

"May I sit beside you?" he asked them. "I have met this young lady before," he said, shaking hands with Mrs. Copperfield, "but I am afraid that I have not yet met her friend." He turned and nodded to Miss Goering.

Mrs. Copperfield was so annoyed at the interruption that she neglected to introduce Miss Goering to the gentleman. He drew up a chair next to Miss Goering's and looked at her.

"I have just come from a most wonderful dinner," he said to her, "moderate in price, but served with care and excellently prepared. If it would interest you I can write down the name of the little restaurant for you."

He reached into his vest pocket and pulled out a leather billfold. He found only one slip of paper which was not already covered with addresses.

"I will write this down for you," he said to Miss Goering. "Undoubtedly you will be seeing Mrs. Copperfield and then you can pass the information on to her, or perhaps she can telephone to you."

Miss Goering took the slip of paper in her hand and looked carefully at the writing.

He had not written down the name of a restaurant at all; instead he had asked Miss Goering to consent to go home with him later to his apartment. This pleased her greatly as she was usually delighted to stay out as late as possible once she had left her home.

She looked up at the man, whose face was now inscrutable. He sipped his drink with calm, and looked around the room like someone who has finally brought a business conversation to a close. However, there were some sweat beads on his forehead.

Mrs. Copperfield stared at him with distaste, but Miss Goering's face suddenly brightened. "Let me tell you," she said to them, "about a strange experience I had this morning. Sit still, little Mrs. Copperfield, and listen to me." Mrs. Copperfield looked up at Miss Goering and took her friend's hand in her own.

"I stayed in town with my sister Sophie last night," said Miss Goering, "and this morning I was standing in front of the window drinking a cup of coffee. The building next to Sophie's house is being torn down. I believe that they are intending to put an apartment house in its place. It was not only extremely windy this morning, but it was raining intermittently. From my window I could see into the rooms of this building, as the wall opposite me had already been torn down. The rooms were still partially furnished, and I stood looking at them, watching the rain spatter the wallpaper. The wallpaper was flowered and already covered with dark spots, which were growing larger."

"How amusing," said Mrs. Copperfield, "or perhaps it was depressing."

"I finally felt rather sad watching this and I was about to go away when a man came into one of these rooms and, walking deliberately over to the bed, took up a coverlet which he folded under his arm. It was undoubtedly a personal possession which he had neglected to pack and had just now returned to fetch. Then he walked around the room aimlessly for a bit and finally he stood at the very edge of his room looking down into the yard with his arms akimbo. I could see him more clearly now, and I could easily tell that he was an artist. As he stood there, I was increasingly filled with horror, very much as though I were watching a scene in a nightmare."

At this point Miss Goering suddenly stood up.

"Did he jump, Miss Goering?" Mrs. Copperfield asked with feeling.

"No, he remained there for quite a while looking down into

the courtyard with an expression of pleasant curiosity on his face."

"Amazing, Miss Goering," said Mrs. Copperfield. "I do think it's such an interesting story, really, but it has quite scared me out of my wits and I shouldn't enjoy hearing another one like it." She had scarcely finished her sentence when she heard her husband say:

"We will go to Panama and linger there awhile before we penetrate into the interior." Mrs. Copperfield pressed Miss Goering's hand.

"I don't think I can bear it," she said. "Really, Miss Goering, it frightens me so much to go."

"I would go anyway," said Miss Goering.

Mrs. Copperfield jumped off the arm of the chair and ran into the library. She locked the door behind her carefully and then she fell in a little heap on the sofa and sobbed bitterly. When she had stopped crying she powdered her nose, seated herself on the window-sill, and looked down into the dark garden below.

An hour or two later Arnold, the stout man in the blue suit, was still talking to Miss Goering. He suggested to her that they leave the party and go to his own house. "I think that we will have a much nicer time there," he said to her. "There will be less noise and we will be able to talk more freely."

As yet Miss Goering had no desire at all to leave, she enjoyed so much being in a room full of people, but she did not quite know how to get out of accepting his invitation.

- "Certainly," she said, "let's be on our way." They rose and left the room together in silence.

"Don't say anything to Anna about our leaving," Arnold told Miss Goering. "It will only cause a commotion. I promise you I'll send some sweets to her tomorrow, or some flowers." He pressed Miss Goering's hand and smiled at her. She was not sure that she did not find him a bit too familiar.

•

After leaving Anna's party, Arnold walked awhile with Miss
Goering and then hailed a cab. The road to his home led
through many dark and deserted streets. Miss Goering was so
nervous and hysterical about this that Arnold was alarmed.

"I always think," said Miss Goering, "that the driver is only
waiting for the passengers to become absorbed in conversation
in order to shoot down some street, to an inaccessible and
lonely place where he will either torture or murder them. I am
certain that most people feel the same way about it that I do,
but they have the good taste not to mention it."

"Since you live so far out of town," said Arnold, "why don't
you spend the night at my house? We have an extra bedroom."

"I probably shall," said Miss Goering, "although it is against
my entire code, but then, I have never even begun to use my
code, although I judge everything by it." Miss Goering looked
a little morose after having said this and they drove on in silence until they reached their destination.

Arnold's flat was on the second floor. He opened the door
and they walked into a room lined to the ceiling with book-
shelves. The couch had been made up and Arnold's slippers
were lying on the rug beside it. The furniture was heavy and
some small Oriental rugs were scattered here and there.

"I sleep in here," said Arnold, "and my mother and father
occupy the bedroom. We have a small kitchen, but generally
we prefer to eat out. There is another tiny bedroom, originally
intended for a maid's room, but I would rather sleep in here
and let my eye wander from book to book; books are a great
solace to me." He sighed heavily and laid both his hands on
Miss Goering's shoulders. "You see, my dear lady," he said,
"I'm not exactly doing the kind of thing that I would like to
do. . . . I'm in the real-estate business."

"What is it that you would like to do?" asked Miss Goering,
looking weary and indifferent.

"Something, naturally," said Arnold, "in the book line, or in the painting line."

"And you can't?"

"No," said Arnold, "my family doesn't believe that such an occupation is serious, and since I must earn my living and pay for my share of this flat, I have been obliged to accept a post in my uncle's office, where I must say I very quickly have become his prize salesman. In the evenings, however, I have plenty of time to move among people who have nothing to do with real estate. As a matter of fact, they think very little about earning money at all. Naturally, these people are interested in having enough to eat. Even though I am thirty-nine years old I still am hoping very seriously that I will be able to make a definite break with my family. I do not see life through the same pair of eyes that they do. And I feel more and more that my life here with them is becoming insupportable in spite of the fact that I am free to entertain whom I please since I pay for part of the upkeep of the flat."

He sat down on the couch and rubbed his eyes with his hands.

"You'll forgive me, Miss Goering, but I'm feeling very sleepy suddenly. I'm sure the feeling will go away."

Miss Goering's drinks were wearing off and she thought it high time that she got back to Miss Gamelon, but she had not the courage to ride all the way out to her home by herself.

"Well, I suppose this is a great disappointment to you," said Arnold, "but you see I have fallen in love with you. I wanted to bring you here and tell you about my whole life, but now I don't feel like talking about anything."

"Perhaps some other time you'll tell me about your life," said Miss Goering, beginning to walk up and down very quickly. She stopped and turned towards him. "What do you advise me to do?" she asked him. "Do you advise me to go home or stay here?"

Arnold studied his watch. "Stay here by all means," he said.

Just then Arnold's father came in, wearing a lounging-robe and carrying a cup of coffee in his hand. He was very slender and he wore a small pointed beard. He was a more distinguished figure than Arnold.

"Good evening, Arnold," said his father. "Will you introduce me, please, to this young lady?"

Arnold introduced them and then his father asked Miss Goering why she did not take off her cloak.

"As long as you are up so late at night," he said, "and not enjoying the comfort and the security of your own bed, you might as well be at ease. Arnold, my son, never thinks of things like this." He took Miss Goering's cloak off and complimented her on her lovely dress.

"Now tell me where you have been and what you have done. I myself don't go out in society, being content with the company of my wife and son."

Arnold shrugged his shoulders and pretended to look absently around the room. But any person even a little observant could have seen that his face was decidedly hostile.

"Now tell me about this party," said Arnold's father adjusting the scarf that he was wearing around his neck. "*You* tell me." He pointed at Miss Goering, who was beginning to feel much gayer already. She had instantly preferred Arnold's father to Arnold himself.

"I'll tell you about it," said Arnold. "There were many people there, the majority of whom were creative artists, some successful and rich, others rich simply because they had inherited money from some member of the family, and others with just barely enough to eat. None of these people, however, were interested in money as an objective but would have been content, all of them, with just enough to eat."

"Like wild animals," said his father, rising to his feet. "Like wolves! What separates a man from a wolf if it is not that a man wants to make a profit?"

Miss Goering laughed until the tears streamed down her

face. Arnold took some magazines from the table and began looking through them very quickly.

Just then Arnold's mother came into the room carrying in one hand a plate heaped with cakes and in the other a cup of coffee.

She was dowdy and unimpressive and of very much the same build as Arnold. She was wearing a pink wrapper.

"Welcome," said Miss Goering to Arnold's mother. "May I have a piece of your cake?"

Arnold's mother, who was a very gauche woman, did not offer Miss Goering any of the cake; instead, hugging the platter close to her, she said to Miss Goering: "Have you known Arnold for long?"

"No, I met your son tonight, at a party."

"Well," said Arnold's mother, putting the tray down and sitting on the sofa, "I guess that isn't long, is it?"

Arnold's father was annoyed with his wife and showed it plainly in his face.

"I hate that pink wrapper," he said.

"Why do you talk about that now when there is company?"

"Because the company doesn't make the wrapper look any different." He winked broadly at Miss Goering and then burst out laughing. Miss Goering again laughed heartily at his remark. Arnold was even glummer than he had been a moment before.

"Miss Goering," said Arnold, "was afraid to go home alone, so I told her that she was welcome to sleep in the extra room. Although the bed isn't very comfortable in there, I think that she will at least have privacy."

"And *why,*" said Arnold's father, "was Miss Goering afraid to go home alone?"

"Well," said Arnold, "it is not really very safe for a lady to wander about the streets or even to be in a taxi without an escort at so late an hour. Particularly if she has very far to go.

Of course if she hadn't had so far to go I should naturally have
accompanied her myself."

"You sound like a sissy, the way you talk," said his father. "I
thought that you and your friends were not afraid of such
things. I thought you were wild ones and that rape meant no
more to you than flying a balloon."

"Oh, don't talk like that," said Arnold's mother, looking
really horrified. "Why do you talk like that to them?"

"I wish you would go to bed," Arnold's father said. "As a
matter of fact, I am going to order you to go to bed. You are
getting a cold."

"Isn't he terrible?" said Arnold's mother, smiling at Miss
Goering. "Even when there is company in the house he can't
control his lion nature. He *has* a nature like a lion, roaring in
the apartment all day long, and he gets so upset about Arnold
and his friends."

Arnold's father stamped out of the room and they heard a
door slam down the hall.

"Excuse me," said Arnold's mother to Miss Goering, "I
didn't want to upset the party."

Miss Goering was very annoyed, for she found the old man
quite exhilarating, and Arnold himself was depressing her
more and more.

"I think I'll show you where you're going to sleep," said Arnold, getting up from the sofa and in so doing allowing some
magazines to slide from his lap to the floor. "Oh, well," he said,
"come this way. I'm pretty sleepy and disgusted with this
whole affair."

Miss Goering followed Arnold reluctantly down the hall.

"Dear me," she said to Arnold, "I must confess that I am not
sleepy. There is really nothing worse, is there?"

"No, it's dreadful," said Arnold. "I personally am ready to
fall down on the carpet and lie there until tomorrow noon, I
am so completely exhausted."

Miss Goering thought this remark a very inhospitable one and she began to feel a little frightened. Arnold was obliged to search for the key to the spare room, and Miss Goering was left standing alone in front of the door for some time.

"Control yourself," she whispered out loud, for her heart was beginning to beat very quickly. She wondered how she had ever allowed herself to come so far from her house and Miss Gamelon. Arnold returned finally with the key and opened the door to the room.

It was a very small room and much colder than the room in which they had been sitting. Miss Goering expected that Arnold would be extremely embarrassed about this, but although he shivered and rubbed his hands together, he said nothing. There were no curtains at the window, but there was a yellow shade, which had already been pulled down. Miss Goering threw herself down on the bed.

"Well, my dear," said Arnold, "good night. I'm going to bed Maybe we'll go and see some paintings tomorrow, or if you like I'll come out to your house." He put his arms around her neck and kissed her very lightly on the lips and left the room.

She was so angry that there were tears in her eyes. Arnold stood outside of the door for a little while and then after a few minutes he walked away.

Miss Goering went over to the bureau and leaned her head on her hands. She remained in this position for a long time in spite of the fact that she was shivering with the cold. Finally there was a light tap on the door. She stopped crying as abruptly as she had begun and hurried to open the door. She saw Arnold's father standing outside in the badly lighted hall. He was wearing pink striped pajamas and he gave her a brief salute as a greeting. After that he stood very still, waiting apparently for Miss Goering to ask him in.

"Come in, come in," she said to him, "I'm delighted to see you. Heavens! I've had such a feeling of being deserted."

Arnold's father came in and balanced himself on the foot of

Miss Goering's bed, where he sat swinging his legs. He lit his pipe in rather an affected manner and looked around him at the walls of the room.

"Well, lady," he said to her, "are you an artist too?"

"No," said Miss Goering. "I wanted to be a religious leader when I was young and now I just reside in my house and try not to be too unhappy. I have a friend living with me, which makes it easier."

"What do you think of my son?" he asked, winking at her.

"I have only just met him," said Miss Goering.

"You'll discover soon enough," said Arnold's father, "that he's a rather inferior person. He has no conception of what it is to fight. I shouldn't think women would like that very much. As a matter of fact, I don't think Arnold has had many women in his life. If you'll forgive me for passing this information on to you. I myself am used to fighting. I've fought my neighbors all my life instead of sitting down and having tea with them like Arnold. And my neighbors have fought me back like tigers too. Now that's not Arnold's kind of thing. My life's ambition always has been to be a notch higher on the tree than my neighbors and I was willing to admit complete disgrace too when I ended up perching a notch lower than anybody else I knew. I haven't been out in a good many years. Nobody comes to see me and I don't go to see anybody. Now, with Arnold and his friends nothing ever really begins or finishes. They're like fish in dirty water to me. If life don't please them one way and nobody likes them one place, then they go someplace else. They aim to please and be pleased; that's why it's so easy to come and bop them on the head from behind, because they've never done any serious hating in their lives."

"What a strange doctrine!" said Miss Goering.

"This is no doctrine," said Arnold's father. "These are my own ideas, taken from my own personal experience. I'm a great believer in personal experience, aren't you?"

"Oh, yes," said Miss Goering, "and I do think you're right

about Arnold." She felt a curious delight in running down Arnold.

"Now Arnold," continued his father, and he seemed to grow gayer as he talked, "Arnold could never bear to have anyone catch him sitting on the lowest notch. Everyone knows how big your house is, and men who are willing to set their happiness by that are men of iron."

"Arnold is not an artist, anyway," put in Miss Goering.

"No, that is just it," said Arnold's father, getting more and more excited. "That's just it! He hasn't got the brawn nor the nerve nor the perseverance to be a good artist. An artist must have brawn and pluck and character. Arnold is like my wife," he continued. "I married her when she was twenty years old because of certain business interests. Every time I tell her that, she cries. She's another fool. She doesn't love me a bit, but it scares her to think of it, so that she cries. She's green-eyed with jealousy too and she's coiled around her family and her house like a python, although she doesn't have a good time here. Her life, as a matter of fact, is a wretched one, I must admit. Arnold's ashamed of her and I knock her around all day long. But in spite of the fact that she is a timid woman, she is capable of showing a certain amount of violence and brawn. Because she too, like myself, is faithful to one ideal, I suppose."

Just then there was a smart rap on the door. Arnold's father did not say a word, but Miss Goering called out in a clear voice: "Who is it?"

"It's me, Arnold's mother," came the answer. "Please let me in right away."

"Just one moment," said Miss Goering, "and I certainly shall."

"No," said Arnold's father. "Don't open the door. She has no right whatsoever to command anyone to open the door."

"You had better open it," said his wife. "Otherwise, I'll call the police, and I mean that very seriously. I have never threatened to call them before, you know."

"Yes, you did threaten to call them once before," said Arnold's father, looking very worried.

"The way I feel about my life," said Arnold's mother, "I'd just as soon open all the doors and let everyone come in the house and witness my disgrace."

"That's the last thing she'd ever do," said Arnold's father. "She talks like a fool when she's angry."

"I'll let her in," said Miss Goering, walking towards the door. She did not feel very frightened because Arnold's mother, judging from her voice, sounded more as though she was sad than angry. But when Miss Goering opened the door she was surprised to see that, on the contrary, her face was blanched with anger and her eyes were little narrow slits.

"Why do you pretend always to sleep so well?" said Arnold's father. This was the only remark he was able to think of, although he realized himself how inadequate it must have sounded to his wife.

"You're a harlot," said his wife to Miss Goering. Miss Goering was gravely shocked by this remark, and very much to her own amazement, for she had always thought that such things meant nothing to her.

"I am afraid you are entirely on the wrong track," said Miss Goering, "and I believe that some day we shall be great friends."

"I'll thank you to let me choose my own friends," Arnold's mother answered her. "I already have my friends, as a matter of fact, and I don't expect to add any more to my list, and least of all, you."

"Still, you can't tell," said Miss Goering rather weakly backing up a bit, and trying to lean in an easy manner against the bureau. Unfortunately, in calling Miss Goering a harlot Arnold's mother had suggested to her husband the stand that he would take to defend himself.

"How dare you!" he said. "How dare you call anyone that is staying in our house a harlot! You are violating the laws of hospitality to the hundredth degree and I am not going to stand for it."

"Don't bully me," said Arnold's mother. "She's got to go right away this minute or I will make a scandal and you'll be sorry."

"Look, my dear," said Arnold's father to Miss Goering. "Perhaps it would be better if you did go, for your own sake. It is beginning to grow light, so that you needn't be at all frightened."

Arnold's father looked around nervously and then hurried out of the room and down the hall, followed by his wife. Miss Goering heard a door slam and she imagined that they would continue their argument in private.

She herself ran headlong down the hall and out of the house. She found a taxicab after walking a little while and she hadn't been riding more than a few minutes before she fell asleep.

•

On the following day the sun was shining and both Miss Gamelon and Miss Goering were sitting on the lawn arguing. Miss Goering was stretched out on the grass. Miss Gamelon seemed the more discontented of the two. She was frowning and looking over her shoulder at the house, which was behind them. Miss Goering had her eyes shut and there was a faint smile on her face.

"Well," said Miss Gamelon turning around, "you know so little about what you're doing that it's a real crime against society that you have property in your hands. Property should be in the hands of people who like it."

"I think," said Miss Goering, "that I like it more than most people. It gives me a comfortable feeling of safety, as I have explained to you at least a dozen times. However, in order to work out my own little idea of salvation I really believe that it is necessary for me to live in some more tawdry place and particularly in some place where I was not born."

"In my opinion," said Miss Gamelon, "you could perfectly well work out your salvation during certain hours of the day without having to move everything."

"No," said Miss Goering, "that would not be in accordance with the spirit of the age."

Miss Gamelon shifted in her chair.

"The spirit of the age, whatever that is," she said, "I'm sure it can get along beautifully without you—probably would prefer it."

Miss Goering smiled and shook her head.

"The idea," said Miss Goering, "is to change first of our own volition and according to our own inner promptings before they impose completely arbitrary changes on us."

"I have no such promptings," said Miss Gamelon, "and I think you have a colossal nerve to identify yourself with anybody else at all. As a matter of fact, I think that if you leave this house, I shall give you up as a hopeless lunatic. After all, I am not the sort of person that is interested in living with a lunatic, nor is anyone else."

"When I have given you up," said Miss Goering, sitting up and throwing her head back in an exalted manner, "when I have given you up, I shall have given up more than my house, Lucy."

"That's one of your nastinesses," said Miss Gamelon. "It goes in one of my ears and then out the other."

Miss Goering shrugged her shoulders and went inside the house.

She stood for a while in the parlor rearranging some flowers in a bowl and she was just about to go to her room and sleep when Arnold appeared.

"Hello," said Arnold, "I meant to come and see you earlier, but I couldn't quite make it. We had one of those long family lunches. I think flowers look beautiful in this room."

"How is your father?" Miss Goering asked him.

"Oh," said Arnold, "he's all right, I guess. We have very

little to do with each other." Miss Goering noticed that he was sweating again. He had evidently been terribly excited about arriving at her house, because he had forgotten to remove his straw hat.

"This is a really beautiful house," he told her. "It has a quality of past splendor about it that thrills me. You must hate to leave it ever. Well, Father seemed to be quite taken with you. Don't let him get too cocky. He thinks the girls are crazy about him."

"I'm devoted to him," said Miss Goering.

"Well, I hope that the fact that you're devoted to him," said Arnold, "won't interfere with our friendship, because I have decided to see quite a bit of you, providing of course that it is agreeable to you that I do."

"Of course," said Miss Goering, "whenever you like."

"I think that I shall like being here in your home, and you needn't feel that it's a strain. I'm quite happy to sit alone and think, because as you know I'm very anxious to establish myself in some other way than I am now established, which is not satisfactory to me. As you can well imagine, it is even impossible for me to give a dinner party for a few friends because neither Father nor Mother ever stirs from the house unless I do."

Arnold seated himself in a chair by a big bay window and stretched his legs out.

"Come here!" he said to Miss Goering, "and watch the wind rippling through the tops of the trees. There is nothing more lovely in the world." He looked up at her very seriously for a little while.

"Do you have some milk and some bread and marmalade?" he asked her. "I hope there is to be no ceremony between us."

Miss Goering was surprised that Arnold should ask for something to eat so shortly after his luncheon, and she decided that this was undoubtedly the reason why he was so fat.

"Certainly we have," she said sweetly, and she went away to give the servant the order.

Meanwhile Miss Gamelon had decided to come inside and if possible pursue Miss Goering with her argument. When Arnold saw her he realized that she was the companion about whom Miss Goering had spoken the night before.

He rose to his feet immediately, having decided that it was very important for him to make friends with Miss Gamelon.

Miss Gamelon herself was very pleased to see him, as they seldom had company and she enjoyed talking to almost anyone better than to Miss Goering.

They introduced themselves and Arnold pulled up a chair for Miss Gamelon near his own.

"You are Miss Goering's companion," he said to Miss Gamelon. "I think that's lovely."

"Do you think it's lovely?" asked Miss Gamelon. "That's very interesting indeed."

Arnold smiled happily at this remark of Miss Gamelon's and sat on without saying anything for a little while.

"This house is done in exquisite taste," he said finally, "and it is filled with rest and peace."

"It all depends on how you look at it," said Miss Gamelon quickly, jerking her head around and looking out of the window.

"There are certain people," she said, "who turn peace from the door as though it were a red dragon breathing fire out of its nostrils and there are certain people who won't leave God alone either."

Arnold leaned forward trying to appear deferential and interested at the same time.

"I think," he said gravely, "I think I understand what you mean to say."

Then they both looked out of the window at the same time and they saw Miss Goering in the distance wearing a cape over her shoulders and talking to a young man whom they were scarcely able to distinguish because he was directly against the sun.

"That's the agent," said Miss Gamelon. "I suppose there is nothing to look forward to from now on."

"What agent?" asked Arnold.

"The agent through whom she's going to sell her house," said Miss Gamelon. "Isn't it all too dreadful for words?"

"Oh, I'm sorry," said Arnold. "I think it's very foolish of her, but I suppose it's not my affair."

"We're going to live," added Miss Gamelon, "in a four-room frame house and do our own cooking. It's to be in the country surrounded by woods."

"That does sound gloomy, doesn't it?" said Arnold. "But why should Miss Goering have decided to do such a thing?"

"She says it is only a beginning in a tremendous scheme."

Arnold seemed to be very sad. He no longer spoke to Miss Gamelon but merely pursed his lips and looked at the ceiling.

"I suppose the most important thing in the world," he said at length, "is friendship and understanding." He looked at Miss Gamelon questioningly. He seemed to have given up something.

"Well, Miss Gamelon," he said again, "do you not agree with me that friendship and understanding are the most important things in the world?"

"Yes," said Miss Gamelon, "and keeping your head is, too."

Soon Miss Goering came in with a batch of papers under her arm.

"These," she said, "are the contracts. My, they are lengthy, but I think the agent is a sweet man. He said he thought this house was lovely." She held out the contracts first to Arnold and then to Miss Gamelon.

"I should think," said Miss Gamelon, "that you would be afraid to look in the mirror for fear of seeing something too wild and peculiar. I don't want to have to look at these contracts. Please take them off my lap right away. Jesus God Almighty!"

Miss Goering, as a matter of fact, did look a little wild, and Miss Gamelon with a wary eye had noticed immediately that the hand in which she held the contracts was trembling.

"Where is your little house, Miss Goering?" Arnold asked her, trying to introduce a more natural note into the conversation.

"It's on an island," said Miss Goering, "not far from the city by ferryboat. I remember having visited this island as a child and always having disliked it because one can smell the glue factories from the mainland even when walking through the woods or across the fields. One end of the island is very well populated, although you can only buy third-rate goods in any of the stores. Farther out the island is wilder and more old-fashioned; nevertheless there is a little train that meets the ferry frequently and carries you out to the other end. There you land in a little town that is quite lost and looks very tough, and you feel a bit frightened, I think, to find that the mainland opposite the point is as squalid as the island itself and offers you no protection at all."

"You seem to have looked the situation over very carefully and from every angle," said Miss Gamelon. "My compliments to you!" She waved at Miss Goering from her seat, but one could easily see that she was not feeling frivolous in the least.

Arnold shifted about uneasily in his chair. He coughed and then he spoke very gently to Miss Goering.

"I am sure that the island has certain advantages too, which you know about, but perhaps you prefer to surprise us with them rather than disappoint us."

"I know of none at the moment," said Miss Goering. "Why, are you coming with us?"

"I think that I would like to spend quite a bit of time with you out there; that is, if you will invite me."

Arnold was sad and uneasy, but he felt that he must at any

cost remain close to Miss Goering in whatever world she chose to move.

"If you will invite me," he said again, "I will be glad to come out with you for a little while anyway and we will see how it goes. I could continue to keep up my end of the apartment that I share with my parents without having to spend all my time there. But I don't advise you to sell your beautiful house; rather rent it or board it up while you are away. Certainly you might have a change of heart and want to return to it."

Miss Gamelon flushed with pleasure.

"That would be too human a thing for her to consider doing," she said, but she looked a little more hopeful.

Miss Goering seemed to be dreaming and not listening to what either of them was saying.

"Well," said Miss Gamelon, "aren't you going to answer him? He said: why not board your house up or rent it and then if you have a change of heart you can return to it."

"Oh, no," said Miss Goering. "Thank you very much, but I couldn't do that. It wouldn't make much sense to do that."

Arnold coughed to hide his embarrassment at having suggested something so obviously displeasing to Miss Goering.

"I mustn't," he said to himself, "I mustn't align myself too much on the side of Miss Gamelon, or Miss Goering will begin to think that my mind is of the same caliber."

"Perhaps it is better after all," he said aloud, "to sell everything."

· 2

Mr. and Mrs. Copperfield stood on the foredeck of the boat as it sailed into the harbor at Panama. Mrs. Copperfield was very glad to see land at last.

"You must admit now," she said to Mr. Copperfield, "that the land is nicer than the sea." She herself had a great fear of drowning.

"It isn't only being afraid of the sea," she continued, "but it's boring. It's the same thing all the time. The colors are beautiful, of course."

Mr. Copperfield was studying the shore line.

"If you stand still and look between the buildings on the docks," he said, "you'll be able to catch a glimpse of some green trains loaded with bananas. They seem to go by every quarter of an hour."

His wife did not answer him; instead she put on the sun-helmet which she had been carrying in her hand.

"Aren't you beginning to feel the heat already? I am," she said to him at last. As she received no answer she moved along the rail and looked down at the water.

Presently a stout woman whose acquaintance she had made on the boat came up to talk with her. Mrs. Copperfield brightened.

"You've had your hair marcelled!" she said. The woman smiled.

"Now remember," she said to Mrs. Copperfield, "the minute you get to your hotel, stretch yourself out and rest. Don't let them drag you through the streets, no matter what kind of a wild time they promise you. Nothing but monkeys in the streets anyway. There isn't a fine-looking person in the whole town that isn't connected with the American Army, and the Americans stick pretty much in their own quarter. The American quarter is called Cristobal. It's separated from Colon. Colon is full of nothing but half-breeds and monkeys. Cristobal is nice. Everyone in Cristobal has got his own little screened-in porch. They'd never dream of screening themselves in, the monkeys in Colon. They don't know when a mosquito's biting them anyway, and even if they did know they wouldn't lift their arm up to shoo him off. Eat plenty of fruit and be careful of the stores. Most of them are owned by Hindus. They're just like Jews, you know. They'll gyp you right and left."

"I'm not interested in buying anything," said Mrs. Copperfield, "but may I come and visit you while I'm in Colon?"

"I love you, dear," answered the woman, "but I like to spend every minute with my boy while I'm here."

"That's all right," said Mrs. Copperfield.

"Of course it's all right. You've got that beautiful husband of yours."

"That doesn't help," said Mrs. Copperfield, but no sooner had she said this than she was horrified at herself.

"Well now, you've had a tussle?" said the woman.

"No."

"Then I think you're a terrible little woman talking that way about your husband," she said, walking away. Mrs. Copperfield hung her head and went back to stand beside Mr. Copperfield.

"Why do you speak to such dopes?" he asked.

She did not answer.

"Well," he said, "for Heaven's sake, look at the scenery now, will you?"

They got into a taxicab and Mr. Copperfield insisted on going to a hotel right in the center of town. Normally all tourists with even a small amount of money stayed at the Hotel Washington, overlooking the sea, a few miles out of Colon.

"I don't believe," Mr. Copperfield said to his wife, "I don't believe in spending money on a luxury that can only be mine for a week at the most. I think it's more fun to buy objects which will last me perhaps a lifetime. We can certainly find a hotel in the town that will be comfortable. Then we will be free to spend our money on more exciting things."

"The room in which I sleep is so important to me," Mrs. Copperfield said. She was nearly moaning.

"My dear, a room is really only a place in which to sleep and dress. If it is quiet and the bed is comfortable, nothing more is necessary. Don't you agree with me?"

"You know very well I don't agree with you."

"If you are going to be miserable, we'll go to the Hotel Washington," said Mr. Copperfield. Suddenly he lost his dignity. His eyes clouded over and he pouted. "But I'll be wretched there, I can assure you. It's going to be so God-damned dull." He was like a baby and Mrs. Copperfield was obliged to comfort him. He had a trick way of making her feel responsible.

"After all, it's mostly my money," she said to herself. "I'm footing the bulk of the expenditures for this trip." Nevertheless, she was unable to gain a sense of power by reminding herself of this. She was completely dominated by Mr. Copperfield, as she was by almost anyone with whom she came in contact. Still, certain people who knew her well affirmed that she was capable of suddenly making a very radical and independent move without a soul to back her up.

She looked out the window of the taxicab and she noticed that there was a terrific amount of activity going on around her in the streets. The people, for the most part Negroes and uniformed men from the fleets of all nations, were running in and out and making so much noise that Mrs. Copperfield wondered if it was not a holiday of some kind.

"It's like a city that is being constantly looted," said her husband.

The houses were painted in bright colors and they had wide porches on the upper floors, supported beneath by long wooden posts. Thus they formed a kind of arcade to shade the people walking in the street.

"This architecture is ingenious," remarked Mr. Copperfield. "The streets would be unbearable if one had to walk along them with nothing overhead."

"You could not stand that, mister," said the cab-driver, "to walk along with nothing over your head."

"Anyway," said Mrs. Copperfield, "do let's choose one of these hotels quickly and get into it."

They found one right in the heart of the red-light district and agreed to look at some rooms on the fifth floor. The manager had told them that these were sure to be the least noisy. Mrs. Copperfield, who was afraid of lifts, decided to go up the stairs on foot and wait for her husband to arrive with the luggage. Having climbed to the fifth floor, she was surprised to find that the main hall contained at least a hundred straight-backed dining-room chairs and nothing more. As she looked around, her anger mounted and she could barely wait for Mr. Copperfield to arrive on the lift in order to tell him what she thought of him. "I must get to the Hotel Washington," she said to herself.

Mr. Copperfield finally arrived, walking beside a boy with the luggage. She ran up to him.

"It's the ugliest thing I've ever seen," she said.

"Wait a second, please, and let me count the luggage; I want to make sure it's all here."

"As far as I'm concerned, it could be at the bottom of the sea—all of it."

"Where's my typewriter?" asked Mr. Copperfield.

"Talk to me this minute," said his wife, beside herself with anger.

"Do you care whether or not you have a private bath?" asked Mr. Copperfield.

"No, no. I don't care about that. It's not a question of comfort at all. It's something much more than that."

Mr. Copperfield chuckled. "You're so crazy," he said to her with indulgence. He was delighted to be in the tropics at last and he was more than pleased with himself that he had managed to dissuade his wife from stopping at a ridiculously expensive hotel where they would have been surrounded by tourists. He realized that this hotel was sinister, but that was what he loved.

They followed the bellhop to one of the rooms, and no sooner had they arrived there than Mrs. Copperfield began pushing the door backwards and forwards. It opened both ways and could only be locked by means of a little hook.

"Anyone could break into this room," said Mrs. Copperfield.

"I dare say they could, but I don't think they would be very likely to, do you?" Mr. Copperfield made a point of never reassuring his wife. He gave her fears their just due. However, he did not insist, and they decided upon another room, with a stronger door.

•

Mrs. Copperfield was amazed at her husband's vivacity. He had washed and gone out to buy a papaya.

She lay on the bed thinking.

"Now," she said to herself, "when people believed in God they carried Him from one place to another. They carried Him through the jungles and across the Arctic Circle. God watched over everybody, and all men were brothers. Now there is nothing to carry with you from one place to another, and as far as I'm concerned, these people might as well be kangaroos; yet somehow there must be someone here who will remind me of something . . . I must try to find a nest in this outlandish place."

Mrs. Copperfield's sole object in life was to be happy, although people who had observed her behavior over a period of years would have been surprised to discover that this was all.

She rose from her bed and pulled Miss Goering's present, a manicuring set, from her grip. "Memory," she whispered. "Memory of the things I have loved since I was a child. My husband is a man without memory." She felt intense pain at the thought of this man whom she liked above all other people, this man for whom each thing he had not yet known was a joy. For her, all that which was not already an old dream was an outrage. She got back on her bed and fell sound asleep.

When she awoke, Mr. Copperfield was standing near the foot of the bed eating a papaya.

"You must try some," he said. "It gives you lots of energy and besides it's delicious. Won't you have some?" He looked at her shyly.

"Where have you been?" she asked him.

"Oh, walking through the streets. As a matter of fact, I've walked for miles. You should come out, really. It's a madhouse. The streets are full of soldiers and sailors and whores. The

women are all in long dresses . . . incredibly cheap dresses.
They'll all talk to you. Come on out."

•

They were walking through the streets arm in arm. Mrs. Copperfield's forehead was burning hot and her hands were cold.
She felt something trembling in the pit of her stomach. When
she looked ahead of her the very end of the street seemed to
bend and then straighten out again. She told this to Mr. Copperfield and he explained that it was a result of their having so
recently come off the boat. Above their heads the children were
jumping up and down on the wooden porches and making the
houses shake. Someone bumped against Mrs. Copperfield's
shoulder and she was almost knocked over. At the same time
she was very much aware of the strong and fragrant odor of
rose perfume. The person who had collided with her was a Negress in a pink silk evening dress.

"I can't tell you how sorry I am. I can't tell you," she said to
them. Then she looked around her vaguely and began to hum.

"I told you it was a madhouse," Mr. Copperfield said to his
wife.

"Listen," said the Negress, "go down the next street and
you'll like it better. I've got to meet my beau over at that bar."
She pointed it out to them. "That's a beautiful barroom.
Everyone goes in there," she said. She moved up closer and
addressed herself solely to Mrs. Copperfield. "You come along
with me, darling, and you'll have the happiest time you've ever
had before. I'll be your type. Come on."

She took Mrs. Copperfield's hand in her own and started to
drag her away from Mr. Copperfield. She was bigger than
either of them.

"I don't believe that she wants to go to a bar just now," said
Mr. Copperfield. "We'd like to explore the town awhile first."

The Negress caressed Mrs. Copperfield's face with the palm

of her hand. "Is that what you want to do, darling, or do you want to come along with me?" A policeman stopped and stood a few feet away from them. The Negress released Mrs. Copperfield's hand and bounded across the street laughing.

"Wasn't that the strangest thing you've ever seen?" said Mrs. Copperfield, breathlessly.

"You better mind your own business," said the policeman. "Why don't you go over and look at the stores? Everybody walks along the streets where the stores are. Buy something for your uncle or your cousin."

"No, that's not what I want to do," said Mrs. Copperfield.

"Well, then, go to a movie," said the policeman, walking away.

Mr. Copperfield was hysterical with laughter. He had his handkerchief up to his mouth. "This is the sort of thing I love," he managed to say. They walked along farther and turned down another street. The sun was setting and the air was still and hot. On this street there were no balconies, only little one-story houses. In front of every door at least one woman was seated. Mrs. Copperfield walked up to the window of one house and looked in. The room inside was almost entirely filled by a large double bed with an extremely bumpy mattress over which was spread a lace throw. An electric bulb under a lavender chiffon lamp shade threw a garish light over the bed, and there was a fan stamped *Panama City* spread open on the pillow.

The woman seated in front of this particular house was rather old. She sat on a stool with her elbows resting on her knees, and it seemed to Mrs. Copperfield, who had now turned to look at her, that she was probably a West Indian type. She was flat-chested and raw-boned, with very muscular arms and shoulders. Her long disgruntled-looking face and part of her neck were carefully covered with a light-colored face powder, but her chest and arms remained dark. Mrs. Copperfield was amused to see that her dress was of lavender theatrical gauze. There was an attractive gray streak in her hair.

The Negress turned around, and when she saw that both Mr. and Mrs. Copperfield were watching her, she stood up and smoothed the folds of her dress. She was almost a giantess.

"Both of you for a dollar," she said.

"A dollar," Mrs. Copperfield repeated after her. Mr. Copperfield, who had been standing nearby at the curb, came closer to them.

"Frieda," he said, "let's walk down some more streets."

"Oh, please!" said Mrs. Copperfield. "Wait a minute."

"A dollar is the best price I can make," said the Negress.

"If you care to stay here," suggested Mr. Copperfield, "I'll walk around a bit and come back for you in a little while. Maybe you'd better have some money with you. Here is a dollar and thirty-five cents, just in case. . . ."

"I want to talk to her," said Mrs. Copperfield, looking fixedly into space.

"I'll see you, then, in a few minutes. I'm restless," he announced, and he walked away.

"I love to be free," Mrs. Copperfield said to the woman after he had left. "Shall we go into your little room? I've been admiring it through the window. . . ."

Before she had finished her phrase the woman was pushing her through the door with both hands and they were inside the room. There was no rug on the floor, and the walls were bare. The only adornments were those which had been visible from the street. They sat down on the bed.

"I had a little gramophone in that corner over there," said the woman. "Someone who came off a ship lent it to me. His friend came and took it back."

"Te-ta-ta-tee-ta-ta," she said and tapped her heels for a few seconds. She took both Mrs. Copperfield's hands in her own and pulled her off the bed. "Come on now, honey." She hugged Mrs. Copperfield to her. "You're awful little and very sweet. You *are* sweet, and maybe you are lonesome." Mrs. Copperfield put her cheek on the woman's breast. The smell of the theatrical gauze reminded her of her first part in a school play. She smiled up at the Negress, looking as tender and as gentle as she was able.

"What do you do in the afternoons?" she asked the woman.

"Play cards. Go to a movie. . . ."

Mrs. Copperfield stepped away from her. Her cheeks were flamed-red. They both listened to the people walking by. They could now hear every word that was being said outside the window. The Negress was frowning. She wore a look of deep concern.

"Time is gold, honey," she said to Mrs. Copperfield, "but maybe you're too young to realize that."

Mrs. Copperfield shook her head. She felt sad, looking at the Negress. "I'm thirsty," she said. Suddenly they heard a man's voice saying:

"You didn't expect to see me back so soon, Podie?" Then several girls laughed hysterically. The Negress's eyes came to life.

"Give me one dollar! Give me one dollar!" she screamed excitedly at Mrs. Copperfield. "You have stayed your time here anyway." Mrs. Copperfield hurriedly gave her a dollar and the Negress rushed out into the street. Mrs. Copperfield followed her.

In front of the house several girls were hanging onto a heavy man who was wearing a crushed linen suit. When he saw Mrs. Copperfield's Negress in the lavender dress, he broke away from the others and put his arms around her. The Negress rolled her eyes joyously and led him into the house without so much as nodding good-by to Mrs. Copperfield. Very shortly the others ran down the street and Mrs. Copperfield was left alone. People passed by on either side of her, but none of them interested her yet. On the other hand, she herself was of great interest to everyone, particularly to those women who were seated in front of their doors. She was soon accosted by a girl with fuzzy hair.

"Buy me something, Momma," said the girl.

As Mrs. Copperfield did not answer but simply gave the girl a long sad look, the girl said:

"Momma, you can pick it out yourself. You can buy me even a feather, I don't care." Mrs. Copperfield shuddered. She thought she must be dreaming.

"What do you mean, a feather? What do you mean?"

The girl squirmed with delight.

"Oh, Momma," she said in a voice which broke in her throat. "Oh, Momma, you're funny! You're so funny! I don't know what is a feather, but anything you want with your heart, you know."

They walked down the street to a store and came out with a little box of face powder. The girl said good-by and disappeared round the corner with some friends. Once again Mrs. Copperfield was alone. The hacks went past filled with tourists. "Tourists, generally speaking," Mrs. Copperfield had written in her journal, "are human beings so impressed with the importance and immutability of their own manner of living that they are capable of traveling through the most fantastic places without experiencing anything more than a visual reaction. The hardier tourists find that one place resembles another."

Very soon Mr. Copperfield came back and joined her. "Did you have a wonderful time?" he asked her.

She shook her head and looked up at him. Suddenly she felt so tired that she began to cry.

"Cry-baby," said Mr. Copperfield.

Someone came up behind them. A low voice said: "She was lost?" They turned around to see an intelligent-looking girl with sharp features and curly hair standing right behind them. "I wouldn't leave her in the streets here if I were you," she said.

"She wasn't lost; she was just depressed," Mr. Copperfield explained.

"Would you think I was fresh if I asked you to come to a nice restaurant where we can all eat dinner?" asked the girl. She was really quite pretty.

"Let's go," said Mrs. Copperfield vehemently. "By all means." She was now excited; she had a feeling that this girl would be all right. Like most people, she never really believed that one terrible thing would happen after another.

The restaurant wasn't really nice. It was very dark and very long and there was no one in it at all.

"Wouldn't you rather eat somewhere else?" Mrs. Copperfield asked the girl.

"Oh no! I would never go anywhere else. I'll tell you if you are not angry. I can get a little bit of money here when I come and bring some people."

"Well, let me give you the money and we'll go somewhere else. "I'll give you whatever he gives you," said Mrs. Copperfield.

"That's silly," said the girl. "That's very silly."

"I have heard there is a place in this city where we can order wonderful lobster. Couldn't we go there?" Mrs. Copperfield was pleading with the girl now.

"No—that's silly." She called a waiter who had just arrived with some newspapers under his arm.

"Adalberto, bring us some meat and some wine. Meat first." This she said in Spanish.

"How well you speak English!" said Mr. Copperfield.

"I always love to be with Americans when I can," said the girl.

"Do you think they're generous?" asked Mr. Copperfield.

"Oh, sure," said the girl. "Sure they're generous. They're generous when they have the money. They're even more generous when they've got their family with them. I once knew a

man. He was an American man. A real one, and he was staying
at the Hotel Washington. You know that's the most beautiful
hotel in the world. In the afternoon every day his wife would
take a siesta. He would come quickly in a taxicab to Colon and
he was so excited and frightened that he would not get back to
his wife on time that he would never take me into a room and
so he would go with me instead to a store and he would say to
me: 'Quick, quick—pick something—anything that you want,
but be in a hurry about it."

"How terrifying!" said Mrs. Copperfield.

"It was terrible," said the Spanish girl. "I always went so
crazy that once I was really crazy and I said to him: 'All right, I
will buy this pipe for my uncle.' I don't like my uncle, but I
had to give it to him."

Mr. Copperfield roared with laughter.

"Funny, isn't it?" said the girl. "I tell you if he ever comes
back I will never buy another pipe for my uncle when he takes
me to the store. She's not a bad-looker."

"Who?" asked Mr. Copperfield.

"Your wife."

"I look terrible tonight," said Mrs. Copperfield.

"Anyway it does not matter because you are married. You
have nothing to worry about."

"She'll be furious with you if you tell her that," said Mr.
Copperfield.

"Why will she be furious? That is the most beautiful thing
in the whole world, not to have something to worry about."

"That is not what beauty is made of," interposed Mrs. Copperfield. "What has the absence of worry to do with beauty?"

"That has everything to do with what is beautiful in the
world. When you wake up in the morning and the first minute
you open your eyes and you don't know who you are or what
your life has been—that is beautiful. Then when you know
who you are and what day in your life it is and you still think

you are sailing in the air like a happy bird—that is beautiful. That is, when you don't have any worries. You can't tell me you like to worry."

Mr. Copperfield simpered. After dinner he suddenly felt very tired and he suggested that they go home, but Mrs. Copperfield was much too nervous, so she asked the Spanish girl if she would not consent to spend a little more time in her company. The girl said that she would if Mrs. Copperfield did not mind returning with her to the hotel where she lived.

They said good-by to Mr. Copperfield and started on their way.

The walls of the Hotel de las Palmas were wooden and painted a bright green. There were a good many bird-cages standing in the halls and hanging from the ceilings. Some of them were empty. The girl's room was on the second floor and had brightly painted wooden walls the same as the corridors.

"Those birds sing all day long," said the girl, motioning to Mrs. Copperfield to sit down on the bed beside her. "Sometimes I say to myself: 'Little fools, what are you singing about in your cages?' And then I think: 'Pacifica, you are just as much a fool as those birds. You are also in a cage because you don't have any money. Last night you were laughing for three hours with a German man because he had given you some drinks. And you thought he was stupid.' I laugh in my cage and they sing in their cage."

"Oh well," said Mrs. Copperfield, "there really is no rapport between ourselves and birds."

"You don't think it is true?" asked Pacifica with feeling. "I tell you it is true."

She pulled her dress over her head and stood before Mrs. Copperfield in her underslip.

"Tell me," she said, "What do you think of those beautiful silk kimonos that the Hindu men sell in their shops? If I were with such a rich husband I would tell him to buy me one of those kimonos. You don't know how lucky you are. I would go

with him every day to the stores and make him buy me pretty
things instead of standing around and crying like a little baby.
Men don't like to see women cry. You think they like to see
women cry?"

Mrs. Copperfield shrugged her shoulders. "I can't think,"
she said.

"You're right. They like to see women laugh. Women have
got to laugh all night. You watch some pretty girl one time.
When she laughs she is ten years older. That is because she
does it so much. You are ten years older when you laugh."

"True," said Mrs. Copperfield.

"Don't feel bad," said Pacifica. "I like women very much. I
like women sometimes better than men. I like my grandmother
and my mother and my sisters. We always had a good time together, the women in my house. I was always the best one. I
was the smartest one and the one who did the most work. Now
I wish I was back there in my nice house, contented. But I still
want too many things, you know. I am lazy but I have a terrible temper too. I like these men that I meet very much.
Sometimes they tell me what they will do in their future life
when they get off the boat. I always wish for them that it will
happen very soon. The damn boats. When they tell me they
just want to go around the world all their life on a boat I tell
them: 'You don't know what you're missing. I'm through with
you, boy.' I don't like them when they are like that. But now I
am in love with this nice man who is here in business. Most of
the time he can pay my rent for me. Not always every week. He
is very happy to have me. Most of the men are very happy to
have me. I don't hold my head too high for that. It's from God
that it comes." Pacifica crossed herself.

"I once was in love with an older woman," said Mrs. Copperfield eagerly. "She was no longer beautiful, but in her face I
found fragments of beauty which were much more exciting to
me than any beauty that I have known at its height. But who
hasn't loved an older person? Good Lord!"

"You like things which are not what other people like, don't you? I would like to have this experience of loving an older woman. I think that is sweet, but I really am always in love with some nice man. It is lucky for me, I think. Some of the girls, they can't fall in love any more. They only think of money, money, money. You don't think so much about money, do you?" She asked Mrs. Copperfield.

"No, I don't."

"Now we rest a little while, yes?" The girl lay down on the bed and motioned to Mrs. Copperfield to lie down beside her. She yawned, folded Mrs. Copperfield's hand in her own, and fell asleep almost instantly. Mrs. Copperfield thought that she might as well get some sleep too. At that moment she felt very peaceful.

They were awakened by a terrific knocking at the door. Mrs. Copperfield opened her eyes and in a second she was a prey to the most overwhelming terror. She looked at Pacifica, and her friend's face was not very much more reassuring than her own.

"Callate!" she whispered to Mrs. Copperfield reverting to her native tongue.

"What is it? What is it?" asked Mrs. Copperfield in a harsh voice. "I don't understand Spanish."

"Don't say a word," repeated Pacifica in English.

"I can't lie here without saying a word. I know I can't. What is it?"

"Drunken man. In love with me. I know him well. He hurt me very bad when I sleep with him. His boat has come in again."

The knocking grew more insistent and they heard a man's voice saying:

"I know you are there, Pacifica, so open the bloody door."

"Oh, open it, Pacifica!" pleaded Mrs. Copperfield, jumping up from the bed. "Nothing could be worse than this suspense."

"Don't be crazy. Maybe he is drunk enough and he will go away."

Mrs. Copperfield's eyes were glazed. She was becoming hysterical.

"No, no—I have always promised myself that I would open the door if someone was trying to break in. He will be less of an enemy then. The longer he stays out there, the angrier he will get. The first thing I will say to him when I open the door is: 'We are your friends,' and then perhaps he will be less angry."

"If you make me even more crazy than I am I don't know what to do," said Pacifica. "Now we just wait here and see if he goes away. We might move this bureau against the door. Will you help me move it against the door?"

"I can't push anything!" Mrs. Copperfield was so weak that she slid along the wall onto the floor.

"Have I got to break the God-damned door in?" the man was saying.

Mrs. Copperfield rose to her feet, staggered over to the door, and opened it.

The man who came in was hatchet-faced and very tall. He had obviously had a great deal to drink.

"Hello, Meyer," said Pacifica. "Can't you let me get some sleep?" She hesitated a minute, and as he did not answer her she said again: "I was trying to get some sleep."

"I was tight asleep," said Mrs. Copperfield. Her voice was higher than usual and her face was very bright. "I am sorry we did not hear you right away. We must have kept you waiting a long time."

"Nobody ever kept me waiting a long time," said Meyer, getting redder in the face. Pacifica's eyes were narrowing. She was beginning to lose her temper.

"Get out of my room," she said to Meyer.

In answer to this, Meyer fell diagonally across the bed, and the impact of his body was so great that it almost broke the slats.

"Let's get out of here quickly," said Mrs. Copperfield to Pacifica. She was no longer able to show any composure. For one moment she had hoped that the enemy would suddenly burst into tears as they do sometimes in dreams, but now she was convinced that this would not happen. Pacifica was growing more and more furious.

"Listen to me, Meyer," she was saying. "You go back into the street right away. Because I'm not going to do anything with you except hit you in the nose if you don't go away. If you were not such hot stuff we could sit downstairs together and drink a glass of rum. I have hundreds of boy friends who just like to talk to me and drink with me until they are stiffs under the table. But you always try to bother me. You are like an ape-man. I want to be quiet."

"Who the hell cares about your house!" Meyer bellowed at her. "I could put all your houses together in a row and shoot at them like they were ducks. A boat's better than a house any day! Any time! Come rain, come shine! Come the end of the world!"

"No one is talking about houses except you," said Pacifica, stamping her foot, "and I don't want to listen to your foolish talk."

"Why did you lock the door, then, if you weren't living in this house like you were duchesses having tea together, and praying that none of us were ever going to come on shore again. You were afraid I'd spoil the furniture and spill something on the floor. My mother had a house, but I always slept in the house next door to her house. That's how much I care about houses!"

"You misunderstand," said Mrs. Copperfield in a trembling voice. She wanted very much to remind him gently that this was not a house but a room in a hotel. However, she felt not only afraid but ashamed to make this remark.

"Jesus Christ, I'm disgusted," Pacifica said to Mrs. Copperfield without even bothering to lower her voice.

Meyer did not seem to hear this, but instead he leaned over the edge of the bed with a smile on his face and stretched one arm towards Pacifica. He managed to get hold of the hem of her slip and pull her towards him.

"Not as long as I live!" Pacifica screamed at him, but he had already wrapped his arms around her waist and he was kneeling on the bed, pulling her towards him.

"Housekeeper," he said, laughing, "I'll bet if I took you out to sea you'd vomit. You'd mess up the boat. Now lie down here and stop talking."

Pacifica looked darkly at Mrs. Copperfield for a moment. "Well then," she said, "give me first the money, because I don't trust you. I will sleep with you only for my rent."

He dealt her a terrific blow on the mouth and split her lip. The blood started to run down her chin.

Mrs. Copperfield rushed out of the room. "I'll get help, Pacifica," she yelled over her shoulder. She ran down the hall and down the stairs, hoping to find someone to whom she could report Pacifica's plight, but she knew she would not have the courage to approach any men. On the ground floor she caught sight of a middle-aged woman who was knitting in her room with the door ajar, Mrs. Copperfield rushed in to her.

"Do you know Pacifica?" she gasped.

"Certainly I know Pacifica," said the woman. She spoke like an Englishwoman who has lived for many years among Americans. "I know everybody that lives here for more than two nights. I'm the proprietor of this hotel."

"Well then, do something quickly. Mr. Meyer is in there and he's very drunk."

"I don't do anything with Meyer when he's drunk." The woman was silent for a moment and the idea of doing something with Meyer struck her sense of humor and she chuckled. "Just imagine it," she said, " 'Mr. Meyer, will you kindly leave the room? Pacifica is tired of you. Ha-ha-ha—*Pacifica* is tired of you.' Have a seat, lady, and calm down. There's some gin in that cut-glass decanter over there next to the avocados. Would you like some?"

"You know I'm not used to violence," Mrs. Copperfield said. She helped herself to some gin, and repeated that she was not used to violence. "I doubt that I shall ever get over this evening. The stubbornness of that man. He was like an insane person."

"Meyer isn't insane," said the proprietress. "Some of them are much worse. He told me he was very fond of Pacifica. I've always been decent to him and he's never given me any trouble."

They heard screams from the next floor. Mrs. Copperfield recognized Pacifica's voice.

"Oh, please, let's get the police," pleaded Mrs. Copperfield.

"Are you crazy?" said the woman. "Pacifica doesn't want to get mixed up with the police. She would rather have both legs chopped off. I can promise you that is true."

"Well then, let's go up there," said Mrs. Copperfield. "I'm ready to do anything."

"Keep seated, Mrs.—what's your name? My name is Mrs. Quill."

"I'm Mrs. Copperfield."

"Well, you see, Mrs. Copperfield, Pacifica can take care of herself better than we can take care of her. The fewer people that get involved in a thing, the better off everybody is. That's one law I have here in the hotel."

"All right," said Mrs. Copperfield, "but meanwhile she might be murdered."

"People don't murder as easy as that. They do a lot of hitting around but not so much murdering. I've had some murders here, but not many. I've discovered that most things turn out all right. Of course some of them turn out bad."

"I wish I could feel as relaxed as you about everything. I don't understand how you can sit here, and I don't understand

how Pacifica can go through things like this without ending up
in an insane asylum."

"Well, she's had a lot of experience with these men. I don't
think she's scared really. She's much tougher than us. She's just
bothered. She likes to be able to have her room and do what
she likes. I think sometimes women don't know what they
want. Do you think maybe she has a little yen for Meyer?"

"How could she possibly? I don't understand what you
mean."

"Well now, that boy she says she's in love with; now, I don't
really think she's in love with him at all. She's had one after
another of them like that. All nice dopes. They worship the
ground she walks on. I think she gets so jealous and nervous
while Meyer's away that she likes to pretend to herself that she
likes these other little men better. When Meyer comes back she
really believes she's mad at him for interfering. Now, maybe
I'm right and maybe I'm wrong, but I think it goes a little
something like that."

"I think it's impossible. She wouldn't allow him to hurt her,
then, before she went to bed with him."

"Sure she would," said Mrs. Quill, "but I don't know anything about such things. Pacifica's a nice girl, though. She
comes from a nice family too."

Mrs. Copperfield drank her gin and enjoyed it.

"She'll be coming down here soon to have a talk," said Mrs.
Quill. "It's balmy here and they all enjoy themselves. They
talk and they drink and they make love; they go on picnics;
they go to the movies; they dance, sometimes all night long.
. . . I need never be lonely unless I want to. . . . I can always go and dance with them if I feel like it. I have a fellow
who takes me out to the dancing places whenever I want to go
and I can always string along. I love it here. Wouldn't go back
home for a load of monkeys. It's hot sometimes, but mostly
balmy, and nobody's in a hurry. Sex doesn't interest me and I
sleep like a baby. I am never bothered with dreams unless I eat

something which sits on my stomach. You have to pay a price when you indulge yourself. I have a terrific yen for lobster à la Newburg, you see. I know exactly what I'm doing when I eat it. I go to Bill Grey's restaurant I should say about once every month with this fellow."

"Go on," said Mrs. Copperfield, who was enjoying this.

"Well, we order lobster à la Newburg. I tell you it's the most delicious thing in the world. . . ."

"How do you like frogs' legs?" asked Mrs. Copperfield.

"Lobster à la Newburg for me."

"You sound so happy I have a feeling I'm going to nestle right in here, in this hotel. How would you like that?"

"You do what you want to with your own life. That's my motto. For how long would you want to stay?"

"Oh, I don't know," said Mrs. Copperfield. "Do you think I'd have fun here?"

"Oh, no end of fun," said the proprietess. "Dancing, drinking . . . all the things that are pleasant in this world. You don't need much money, you know. The men come off the ships with their pockets bulging. I tell you this place is God's own town, or maybe the Devil's." She laughed heartily.

"No end of fun," she repeated. She got up from her chair with some difficulty and went over to a box-like phonograph which stood in the corner of the room. After winding it up she put on a cowboy song.

"You can always listen to this," she said to Mrs. Copperfield, "whenever your little heart pleases. There are the needles and the records and all you've got to do is wind it up. When I'm not here, you can sit in this rocker and listen. I've got famous people singing on those records like Sophie Tucker and Al Jolson from the United States, and I say that music is the ear's wine."

"And I suppose reading would be very pleasant in this room —at the same time that one listened to the gramophone," said Mrs. Copperfield.

"Reading—you can do all the reading you want."

They sat for some time listening to records and drinking gin. After an hour or so Mrs. Quill saw Pacifica coming down the hall. "Now," she said to Mrs. Copperfield, "here comes your friend."

Pacifica had on a little silk dress and bedroom slippers. She had made up her face very carefully and she had perfumed herself.

"Look what Meyer brought me," she said, coming towards them and showing them a very large wrist watch with a radium dial. She seemed to be in a very pleasant mood.

"You been talking here one to the other," she said, smiling at them kindly. "Now suppose we all three of us go and take a walk through the street and get some beer or whatever we want."

"That would be nice," said Mrs. Copperfield. She was beginning to worry a bit about Mr. Copperfield. He hated her to disappear this way for a long time because it gave him an unbalanced feeling and interfered very much with his sleep. She promised herself to drop by the room and let him know that she was still out, but the very idea of going near the hotel made her shudder.

"Hurry up, girls," said Pacifica.

They went back to the quiet restaurant where Pacifica had taken Mr. and Mrs. Copperfield to dinner. Opposite was a very large saloon all lighted up. There was a ten-piece band playing there, and it was so crowded that the people were dancing in the streets.

Mrs. Quill said: "Oh boy, Pacifica! There's the place where you could have the time of your life tonight. Look at the time *they're* having."

"No, Mrs. Quill," said Pacifica. "We can stay here fine. The light is not so bright and it is more quiet and then we will go to bed."

"Yes," said Mrs. Quill, her face falling. Mrs. Copperfield

thought she saw in Mrs. Quill's eyes a terribly pained and thwarted look.

"I'll go there tomorrow night," said Mrs. Quill softly. "It doesn't mean a thing. Every night they have those dances. That's because the boats never stop coming in. The girls are never tired either," she said to Mrs. Copperfield. "That's because they sleep all they want in the daytime. They can sleep as well in the daytime as they do at night. They don't get tired. Why should they? It doesn't make you tired to dance. The music carries you along."

"Don't be a fool," said Pacifica. "They're always tired."

"Well, which is it?" asked Mrs. Copperfield.

"Oh," said Mrs. Quill, "Pacifica is always looking on the darkest side of life. She's the gloomiest thing I ever knew."

"I don't look at the dark side, I look at the truth. You're a little foolish sometimes, Mrs. Quill."

"Don't talk to me that way when you know how much I love you," said Mrs. Quill, her lips beginning to tremble.

"I'm sorry, Mrs. Quill," said Pacifica gravely.

"There is something very lovable about Pacifica," Mrs. Copperfield thought to herself. "I believe she takes everyone quite seriously."

She took Pacifica's hand in her own.

"In a minute we're going to have something nice to drink," she said, smiling up at Pacifica. "Aren't you glad?"

"Yes, it will be nice to have something to drink," said Pacifica politely; but Mrs. Quill understood the gaiety of it. She rubbed her hands together and said: "I'm with you."

Mrs. Copperfield looked out into the street and saw Meyer walking by. He was with two blondes and some sailors.

"There goes Meyer," she said. The other two women looked across the street and they all watched him disappear.

•

Mr. and Mrs. Copperfield had gone over to Panama City for two days. The first day after lunch Mr. Copperfield proposed a walk towards the outskirts of the city. It was the first thing he always did when he arrived in a new place. Mrs. Copperfield hated to know what was around her, because it always turned out to be even stranger than she had feared.

They walked for a long time. The streets began to look all alike. On one side they went gradually uphill, and on the other they descended abruptly to the muddy regions near the sea. The stone houses were completely colorless in the hot sun. All the windows were heavily grilled; there was very little sign of life anywhere. They came to three naked boys struggling with a football, and turned downhill towards the water. A woman dressed in black silk came their way slowly. When they had passed her she turned around and stared at them shamelessly. They looked over their shoulders several times and they could still see her standing there watching them.

The tide was out. They made their way along the muddy beach. Back of them there was a huge stone hotel built in front of a low cliff, so that it was already in the shade. The mud flats and the water were still in the sunlight. They walked along until Mr. Copperfield found a large, flat rock for them to sit on.

"It's so beautiful here," he said.

A crab ran along sideways in the mud at their feet.

"Oh, look!" said Mr. Copperfield. "Don't you love them?"

"Yes, I do love them," she answered, but she could not suppress a rising feeling of dread as she looked around her at the landscape. Someone had painted the words *Cerveza—Beer* in green letters on the façade of the hotel.

Mr. Copperfield rolled up his trousers and asked if she would care to go barefoot to the edge of the water with him.

"I think I've gone far enough," she said.

"Are you tired?" he asked her.

"Oh, no. I'm not tired." There was such a pained expression on her face as she answered him that he asked her what the trouble was.

"I'm unhappy," she said.

"Again?" asked Mr. Copperfield. "What is there to be unhappy about now?"

"I feel so lost and so far away and so frightened."

"What's frighening about this?"

"I don't know. It's all so strange and it has no connection with anything."

"It's connected with Panama," observed Mr. Copperfield acidly. "Won't you ever understand that?" He paused. "I don't think really that I'm going to try to make you understand any more. . . . But I'm going to walk to the water's edge. You spoil all my fun. There's absolutely nothing anyone can do with you." He was pouting.

"Yes, I know. I mean go to the water's edge. I guess I am tired after all." She watched him picking his way among the tiny stones, his arms held out for balance like a tight-rope walker's, and wished that she were able to join him because she was so fond of him. She began to feel a little exalted. There was a strong wind, and some lovely sailboats were passing by very swiftly not far from the shore. She threw her head back and closed her eyes, hoping that perhaps she might become exalted enough to run down and join her husband. But the wind did not blow quite hard enough, and behind her closed eyes she saw Pacifica and Mrs. Quill standing in front of the Hotel de las Palmas. She had said good-by to them from the old-fashioned hack that she had hired to drive her to the station. Mr. Copperfield had preferred to walk, and she had been alone with her two friends. Pacifica had been wearing the satin kimono which Mrs. Copperfield had bought her, and a pair of bedroom slippers decorated with pompons. She had stood near the wall of the hotel squinting, and complaining

about being out in the street dressed only in a kimono, but Mrs.
Copperfield had had only a minute to say good-by to them and
she would not descend from the carriage.

"Pacifica and Mrs. Quill," she had said to them, leaning out
of the victoria, "you can't imagine how I dread leaving you
even for only two days. I honestly don't know how I'll be able
to stand it."

"Listen, Copperfield," Mrs. Quill had answered, "you go
and have the time of your life in Panama. Don't you think
about us for one minute. Do you hear me? My, oh my, if I was
young enough to be going to Panama City with my husband,
I'd be wearing a different expression on my face than you are
wearing now."

"That means nothing to be going to Panama City with your
husband," Pacifica had insisted very firmly. "That does not
mean that she is happy. Everyone likes to do different things.
Maybe Copperfield likes better to go fishing or buy dresses."
She had then smiled gratefully at Pacifica.

"Well," Mrs. Quill had retorted somewhat feebly, "I'm sure
you would be happy, Pacifica, if you were going to Panama
City with your husband. . . . It's beautiful over there."

"Anyway, she has been in Paris," Pacifica had answered.

"Well, promise me you will be here when I get back," Mrs.
Copperfield had begged them. "I'm so terrified that you might
suddenly vanish."

"Don't make up such stories to yourself, my dear; life is difficult enough. Where are we going away?" Pacifica had said to
her, yawning and starting to go inside. Then she had blown a
kiss to Mrs. Copperfield from the doorway and waved her
hand.

"Such fun, to be with them," she said, audibly, opening her
eyes. "They are a great comfort."

Mr. Copperfield was on his way back to the flat rock where
she was sitting. He had a stone of strange texture and forma-
tion in his hand. He was smiling as he came towards her.

"Look," he said, "isn't this an amusing stone? It's really quite beautiful. I thought you would like to see it, so I brought it to you." Mrs. Copperfield examined the stone and said: "Oh, it is beautiful and very strange. Thanks ever so much." She looked at it lying in the palm of her hand. As she examined it Mr. Copperfield pressed her shoulder and said: "Look at the big steamer plowing through the water. Do you see it?" He twisted her neck slightly so that she might look in the right direction.

"Yes, I see it. It's wonderful too. . . . I think we had better be walking back home. It's going to be dark soon."

They left the beach and started walking through the streets again. It was getting dark, but there were more people standing around now. They commented openly on Mr. and Mrs. Copperfield as they passed by.

"It's really been the most wonderful day," Mr. Copperfield said. "You must have enjoyed some of it, because we've seen such incredible things." Mrs. Copperfield squeezed his hand harder and harder.

"I don't have wingèd feet like you," she said to him. "You must forgive me. I can't move about so easily. At thirty-three I have certain habits."

"That's bad," he answered. "Of course, I have certain habits too—habits of eating, habits of sleeping, habits of working— but I don't think that is what you meant, was it?"

"Let's not talk about it. That isn't what I meant, no."

•

The next day Mrs. Copperfield said that they would go out and see some of the jungle. Mrs. Copperfield said they hadn't the proper equipment and he explained that he hadn't meant that they would go exploring into the jungle but only around the edges where there were paths.

"Don't let the word 'jungle' frighten you," he said. "After all it only means tropical forest."

"If I don't feel like going in I won't. It doesn't matter. To-night we are going back to Colon, aren't we?"

"Well, maybe we'll be too tired and we'll have to stay here another night."

"But I told Pacifica and Mrs. Quill that we would be back tonight. They'll be so disappointed if we aren't."

"You aren't really considering *them,* are you? . . . After all, Frieda! Anyway, I don't think they'll mind. They'll understand."

"Oh, no, they won't," answered Mrs. Copperfield. "They'll be disappointed. I told them I would be back before midnight and that we would go out and celebrate. I'm positive that Mrs. Quill will be very disappointed. She loves to celebrate."

"Who on earth is Mrs. Quill?"

"Mrs. Quill . . . Mrs. Quill and Pacifica."

"Yes, I know, but it's so ridiculous. It seems to me you wouldn't care to see them for more than one evening. I should think it would be easy to know what they were like in a very short time."

"Oh, I know what they're like, but I do have so much fun with them." Mr. Copperfield did not answer.

They went out and walked through the streets until they came to a place where there were some buses. They inquired about schedules, and boarded a bus called *Shirley Temple.* On the insides of the doors were painted pictures of Mickey Mouse. The driver had pasted postcards of the saints and the holy virgin on the windshield above his head. He was drinking a Coca-Cola when they got in the bus.

"*¿En que barco vinieron?*" asked the driver.

"*Venimos de Colon,*" said Mr. Copperfield.

"What was that?" Mrs. Copperfield asked him.

"Just what boat did we come on, and I answered we have just arrived from Colon. You see, most people have just come off a boat. It corresponds to asking people where they live, in other places."

"*J'adore Colon, c'est tellement . . .*" began Mrs. Copperfield. Mr. Copperfield looked embarrassed. "Don't speak in French to him. It doesn't make any sense. Speak to him in English."

"I adore Colon."

The driver made a face. "Dirty wooden city. I am sure you have made a big mistake. You will see. You will like Panama City better. More stores, more hospitals, wonderful cinemas, big clean restaurants, wonderful houses in stone; Panama City is a big place. When we drive through Ancon I will show you how nice the lawns are and the trees and the sidewalks. You can't show me anything like that in Colon. You know who likes Colon?" He leaned way over the back of his seat, and as they were sitting behind him he was breathing right in their faces.

"You know who likes Colon?" He winked at Mr. Copperfield. "They're all over the streets. That is what it is there; nothing else much. We have that here too, but in a separate place. If you like that you can go. We have everything here."

"You mean the whores?" asked Mrs. Copperfield in a clear voice.

"*Las putas,*" Mr. Copperfield explained in Spanish to the driver. He was delighted at the turn in the conversation and fearful lest the driver should not get the full savor of it.

The driver covered his mouth with his hand and laughed.

"She loves that," said Mr. Copperfield, giving his wife a push.

"No—no," said the driver, "she could not."

"They've all been very sweet to me."

"*Sweet!*" said the driver, almost screaming. "There is not this much sweet in them." He made a tiny little circle with his thumb and forefinger. "No, not sweet—someone has been fooling you. He knows." He put his hand on Mr. Copperfield's leg.

"I'm afraid I don't know anything about it," said Mr. Copperfield. The driver winked at him again, and then he said,

"She thinks she knows *las*—I will not say the word, but she has never met one of them."

"But I have. I have even taken a siesta with one."

"*Siesta!*" the driver roared with laughter. "Don't make fun please, lady. That is not very nice, you know." He suddenly looked very sober. "No, no, no." He shook his head sadly.

By now the bus had filled up and the driver was obliged to start off. Every time they stopped he would turn around and wag a finger at Mrs. Copperfield. They went through Ancon and passed several long low buildings set up on some small hills.

"Hospitals," yelled the driver for the benefit of Mr. and Mrs. Copperfield. "They have doctors here for every kind of thing in the world. The Army can go there for nothing. They eat and they sleep and they get well all for nothing. Some of the old ones live there for the rest of their lives. I dream to be in the American Army and not driving this dirty bus."

"I should hate to be regimented," said Mr. Copperfield with feeling.

"They are always going to dinners and balls, balls and dinners," commented the driver. There was a murmuring from the back of the bus. The women were all eager to know what the driver had said. One of them who spoke English explained rapidly to the others in Spanish. They all giggled about it for fully five mintues afterwards. The driver started to sing *Over There,* and the laughter reached the pitch of hysteria. They were now almost in the country, driving alongside a river. Across the river was a very new road and behind that a tremendous thick forest.

"Oh, look," said Mr. Copperfield, pointing to the forest. "Do you see the difference? Do you see how enormous the trees are and how entangled the undergrowth is? You can tell that even from here. No northern forests ever look so rich."

"That's true, they don't," said Mrs. Copperfield.

The bus finally stopped at a tiny pier. Only three women and the Copperfields remained inside by now. Mrs. Copperfield looked at them hoping that they were going to the jungle, too.

Mr. Copperfield descended from the bus and she followed reluctantly. The driver was already in the street smoking. He was standing beside Mr. Copperfield, hoping that he would start another conversation. But Mr. Copperfield was much too excited at being so near the jungle to think of anything else. The three women did not get out. They remained in their seats talking. Mrs. Copperfield looked back into the bus and stared at them with a perplexed expression on her face. She seemed to be saying: "Please come out, won't you?" They were embarrassed and they started to giggle again.

Mrs. Copperfield went over to the driver and said to him: "Is this the last stop?"

"Yes," he said.

"And they?"

"Who?" he asked, looking dumb.

"Those three ladies in the back."

"They ride. They are very nice ladies. This is not the first time they are riding on my bus."

"Back and forth?"

"Sure," said the driver.

Mr. Copperfield took Mrs. Copperfield's hand and led her onto the pier. A little ferry was coming towards them. There seemed to be no one on the ferry at all.

Suddenly Mrs. Copperfield said to her husband: "I just don't want to go to the jungle. Yesterday was such a strange, terrible day. If I have another day like it I shall be in an awful state. Please let me go back on the bus."

"But," said Mr. Copperfield, "after you've come all the way here, it seems to me so silly and so senseless to go back. I can assure you that the jungle will be of some interest to you. I've been in them before. You see the strangest-shaped leaves and

flowers. And I'm sure you would hear wonderful noises. Some
of the birds in the tropics have voices like xylophones, others
like bells."

"I thought maybe when I arrived here I would feel inspired;
that I would feel the urge to set out. But I don't in the least.
Please let's not discuss it."

"All right," said Mr. Copperfield. He looked sad and lonely.
He enjoyed so much showing other people the things he liked
best. He started to walk away towards the edge of the water
and stared out across the river at the opposite shore. He was
very slight and his head was beautifully shaped.

"Oh, please don't be sad!" said Mrs. Copperfield, hurrying
over to him. "I refuse to allow you to be sad. I feel like an ox.
Like a murderer. But I would be such a nuisance over on the
other side of the river in the jungle. You'll love it once you're
over there and you will be able to go much farther in without
me."

"But my dear—I don't mind . . . I only hope you will be
able to get home all right on the bus. Heaven knows when I'll
get home. I might decide to just wander around and around
. . . and you don't like to be alone in Panama."

"Well then," said Mrs. Copperfield, "suppose I take the
train back to Colon. It's a simple trip, and I have only one grip
with me. Then you can follow me tonight if you get back early
from the jungle, and if you don't you can come along tomorrow morning. We had planned to go back tomorrow anyway.
But you must give me your word of honor that you will come."

"It's all so complicated," said Mr. Copperfield. "I thought
we were going to have a nice day in the jungle. I'll come back
tomorrow. The luggage is there, so there is no danger of my
not coming back. Good-by." He gave her his hand. The ferry
was scraping against the dock.

"Listen," she said, "if you're not back by twelve tonight, I
shall sleep at the Hotel de las Palmas. I'll phone our hotel at
twelve and see if you're there, in case I'm out."

"I won't be there until tomorrow."

"I'm at the Hotel de las Palmas if I'm not home, then."

"All right, but be good and get some sleep."

"Yes, of course I will."

He got into the boat and it pulled out.

"I hope his day has not been spoiled," she said to herself. The tenderness that she was feeling for him now was almost overwhelming. She got back on the bus and stared fixedly out the window because she did not want anyone to see that she was crying.

•

Mrs. Copperfield went straight to the Hotel de las Palmas. As she descended from the carriage she saw Pacifica walking towards her alone. She paid the driver and rushed up to her.

"Pacifica! How glad I am to see you!"

Pacifica's forehead had broken out. She looked tired.

"Ah, Copperfield," she said, "Mrs. Quill and I did not think we would ever see you again and now you are back."

"But, Pacifica, how can you say a thing like that? I'm surprised at both of you. Didn't I promise you I would be back before midnight and that we would celebrate?"

"Yes, but people often say this. After all, nobody gets angry if they don't come back."

"Let's go and say hello to Mrs. Quill."

"All right, but she has been in a terrible humor all the day, crying a lot and not eating anything."

"What on earth is the matter?"

"She had some fight, I think, with her boy friend. He don't like her. I tell her this but she won't listen."

"But the first thing she told me was that sex didn't interest her."

"To go to bed she don't care so much, but she is terribly sentimental, like she was sixteen years old. I feel sorry to see an old woman making such a fool."

Pacifica was still wearing her bedroom slippers. They went past the bar, which was filled with men smoking cigars and drinking.

"My God! how in one minute they make a place stink," said Pacifica. "I wish I could go and have a nice little house with a garden somewhere."

"I'm going to live here, Pacifica, and we'll all have lots of fun."

"The time for fun is over," said Pacifica gloomily.

"You'll feel better after we've all had a drink," said Mrs. Copperfield.

They knocked on Mrs. Quill's door.

They heard her moving about in her room and rattling some papers. Then she came to the door and opened it. Mrs. Copperfield noticed that she looked weaker than usual.

"Do come in," she said to them, "although I have nothing to offer you. You can sit down for a while."

Pacifica nudged Mrs. Copperfield. Mrs. Quill went back to her chair and took up a handful of bills which had been lying on the table near her.

"I must look over these. You will excuse me, but they're terribly important."

Pacifica turned to Mrs. Copperfield and talked softly.

"She can't even see them, because she does not have her glasses on. She is behaving like a child. Now she will be mad at us because her boy friend, like she calls him, has left her alone. I will not be treated like a dog very long."

Mrs. Quill overheard what Pacifica was saying, and reddened. She turned to Mrs. Copperfield.

"Do you still intend to come and live in this hotel?" she asked her.

"Yes," said Mrs. Copperfield buoyantly, "I wouldn't live anywhere else for the world. Even if you do growl at me."

"You probably will not find it comfortable enough."

"Don't growl at Copperfield," put in Pacifica. "First, she's been away for two days, and second, she doesn't know, like I do, what you are like."

"I'll thank you to keep your common little mouth shut," retorted Mrs. Quill, shuffling the bills rapidly.

"I am sorry to have disturbed you, Mrs. Quill," said Pacifica, rising to her feet and going towards the door.

"I wasn't yelling at Copperfield, I just said that I didn't think she would be comfortable here." Mrs. Quill laid down the bills. "Do you think she would be comfortable here, Pacifica?"

"A common little thing does not know anything about these questions," answered Pacifica and she left the room, leaving Mrs. Copperfield behind with Mrs. Quill.

Mrs. Quill took some keys from the top of her dresser and motioned to Mrs. Copperfield to follow her. They walked through some halls and up a flight of stairs and Mrs. Quill opened the door of one of the rooms.

"Is it near Pacifica's?" asked Mrs. Copperfield.

Mrs. Quill without answering led her back through the halls and stopped near Pacifica's room.

"This is dearer," said Mrs. Quill, "but it's near Miss Pacifica's room if that's your pleasure and you can stand the noise."

"What noise?"

"She'll start yammering away and heaving things around the minute she wakes up in the morning. It don't affect her any. She's tough. She hasn't got a nerve in her body."

"Mrs. Quill—"

"Yes."

"Could you have someone bring me a bottle of gin to my room?"

"I think I can do that. . . . Well, I hope you are comfortable." Mrs. Quill walked away. "I'll have your bag sent up," she said, looking over her shoulder.

Mrs. Copperfield was appalled at the turn of events.

"I thought," she said to herself, "that they would go on the way they were forever. Now I must be patient and wait until everything is all right again. The longer I live, the less I can foresee anything." She lay down on the bed, put her knees up, and held onto her ankles with her hands.

"Be gay . . . be gay . . . be gay," she sang, rocking back and forth on the bed. There was a knock on the door and a man in a striped sweater entered the room without waiting for an answer to his knock.

"You ask for a bottle of gin?" he said.

"I certainly did—hooray!"

"And here's a suitcase. I'm putting it down here."

Mrs. Copperfield paid him and he left.

"Now," she said, jumping off the bed, "now for a little spot of gin to chase my troubles away. There just isn't any other way that's as good. At a certain point gin takes everything off your hands and you flop around like a little baby. Tonight I want to be a little baby." She took a hookerful, and shortly after that another. The third one she drank more slowly.

The brown shutters of her window were wide open and a small wind was bringing the smell of frying fat into the room. She went over to the window and looked down into the alleyway which separated the Hotel de las Palmas from a group of shacks.

There was an old lady seated in a chair in the alleyway, eating her dinner.

"Eat every bit of it!" Mrs. Copperfield said. The old lady looked up dreamily, but she did not answer.

Mrs. Copperfield put her hand over her heart. *"Le bonheur,"* she whispered, *"le bonheur . . .* what an angel a happy moment is—and how nice not to have to struggle too much for inner peace! I know that I shall enjoy certain moments of gaiety, willy-nilly. No one among my friends speaks any longer of character—and what interests us most, certainly, is finding out what we are like."

"Copperfield!" Pacifica burst into the room. Her hair was messy and she seemed to be out of breath. "Come on downstairs and have some fun. Maybe they are not the kind of men you like to be with, but if you don't like them you just walk away. Put some rouge on your face. Can I have some of your gin, please?"

"But a moment ago you said the time for fun was over!"

"What the hell!"

"By all means what the hell," said Mrs. Copperfield. "That's music to anyone's ears. . . . If you could only stop me from thinking, always, Pacifica."

"You don't want to stop thinking. The more you can think, the more you are better than the other fellow. Thank your God that you can think."

Downstairs in the bar Mrs. Copperfield was introduced to three or four men.

"This man is Lou," said Pacifica, pulling out a stool from under the bar and making her sit next to him.

Lou was small and over forty. He wore a light-weight gray suit that was too tight for him, a blue shirt, and a straw hat.

"She wants to stop thinking," said Pacifica to Lou.

"Who wants to stop thinking?" asked Lou.

"Copperfield. The little girl who is sitting on a stool, you big boob."

"Boob yourself. You're gettin' just like one of them New York girls," said Lou.

"Take me to Nueva York, take me to Nueva York," said Pacifica, bouncing up and down on her stool.

Mrs. Copperfield was shocked to see Pacifica behaving in this kittenish manner.

"Remember the belly buttons," said Lou to Pacifica.

"The belly buttons! The belly buttons!" Pacifica threw up her arms and screeched with delight.

"What about the belly buttons?" asked Mrs. Copperfield.

"Don't you think those two are the funniest words in the whole world? Belly and button—belly and button—in Spanish it is only *ombligo.*"

"I don't think anything's *that* funny. But you like to laugh, so go ahead and laugh," said Lou, who made no attempt to talk to Mrs. Copperfield at all.

Mrs. Copperfield pulled at his sleeve. "Where do you come from?" she asked him.

"Pittsburgh."

"I don't know anything about Pittsburgh," said Mrs. Copperfield. But Lou was already turning his eyes in Pacifica's direction.

"Belly button," he said suddenly without changing his expression. This time Pacifica did not laugh. She did not seem to have heard him. She was standing up on the rail of the bar waving her arms in an agitated and officious manner.

"Well, well," she said, "I see that nobody has yet bought for Copperfield a drink. Am I with grown men or little boys? No, no . . . Pacifica will find other friends." She started to climb down from the bar, commanding Mrs. Copperfield to follow her. In the meantime she knocked off the hat of the man who was seated next to her with her elbow.

"Toby," she said to him, "you ought to be ashamed." Toby had a sleepy fat face and a broken nose. He was dressed in a dark brown heavy-weight suit.

"What? Did you want a drink?"

"Of course I wanted a drink." Pacifica's eyes were flashing.

Everyone was served and she settled back on her stool. "Come on now," she said, "what are we going to sing?"

"I'm a monotone," said Lou.

"Singing ain't in my line," said Toby.

They were all surprised to see Mrs. Copperfield throw her head back as though filled with a sudden feeling of exaltation and start to sing.

"Who cares if the sky cares to fall into the sea
Who cares what banks fail in Yonkers
As long as you've got the kiss that conquers
Why should I care?
Life is one long jubilee
As long as I care for you
And you care for me."

"Good, fine . . . now another one," said Pacifica in a snappy voice.

"Did you ever sing in a club?" Lou asked Mrs. Copperfield. Her cheeks were very red.

"Actually, I didn't. But when I was in the mood, I used to sing very loudly at a table in a restaurant and attract a good bit of attention."

"You wasn't such good friends with Pacifica the last time I was in Colon."

"My dear man, I wasn't here. I was in Paris, I suppose."

"She didn't tell me you were in Paris. Are you a screwball or were you really in Paris?"

"I was in Paris. . . . After all, stranger things have happened."

"Then you're fancy?"

"What do you mean, fancy?"

"Fancy is what fancy does."

"Well, if you care to be mysterious it's your right, but the word 'fancy' doesn't mean a thing to me."

"Hey," said Lou to Pacifica, "is she tryin' to be highhat with me?"

"No, she's very intelligent. She's not like you."

For the first time Mrs. Copperfield sensed that Pacifica was proud of her. She realized that all this time Pacifica had been waiting to show her to her friends and she was not so sure that she was pleased. Lou turned to Mrs. Copperfield again.

"I'm sorry, Duchess. Pacifica says you got something on the ball and that I shouldn't address myself to you."

Mrs. Copperfield was bored with Lou, so she jumped down and went and stood between Toby and Pacifica. Toby was talking in a thick low voice with Pacifica.

"I'm tellin' you if she gets a singer in here and paints the place up a little she could make a lot of money on the joint. Everybody knows it's a good place to hit the hay in, but there ain't no music. You're here, you got a lot of friends, you got a way with you. . . ."

"Toby, I don't want to start with music and a lot of friends. I'm quiet. . . ."

"Yeah, you're quiet. This week you're quiet and maybe next week you won't want to be so quiet."

"I don't change my mind like that, Toby. I have a boy friend. I don't want to live in here much longer, you know."

"But you're livin' here now."

"Yes."

"Well, you want to make a little money. I'm tellin' you, with a little money we could fix up the joint."

"But why must I be here?"

"Because you got contacts."

"I never saw such a man. Talking all the time about business."

"You're not such a bad one for business yourself. I saw you hustlin' up a drink for that pal of yours. You get your cut, don't you?"

Pacifica kicked Toby with her heel.

"Listen, Pacifica, I like to have fun. But I can't see somethin' that could be coinin' the money takin' in petty cash."

"Stop being so busy." Pacifica pushed his hat off his head. He realized there was nothing to be done and sighed.

"How's Emma?" he asked her listlessly.

"Emma? I have not seen her since that night on the boat. She looked so gorgeous dressed up like a sailor."

"Women look fantastic dressed up in men's clothes," put in Mrs. Copperfield with enthusiasm.

"That's what you think," said Toby. "They look better to me in ruffles."

"She was only talking for a *minute* they look nice," said Pacifica.

"Not for me," said Toby.

"All right, Toby, maybe not for you, but for her they look nice that way."

"I still think I'm right. It ain't only a matter of opinion."

"Well, you can't prove it mathematically," said Mrs. Copperfield. Toby looked at her with no interest in his face.

"What about Emma?" said Pacifica. "You are really not interested finally in somebody?"

"You asked me to talk about somethin' besides business, so I asked you about Emma, just to show how sociable I am. We both know her. We were on a party together. Ain't that the right thing to do? How's Emma, how's your momma and poppa. That's the kind of talk you like. Next I tell you how my family is gettin' along and maybe I bring in another friend who we both forgot we knew, and then we say prices are goin' up and comes the revolution and we all eat strawberries. Prices are goin' up fast and that's why I wanted you to cash in on this joint."

"My God!" said Pacifica, "my life is hard enough and I am all alone, but I can still enjoy myself like a young girl. *You,* you are an old man."

"Your life don't have to be hard, Pacifica."

"Well, your life is still very hard and you are always trying to make it easy. That's the hardest part even of your life."

"I'm just waitin' to get a break. With my ideas and a break my life can be easy overnight."

"And then what will you do?"

"Keep it that way or maybe make it even easier. I'll be plenty busy."

"You will never have any time for anything."

"What's a guy like me want time for—plantin' tulips?"

"You don't enjoy to talk to me, Toby."

"Sure. You're friendly and cute and you got a good brain aside from a few phony ideas."

"And what about me? Am I friendly and cute too?" asked Mrs. Copperfield.

"Sure. You're all friendly and cute."

"Copperfield, I think we have just been insulted," said Pacifica, drawing herself up.

Mrs. Copperfield started to march out of the room in mock anger, but Pacifica was already thinking of something else and Mrs. Copperfield found herself to be in the ridiculous position of the performer who is suddenly without an audience. She came back to the bar.

"Listen," said Pacifica, "go upstairs and knock on Mrs. Quill's door. Tell her that Mr. Toby wants to meet her very much. Don't say Pacifica sent you. She will know this anyway and it will be easier for her if you don't say it. She will love to come down. That I know like if she was my mother."

"Oh, I'd love to, Pacifica," said Mrs. Copperfield, running out of the room.

When Mrs. Copperfield arrived in Mrs. Quill's room, Mrs. Quill was busy cleaning the top drawer of her dresser. It was very quiet in her room and very hot.

"I never have the heart to throw these things away," said Mrs. Quill, turning around and patting her hair. "I suppose you've met half of Colon," she said sadly, studying Mrs. Copperfield's flushed face.

"No, I haven't, but would you care to come down and meet Mr. Toby?"

"Who is Mr. Toby, dear?"

"Oh, please come, please come just for me."

"I will, dear, if you'll sit down and wait while I change into something better."

Mrs. Copperfield sat down. Her head was spinning. Mrs. Quill pulled out a long black silk dress from her closet. She drew it over her head and then selected some strings of black beads from her jewel-box, and a cameo pin. She powdered her face carefully and stuck several more hairpins into her hair.

"I'm not going to bother to take a bath," she said when she had finished. "Now, do you really think that I should meet this Mr. Toby, or do you think perhaps another night would be better?"

Mrs. Copperfield took Mrs. Quill's hand and pulled her out of the room. Mrs. Quill's entrance into the barroom was gracious and extremely formal. She was already using the hurt that her beau had caused her to good advantage.

"Now, dear," she said quietly to Mrs. Copperfield, "tell me which one is Mr. Toby."

"That one over there, sitting next to Pacifica," Mrs. Copperfield said hesitantly. She was fearful lest Mrs. Quill should find him completely unattractive and leave the room.

"I see. The stout gentleman."

"Do you hate fat people?"

"I don't judge people by their bodies. Even when I was a young girl I liked men for their minds. Now that I'm middle-aged I see how right I was."

"I've always been a body-worshipper," said Mrs. Copperfield, "but that doesn't mean that I fall in love with people who have beautiful bodies. Some of the bodies I've liked have been awful. Come, let's go over to Mr. Toby."

Toby stood up for Mrs. Quill and took off his hat.

"Come sit down with us and have a drink."

"Let me get my bearings, young man. Let me get my bearings."

"This bar belongs to you, don't it?" said Toby, looking worried.

"Yes, yes," said Mrs. Quill blandly. She was staring at the top of Pacifica's head. "Pacifica," she said, "don't you drink too much. I have to watch out for you."

"Don't you worry, Mrs. Quill. I have been taking care of myself for a long time." She turned to Lou and said solemnly: "Fifteen years." Pacifica was completely natural. She behaved as though nothing had occurred between her and Mrs. Quill. Mrs. Copperfield was enchanted. She put her arms around Mrs. Quill's waist and hugged her very tight.

"Oh," she said, "oh, you make me so happy!"

Toby smiled. "The girl's feelin' good, Mrs. Quill. Now don't you want a drink?"

"Yes, I'll have a glass of gin. It pains me the way these girls come away from their homes so young. I had my home and my mother and my sisters and my brothers until the age of twenty-six. Even so, when I got married I felt like a scared rabbit. As if I was going out into the world. Mr. Quill was like a family to me, though, and it wasn't until he died that I really got out into the world. I was in my thirties then, and more of a scared rabbit than ever. Pacifica's really been out in the world much longer than I have. You know, she is like an old sea captain. Sometimes I feel very silly when she tells me of some of her experiences. My eyes almost pop right out of my head. It isn't so much a question of age as it is a question of experience. The Lord has spared me more than he has spared Pacifica. She hasn't been spared a single thing. Still, she's not as nervous as I am."

"Well, she certainly don't know how to look out for herself for someone who's had so much experience," said Toby. "She don't know a good thing when she sees it."

"Yes, I expect you're right," said Mrs. Quill, warming up to Toby.

"Sure I'm right. But she's got lots of friends here in Panama, ain't she?"

"I dare say Pacifica has a great many friends," said Mrs. Quill.

"Come on, you know she's got lots of friends, don't you?"

As Mrs. Quill looked as though she had been somewhat startled by the pressing tone in his voice, Toby decided he was
hurrying things too much.

"Who the hell cares, anyway?" he said, looking at her out of
the corner of his eye. This seemed to have the right effect on
Mrs. Quill, and Toby breathed a sigh of relief.

Mrs. Copperfield went over to a bench in the corner and lay
down. She shut her eyes and smiled.

"That's the best thing for her," said Mrs. Quill to Toby.
"She's a nice woman, a dear sweet woman, and she'd had a
little too much to drink. Pacifica, she can really take care of
herself like she says. I've seen her drink as much as a man, but
with her it's different. As I said, she's had all the experience in
the world. Now, Mrs. Copperfield and me, we have to watch
ourselves more carefully or else have some nice man watching
out for us."

"Yeah," said Toby, twisting around on his stool. "Bartender, another gin. You want one, don't you?" he asked Mrs.
Quill.

"Yes, if you'll watch out for me."

"Sure I will. I'll even take you home in my arms if you fall
down."

"Oh, no." Mrs. Quill giggled and flushed. "You wouldn't try
that, young man. I'm heavy, you know."

"Yeah. . . . Say—"

"Yes?"

"Would you mind telling me something?"

"I'd be delighted to tell you anything you'd like to hear."

"How is it you ain't never bothered to fix this place up?"

"Oh, dear, isn't it awful? I've always promised myself I
would and I never get around to it."

"No dough?" asked Toby. Mrs. Quill looked vague. "Haven't
you got no money to fix it up with?" he repeated.

"Oh yes, certainly I have." Mrs. Quill looked around at the
bar. "I even have some things upstairs that I always promised

myself to hang up on the walls here. Everything is so dirty, isn't it? I feel ashamed."

"No, no," said Toby impatiently. He was now very animated. "That ain't what I mean at all."

Mrs. Quill smiled at him sweetly.

"Listen," said Toby, "I been handlin' restaurants and bars and clubs all my life, and I can make them go."

"I'm certain that you can."

"I'm tellin' you that I can. Listen, let's get out of here; let's go some place else where we can really talk. Any place in town you name I'll take you to. It's worth it to me and it'll be worth it to you even more. You'll see. We can have more to drink or maybe a little bite to eat. Listen"—he grabbed hold of Mrs. Quill's upper arm—"would you like to go to the Hotel Washington?"

At first Mrs. Quill did not react, but when she realized what he had said, she answered that she would enjoy it very much, in a voice trembling with emotion. Toby jumped off the stool, pulled his hat down over his face, and started walking out of the bar, saying: "Come on, then," over his shoulder to Mrs. Quill. He looked annoyed but resolute.

Mrs. Quill took Pacifica's hand in her own and told her that she was going to the Hotel Washington.

"If there was any possible way I would take you with us, I would, Pacifica. I feel very badly to be going there without you, but I don't see how you can come, do you?"

"Now, don't you worry about that, Mrs. Quill. I'm having a very good time here," said Pacifica in a sincerely world-weary tone of voice.

"That's a hocus-pocus joint," said Lou.

"Oh no," said Pacifica, "it is very nice there, very beautiful. She will have a lovely time." Pacifica pinched Lou. "You don't know," she said to him.

Mrs. Quill walked out of the bar slowly and joined Toby on the sidewalk. They got into a hack and started for the hotel.

Toby was silent. He sprawled way back in his seat and lighted a cigar.

"I regret that automobiles were ever invented," said Mrs. Quill.

"You'd go crazy tryin' to get from one place to another if they wasn't."

"Oh, no. I always take my time. There isn't anything that can't wait."

"That's what you think," said Toby in a surly tone of voice, sensing that this was just the thing that he would have to combat in Mrs. Quill. "It's just that extra second that makes Man O'War or any other horse come in first," he said.

"Well, life isn't a horse race."

"Nowadays that's just what life is."

"Well, not for me," said Mrs. Quill.

Toby was disgusted.

The walk which led up to the veranda of the Hotel Washington was lined with African date-palms. The hotel itself was very impressive. They descended from the carriage. Toby stood in the middle of the walk between the scraping palms and looked towards the hotel. It was all lighted up. Mrs. Quill stood beside Toby.

"I'll bet they soak you for drinks in there," said Toby. "I'll bet they make two hundred per cent profit."

"Oh, please," said Mrs. Quill, "if you don't feel you can afford it let's take a carriage and go back. The ride is so pleasant anyway." Her heart was beating very quickly.

"Don't be a God-damn fool!" Toby said to her, and they headed for the hotel.

The floor in the lobby was of imitation yellow marble. There was a magazine stand in one corner where the guests were able to buy chewing gum and picture postcards, maps, and souvenirs. Mrs. Quill felt as though she had just come off a ship. She wandered about in circles, but Toby went straight up to the man behind the magazine stand and asked him where he could get a drink. He suggested to Toby that they go out on the terrace.

"It's generally where everyone goes," he said.

They were seated at a table on the edge of the terrace, and they had a very nice view of a stretch of beach and the sea.

Between them on the table there was a little lamp with a rose-colored shade. Toby began at once to twirl the lamp shade. His cigar by now was very short and very wet.

Here and there on the terrace small groups of people were talking together in low voices.

"Dead!" said Toby.

"Oh, I think it's lovely," said Mrs. Quill. She was shivering a little, as the wind kept blowing over her shoulder, and it was a good deal cooler than in Colon.

A waiter was standing beside them with his pencil poised in the air waiting for an order.

"What do you want?" asked Toby.

"What would you suggest, young man, that's really delicious?" said Mrs. Quill, turning to the waiter.

"Fruit punch à la Washington Hotel," said the waiter abruptly.

"That *does* sound good."

"O.K.," said Toby, "bring one, and a straight rye for me."

When Mrs. Quill had sipped quite a bit of her drink Toby spoke to her. "So you got the dough, but you never bothered to fix it up."

"Mmmmmm!" said Mrs. Quill. "They've got every kind of fruit in the world in this drink. I'm afraid I'm behaving just like a baby, but there's no one who likes the good things in this world better than me. Of course, I've never had to do without them, you know."

"You don't call livin' the way you're livin' havin' the good things in life, do you?" said Toby.

"I live much better than you think. How do you know how I live?"

"Well, you could have more style," said Toby, "and you could have that easy. I mean the place could be better very easy."

"It probably would be easy, wouldn't it?"

"Yeah." Toby waited to see if she would say anything more by herself before he addressed her again.

"Take all these people here," said Mrs. Quill. "There aren't many of them, but you'd think they'd all get together instead of staying in twos and threes. As long as they're all living here in this gorgeous hotel, you'd think they'd have on their ball dresses and be having a wonderful time every minute, instead of looking out over the terrace or reading. You'd think they'd always be dressed up to the hilt and flirting together instead of wearing those plain clothes."

"They got on sport clothes," said Toby. "They don't want to be bothered dressin'. They probably come here for a rest. They're probably business people. Maybe some of them belong to society. They got to rest too. They got so many places they got to show up at when they're home."

"Well, I wouldn't pay out all that money just to rest. I'd stay in my own house."

"It don't make no difference. They got plenty."

"That's true enough. Isn't it sad?"

"I don't see nothin' sad about it. What looks sad to me," said Toby, leaning way over and crushing his cigar out in the ash-tray, "what looks sad to me is that you've got that bar and hotel set-up and you ain't makin' enough money on it."

"Yes, isn't it terrible?"

"I like you and I don't like to see you not gettin' what you could." He took hold of her hand with a certain amount of gentleness. "Now, I know what to do with your place. Like I told you before. Do you remember what I told you before?"

"Well, you've told me so many things."

"I'll tell you again. I've been working with restaurants and

bars and hotels all my life and makin' them go. I said makin'
them go. If I had the dough right now, if it wasn't that I'm
short because I had to help my brother and his family out of a
jam, I'd take my own dough before you could say Jack Robin-
son and sink it into your joint and fix it up. I know that I'd get
it right back anyway, so it wouldn't be no act of charity."

"Certainly it wouldn't," said Mrs. Quill. Her head was swaying gently from side to side. She looked at Toby with luminous
eyes.

"Well, I got to go easy now until next October, when I got a
big contract comin'. A contract with a chain. I could use a
little money now, but that ain't the point."

"Don't bother to explain, Toby," said Mrs. Quill.

"What do you mean, don't bother to explain? Ain't you interested in what I've got to tell you?"

"Toby, I'm interested in every word you have to say. But
you must not worry about the drinks. Your friend Flora Quill
tells you that you needn't worry. We're out to enjoy ourselves
and Heaven knows we're going to, aren't we, Toby?"

"Yeah, but just let me explain this to you. I think the reason
you ain't done nothin' about the place is because you didn't
know where to begin, maybe. Understand? You don't know the
ropes. Now, I know all about gettin' orchestras and carpenters
and waiters, cheap. I know how to do all that. You got a name,
and lots of people like to come there even now because they
can go right from the bar upstairs. Pacifica is a big item because she knows every bloke in town and they like her and they
trust her. The trouble is, you ain't got no atmosphere, no
bright lights, no dancin'. It ain't pretty or big enough. People
go to the other places and then they come to your place late.
Just before they go to bed. If I was you, I'd turn over in my
grave. It's the other guys that are gettin' the meat. You only
get a little bit. What's left near the bone, see?"

"The meat nearest the bone is the sweetest," said Mrs. Quill.

"Hey, is there any use my talkin' to you or are you gonna be silly? I'm serious. Now, you got some money in the bank. You got money in the bank, ain't you?"

"Yes, I've got money in the bank," said Mrs. Quill.

"O.K. Well, you let me help you fix up the joint. I'll take everything off your hands. All you got to do is lie back and enjoy the haul."

"Nonsense," said Mrs. Quill.

"Now come on," said Toby, beginning to get angry. "I'm not askin' you for nothin' except maybe a little percentage in the place and a little cash to pay expenses for a while. I can do it all for you cheap and quick and I can manage the joint for you so that it won't cost you much more than it's costin' you now."

"But I think that's wonderful, Toby. I think it's so wonderful."

"You don't have to tell me it's wonderful. I know it's wonderful. It ain't wonderful, it's swell. It's marvelous. We ain't got no time to lose. Have another drink."

"Yes, yes."

"I'm spendin' my last cent on you," he said recklessly.

Mrs. Quill was drunk by now and she just nodded her head.

"It's worth it." He sat back in his chair and studied the horizon. He was very busy calculating in his head. "What percentage in the place do you think I ought to get? Don't forget I'm gonna manage the whole thing for you for a year."

"Oh, dear," said Mrs. Quill, "I'm sure I haven't got any idea." She smiled at him blissfully.

"O.K. How much advance will you give me just so I can stay on here until I get the place goin'?"

"I don't know."

"Well, we'll figure it this way," said Toby cautiously. He was not sure yet that he had taken the right move. "We'll figure it this way. I don't want you to do more than you can. I

want to go in this deal with you. You tell me how much money
you got in the bank. Then I'll figure out how much fixin' the
place up will cost you and then how much I think is a mini-
mum for me. If you ain't got much I'm not gonna let you go
busted. You be honest with me and I'll be honest with you."

"Toby," said Mrs. Quill seriously, "don't you think I'm an
honest woman?"

"What the hell," said Toby, "do you think I'd put a propo-
sition like that to you if I didn't think you were?"

"No, I guess you wouldn't," said Mrs. Quill sadly.

"How much you got?" asked Toby, looking at her intently.

"What?" asked Mrs. Quill.

"How much money you got in the bank?"

"I'll show you, Toby. I'll show you right away." She started
to fumble in her big black leather pocketbook.

Toby had his jaw locked and his eyes averted from the face
of Mrs. Quill.

"Messy—messy—messy," Mrs. Quill was saying. "I have everything in this pocketbook but the kitchen stove."

There was a very still look in Toby's eyes as he stared first at
the water and then at the palm trees. He considered that he
had already won, and he was beginning to wonder whether or
not it was really a good thing.

"Dear me," said Mrs. Quill, "I live just like a gypsy. Twenty-
two fifty in the bank and I don't even care."

Toby snatched the book from her hands. When he saw that
the balance was marked twenty-two dollars and fifty cents, he
rose to his feet and, clutching his napkin in one hand and his
hat in the other, he walked off the terrace.

After Toby had left the table so abruptly, Mrs. Quill felt
deeply ashamed of herself.

"He's just so disgusted," she decided, "that he can't even
look me in the face without feeling like throwing up. It's because he thinks I'm balmy to go around gay as a lark with only

twenty-two fifty in the bank. Well, well, I expect I'd better start worrying a little more. When he comes back I'll tell him I'll turn over a new leaf."

Everyone had left the terrace by now with the exception of the waiter who had served Mrs. Quill. He stood with his hands behind his back and stared straight ahead of him.

"Sit down for a bit and talk to me," said Mrs. Quill to him. "I'm lonesome on this dark old terrace. It's really a beautiful terrace. You might tell me something about yourself. How much money have you got in the bank? I know you think I'm fresh to ask you, but I'd really like to know."

"Why not?" answered the waiter. "I've got about three hundred and fifty dollars in the bank." He did not sit down.

"Where did you get it?" asked Mrs. Quill.

"From my uncle."

"I guess you feel pretty secure."

"No."

Mrs. Quill began to wonder whether or not Toby would come back at all. She pressed her hands together and asked the young waiter if he knew where the gentleman who had been sitting next to her had gone.

"Home, I guess," said the waiter.

"Well, let's just have one look in the lobby," said Mrs. Quill nervously. She beckoned to the waiter to follow her.

They went into the lobby and together they searched the faces of the guests, who were either standing around in groups or sitting along the wall in armchairs. The hotel was much livelier now than it had been when Mrs. Quill first arrived with Toby. She was deeply troubled and hurt at not seeing Toby anywhere.

"I guess I'd better go home and let you get some sleep," she said absentmindedly to the waiter, "but not before I've bought something for Pacifica. . . ." She had been trembling a little, but the thought of Pacifica filled her with assurance.

"Such an awful, dreadful, mean thing to be alone in the

world even for a minute," she said to the waiter. "Come with me and help me choose something, nothing important, just some remembrance of the hotel."

"They're all the same," said the waiter, following her reluctantly. "Just a lot of junk. I don't know what your friend wants. You might get her a little pocketbook with *Panama* painted on it."

"No, I want it to be specially marked with the name of the hotel."

"Well," said the waiter, "most people don't go in for that."

"Oh my—oh my," said Mrs. Quill emphatically, "must I always be told what other people do? I've had just about enough of it." She marched up to the magazine stand and said to the young man behind the counter: "Now, I want something with *Hotel Washington* written on it. For a woman."

The man looked through his stock and pulled out a handkerchief on the corner of which were painted two palm trees and the words: *Souvenir of Panama.*

"Most people prefer this, though," he said, drawing a tremendous straw hat from under the counter and placing it on his own head.

"You see, it gives you as much shadow as an umbrella and it is very becoming." There was nothing written on the hat at all.

"That handkerchief," continued the young man, "most people consider it kind of, you know . . ."

"My dear young man," said Mrs. Quill, "I expressly told you that I wanted this gift to bear the words *Hotel Washington* and if possible also a picture of the hotel."

"But, lady, nobody wants that. People don't want pictures of hotels on their souvenirs. Palm trees, sunsets, sometimes even bridges, but not hotels."

"Do you or do you not have anything that bears the words *Hotel Washington?*" said Mrs. Quill, raising her voice.

The salesman was beginning to get angry. "I *do* have," he

said, his eyes flashing, "if you will wait one minute please, madam." He opened a little gate and went out into the lobby. He was back in a short time carrying a heavy black ash-tray which he set on the counter in front of Mrs. Quill. The name of the hotel was stamped in the center of the ash-tray in yellow lettering.

"Is this the type of thing you wanted?" asked the salesman.

"Why, yes," said Mrs. Quill, "it is."

"All right, madam, that'll be fifty cents."

"That's not worth fifty cents." whispered the waiter to Mrs. Quill.

Mrs. Quill looked through her purse; she was able to find no more than a quarter in change and no bills at all.

"Look," she said to the young man, "I'm the proprietress of the Hotel de las Palmas. I will show you my bank book with my address written in the front of it. Are you going to trust me with this ash-tray just this once? You see, I came with a gentleman friend and we had a falling out and he went home ahead of me."

"I can't help that, madam," said the salesman.

Meanwhile one of the assistant managers who had been watching the group at the magazine stand from another corner of the lobby thought it time to intervene. He was exceedingly suspicious of Mrs. Quill, who did not appear to him to measure up to the standard of the other guests in any way, not even from a distance. He also wondered what could possibly be keeping the waiter standing in front of the magazine stand for such a long while. He walked over to them looking as serious and as thoughtful as he was able.

"Here's my bank book," Mrs. Quill was saying to the salesman.

The waiter, seeing the assistant manager approaching, was frightened and immediately presented Mrs. Quill with the check for the drinks she and Toby had consumed together.

"You owe six dollars on the terrace," he said to Mrs. Quill.

"Didn't he pay for them?" she said. "I guess he must have been in an awful state."

"Can I help you?" the assistant manager asked of Mrs. Quill.

"I'm sure you can," she said. "I'm the owner of the Hotel de las Palmas."

"I'm sorry," the manager said, "but I'm not familiar with the Hotel de las Palmas."

"Well," said Mrs. Quill, "I have no money with me. I came here with a gentleman, we had a falling out, but I have my bank book here with me which will prove to you that I will have the money as soon as I can run over to the bank tomorrow. I can't sign a check because it's in the savings bank."

"I'm sorry," said the assistant manager, "but we extend credit only to guests residing in the hotel."

"I do that too, in my hotel," said Mrs. Quill, "unless it is something out of the ordinary."

"We make a rule of never extending credit . . ."

"I wanted to take this ash-tray home to my girl friend. She admires your hotel."

"That ash-tray is the property of the Hotel Washington," said the assistant manager, frowning sternly at the salesman, who said quickly: "She wanted something with *Hotel Washington* written on it. I didn't have anything so I thought I'd sell her one of these—for fifty cents," he added, winking at the assistant manager, who was standing farther and farther back on his heels.

"These ash-trays," he repeated, "are the property of the Hotel Washington. We have only a limited number of them in stock and every available tray is in constant use."

The salesman, not caring to have anything more to do with the ash-tray lest he lose his job, carried it back to the table from which he had originally removed it and took up his position again behind the counter.

"Do you want either the handkerchief or the hat?" he asked of Mrs. Quill as though nothing had happened.

"She's got all the hats and the hankies she needs," said Mrs. Quill. "I suppose I'd better go home."

"Would you care to come to the desk with me and settle the bill?" asked the assistant manager.

"Well, if you'll just wait until tomorrow—"

"I'm afraid it is definitely against the rules of the hotel, madam. If you'll just step this way with me." He turned to the waiter, who was following the conversation intently. "*Te necesitan afuera*," he said to him, "go on."

The waiter was about to say something, but he decided against it and walked slowly away towards the terrace. Mrs. Quill began to cry.

"Wait a minute," she said, taking a handkerchief from her bag. "Wait a minute—I would like to telephone to my friend Pacifica."

The assistant manager pointed in the direction of the telephone booths, and she hurried away, her face buried in her handkerchief. Fifteen minutes later she returned, crying more pitifully than before.

"Mrs. Copperfield is coming to get me—I told her all about it. I think I'll sit down somewhere and wait."

"Does Mrs. Copperfield have the necessary funds with which to cover your bill?"

"I don't know," said Mrs. Quill, walking away from him.

"You mean you don't know whether or not she will be able to pay your bill?"

"Yes, yes, she'll pay my bill. Please let me sit down over there."

The manager nodded. Mrs. Quill fell into an armchair that stood beside a tall palm tree. She covered her face with her hands and continued to cry.

Twenty minutes later Mrs. Copperfield arrived. In spite of

the heat she was wearing a silver-fox cape which she had brought with her for use only in higher altitudes.

Although she was perspiring and badly made up, she felt assured of being treated with a certain amount of deference by the hotel employees because of the silver-fox cape.

She had awakened quite some time before and was again a little drunk. She rushed up to Mrs. Quill and kissed her on the top of her head.

"Where's the man who made you cry?" she asked.

Mrs. Quill looked around through her tear-veiled eyes and pointed to the assistant manager. Mrs. Copperfield beckoned to him with her index finger.

He came over to them and she asked him where she could get some flowers for Mrs. Quill.

"There's nothing like flowers when you're either sick at heart or physically ill," she said to him. "She's been under a terrible strain. Would you get some flowers?" she asked, taking a twenty-dollar bill from her purse.

"There is no florist in the hotel," said the assistant manager.

"That's not very luxurious," said Mrs. Copperfield.

He did not reply.

"Well then," she continued, "the next best thing to do is to buy her something nice to drink. I suggest that we all go to the bar."

The assistant manager declined.

"But," said Mrs. Copperfield, "I insist that you come along. I want to talk things over with you. I think you've been horrid."

The assistant manager stared at her.

"The most horrid thing about you," continued Mrs. Copperfield, "is that you're just as grouchy now that you know your bill will be paid as you were before. You were mean and worried then and you're mean and worried now. The expression on your face hasn't changed one bit. It's a dangerous man who reacts more or less in the same way to good news or bad news."

Since he still made no effort to speak, she continued: "You've not only made Mrs. Quill completely miserable for no reason at all, but you've spoiled my fun too. You don't even know how to please the rich." The assistant manager raised his eyebrows.

"You won't understand this but I shall tell it to you anyway. I came here for two reasons. The first reason, naturally, was in order to get my friend Mrs. Quill out of trouble; the second reason was in order to see your face when you realized that a bill which you never expected to be paid was to be paid after all. I expected to be able to watch the transition. You understand—enemy into friend—that's always terribly exciting. That's why in a good movie the hero often hates the heroine until the very end. But you, of course, wouldn't dream of lowering your standards. You think it would be cheap to turn into an affable human being because you discovered there was money where you had been sure there was no money to be forthcoming. Do you think the rich mind? They never get enough of it. They want to be liked for their money too, and not only for themselves. You're not even a good hotel manager. You're definitely a boor in every way."

The assistant manager looked down with loathing at Mrs. Copperfield's upturned face. He hated her sharp features and her high voice. He found her even more disgusting than Mrs. Quill. He was not fond of women anyway.

"You have no imagination," she said, *"none whatever!* You are missing everything. Where do I pay my bill?"

All the way home Mrs. Copperfield felt sad because Mrs. Quill was dignified and remote and did not give her the lavish thanks which she had been expecting.

•

Early the next morning Mrs. Copperfield and Pacifica were together in Pacifica's bedroom. The sky was beginning to grow
light. Mrs. Copperfield had never seen Pacifica this drunk. Her
hair was pushed up on her head. It looked now somewhat like
a wig which is a little too small for the wearer. Her pupils were
very large and slightly filmed. There was a large dark spot on
the front of her checked skirt, and her breath smelled very
strongly of whisky. She stumbled over to the window and
looked out. It was quite dark in the room. Mrs. Copperfield
could barely discern the red and purple squares in Pacifica's
skirt. She could not see her legs at all, the shadows were so
deep, but she knew the heavy yellow silk stockings and the
white sneakers well.

"It's so lovely," said Mrs. Copperfield.

"Beautiful," said Pacifica, turning around, "beautiful." She
moved unsteadily around the room. "Listen," she said, "the
most wonderful thing to do now is to go to the beach and swim
in the water. If you have enough money we can take a taxicab
and go. Come on. Will you?"

Mrs. Copperfield was very startled indeed, but Pacifica was
already pulling a blanket from the bed. "Please," she said.
"You cannot know how much pleasure this would give me.
You must take that towel over there."

The beach was not very far away. When they arrived, Pacifica told the cab-driver to come back in two hours.

The shore was strewn with rocks; this was a disappointment
to Mrs. Copperfield. Although the wind was not very strong,
she noticed that the top branches of the palm trees were shaking.

Pacifica took her clothes off and immediately walked into
the water. She stood for a time with her legs wide apart, the
water scarcely reaching to her shins, while Mrs. Copperfield sat
on a rock trying to decide whether or not to remove her own

clothes. There was a sudden splash and Pacifica started to swim. She swam first on her back and then on her stomach, and Mrs. Copperfield was certain that she could hear her singing. When at last Pacifica grew tired of splashing about in the water, she stood up and walked towards the beach. She took tremendous strides and her pubic hair hung between her legs sopping wet. Mrs. Copperfield looked a little embarrassed, but Pacifica plopped down beside her and asked her why she did not come in the water.

"I can't swim," said Mrs. Copperfield.

Pacifica looked up at the sky. She could see now that it was not going to be a completely fair day.

"Why do you sit on that terrible rock?" said Pacifica. "Come, take your clothes off and we go in the water. I will teach you to swim."

"I was never able to learn."

"I will teach you. If you cannot learn I will let you sink. No, this is only a joke. Don't take it serious."

Mrs. Copperfield undressed. She was very white and thin, and her spine was visible all the way along her back. Pacifica looked at her body without saying a word.

"I know I have an awful figure," said Mrs. Copperfield.

Pacifica did not answer. "Come," she said, getting up and putting her arm around Mrs. Copperfield's waist.

They stood with the water up to their thighs, facing the beach and the palm trees. The trees appeared to be moving behind a mist. The beach was colorless. Behind them the sky was growing lighter very rapidly, but the sea was still almost black. Mrs. Copperfield noticed a red fever sore on Pacifica's lip. Water was dripping from her hair onto her shoulders.

She turned away from the beach and pulled Mrs. Copperfield farther out into the water.

Mrs. Copperfield held onto Pacifica's hand very hard. Soon the water was up to her chin.

"Now lie on your back. I will hold you under your head," said Pacifica.

Mrs. Copperfield looked around wildly, but she obeyed, and floated on her back with only the support of Pacifica's open hand under her head to keep her from sinking. She could see her own narrow feet floating on top of the water. Pacifica started to swim, dragging Mrs. Copperfield along with her. As she had only the use of one arm, her task was an arduous one and she was soon breathing like a bull. The touch of her hand underneath the head of Mrs. Copperfield was very light—in fact, so light that Mrs. Copperfield feared that she would be left alone from one minute to the next. She looked up. The sky was packed with gray clouds. She wanted to say something to Pacifica, but she did not dare to turn her head.

Pacifica swam a little farther inland. Suddenly she stood up and placed both her hands firmly in the small of Mrs. Copperfield's back. Mrs. Copperfield felt happy and sick at once. She turned her face and in so doing she brushed Pacifica's heavy stomach with her cheek. She held on hard to Pacifica's thigh with the strength of years of sorrow and frustration in her hand.

"Don't leave me," she called out.

At this moment Mrs. Copperfield was strongly reminded of a dream that had recurred often during her life. She was being chased up a short hill by a dog. At the top of the hill there stood a few pine trees and a mannequin about eight feet high. She approached the mannequin and discovered her to be fashioned out of flesh, but without life. Her dress was of black velvet, and tapered to a very narrow width at the hem. Mrs. Copperfield wrapped one of the mannequin's arms tightly around her own waist. She was startled by the thickness of the arm and very pleased. The mannequin's other arm she bent upward from the elbow with her free hand. Then the mannequin began to sway backwards and forwards. Mrs. Copperfield clung all the more tightly to the mannequin and together they fell off the top of the hill and continued rolling for quite a distance until they landed on a little walk, where they remained locked in each other's arms. Mrs. Copperfield loved this part of the dream best; and the fact that all the way down the hill the mannequin acted as a buffer between herself and the broken bottles and little stones over which they fell gave her particular satisfaction.

Pacifica had resurrected the emotional content of her dream for a moment, which Mrs. Copperfield thought was certainly the reason for her own peculiar elation.

"Now," said Pacifica, "if you don't mind I will take one more swim by myself." But first she helped Mrs. Copperfield to her feet and led her back to the beach, where Mrs. Copperfield collapsed on the sand and hung her head like a wilted flower. She was trembling and exhausted as one is after a love experience. She looked up at Pacifica, who noticed that her eyes were more luminous and softer than she had ever seen them before.

"You should go in the water more," said Pacifica; "you stay in the house too much."

She ran back into the water and swam back and forth many times. The sea was now blue and much rougher than it had been earlier. Once during the course of her swimming Pacifica rested on a large flat rock which the outgoing tide had uncovered. She was directly in the line of the hazy sun's pale rays. Mrs. Copperfield had a difficult time being able to see her at all and soon she fell asleep.

•

Upon arriving back at the hotel, Pacifica announced to Mrs. Copperfield that she was going to sleep like a dead person. "I hope I don't wake up for ten days," she said.

Mrs. Copperfield watched her stumble down the bright green corridor, yawning and tossing her head.

"Two weeks I'll sleep," she said again, and then she went

into her room and shut the door behind her. In her own room
Mrs. Copperfield decided that she had better call on Mr. Copperfield. She went downstairs and walked out into the street,
which seemed to be moving as it had on the first day of her
arrival. There were a few people already seated on their balconies who were looking down at her. A very thin girl, wearing a
red silk dress which hung down to her ankles, was crossing the
street towards her. She looked surprisingly young and fresh.
When Mrs. Copperfield was nearer to her she decided that she
was a Malayan. She was rather startled when the girl stopped
directly in front of her and addressed her in perfect English.

"Where have you been that you got your hair all wet?" she
said.

"I've been taking a swim with a friend of mine. We—we
went early to the beach." Mrs. Copperfield didn't feel much
like talking.

"What beach?" asked the girl.

"I don't know," said Mrs. Copperfield.

"Well, did you walk there or did you ride?"

"We rode."

"There isn't any beach really near enough to walk to, I
guess," said the girl.

"No, I guess there isn't," said Mrs. Copperfield, sighing and
looking around her. The girl was walking along with her.

"Was the water cold?" asked the girl.

"Yes and no," said Mrs. Copperfield.

"Did you swim in the water naked with your friend?"

"Yes."

"Then there weren't any people around, I suppose."

"No, there wasn't a soul there. Do you swim?" Mrs. Copperfield asked the girl.

"No," she said, "I never go near the water." The girl had a
shrill voice. She had light hair and brows. She could easily
have been partly English. Mrs. Copperfield decided not to ask
her. She turned to the girl.

"I'm going to make a telephone call. Where is the nearest place with a phone?"

"Come to Bill Grey's restaurant. They keep it very cool. I generally spend my mornings there drinking like a fish. By the time it's noon I'm cockeyed drunk. I shock the tourists. I'm half Irish and half Javanese. They make bets about what I am. Whoever wins has to buy me a drink. Guess how old I am."

"God knows," said Mrs. Copperfield.

"Well, I'm sixteen."

"Very possible," said Mrs. Copperfield. The girl seemed peeved. They walked in silence to Bill Grey's restaurant, where the girl pushed Mrs. Copperfield through the door and along the floor towards a table in the middle of the restaurant.

"Sit down and order whatever you like. It's on me," said the girl.

There was an electric fan whirling above their heads.

"Isn't it delicious in here?" she said to Mrs. Copperfield.

"Let me make my phone call," said Mrs. Copperfield, who was terrified lest Mr. Copperfield should have come in a few hours ago and be waiting impatiently for her call even at this very moment.

"Make all the phone calls you like," said the girl.

Mrs. Copperfield went into the booth and phoned her husband. He said that he had arrived a short time ago, and that he would have breakfast and join her afterwards at Bill Grey's. He sounded cold and tired.

The girl, while waiting anxiously for her return, had ordered two old-fashioneds. Mrs. Copperfield came back to the table and flopped into her seat.

"I never can sleep late in the mornings," said the girl. "I don't even like to sleep at night if I have anything better to do. My mother told me that I was as nervous as a cat, but very healthy. I went to dancing school but I was too lazy to learn the steps."

"Where do you live?" asked Mrs. Copperfield.

"I live alone in a hotel. I've got plenty of money. A man in the Army is in love with me. He's married but I never go with anyone else. He gives me plenty of money. He's even got more money at home. I'll buy you what you want. Don't tell anyone around here, though, that I've got money to spend on other people. I never buy them anything. They give me a pain. They live such terrible lives. So cheap; so stupid; so very stupid! They don't have any privacy. I have two rooms. You can use one of them if you like."

Mrs. Copperfield said she wouldn't need to, very firmly. She wasn't fond of this girl in the least.

"What is your name?" the girl asked her.

"Frieda Copperfield."

"My name is Peggy—Peggy Gladys. You looked kind of adorable to me with your hair all wet and your little nose as shiny as it was. That's why I asked you to drink with me."

Mrs. Copperfield jumped. "Please don't embarrass me," she said.

"Oh, let me embarrass you, adorable. Now finish your drink and I'll get you some more. Maybe you're hungry and would like some steak."

The girl had the bright eyes of an insatiable nymphomaniac. She wore a ridiculous little watch on a black ribbon around her wrist.

"I live at the Hotel de las Palmas," said Mrs. Copperfield. "I am a friend of the manager there, Mrs. Quill, and one of her guests, Pacifica."

"That's no good, that hotel," said Peggy. "I went in there with some fellows for drinks one night and I said to them: 'If you don't turn right around and leave this hotel, I'll never allow you to take me out again.' It's a cheap place; awful place; it's filthy dirty besides. I'm surprised at you living there. My hotel is much nicer. Some Americans stay there when they come off the boat if they don't go to the Hotel Washington. It's the Hotel Granada."

"Yes, that is where we were staying originally," said Mrs. Copperfield. "My husband is there now. I think it is the most depressing place I have ever set foot in. I think the Hotel de las Palmas is a hundred million times nicer."

"But," said the girl, opening her mouth wide in dismay, "I think you have not looked very carefully. I've put all my own things around in my room of course, and that makes a lot of difference."

"How long have you been living there?" asked Mrs. Copperfield. She was completely puzzled by this girl and a little bit sorry for her.

"I have been living there for a year and a half. It seems like a lifetime. I moved in a little while after I met the man in the Army. He's very nice to me. I think I'm smarter than he is. That's because I'm a girl. Mother told me that girls were never dumb like men, so I just go ahead and do whatever I think is right."

The girl's face was elfin and sweet. She had a cleft chin and a small snub-nose.

"Honestly," she said, "I've got lots of money. I can always get more. I'd love to get you anything you like, because I love the way you talk and look and the way you move; you're elegant." She giggled and put her own dry rough hand in Mrs. Copperfield's.

"Please," she said, "be friendly to me. I don't often see people I like. I never do the same thing twice, really I don't. I haven't asked anyone up to my rooms in the longest while because I'm not interested and because they get everything so dirty. I know you wouldn't get everything dirty because I can tell that you come from a nice class of people. I love people with a good education. I think it's wonderful."

"I have so much on my mind," said Mrs. Copperfield. "Generally I haven't."

"Well, forget it," said the young girl imperiously. "You're with Peggy Gladys and she's paying for your drinks. Because she wants to pay for your drinks with all her heart. It's such a beautiful morning. Cheer up!" She took Mrs. Copperfield by the sleeve and shook her.

Mrs. Copperfield was still deep in the magic of her dream and in thoughts of Pacifica. She was uneasy and the electric fan seemed to blow directly on her heart. She sat staring ahead of her, not listening to a word the girl was saying.

She could not tell how long she had been dreaming when she looked down and saw a lobster lying on a plate in front of her.

"Oh," she said, "I can't eat this. I can't possibly eat this."

"But I ordered it for you," said Peggy, "and there is some beer coming along. I had your old-fashioned taken away because you weren't touching it." She leaned across the table and tucked Mrs. Copperfield's napkin under her chin.

"Please eat, dearest," said Peggy, "you'll give me such great pleasure if you do."

"What do you think you're doing?" said Mrs. Copperfield fretfully. "Playing house?"

Peggy laughed.

"You know," said Mrs. Copperfield, "my husband is coming here to join us. He'll think we're both stark raving mad to be eating lobster in the morning. He doesn't understand such things."

"Well, let's eat it up quickly, then," said Peggy. She looked wistfully at Mrs. Copperfield. "I wish he wasn't coming," she said. "Couldn't you telephone him and tell him not to come?"

"No, my dear, that would be impossible. Besides, I don't have any reason to tell him not to come. I am very anxious to see him." Mrs. Copperfield could not resist being just a little bit sadistic with Peggy Gladys.

"Of course you want to see him," said Peggy, looking very shy and demure. "I'll be quiet while he's here, I'll promise you."

"That's just what I don't want you to do. Please continue to prattle when he's here."

"Of course, darling. Don't be so nervous."

Mr. Copperfield arrived as they were eating their lobster. He was wearing a dark green suit and looking extremely well. He came over to them smiling pleasantly.

"Hello," said Mrs. Copperfield. "I'm very glad to see you. You look very well. This is Peggy Gladys; we've just met."

He shook hands with her and seemed very pleased. "What on earth are you eating?" he asked them.

"Lobster," they answered. He frowned. "But," he said, "you'll have indigestion, and you're drinking beer too! Good God!" He sat down.

"I don't mean to interfere, of course," said Mr. Copperfield, "but it's very bad. Have you had breakfast?"

"I don't know," said Mrs. Copperfield purposely. Peggy Gladys laughed. Mr. Copperfield raised his brows.

"You must know," he murmured. "Don't be ridiculous."

He asked Peggy Gladys where she was from.

"I'm from Panama," she told him, "but I'm half Irish and half Javanese."

"I see," said Mr. Copperfield. He kept smiling at her.

"Pacifica's asleep," said Mrs. Copperfield suddenly.

Mr. Copperfield frowned. "Really," he said, "are you going back there?"

"What do you think I'm going to do?"

"There isn't any point in staying here much longer. I thought we'd pack. I've made arrangements in Panama. We can sail tomorrow. I have to phone them tonight. I've found out a lot about the various countries in Central America. It might be possible for us to stay on a kind of cattle ranch in Costa Rica. A man told me about it. It's completely isolated. You have to get there on a river boat."

Peggy Gladys looked bored.

Mrs. Copperfield put her head in her hands.

"Imagine red and blue guacamayos flying over the cattle," Mr. Copperfield laughed. "Latin Texas. It must be completely crazy."

"Red and blue guacamayos flying over the cattle," Peggy Gladys repeated after him. "What are guacamayos?" she asked.

"They're tremendous red and blue birds, more or less like parrots," said Mr. Copperfield. "As long as you are eating lobster I think I shall have ice cream with whipped cream on top."

"He's nice," said Peggy Gladys.

"Listen," said Mrs. Copperfield, "I feel sick. I don't think I can sit through the ice cream."

"I won't take long," said Mr. Copperfield. He looked at her. "It must be the lobster."

"Maybe I'd better take her to my Hotel Granada," said Peggy Gladys, jumping to her feet with alacrity. "She'll be very comfortable there. Then you can come after you've eaten your ice cream."

"That seems sensible, don't you think so, Frieda?"

"No," said Mrs. Copperfield vehemently, clutching at the chain she wore around her neck. "I think I'd better go right straight back to the Hotel de las Palmas. I *must* go. I must go immediately. . . ." She was so distraught that she rose from the table, forgetting her pocketbook and her scarf, and started to leave the restaurant.

"But you've left everything behind you," Mr. Copperfield called out after her.

"I'll take them," exclaimed Peggy Gladys. "You eat your ice cream and come later." She rushed after Mrs. Copperfield and together they ran down the suffocatingly hot street towards the Hotel de las Palmas.

Mrs. Quill was standing in the doorway drinking something out of a bottle.

"I'm on the cherry-pop wagon until dinner time," she said.

"Oh, Mrs. Quill, come up to my room with me!" said Mrs.

Copperfield, putting her arms around Mrs. Quill and sighing deeply. "Mr. Copperfield is back."

"Why don't you come upstairs with *me?*" said Peggy Gladys. "I promised your husband I'd take care of you."

Mrs. Copperfield wheeled round. "Please be quiet," she shouted, looking fixedly at Peggy Gladys.

"Now, now," said Mrs. Quill, "don't upset the little girl. We'll have to be giving her a honey bun to quiet her. Of course it took more than a honey bun to quiet me at her age."

"I'm all right," said Peggy Gladys. "Will you kindly take us to her room? She's supposed to be flat on her back."

The young girl sat on the edge of Mrs. Copperfield's bed with her hand on Mrs. Copperfield's forehead.

"I'm sorry," she said. "You look very badly. I wish you wouldn't be so unhappy. Couldn't you possibly not think about it now and think about it some other day? Sometimes if you let things rest . . . I'm not sixteen, I'm seventeen. I feel like a child. I can't seem to say anything unless people think I'm very young. Maybe you don't like the fact that I'm so fresh. You're white and green. You don't look pretty. You looked much prettier before. After your husband has been here I'll take you for a ride in a carriage if you like. My mother's dead," she said softly.

"Listen," said Mrs. Copperfield. "If you don't mind going away now . . . I'd like to be by myself. You can come back later."

"What time can I come back?"

"I don't know; come back later; can't you see? I don't know."

"All right," said Peggy Gladys. "Maybe I should just go downstairs and talk to that fat woman, or drink. Then when you're ready you can come down. I have nothing to do for three days. You really want me to go?"

Mrs. Copperfield nodded.

The girl left the room reluctantly.

Mrs. Copperfield started to tremble after the girl had closed the door behind her. She trembled so violently that she shook the bed. She was suffering as much as she had ever suffered before, because she was going to do what she wanted to do. But it would not make her happy. She did not have the courage to stop from doing what she wanted to do. She knew that it would not make her happy, because only the dreams of crazy people come true. She thought that she was only interested in duplicating a dream, but in doing so she necessarily became the complete victim of a nightmare.

Mr. Copperfield came very quietly into her room. "How do you feel now?" he asked.

"I'm all right," she said.

"Who was that young girl? She was very pretty—from a sculptural point of view."

"Her name is Peggy Gladys."

"She spoke very well, didn't she? Or am I wrong?"

"She spoke beautifully."

"Have you been having a nice time?"

"I've had the most wonderful time in my whole life," said Mrs. Copperfield, almost weeping.

"I had a nice time too, exploring Panama City. But my room was so uncomfortable. There was too much noise. I couldn't sleep."

"Why didn't you take a nicer room in a better hotel?"

"You know me. I hate to spend money. I never think it's worth it. I guess I should have. I should have been drinking too. I'd have had a better time. But I didn't."

They were silent. Mr. Copperfield drummed on the bureau. "I guess we should be leaving tonight," he said, "instead of staying on here. It's terribly expensive here. There won't be another boat for quite a few days."

Mrs. Copperfield did not answer.

"Don't you think I'm correct?"

"I don't want to go," she said, twisting on the bed.

"I don't understand," said Mr. Copperfield.

"I can't go. I want to stay here."

"For how long?"

"I don't know."

"But you can't plan a trip that way. Perhaps you don't intend to plan a trip."

"Oh, I'll plan a trip," said Mrs. Copperfield vaguely.

"You will?"

"No, I won't."

"It's up to you," said Mr. Copperfield. "I just think you'll be
missing a great deal by not seeing Central America. You're certain to get bored here unless you start to drink. You probably
will start to drink."

"Why don't you go, and then come back when you've seen
enough?" she suggested.

"I won't come back because I can't look at you," said Mr.
Copperfield. "You're a horror." So saying, he took an empty
pitcher from the bureau, threw it out of the window into the
alley, and left the room.

An hour later Mrs. Copperfield went downstairs into the
bar. She was surprised and glad to see Pacifica there. Although
Pacifica had powdered her face very heavily, she looked tired.
She was sitting at a little table holding her pocketbook in her
hands.

"Pacifica," said Mrs. Copperfield, "I didn't know that you
were awake. I was certain that you were asleep in your room.
I'm so glad to see you."

"I could not close my eyes. I was sleeping for fifteen minutes
and then after that I could not close my eyes. Someone came to
see me."

Peggy Gladys walked over to Mrs. Copperfield. "Hello," she
said, running her fingers through Mrs. Copperfield's hair. "Are
you ready to take that ride yet?"

"What ride?" asked Mrs. Copperfield.

"The ride in the carriage with me."

"No, I'm not ready," said Mrs. Copperfield.

"When will you be?" asked Peggy Gladys.

"I'm going to buy some stockings," said Pacifica. "You want to come with me, Copperfield?"

"Yes. Let's go."

"Your husband looked upset when he left the hotel," said Peggy Gladys. "I hope you didn't have a fight."

Mrs. Copperfield was walking out of the door with Pacifica. "Excuse us," she called over her shoulder to Peggy Gladys. She was standing still and looking after them like a hurt animal!

It was so hot out that even the most conservative women tourists, their faces and chests flame-red, were pulling off their hats and drying their foreheads with their handkerchiefs. Most of them, to escape the heat, were dropping into the little Hindu stores where, if the shop wasn't too crowded, the salesman offered them a little chair so that they might view twenty or thirty kimonos without getting tired.

"*Qué calor!*" said Pacifica.

"To hell with stockings," said Mrs. Copperfield, who thought she was about to faint. "Let's get some beer."

"If you want, go and get yourself some beer. I must have stockings. I think bare legs on a woman is something terrible."

"No, I'll come with you." Mrs. Copperfield put her hand in Pacifica's.

"Ay!" cried Pacifica, releasing her hand. "We are both too wet, darling. *Qué barbaridad!*"

The store into which Pacifica took Mrs. Copperfield was very tiny. It was even hotter in there than on the street.

"You see you can buy many things here," said Pacifica. "I come here because he knows me and I can get my stockings for very little money."

While Pacifica was buying her stockings Mrs. Copperfield looked at all the other little articles in the store. Pacifica took such a long time that Mrs. Copperfield grew more and more bored. She stood first on one foot and then on the other. Pacifica argued and argued. There were dark perspiration stains under her arms, and the wings of her nose were streaming.

When it was all over and Mrs. Copperfield saw that the salesman was wrapping the package, she went over and paid the bill. The salesman wished her good luck and they left the store.

There was a letter for her at home. Mrs. Quill gave it to her.

"Mr. Copperfield left this for you," she said. "I tried to urge him to stay and have a cup of tea or some beer, but he was in a hurry. He's one handsome fellow."

Mrs. Copperfield took the letter and started towards the bar.

"Hello, sweet," said Peggy Gladys softly.

Mrs. Copperfield could see that Peggy was very drunk. Her hair was hanging over her face and her eyes were dead.

"Maybe you're not ready yet . . . but I can wait a long time. I love to wait. I don't mind being by myself."

"You'll excuse me a minute if I read a letter which I just received from my husband," said Mrs. Copperfield.

She sat down and tore open the envelope.

> Dear Frieda [she read],
>
> I do not mean to be cruel but I shall write to you exactly what I consider to be your faults and I hope sincerely that what I have written will influence you. Like most people, you are not able to face more than one fear during your lifetime. You also spend your life fleeing from your first fear towards your first hope. Be careful that you do not, through your own wiliness, end up always in the same position in which you began. I do not advise you to spend your life surrounding yourself with those things which you term necessary to your existence, regardless of whether or not they are objectively interesting in themselves or even to your own particular intellect. I believe sincerely that only those men who reach the stage where it is possible for them to combat a second tragedy within themselves, and not the first over

again, are worthy of being called mature. When you think someone is going ahead, make sure that he is not really standing still. In order to go ahead, you must leave things behind which most people are unwilling to do. Your first pain, you carry it with you like a lodestone in your breast because all tenderness will come from there. You must carry it with you through your whole life but you must not circle around it. You must give up the search for those symbols which only serve to hide its face from you. You will have the illusion that they are disparate and manifold but they are always the same. If you are only interested in a bearable life, perhaps this letter does not concern you. For God's sake, a ship leaving port is still a wonderful thing to see.

J.C.

Mrs. Copperfield's heart was beating very quickly. She crushed the letter in her hand and shook her head two or three times.

"I'll never bother you unless you ask me to bother you," Peggy Gladys was saying. She did not seem to be addressing anyone in particular. Her eyes wandered from the ceiling to the walls. She was smiling to herself.

"She is reading a letter from her husband," she said, letting her arm fall down heavily on the bar. "I myself don't want a husband—never—never—never. . . ."

Mrs. Copperfield rose to her feet.

"*Pacifica,*" she shouted, "*Pacifica!*"

"Who is Pacifica?" asked Peggy Gladys. "I want to meet her. Is she as beautiful as you are? Tell her to come here. . . ."

"Beautiful?" the bartender laughed. "Beautiful? Neither of them is beautiful. They're both old hens. You're beautiful even if you are blind drunk."

"Bring her in here, darling," said Peggy Gladys, letting her head fall down on the bar.

"Listen, your pal's been out of the room two whole minutes already. She's gone to look for Pacifica."

· 3

It was several months later, and Miss Goering, Miss Gamelon, and Arnold had been living for nearly four weeks in the house which Miss Goering had chosen.

This was gloomier even than Miss Gamelon had expected it would be, since she hadn't much imagination, and reality was often more frightening to her than her wildest dreams. She was now more incensed against Miss Goering than she had been before they had changed houses, and her disposition was so bad that scarcely an hour went by that she did not complain bitterly about her life, or threaten to leave altogether. Behind the house was a dirt bank and some bushes, and if one walked over the bank and followed a narrow path through some more bushes, one soon came to the woods. To the right of the house was a field that was filled with daisies in the summertime. This field might have been quite pleasant to look at had there not been lying right in the middle of it the rusted engine of an old

car. There was very little place to sit out of doors, since the
front porch had rotted away, so they had, all three of them, got
into the habit of sitting close by the kitchen door, where the
house protected them from the wind. Miss Gamelon had been
suffering from the cold ever since she had arrived. In fact, there
was no central heating in the house: only a few little oil stoves,
and although it was still only early fall, on certain days it was
already quite chilly.

Arnold returned to his own home less and less frequently,
and more and more often he took the little train and the ferry
boat into the city from Miss Goering's house and then returned again after his work was done to have his dinner and
sleep on the island.

Miss Goering never questioned his presence. He became
more careless about his clothing, and three times in the last
week he had neglected to go in to his office at all. Miss Gamelon had made a terrible fuss over this.

One day Arnold was resting upstairs in one of the little bedrooms directly under the roof and she and Miss Goering were
seated in front of the kitchen door warming themselves in the
afternoon sun.

"That slob upstairs," said Miss Gamelon, "is eventually
going to give up going to the office at all. He's going to move in
here completely and do nothing but eat and sleep. In another
year he's going to be as big as an elephant and you won't be
able to rid yourself of him. Thank the Lord I don't expect to
be here then."

"Do you really think that he will be so very, very fat in one
year?" said Miss Goering.

"I know it!" said Miss Gamelon. There was a sudden blast
of wind which blew the kitchen door open. "Oh, I hate this,"
said Miss Gamelon vehemently, getting up from her seat to fix
the door.

"Besides," she continued, "who ever heard of a man living
together with two ladies in a house which does not even con-

tain one extra bedroom, so that he is obliged to sleep fully clothed on the couch! It is enough to take one's appetite away, just to walk through the parlor and see him there at all hours of the day, eyes open or shut, with not a care in the world. Only a man who is a slob could be willing to live in such a way. He is even too lazy to court either of us, which is a most unnatural thing you must admit—if you have any conception at all of the male physical make-up. Of course he is not a man. He is an elephant."

"I don't think," said Miss Goering, "that he is as big as all that."

"Well, I told him to rest in my room because I couldn't stand seeing him on the couch any more. And as for you," she said to Miss Goering, "I think you are the most insensitive person that I have ever met in my life."

At the same time Miss Gamelon was really worried—although she scarcely admitted this to herself—that Miss Goering was losing her mind. Miss Goering seemed thinner and more nervous and she insisted on doing most of the housework all by herself. She was constantly cleaning the house and polishing the doorknobs and the silver; she tried in many small ways to make the house livable without buying any of the things which were needed to make it so; she had in these last few weeks suddenly developed an extreme avarice and drew only enough money from the bank to enable them to live in the simplest manner possible. At the same time she seemed to think nothing of paying for Arnold's food, as he scarcely ever offered to contribute anything to the upkeep of the house. It was true that he went on paying his own share in his family's apartment, which perhaps left him very little to pay for anything else. This made Miss Gamelon furious, because although she did not understand why it was necessary for Miss Goering to live on less than one tenth of her income, she had nevertheless adjusted herself to this tiny scale of living and was trying desperately to make the money stretch as far as possible.

They sat in silence for a few minutes. Miss Gamelon was thinking seriously about all these things when suddenly a bottle broke against her head, inundating her with perfume and making quite a deep cut just above her forehead. She started to bleed profusely and sat for a moment with her hands over her eyes.

"I didn't actually mean to draw blood," said Arnold leaning out of the window. "I just meant to give her a start."

Miss Goering, although she was beginning to regard Miss Gamelon more and more as the embodiment of evil, made a swift and compassionate gesture towards her friend.

"Oh, my dear, let me get you something to disinfect the cut with." She went into the house and passed Arnold in the hall. He was standing with his hand on the front door, unable to decide whether to stay in or go out. When Miss Goering came down again with the medicine, Arnold had disappeared.

•

It was near evening, and Miss Gamelon, with a bandaged head, was standing in front of the house. She could see the road between the trees, from where she was standing. Her face was very white and her eyes were swollen because she had been weeping bitterly. She was weeping because it was the first time in her life that anyone had ever struck her physically. The more she thought about it, the more serious it became in her mind, and while she stood in front of the house she was suddenly frightened for the first time in her life. How far she had traveled from her home! Twice she had begun to pack her bags and twice she had decided not to do so, only because she could not bring herself to leave Miss Goering, since in her own way, though she scarcely knew it herself, she was deeply attached to her. It was dark before Miss Gamelon went into the house.

Miss Goering was terribly upset because Arnold had not yet returned, although she did not care for him very much more than she had in the beginning. She, too, stood outside in the dark for nearly an hour because her anxiety was so great that she was unable to remain in the house.

While she was still outside, Miss Gamelon, seated in the parlor before an empty fireplace, felt that all of God's wrath had descended upon her own head. The world and the people in it had suddenly slipped beyond her comprehension and she felt in great danger of losing the whole world once and for all—a feeling that is difficult to explain.

Each time that she looked over her shoulder into the kitchen and saw Miss Goering's dark shape still standing in front of the door, her heart failed her a little more. Finally Miss Goering came in.

"Lucy!" she called. Her voice was very clear and a little higher than usual. "Lucy, let's go and find Arnold." She sat opposite Miss Gamelon, and her face looked extraordinarily bright.

Miss Gamelon said: "Certainly not."

"Well, after all," said Miss Goering, "he lives in my house."

"Yes, that he does," said Miss Gamelon.

"And it is only right," said Miss Goering, "that people in the same house should look after each other. They always do, I think, don't they?"

"They're more careful about who gets under the same roof with them," said Miss Gamelon, coming to life again.

"I don't think so, really," said Miss Goering. Miss Gamelon breathed a deep sigh and got up. "Never mind," she said, "soon I'll be in the midst of real human beings again."

They started through the woods along a path which was a short cut to the nearest town, about twenty minutes from their house on foot. Miss Goering screeched at every strange noise and clutched at Miss Gamelon's sweater all the way. Miss Gamelon was sullen and suggested that they take the long way around on their way back.

At last they came out of the woods and walked a short

stretch along the highway. On either side of the road were restaurants which catered mainly to automobilists. In one of these
Miss Goering saw Arnold seated at a table near the window,
eating a sandwich.

"There's Arnold," said Miss Goering. "Come along!" She
took hold of Miss Gamelon's hand and almost skipped in the
direction of the restaurant.

"It is really almost too good to be true," said Miss Gamelon;
"he is eating again."

It was terribly hot inside. They removed their sweaters and
went to sit with Arnold at his table.

"Good evening," said Arnold. "I didn't expect to see you
here." This he said to Miss Goering. He avoided looking in the
direction of Miss Gamelon.

"Well," said Miss Gamelon, "are you going to explain yourself?"

Arnold had just taken quite a large bite of his sandwich so
that he was unable to answer her. But he did roll his eyes in
her direction. It was impossible to tell with his cheeks so full
whether or not he looked angry. Miss Gamelon was terribly
annoyed at this, but Miss Goering sat smiling at them because
she was glad to have them both with her again.

Finally Arnold swallowed his food.

"I don't have to explain myself," he said to Miss Gamelon,
looking very grouchy indeed now that he had swallowed his
food. "You owe a profound apology to me for hating me and
telling Miss Goering about it."

"I have a perfect right to hate whom I please," said Miss
Gamelon, "and also, since we live in a free country, I can talk
about it on the street corner if I want to."

"You don't know me well enough to hate me. You've mis-
judged me anyway, which is enough to make any man furious,
and I *am* furious."

"Well then, get out of the house. Nobody wants you there
anyway."

"That's incorrect; Miss Goering, I am sure, wants me there, don't you?"

"Yes, Arnold, of course," said Miss Goering.

"There is no justice," said Miss Gamelon; "you are both outrageous." She sat up very straight, and both Arnold and Miss Goering stared at her bandage.

"Well," said Arnold, wiping his mouth and pushing his plate away, "I am sure there is some way whereby we can arrange it so we can both live in the house together."

"Why are you so attached to the house?" screamed Miss Gamelon. "All you ever do when you're in it is to stretch out in the parlor and go to sleep."

"The house gives me a certain feeling of freedom."

Miss Gamelon looked at him.

"You mean an opportunity to indulge your laziness."

"Now look," said Arnold, "suppose that I am allowed to use the parlor after dinner and in the morning. Then you can use it the rest of the time."

"All right," said Miss Gamelon, "I agree, but see that you don't set your foot in it during the entire afternoon."

On the way home both Miss Gamelon and Arnold seemed quite contented because they had evolved a plan. Each one thought he had got the better of the bargain and Miss Gamelon was already outlining to herself several pleasant ways of spending an afternoon in the parlor.

When they arrived home she went upstairs to bed almost immediately. Arnold lay on the couch, fully dressed, and pulled a knitted coverlet over him. Miss Goering was sitting in the kitchen. After a little while she heard someone sobbing in the parlor. She went inside and found Arnold crying into his sleeve.

"What's the matter, Arnold?"

"I don't know," said Arnold, "it's so disagreeable to have someone hate you. I really think I had perhaps better leave and go back to my house. But I dislike doing that more than

anything in the world and I hate the real-estate business and I
hate for her to be angry with me. Can't you tell her it's just a
period of adjustment for me—to please wait a little bit?"

"Certainly, Arnold, I shall tell her that the very first thing in
the morning. Maybe if you went to business tomorrow, she
might feel better about you."

"Do you think so?" asked Arnold, sitting bolt upright in his
eagerness. "Then I will." He got up and stood by the window
with his feet wide apart. "I just can't stand to have anyone
hate me during this period of adjustment," he said, "and then
of course I'm devoted to you both."

The next evening, when Arnold came home with a box of
chocolates apiece for Miss Goering and Miss Gamelon, he was
surprised to find his father there. He was sitting in a straight-
backed chair next to the fireplace, drinking a cup of tea, and
he had on a motoring cap.

"I came out to see, Arnold, how well you were providing for
these young ladies. They seem to be living in a dung-heap
here."

"I don't see where you have any right to say such a thing as a
guest, Father," said Arnold, gravely handing a box of candy to
each of the women.

"Certainly, because of age, my dear son, I am allowed to say
a great many things. Remember you are all my children to me,
including Princess over here." He hooked Miss Goering's waist
with the top of his cane and drew her over to him. She had
never imagined she would see him in such a rollicking good
humor. He looked to her smaller and thinner than on the
night they had met.

"Well, where do you crazy bugs eat?" he asked them.

"We have a square table," said Miss Gamelon, "in the
kitchen. Sometimes we put it in front of the fireplace, but it's
never very adequate."

Arnold's father cleared his throat and said nothing. He
seemed to be annoyed that Miss Gamelon had spoken.

"Well, you're all crazy," he said, looking at his son and at Miss Goering, and purposely excluding Miss Gamelon, "but I'm rooting for you."

"Where is your wife?" Miss Goering asked him.

"She's at home, I gather," said Arnold's father, "and as sour as a pickle and just as bitter to taste."

Miss Gamelon giggled at his remark. It was the kind of thing that she found amusing. Arnold was delighted to see that she was brightening up a bit.

"Come out with me," said Arnold's father to Miss Goering, "into the wind and the sunshine, my love, or shall I say into the wind and the moonlight, never forgetting to add 'my love.' "

They left the room together and Arnold's father led Miss Goering a little way into the field.

"You see," he said, "I've decided to go back to a number of my boyish tastes. For instance, I took a certain delight in nature when I was young. I can frankly say that I have decided to throw away some of my conventions and ideals and again get a kick out of nature—that is, of course if you are willing to be by my side. It all depends on that."

"Certainly," said Miss Goering, "but what does this involve?"

"It involves," said Arnold's father, "your being a true woman. Sympathetic and willing to defend all that I say and do. At the same time prone to scolding me just a little." He put his ice-cold hand in hers.

"Let's go in," said Miss Goering. "I want to go inside." She began tugging at his arm, but he would not move. She realized that although he looked terribly old-fashioned and a little ridiculous in his motoring cap, he was still very strong. She wondered why he had seemed so much more distinguished the first night that they had met.

She tugged at his arm even harder, half in play, half in earnest, and in so doing she quite unwittingly scratched the inside

of his wrist with her nail. She drew a little blood, which
seemed to upset Arnold's father quite a lot, because he began
stumbling through the field as quickly as he could towards
the house.

Later he announced to everyone his intention of staying the
night in Miss Goering's house. They had lighted a fire and
they were all seated around it together. Twice Arnold had
fallen asleep.

"Mother would be terribly worried," said Arnold.

"Worried?" said Arnold's father. "She will probably die of a
heart attack before morning, but then, what is life but a puff
of smoke or a leaf or a candle soon burned out anyway?"

"Don't pretend you don't take life seriously," said Arnold,
"and don't pretend, just because there are women around, that
you are light-hearted. You're the grim, worrying type and you
know it."

Arnold's father coughed. He looked a little upset.

"I don't agree with you," he said.

Miss Goering took him upstairs to her own bedroom.

"I hope you will sleep in peace," she said to him. "You know
that I'm delighted to have you in my house any time."

Arnold's father pointed to the trees outside the window.

"Oh, night!" he said. "Soft as a maiden's cheek, and as mysterious as the brooding owl, the Orient, the turbaned sultan's
head. How long have I ignored thee underneath my reading
lamp, occupied with various and sundry occupations which I
have now decided to disregard in favor of thee. Accept my
apology and let me be numbered among thy sons and daughters. You see," he said to Miss Goering, "you see what a new
leaf I have really turned over; I think we understand each
other now. You mustn't ever think people have only one nature. Everything I said to you the other night was wrong."

"Oh," said Miss Goering, a little dismayed.

"Yes, I am now interested in being an entirely new personality as different from my former self as A is from Z. This has

been a very lovely beginning. It augurs well, as they say."

He stretched out on the bed, and while Miss Goering was looking at him he fell asleep. Soon he began to snore. She threw a cover over him and left the room, deeply perplexed.

Downstairs she joined the others in front of the fire. They were drinking hot tea into which they had poured a bit of rum.

Miss Gamelon was relaxing. "This is the best thing in the world for your nerves," she said, "and also for softening the sharp angles of your life. Arnold has been telling me about his progress in his uncle's office. How he started as a messenger and has now worked his way up to being one of the chief agents in the office. We've had an extremely pleasant time just sitting here. I think Arnold has been hiding from us a very excellent business sense."

Arnold looked a little distressed. He was still fearful of displeasing Miss Goering.

"Miss Gamelon and I are going to inquire tomorrow whether or not there is a golf course on the island. We have discovered a mutual interest in golf," he said.

Miss Goering could not understand Arnold's sudden change of attitude. It was as though he had just arrived at a summer hotel and was anxious to plan a nice vacation. Miss Gamelon also surprised her somewhat, but she said nothing.

"Golf would be wonderful for you," said Miss Gamelon to Miss Goering; "probably would straighten you out in a week."

"Well," said Arnold apologetically, "she might not like it."

"I don't like sports," said Miss Goering; "more than anything else, they give me a terrific feeling of sinning."

"On the contrary," said Miss Gamelon, "that's exactly what they never do."

"Don't be rude, Lucy dear," said Miss Goering. "After all, I have paid sufficient attention to what happens inside of me and I know better than you about my own feelings."

"Sports," said Miss Gamelon, "can never give you a feeling

of sinning, but what is more interesting is that you can never sit down for more than five minutes without introducing something weird into the conversation. I certainly think you have made a study of it."

.

The next morning Arnold's father came downstairs with his shirt collar open and without a vest. He had rumpled his hair up a bit so that now he looked like an old artist.

"What on earth is Mother going to do?" Arnold asked him at breakfast.

"Fiddlesticks!" said Arnold's father. "You call yourself an artist and you don't even know how to be irresponsible. The beauty of the artist lies in the childlike soul." He touched Miss Goering's hand with his own. She could not help thinking of the speech he had made the night he had come into her bedroom and how opposed it had been to everything he was now saying.

"If your mother has a desire to live, she will live, providing she is willing to leave everything behind her as I have done," he added.

Miss Gamelon was slightly embarrassed by this elderly man who seemed to have just recently made some momentous change in his life. But she was not really curious about him.

"Well," said Arnold, "I imagine you are still providing her with money to pay the rent. I am continuing to contribute my share."

"Certainly," said his father. "I am always a gentleman, although I must say the responsibility weighs heavy on me, like an anchor around my neck. Now," he continued, "let me go out and do the marketing for the day. I feel able to run a hundred-yard dash."

Miss Gamelon sat with furrowed brow, wondering if Miss Goering would permit this crazy old man to live on in the already crowded house. He set out towards town a little while later. They called after him from the window, entreating him to return and put on his coat, but he waved his hand at the sky and refused.

In the afternoon Miss Goering did some serious thinking. She walked back and forth in front of the kitchen door. Already the house, to her, had become a friendly and familiar place and one which she readily thought of as her home. She decided that it was now necessary for her to take little trips to the tip of the island, where she could board the ferry and cross back over to the mainland. She hated to do this as she knew how upsetting it would be, and the more she considered it, the more attractive the life in the little house seemed to her, until she even thought of it as humming with gaiety. In order to assure herself that she would make her excursion that night, she went into her bedroom and put fifty cents on the bureau.

After dinner, when she announced that she was taking a train ride alone, Miss Gamelon nearly wept with indignation. Arnold's father said he thought it was a wonderful idea to take "a train ride into the blue," as he termed it. When Miss Gamelon heard him encouraging Miss Goering, she could no longer contain herself and rushed up into her bedroom. Arnold hastily left the table and lumbered up the steps after her.

Arnold's father begged Miss Goering to allow him to go with her.

"Not this time," she said, "I must go alone"; and Arnold's father, although he said he was very much disappointed, still remained elated. There seemed to be no end to his good humor.

"Well," he said, "setting out into the night like this is just in the spirit of what I'd like to do, and I think that you are cheating me prettily by not allowing me to accompany you."

"It is not for fun that I am going," said Miss Goering, "but because it is necessary to do so."

"Still, I beg you once more," said Arnold's father ignoring

the implications of this remark and getting down on his knees
with difficulty, "I beg you, take me with you."

"Oh, please, my dear," said Miss Goering, "please don't
make it hard for me. I have a weakish personality."

Arnold's father jumped to his feet. "Certainly," he said, "I
would not make anything hard for you." He kissed her wrist
and wished her good luck. "Do you think the two turtle doves
will talk to me?" he asked her, "or do you think they will remain cooped up together all night? I rather hate to be alone."

"So do I," said Miss Goering. "Bang on their door; they'll
talk to you. Good-by. . . ."

Miss Goering decided to walk along the highway, as it was
really too dark to walk through the woods at this hour. She
had proposed this to herself as a stint, earlier in the afternoon,
but had later decided that it was pure folly even to consider it.
It was cold and windy out and she pulled her shawl closer
around her. She continued to affect woolen shawls, although
they had not been stylish for a good many years. Miss Goering
looked up at the sky; she was looking for the stars and hoping
very hard to see some. She stood still for a long time, but she
could not decide whether it was a starlit night or not because
even though she fixed her attention on the sky without once
lowering her eyes, the stars seemed to appear and disappear so
quickly that they were like visions of stars rather than like actual stars. She decided that this was only because the clouds
were racing across the sky so quickly that the stars were obliter-
ated one minute and visible the next. She continued on her
way to the station.

When she arrived she was surprised to find that there were
eight or nine children who had got there ahead of her. Each
one carried a large blue and gold school banner. The children
weren't saying much, but they were engaged in hopping heavily first on one foot and then on the other. Since they were
doing this in unison, the little wooden platform shook abomi-

nably and Miss Goering wondered whether she had not better draw the attention of the children to this fact. Very shortly, however, the train pulled into the station and they all boarded it together. Miss Goering sat in a seat across the aisle from a middle-aged stout woman. She and Miss Goering were the only occupants of the car besides the children. Miss Goering looked at her with interest.

She was wearing gloves and a hat and she sat up very straight. In her right hand she held a long thin package which looked like a fly-swatter. The woman stared ahead of her and not a muscle in her face moved. There were some more packages that she had piled neatly on the seat next to her. Miss Goering looked at her and hoped that she too, was going to the tip of the island. The train started to move and the woman put her free hand on top of the packages next to her so that they would not slide off the seat.

The children had mostly crowded into two seats and those who would have had to sit elsewhere preferred to stand around the already occupied seats. Soon they began to sing songs, which were all in praise of the school from which they had come. They did this so badly that it was almost too much for Miss Goering to bear. She got out of her seat and was so intent upon getting to the children quickly that she paid no attention to the lurching of the car and consequently in her hurry she tripped and fell headlong on the floor right next to where the children were singing.

She managed to get on her feet again although her chin was bleeding. She first asked the children to please stop their singing. They all stared at her. Then she pulled out a little lace handkerchief and started to mop the blood from her chin. Soon the train stopped and the children got off. Miss Goering went to the end of the car and filled a paper cup with water. She wondered nervously, as she mopped her chin in the dark passage, whether or not the lady with the fly-swatter would still be in the car. When she got back to her seat she saw with great relief that the lady was still there. She still held the fly-swatter, but she had turned her head to the left and was looking out at the little station platform.

"I don't think," said Miss Goering to herself, "that it would do any harm if I changed my seat and sat opposite her. After all, I suppose it's quite a natural thing for ladies to approach each other on a suburban train like this, particularly on such a small island."

She slid quietly into the seat opposite the woman and continued to occupy herself with her chin. The train had started again and the woman stared harder and harder out of the window in order to avoid Miss Goering's eye, for Miss Goering was a little disturbing to certain people. Perhaps because of her red and exalted face and her outlandish clothes.

"I'm delighted that the children have left," said Miss Goering; "now it is really pleasant on this train."

It began to rain and the woman pressed her forehead to the glass in order to stare more closely at the slanting drops on the window-pane. She did not answer Miss Goering. Miss Goering began again, for she was used to forcing people into conversation, her fears never having been of a social nature.

"Where are you going?" Miss Goering asked, first because she was really interested in knowing whether or not the woman was traveling to the tip of the island, and also because she thought it a rather disarming question. The woman studied her carefully.

"Home," she said in a flat voice.

"And do you live on this island?" Miss Goering asked her. "It's really enchanting," she added.

The woman did not answer, but instead she started to gather all her packages up in her arms.

"Where exactly do you live?" asked Miss Goering. The woman's eyes shifted about.

"Glensdale," she said hesitatingly, and Miss Goering, although she was not sensitive to slights, realized that the woman was lying to her. This pained her very much.

"Why do you lie to me?" she asked. "I assure you that I am a lady like yourself."

The woman by then had mustered her strength and seemed more sure of herself. She looked straight into Miss Goering's eyes.

"I live in Glensdale," she said, "and I have lived there all my life. I am on my way to visit a friend who lives in a town a little farther along."

"Why do I terrify you so?" Miss Goering asked her. "I would like to have talked to you."

"I won't stand for this another moment," the woman said, more to herself than to Miss Goering. "I have enough real grief in my life without having to encounter lunatics."

Suddenly she grabbed her umbrella and gave Miss Goering a smart rap on the ankles. She was quite red in the face and Miss Goering decided that in spite of her solid bourgeois appearance she was really hysterical, but since she had met many women like this before, she decided not to be surprised from now on at anything that the woman might do. The woman left her seat with all of her packages and her umbrella and walked down the aisle with difficulty. Soon she returned, followed by the conductor.

They stopped beside Miss Goering. The woman stood behind the conductor. The conductor, who was an old man, leaned way over Miss Goering so that he was nearly breathing in her face.

"You can't talk to anyone on these here trains," he said, "unless you know them." His voice sounded very mild to Miss Goering.

Then he looked over his shoulder at the woman, who still seemed annoyed but more calm.

"The next time," said the conductor, who really was at a loss for what to say, "the next time you're on this train, stay in your seat and don't molest anybody. If you want to know the time you can ask them without any to-do about it or you can just make a little signal with your hand and I'll be willing to answer all your questions." He straightened up and stood for a moment trying to think of something more to say. "Remember also," he added, "and tell this to your relatives and to your friends. Remember also that there are no dogs allowed on this train or people in masquerade costume unless they're all covered up with a big heavy coat; and no more hubbubs," he added, shaking a finger at her. He tipped his hat to the woman and went on his way.

A minute or two later the train stopped and the woman got off. Miss Goering looked anxiously out of the window for her, but she could see only the empty platform and some dark bushes. She held her hand over her heart and smiled to herself.

When she arrived at the tip of the island the rain had stopped and the stars were shining again intermittently. She had to walk down a long narrow boardwalk which served as a passage between the train and the landing pier of the ferry. Many of the boards were loose and Miss Goering had to be very careful where she was stepping. She sighed with impatience, because it seemed to her that as long as she was still on this boardwalk it was not certain that she would actually board the ferry. Now that she was approaching her destination she felt that the whole excursion could be made very quickly and that she would soon be back with Arnold and his father and Miss Gamelon.

The boardwalk was only lighted at intervals and there were long stretches which she had to cross in the dark. However, Miss Goering, usually so timorous, was not frightened in the least. She even felt a kind of elation, which is common in certain unbalanced but sanguine persons when they begin to approach the thing they fear. She became more agile in avoiding the loose boards, and even made little leaps around them. She could now see the landing dock at the end of the boardwalk. It was very brightly lighted and the municipality had erected a good-sized flagpole in the center of the platform. The flag was now wrapped around the pole in great folds, but Miss Goering could distinguish easily the red and white stripes and the stars. She was delighted to see the flag in this far-off place, for she hadn't imagined that there would be any organization at all on the tip of the island.

"Why, people have been living here for years," she said to herself. "It is strange that I hadn't thought of this before. They're here naturally, with their family ties, their neighborhood stores, their sense of decency and morality, and they have certainly their organizations for fighting the criminals of the community." She felt almost happy now that she had remembered all this.

She was the only person waiting for the ferry. Once she had got on, she went straight to the prow of the boat and stood watching the mainland until they reached the opposite shore. The ferry dock was at the foot of a road which joined the main street at the summit of a short steep hill. Trucks were still obliged to stop short at the top of the hill and unload their freight into wheelbarrows, which were then rolled cautiously down to the dock. Looking up from the dock, it was possible to see the side walls of the two stores at the end of the main street but not very much more. The road was so brightly lighted on either side that it was possible for Miss Goering to distinguish most of the details on the clothing of the persons who were coming down the hill to board the ferry.

She saw coming towards her three young women holding onto one another's arms and giggling. They were very fancily dressed and were trying to hold onto their hats as well as one another. This made their progress very slow, but half-way down the hill they called to someone on the dock who was standing near the post to which the ferry had been moored.

"Don't you leave without us, George," they yelled to him, and he waved his hand back in a friendly manner.

There were many young men coming down the hill and they too seemed to be dressed for something special. Their shoes were well shined, and many of them wore flowers in their buttonholes. Even those who had started long after the three young women quickly trotted past them. Each time this happened the girls would go into gales of laughter, which Miss Goering could hear only faintly from where she stood. More and more people kept appearing over the top of the hill and most of them, it seemed to Miss Goering, did not exceed the age of thirty. She stepped to the side and soon they were talking and laughing together all over the foredeck and the bridge of the ferry. She was very curious to know where they were going, but her spirits had been considerably dampened by witnessing the exodus, which she took as a bad omen. She finally decided that she would question a young man who was still on the dock and standing not very far away from her.

"Young man," she said to him, "would you mind telling me if you are all actually going on some lark together in a group or if it's a coincidence?"

"We're all going to the same place," said the boy, "as far as I know."

"Well, could you tell me where that is?" asked Miss Goering.

"Pig Snout's Hook," he answered. Just then the ferry whistle blew. He hastily took leave of Miss Goering and ran to join his friends on the foredeck.

Miss Goering struggled up the hill entirely alone. She kept her eye on the wall of the last store on the main street. An advertising artist had painted in vivid pinks a baby's face of giant dimensions on half the surface of the wall, and in the remaining space a tremendous rubber nipple. Miss Goering wondered what Pig Snout's Hook was. She was rather disappointed when she arrived at the top of the hill to find that the main street was rather empty and dimly lighted. She had perhaps been misled by the brilliant colors of the advertisement of the baby's nipple and had half hoped that the entire town would be similarly garish.

Before proceeding down the main street she decided to examine the painted sign more closely. In order to do this she had to step across an empty lot. Very near to the advertisement she noticed that an old man was bending over some crates and trying to wrench the nails loose from the boards. She decided that she would ask him whether or not he knew where Pig Snout's Hook was.

She approached him and stood watching for a little while before asking her question. He was wearing a green plaid jacket and a little cap of the same material. He was terribly busy trying to pry a nail from the crate with only a thin stick as a tool.

"I beg your pardon," said Miss Goering to him finally, "but I would like to know where Pig Snout's Hook is and also why anyone would go there, if you know."

The man continued to bother with the nail, but Miss Goering could tell that he was really interested in her question.

"Pig Snout's Hook?" said the man. "That's easy. It's a new place, a cabaret."

"Does everyone go there?" Miss Goering asked him.

"If they are the kind who are fools, they go."

"Why do you say that?"

"Why do I say that?" said the man, getting up finally and putting his stick in his pocket. "Why do I say that? Because they go there for the pleasure of being cheated out of their last penny. The meat is just horsemeat, you know. This size and it ain't red. It's a kind of gray, without a sign of a potato near it, and it costs plenty too. They're all as poor as church mice besides, without a single ounce of knowledge about life in the whole crowd of them. Like a lot of dogs straining at the leash."

"And then they all go together to Pig Snout's Hook every single night?"

"I don't know when they go to Pig Snout's Hook," said the man, "any more than I know what cockroaches are doing every night."

"Well, what's so wrong about Pig Snout's Hook?" Miss Goering asked him.

"There's one thing wrong," said the man growing more and more interested, "and that's that they've got a nigger there that jumps up and down in front of a mirror in his room all day long until he sweats and then he does the same thing in front of these lads and lassies and they think he's playing them music. He's got an expensive instrument all right, because I know where he bought it and I'm not saying whether or not he paid for it, but I know he sticks it in his mouth and then starts moving around with his long arms like the arms of a spider and they just won't listen to nothin' else but him."

"Well," said Miss Goering, "certain people do like that type of music."

"Yes," said the man, "certain people do like that type of music and there are people who live together and eat at table together stark naked all the year long and there are others who we both know about"—he looked very mysterious—"but," he continued, "in my day money was worth a pound of sugar or butter or lard any time. When we went out we got what we paid for plus a dog jumpin' through burning hoops, and steaks you could rest your chin on."

"What do you mean?" asked Miss Goering—"a dog jumping through burning hoops?"

"Well," said the man, "you can train them to do anything with years of real patience and perseverance and lots of head-aches too. You get a hoop and you light it all around and these poodles, if they're the real thing, will leap through them like birds flying in the air. Of course it's a rare thing to see them doing this, but they've been right here in this town flying right through the centers of burning hoops. Of course people were older then and they cared for their money better and they didn't want to see a black jumping up and down. They would rather prefer to put a new roof on their house." He laughed.

"Well," said Miss Goering, "did this go on in a cabaret that was situated where the Pig Snout's Hook place is now situated? You understand what I mean."

"It surely didn't!" said the man vehemently. "The place was situated right on this side of the river in a real theater with three different prices for the seats and a show every night and three times a week in the afternoon."

"Well, then," said Miss Goering, "that's quite a different thing isn't it? Because, after all, Pig Snout's Hook is a cabaret, as you said yourself a little while ago, and this place where the poodles jumped through the burning hoops was a theater, so in actuality there is really no point of comparison."

The old man knelt down again and continued to pry the nails from the boards by placing his little stick between the head of the nail and the wood.

Miss Goering did not know what to say to him, but she felt that it was pleasanter to go on talking than to start off down the main street alone. She could tell that he was a little annoyed, so that she was prepared to ask her next question in a considerably softer voice.

"Tell me," she said to him, "is that place at all dangerous, or is it merely a waste of time."

"Surely, it's as dangerous as you want," said the old man immediately, and his ill humor seemed to have passed. "Certainly it's dangerous. There are some Italians running it and the place is surrounded by fields and woods." He looked at her as if to say: "That is all you need to know, isn't it?"

Miss Goering for an instant felt that he was an authority and she in turn looked into his eyes very seriously. "But can't you," she asked, "can't you tell very easily whether or not they have all returned safely? After all, you have only if necessary to stand at the top of the hill and watch them disembark from the ferry." The old man picked up his stick once more and took Miss Goering by the arm.

"Come with me," he said, "and be convinced once and for all." He took her to the edge of the hill and they looked down the brightly lighted street that led to the dock. The ferry was not there, but the man who sold the tickets was clearly visible in his booth, and the rope with which they moored the ferry to the post, and even the opposite shore. Miss Goering took in the entire scene with a clear eye and waited anxiously for what the old man was about to say.

"Well," said the old man, lifting his arm and making a vague gesture which included the river and the sky, "you can see where it is impossible to know anything." Miss Goering looked around her and it seemed to her that there could be nothing hidden from their eyes, but at the same time she believed what the old man said to her. She felt both ashamed and uneasy.

"Come along," said Miss Goering, "I'll invite you to a beer."

"Thank you very much, ma'am," said the old man. His tone had changed to that of a servant, and Miss Goering felt even more ashamed of having believed what he had told her.

"Is there any particular place that you would like to go?" she asked him.

"No, ma'am," he said, shuffling along beside her. He no longer seemed in the least inclined to talk.

There was no one walking along the main street except Miss Goering and the old man. They did pass a car parked in front of a dark store. Two people were smoking on the front seat.

The old man stopped in front of the window of a bar and grill and stood looking at some turkey and some old sausages which were on display.

"Shall we go in here and have something to eat with our little drink?" Miss Goering asked him.

"I'm not hungry," the man said, "but I'll go in with you and sit down."

Miss Goering was disappointed because he didn't seem to have any sense of how to give even the slightest festive air to the evening. The bar was dark, but festooned here and there with crepe paper. "In honor of some recent holiday, no doubt," thought Miss Goering. There was a particularly nice garland of bright green paper flowers strung up along the entire length of the mirror behind the bar. The room was furnished with eight or nine tables, each one enclosed in a dark brown booth.

Miss Goering and the old man seated themselves at the bar.

"By the way," said the old man to her, "wouldn't you like better to seat yourself at a table where you ain't so much in view?"

"No," said Miss Goering, "I think this is very, very pleasant indeed. Now order what you want, will you?"

"I will have," said the man, "a sandwich of turkey and a sandwich of pork, a cup of coffee, and a drink of rye whisky."

"What a curious psychology!" thought Miss Goering. "I should think he would be embarrassed after just having finished saying that he wasn't hungry."

She looked over her shoulder out of curiosity and noticed that behind her in a booth were seated a boy and a girl. The boy was reading a newspaper. He was drinking nothing. The girl was sipping at a very nice cherry-colored drink through a straw. Miss Goering ordered herself two gins in succession, and when she had finished these she turned around and looked at the girl again. The girl seemed to have been expecting this because she already had her face turned in Miss Goering's direction. She smiled softly at Miss Goering and opened her eyes wide. They were very dark. The whites of her eyes, Miss Goering noticed, were shot with yellow. Her hair was black and wiry and stood way out all over her head.

"Jewish, Rumanian, or Italian," Miss Goering said to herself. The boy did not lift his eyes from his newspaper, which he held in such a way that his profile was hidden.

"Having a nice time?" the girl asked Miss Goering in a husky voice.

"Well," said Miss Goering, "it wasn't exactly in order to have a good time that I came out. I have more or less forced myself to, simply because I despise going out in the night-time alone and prefer not to leave my own house. However, it has come to such a point that I am forcing myself to make these little excursions—"

Miss Goering stopped because she actually did not know how she could go on and explain to this girl what she meant without talking a very long time indeed, and she realized that this would be impossible right at that moment, since the waiter was constantly walking back and forth between the bar and the young people's booth.

"Anyway," said Miss Goering, "I certainly think it does no harm to relax a bit and have a lovely time."

"Everyone must have a wonderfully marvelous time," said the girl, and Miss Goering noticed that there was a trace of an accent in her speech. "Isn't that true, my angel Pussycat?" she said to the boy.

The boy put his newspaper down; he looked rather annoyed. "Isn't what true?" he asked her. "I didn't hear a word that you said." Miss Goering knew perfectly well that this was a lie and that he was only pretending not to have noticed that his girl friend had been speaking with her.

"Nothing very important, really," she said, looking tenderly into his eyes. "This lady here was saying that after all it did nobody any harm to relax and have a lovely time."

"Perhaps," said the boy, "it does more harm than anything else to date to have a lovely time." He said this straight to the girl and completely ignored the fact that Miss Goering had been mentioned at all. The girl leaned way over and whispered into his ear.

"Darling," she said, "something terrible has happened to that woman. I feel it in my heart. Please don't be bad-tempered with her."

"With whom?" the boy asked her.

She laughed because she knew there was nothing else much that she could do. The boy was subject to bad moods, but she loved him and was able to put up with almost anything.

The old man who had come with Miss Goering had excused himself and had taken his drinks and sandwiches over to a radio, where he was now standing with his ear close to the box.

Away in the back of the room a man was bowling up a small alley all by himself; Miss Goering listened to the rumble of the balls as they rolled along the wooden runway, and she wished that she were able to see him so that she could be at peace for the evening with the certainty that there was no one who could be considered a menace present in the room. Certainly there was a possibility that more clients would enter through the door, but this had entirely slipped her mind. Hard though she tried, it was impossible for her to get a look at the man who was rolling the balls.

The young boy and the girl were having a fight. Miss Goering could tell by the sound of their voices. She listened to them carefully without turning her head.

"I don't see why," said the girl, "that you must be furious immediately just because I have mentioned that I always like to come in here and sit for a little while."

"There is absolutely no reason," said the boy, "why you should want to come in here and sit more than in any other place."

"Then why—then why do you come in?" the girl asked hesitantly.

"I don't know," said the boy; "maybe because it's the first thing we hit after we leave our room."

"No," said the girl, "there are other places. I wish you would just say that you liked it here; I don't know why, but it would make me so happy; we've been coming here for a long time."

"I'll be God-damned if I'll say it, and I'll be God-damned if I'll come here any more if you're going to invest this place with witches' powers."

"Oh, Pussycat," said the girl, and there was real anguish in her tone, "Pussycat, I am not talking about witches and their powers; not even thinking about them. Only when I was a little girl. I should never have told you the story."

The boy shook his head back and forth; he was disgusted with her.

"For God's sake," he said, "that isn't anything near what I mean, Bernice."

"I do not understand *what* you mean," said Bernice. "Many people come into this place or some other place every night for years and years and without doing much but having a drink and talking to each other; it is only because it is like home to them. And we come here only because it is little by little becoming a home to us; a second home if you can call our little room a home; it is to me; I love it very much."

The boy groaned with discontent.

"And," she added, feeling that her words and her tone of voice could not help working a spell over the boy, "the tables and the chairs and the walls here have now become like the familiar faces of old friends."

"What old friends?" said the boy, scowling more and more furiously. "What old friends? To me this is just another shit-house where poor people imbibe spirits in order to forget the state of their income, which is non-existent."

He sat up very straight and glared at Bernice.

"I guess that is true, in a way," she said vaguely, "but I feel that there is something more."

"That's just the trouble."

Meanwhile Frank, the bartender, had been listening to Bernice's conversation with Dick. It was a dull night and the more he thought about what the boy had said, the angrier he felt. He decided to go over to the table and start a row.

"Come on, Dick," he said, grabbing him by the collar of his shirt. "If that's the way you feel about this place, get the hell out of here." He yanked him out of his seat and gave him a terrific shove so that Dick staggered a few steps and fell head-long over the bar.

"You big fat-head," Dick yelled at the bartender, lunging out at him. "You hunk of retrogressive lard. I'll push your white face in for you."

The two were now fighting very hard. Bernice was standing on the table and pulling at the shirts of the fighters in an attempt to separate them. She was able to reach them even when they were quite a distance from the table because the benches terminated in posts at either end, and by grabbing hold of one of them she could swing out over the heads of the fighters.

Miss Goering, from where she was now standing, could see the flesh above Bernice's stocking whenever she leaned particularly far out of her booth. This would not have troubled her so much had she not noticed that the man who had been rolling the wooden balls had now moved away from his post and was staring quite fixedly at Bernice's bare flesh wherever the occasion presented itself. The man had a narrow red face, a pinched and somewhat inflamed nose, and very thin lips. His hair was almost orange in color. Miss Goering could not decide whether he was of an exceedingly upright character or of a criminal nature, but the intensity of his attitude almost scared her to death. Nor was it even possible for Miss Goering to decide whether he was looking at Bernice with interest or with scorn.

Although he was getting in some good punches and his face was streaming with sweat, Frank the bartender appeared to be very calm and it seemed to Miss Goering that he was losing interest in the fight and that actually the only really tense person in the room was the man who was standing behind her.

Soon Frank had a split lip and Dick a bloody nose. Very shortly after this they both stopped fighting and walked unsteadily towards the washroom. Bernice jumped off the table and ran after them.

They returned in a few minutes, all washed and combed and holding dirty handkerchiefs to their mouths. Miss Goering walked up to them and took hold of each man by the arm.

"I'm glad that it's all over now, and I want each of you to have a drink as my guest."

Dick looked very sad now and very subdued. He nodded his head solemnly and they sat down together and waited for Frank to fix them their drinks. He returned with their drinks, and after he had served them, he too seated himself at the table. They all drank in silence for a little while. Frank was dreamy and seemed to be thinking of very personal things that had nothing to do with the events of the evening. Once he took out an address book and looked through its pages several times. It was Miss Goering who first broke the silence.

"Now tell me," she said to Bernice and Dick," "tell me what you are interested in."

"I'm interested in the political struggle," said Dick, "which is of course the only thing that any self-respecting human being could be interested in. I am also on the winning side and on the right side. The side that believes in the redistribution of capital." He chuckled to himself and it was very easy to tell that he thought he was conversing with a complete fool.

"I've heard all about that," said Miss Goering. "And what are you interested in?" she asked the girl.

"Anything he is interested in, but it is true that I had believed the political struggle was very important before I met him. You see, I have a different nature than he has. What makes me happy I seem to catch out of the sky with both hands; I only hold whatever it is that I love because that is all I can really see. The world interferes with me and my happiness, but I never interfere with the world except now since I am with Dick." Bernice put her hand out on the table for Dick to take hold of it. She was already a little drunk.

"It makes me sad to hear you talk like this," said Dick. "You, as a leftist, know perfectly well that before we fight for our own happiness we must fight for something else. We are living in a period when personal happiness means very little because the individual has very few moments left. It is wise to destroy yourself first; at least to keep only that part of you which can be of use to a big group of people. If you don't do this you lose sight of objective reality and so forth, and you fall plunk into the middle of a mysticism which right now would be a waste of time."

"You are right, darling Dickie," said Bernice, "but sometimes I would love to be waited on in a beautiful room. Sometimes I think it would be nice to be a bourgeois." (She said the word "bourgeois," Miss Goering noticed, as though she had just learned it.) Bernice continued: "I am such a human person. Even though I am poor I will miss the same things that they do, because sometimes at night the fact that they are sleeping in their houses with security, instead of making me angry, fills me with peace like a child who is scared at night likes to hear grown people talking down in the street. Don't you think there is some sense in what I say, Dickie?"

"None whatsoever!" said the boy. "We know perfectly well that it is this security of theirs that makes us cry out at night."

Miss Goering by now was very anxious to get into the conversation.

"You," she said to Dick, "are interested in winning a very correct and intelligent fight. I am far more interested in what is making this fight so hard to win."

"They have the power in their hands; they have the press and the means of production."

Miss Goering put her hand over the boy's mouth. He jumped. "This is very true," she said, "but isn't it very obvious that there is something else too that you are fighting? You are fighting their present position on this earth, to which they are all grimly attached. Our race, as you know, is not torpid. They are grim because they still believe the earth is flat and that they are likely to fall off it at any minute. That is why they hold on so hard to the middle. That is, to all the ideals by which they have always lived. You cannot confront men who are still fighting the dark and all the dragons, with a new future."

"Well, well," said Dick, "what should I do then?"

"Just remember," said Miss Goering, "that a revolution won is an adult who must kill his childhood once and for all."

"I'll remember," said Dick, sneering a bit at Miss Goering.

The man who had been rolling the balls was now standing at the bar.

"I better go see what Andy wants," said Frank. He had been whistling softly all through Miss Goering's conversation with Dick, but he seemed to have been listening nevertheless, because as he was leaving the table he turned to Miss Goering.

"I think that the earth is a very nice place to be living on," he said to her, "and I never felt that by going one step too far I was going to fall off it either. You can always do things two or three times on the earth and everybody's plenty patient till you get something right. First time wrong doesn't mean you're sunk."

"Well, I wasn't talking about anything like that," said Miss Goering.

"That's what you're talking about all right. Don't try to pussyfoot it out now. But I tell you it's perfectly all right as far as I'm concerned." He was looking with feeling into Miss Goering's eyes. "My life," he said, "is my own, whether it's a mongrel or a prince."

"What on earth is he talking about?" Miss Goering asked Bernice and Dick. "He seems to think I've insulted him."

"God knows!" said Dick. "At any rate I am sleepy. Bernice, let's go home."

While Dick was paying Frank at the bar, Bernice leaned over Miss Goering and whispered in her ear.

"You know, darling," she said, "he's not really like this when we are home together alone. He makes me really happy. He is a sweet boy and you should see the simple things that delight him when he is in his own room and not with strangers. Well"—she straightened up and seemed to be a little embarassed at her own burst of confidence—"well, I am very glad indeed that I met you and I hope we did not give you too much of a rough time. I promise you that it has never happened before, because underneath, Dick is really like you and me, but he is in a very nervous state of mind. So you must forgive him."

"Certainly," said Miss Goering, "but I do not see what for."

"Well, good-by," said Bernice.

Miss Goering was far too embarrassed and shocked by what Bernice had said behind Dick's back to notice at first that she was now the only person in the barroom besides the man who had been rolling the wooden balls and the old man, who had by now fallen asleep with his head on the bar. When she did notice, however, she felt for one desolate moment that the whole thing had been prearranged and that although she had forced herself to take this little trip to the mainland, she had somehow at the same time been tricked into taking it by the powers above. She felt that she could not leave and that even if she tried, something would happen to interfere with her departure.

She noticed with a faint heart that the man had lifted his drink from the bar and was coming towards her. He stopped about a foot away from her table and stood holding his glass in mid-air.

"You will have a drink with me, won't you?" he asked her without looking particularly cordial.

"I'm sorry," said Frank from behind the bar, "but we're going to close up now. No more drinks served, I'm afraid."

Andy said nothing, but he went out the door and slammed it behind him. They could hear him walking up and down outside of the saloon.

"He's going to have his own way again," said Frank, "damn it all."

"Oh, dear," said Miss Goering, "are you afraid of him?"

"Sure I'm not," said Frank, "but he's disagreeable—that's the only word I can think up for him—disagreeable; and after it's all said and done, life is too short."

"Well," said Miss Goering, "is he dangerous?"

Frank shrugged his shoulders. Soon Andy came back.

"The moon and the stars are out now," he said, "and I could almost see clear to the edge of the town. There are no policemen in sight, so I think we can have our drink."

He slid in, onto the bench opposite Miss Goering.

"It's cold and lifeless without a living thing on the street," he began, "but that's the way I like it nowadays; you'll forgive me if I sound morose to a gay woman like yourself, but I have a habit of never paying attention to whoever I am talking to. I think people would say, about me: 'Lacking in respect for other human beings.' *You* have great respect for your friends, I'm sure, but that is only because you respect yourself, which is always the starting-off point for everything: yourself."

Miss Goering did not feel very much more at ease now that he was talking to her than she had before he had sat down. He seemed to grow more intense and almost angry as he talked, and his way of attributing qualities to her which were not in any way true to her nature gave his conversation an eerie quality and at the same time made Miss Goering feel inconsequential.

"Do you live in this town" Miss Goering asked him.

"I do, indeed," said Andy. "I have three furnished rooms in a new apartment house. It is the only apartment house in this town. I pay rent every month and I live there all alone. In the afternoon the sun shines into my apartment, which is one of

the finest ironies, in my opinion, because of all the apartments
in the building, mine is the sunniest and I sleep there all day
with my shades drawn down. I didn't always live there. I lived
before in the city with my mother. But this is the nearest thing
I could find to a penal island, so it suits me; it suits me fine."
He fumbled with some cigarettes for a few minutes and kept
his eyes purposely averted from Miss Goering's face. He reminded her of certain comedians who are at last given a sec-
ondary tragic role and execute it rather well. She also had a
very definite impression that one thing was cleaving his simple
mind in two, causing him to twist between his sheets instead of
sleeping, and to lead an altogether wretched existence. She had
no doubt that she would soon find out what it was.

"You have a very special type of beauty," he said to her; "a
bad nose, but beautiful eyes and hair. It would please me in
the midst of all this horror to go to bed with you. But in order
to do this we'll have to leave this bar and go to my apartment."

"Well, I can't promise you anything, but I will be glad to go
to your apartment," said Miss Goering.

Andy told Frank to call the hackstand and tell a certain man
who was on duty all night to come over and get them.

The taxi drove down the main street very slowly. It was very
old and consequently it rattled a good deal. Andy stuck his
head out of the window.

"How do you do, ladies and gentlemen?" he shouted at the
empty street, trying to approximate an English accent. "I
hope, I certainly hope that each and every one of you is having
a fine time in this great town of ours." He leaned back against
his seat again and smiled in such a horrid manner that Miss
Goering felt frightened again.

"You could roll a hoop down this street, naked, at midnight
and no one would ever know it," he said to her.

"Well, if you think it is such a dismal place," said Miss
Goering, "why don't you move somewhere else, bag and bag-
gage?"

"Oh, no," he said gloomily, "I'll never do that. There's no use in my doing that."

"Is it that your business ties you down here?" Miss Goering asked him, although she knew perfectly well he was speaking of something spiritual and far more important.

"Don't call me a business man," he said to her.

"Then you are an artist?"

He shook his head vaguely as though not quite sure what an artist was.

"Well, all right," said Miss Goering, "I've had two guesses; now won't you tell me what you are?"

"A bum!" he said stentoriously, sliding lower in his seat. "You knew that all the time, didn't you, being an intelligent woman?"

The taxicab drew up in front of the apartment house, which stood between an empty lot and a string of stores only one story high.

"You see, I get the afternoon sun all day long," he said, "because I have no obstructions. I look out over this empty lot."

"There is a tree growing in the empty lot," said Miss Goering. "I suppose that you are able to see it from your window?"

"Yes," said Andy. "Weird, isn't it?"

The apartment house was very new and very small. They stood together in the lobby while Andy searched his pockets for the keys. The floor was of imitation marble, yellow in color except in the center where the architect had set in a blue peacock in mosaic, surrounded by various long-stemmed flowers. It was hard to distinguish the peacock in the dim light, but Miss Goering crouched down on her heels to examine it better.

"I think those are water lilies around that peacock," said Andy, "But a peacock is supposed to have thousands of colors in him, isn't he? Multicolored, isn't that the point of a peacock? This one's all blue."

"Well," said Miss Goering, "perhaps it is nicer this way."

They left the lobby and went up some ugly iron steps. Andy

lived on the first floor. There was a terrible odor in the hall, which he told her never went away.

"They're cooking in there for ten people," he said, "all day long. They all work at different hours of the day; half of them don't see the other half at all, except on Sundays and holidays."

Andy's apartment was very hot and stuffy. The furniture was brown and none of the cushions appeared to fit the chairs properly.

"Here's journey's end," said Andy. "Make yourself at home. I'm going to take off some of my clothes." He returned in a minute wearing a bathrobe made of some very cheap material. Both ends of his bathrobe cords had been partially chewed away.

"What happened to your bathrobe cords?" Miss Goering asked him.

"My dog chewed them away."

"Oh, have you a dog?" she asked him.

"Once upon a time I had a dog and a future, and a girl," he said, "but that is no longer so."

"Well, what happened?" Miss Goering asked, throwing her shawl off her shoulders and mopping her forehead with her handkerchief. The steam heat had already begun to make her sweat, particularly as she had not been used to central heating for some time.

"Let's not talk about my life," said Andy, putting his hand up like a traffic officer. "Let's have some drinks instead."

"All right, but I certainly think we should talk about your life sooner or later," said Miss Goering. All the while she was thinking that she would allow herself to go home within an hour. "I consider," she said to herself, "that I have done quite well for my first night." Andy was standing up and pulling his bathrobe cord tighter around the waist.

"I was," he said, "engaged to be married to a very nice girl

who worked. I loved her as much as a man can love a woman.
She had a smooth forehead, beautiful blue eyes, and not so
good teeth. Her legs were something to take pictures of. Her
name was Mary and she got along with my mother. She was a
plain girl with an ordinary mind and she used to get a tremendous kick out of life. Sometimes we used to have dinner at
midnight just for the hell of it and she used to say to me:
'Imagine us, walking down the street at midnight to have our
dinner. Just two ordinary people. Maybe there isn't any san-
ity.' Naturally, I didn't tell her that there were plenty of people like the people who live down the hall in 5D who eat dinner at midnight, not because they are crazy, but because
they've got jobs that cause them to do so, because then maybe
she wouldn't have got so much fun out of it. I wasn't going to
spoil it and tell her that the world wasn't crazy, that the world
was medium fair; and I didn't know either that a couple of
months later her sweetheart was going to become one of the
craziest people in it."

The veins in Andy's forehead were beginning to bulge, his
face was redder, and the wings of his nostrils were sweaty.

"All this must really mean something to him," thought Miss
Goering.

"Often I used to go into an Italian restaurant for dinner; it
was right around the corner from my house; I knew mostly all
the people that ate there, and the atmosphere was very conviv-
ial. There were a few of us who always ate together. I always
bought the wine because I was better fixed than most of them.
Then there were a couple of old men who ate there, but we
never bothered with them. There was one man too who wasn't
so old, but he was solitary and didn't mix in with the others.
We knew he used to be in the circus, but we never found out
what kind of a job he had there or anything. Then one night,
the night before he brought her in, I happened to be gazing at
him for no reason on earth and I saw him stand up and fold

his newspaper into his pocket, which was peculiar-looking because he hadn't finished his dinner yet. Then he turned towards us and coughed like he was clearing his throat.

" 'Gentlemen,' he said, 'I have an announcement to make.' I
had to quiet the boys because he had such a thin little voice
you could hardly hear what he was saying.

" 'I am not going to take much of your time,' he continued,
like someone talking at a big banquet, 'but I just want to tell
you and you'll understand why in a minute. I just want to tell
you that I'm bringing a young lady here tomorrow night and
without any reservations I want you all to love her: This lady,
gentleman, is like a broken doll. She has neither arms nor legs.'
Then he sat down very quietly and started right in eating
again."

"How terribly embarrassing!" said Miss Goering. "Dear me,
what did you answer to that?"

"I don't remember," said Andy, "I just remember that it was
embarrassing like you say and we didn't feel that he had to
make the announcement anyway.

"She was already in her chair the next night when we got
there; nicely made up and wearing a very pretty, clean blouse
pinned in front with a brooch shaped like a butterfly. Her hair
was marcelled too and she was a natural blonde. I kept my ear
cocked and I heard her telling the little man that her appetite
got better all the time and that she could sleep fourteen hours
a day. After that I began to notice her mouth. It was like a rose
petal or a heart or some kind of a little shell. It was really
beautiful. Then right away I started to wonder what she
would be like; the rest of her, you understand—without any
legs." He stopped talking and walked around the room once,
looking up at his walls.

"It came into my mind like an ugly snake, this idea, and
curled there to stay. I looked at her head so little and so delicate against the dark grimy wall and it was the apple of sin
that I was eating for the first time."

"Really for the first time?" said Miss Goering. She looked bewildered and was lost in thought for a moment.

"From then on I thought of nothing else but finding out; every other thought left my head."

"And before what were your thoughts like?" Miss Goering asked him a little maliciously. He didn't seem to hear her.

"Well, this went on for some time—the way I felt about her. I was seeing Belle, who came to the restaurant often, after that first night, and I was seeing Mary too. I got friendly with Belle. There was nothing special about her. She loved wine and I actually used to pour it down her throat for her. She talked a little bit too much about her family and was a little good. Not exactly religious, but a little too full of the milk of human kindness sort of thing. It grew and grew, this terrible curiosity or desire of mine until finally my mind started to wander when I was with Mary and I couldn't sleep with her any more. She was swell all the way through it, though, patient as a lamb. She was much too young to have such a thing happen to her. I was like a horrible old man or one of those impotent kings with a history of syphilis behind him."

"Did you tell your sweetheart what was getting on your nerves?" asked Miss Goering, trying to hurry him up a bit.

"I didn't tell her because I wanted the buildings to stay in place for her and I wanted the stars to be over her head and not cockeyed—I wanted her to be able to walk in the park and feed the birdies in years to come with some other fine human being hanging onto her arm. I didn't want her to have to lock something up inside of her and look out at the world through a nailed window. It was not long before I went to bed with Belle and got myself a beautiful case of syphilis, which I spent the next two years curing. I took to bowling along about then and I finally left my mother's house and my work and came out to No-man's Land. I can live in this apartment all right on a little money that I get from a building I own down in the slums of the city."

He sat down in a chair opposite Miss Goering and put his face in his hands. Miss Goering judged that he had finished and she was just about to thank him for his hospitality and wish him good-night when he uncovered his face and began again.

"The worst of all I remember clearly; more and more I couldn't face my mother. I'd stay out bowling all day long and half the night. Then on the fourth day of July I decided that I would make a very special effort to spend the day with her. There was a big parade supposed to go by our window at three in the afternoon. Very near to that time I was standing in the parlor with a pressed suit on, and Mother was sitting as close to the window as she could get. It was a sunny day out and just right for a parade. The parade was punctual because about a quarter to three we began to hear some faint music in the distance. Then soon after that my country's red, white, and blue flag went by, held up by some fine-looking boys. The band was playing *Yankee Doodle*. All of a sudden I hid my face in my hands; I couldn't look at my country's flag. Then I knew, once and for all, that I hated myself. Since then I have accepted my status as a skunk. 'Citizen Skunk' happens to be a little private name I have for myself. You can have some fun in the mud, though, you know, if you just accept a seat in it instead of trying to squirm around."

"Well," said Miss Goering, "I certainly think you could pull yourself together with a bit of an effort. I wouldn't put much stock in that flag episode either."

He looked at her vaguely. "You talk like a society lady," he said to her.

"I am a society lady," said Miss Goering. "I am also rich, but I have purposely reduced my living standards. I have left my lovely home and I have moved out to a little house on the island. The house is in very bad shape and costs me practically nothing. What do you think of that?"

"I think you're cuckoo," said Andy, and not at all in a friendly tone. He was frowning darkly. "People like you shouldn't be allowed to have money."

Miss Goering was surprised to hear him making such a show of righteous indignation.

"Please," she said, "could you possibly open the window?"

"There will be an awfully cold wind blowing through here if I do," said Andy.

"Nevertheless," said Miss Goering, "I think I would prefer it."

"I'll tell you," said Andy, moving uncomfortably around his chair. "I just put in a bad spell of grippe and I'm dead afraid of getting into a draft." He bit his lip and looked terribly worried. "I could go and stand in the next room if you want while you get your breath of fresh air," he added, brightening up a bit.

"That's a jolly good idea," said Miss Goering.

He left and closed the bedroom door softly behind him. She was delighted with the chance to get some cool air, and after she had opened the window she placed her two hands on the sill far apart from each other and leaned out. She would have enjoyed this far more had she not been certain that Andy was standing still in his room consumed with boredom and impatience. He still frightened her a little and at the same time she felt that he was a terrible burden. There was a gas station opposite the apartment house. Although the office was deserted at the moment, it was brightly lighted and a radio on the desk had been left on. There was a folksong coming over the air. Soon there was a short rap at the bedroom door, which was just what she had been expecting to hear. She closed the window regretfully before the tune had finished.

"Come in," she called to him, "come in." She was dismayed to see when Andy opened the door that he had removed all of his clothing with the exception of his socks and his underdrawers. He did not seem to be embarrassed, but behaved as though they had both tacitly understood that he was to appear dressed in this fashion.

He walked with her to the couch and made her sit down beside him. Then he flung his arm around her and crossed his legs. His legs were terribly thin, and on the whole he looked inconsequential now that he had removed his clothing. He pressed his cheek to Miss Goering's.

"Do you think you could make me a little happy?" he asked her.

"For Heaven's sake," said Miss Goering, sitting bolt upright, "I thought you were beyond that."

"Well, no man can really look into the future, you know." He narrowed his eyes and attempted to kiss her.

"Now, about that woman," she said, "Belle, who had neither arms nor legs?"

"Please, darling, let's not discuss her now. Will you do me that favor?" His tone was a little sneering, but there was an undercurrent of excitement in his voice. He said: "Now tell me whatever it is that you like. You know . . . I haven't lost all my time these two years. There are a few little things I pride myself on."

Miss Goering looked very solemn. She was thinking of this very seriously, because she suspected that were she to accept Andy's offer it would be far more difficult for her to put a stop to her excursions, should she feel so disposed. Until recently she had never followed too dangerously far in action any course which she had decided upon as being the morally correct one. She scarcely approved of this weakness in herself, but she was to a certain extent sensible and happy enough to protect herself automatically. She was feeling a little tipsy, however, and Andy's suggestion rather appealed to her. "One must allow that a certain amount of carelessness in one's nature often accomplishes what the will is incapable of doing," she said to herself.

Andy looked towards the bedroom door. His mood seemed
to have changed very suddenly and he seemed confused. "This
does not mean that he is not lecherous," thought Miss Goering.
He got up and wandered around the room. Finally he pulled
an old gramophone out from behind the couch. He took up a
good deal of time dusting it off and collecting some needles
that were scattered around and underneath the turntable. As
he knelt over the instrument he became quite absorbed in what
he was doing and his face took on an almost sympathetic as-
pect.

"It's a very old machine," he mumbled. "I got it a long, long
time ago."

The machine was very small and terribly out of date, and
had Miss Goering been sentimental, she would have felt a little sad watching him; however, she was growing impatient.

"I can't hear a word that you are saying," she shouted at him
in an unnecessarily loud voice.

He got up without answering her and went into his room.
When he returned he was again wearing his bathrobe and
holding a record in his hand.

"You'll think I'm silly," he said, "bothering with that machine so long, when all I've got to play for you is this one
record. It's a march; here." He handed it to her in order that
she might read the title of the piece and the name of the band
that was executing it.

"Maybe," he said, "you'd rather not hear it. A lot of people
don't like march music."

"No, do play it," said Miss Goering. "I'll be delighted,
really."

He put the record on and sat on the edge of a very uncomfortable chair at quite a distance from Miss Goering. The nee-
dle was too loud and the march was the *Washington Post*. Miss
Goering felt as uneasy as one can feel listening to parade music
in a quiet room. Andy seemed to be enjoying it and he kept
time with his feet during the entire length of the record. But

when it was over he seemed to be in an even worse state of confusion than before.

"Would you like to see the apartment?" he asked her.

Miss Goering leaped up from the couch quickly lest he should change his mind.

"A woman who made dresses had this apartment before me, so my bedroom is kind of sissyish for a man."

She followed him into the bedroom. He had turned the bed down rather badly and the slips of the two pillows were gray and wrinkled. On his dresser were pictures of several girls, all of them terribly unattractive and plain. They looked more to Miss Goering like the church-going type of young woman than like the mistresses of a bachelor.

"They're nice-looking girls, aren't they?" said Andy to Miss Goering.

"Lovely-looking," she said, "lovely."

"None of these girls live in this town," he said. "They live in different towns in the vicinity. The girls here are guarded and they don't like bachelors my age. I don't blame them. I go take one of these girls in the pictures out now and then when I feel like it. I even sit in their living-rooms of an evening with them, with their parents right in the house. But they don't see much of me, I can tell you that."

Miss Goering was growing more and more puzzled, but she didn't ask him any more questions because she was suddenly feeling weary.

"I think I'll be on my way now," she said, swaying a little on her feet. She realized immediately how rude and unkind she was being and she saw Andy tightening up. He put his fists into his pockets.

"Well, you can't go now," he said to her. "Stay a little longer and I'll make you some coffee."

"No, no, I don't want any coffee. Anyway, they'll be worrying about me at home."

"Who's they?" Andy asked her.

"Arnold and Arnold's father and Miss Gamelon."

"It sounds like a terrible mob to me," he said. "I couldn't stand living with a crowd like that."

"I love it," said Miss Goering.

He put his arms around her and tried to kiss her, but she pulled away, "No, honestly, I'm much too tired."

"All right," he said, "all right!" His brow was deeply furrowed and he looked completely miserable. He took his bathrobe off and got into his bed. He lay there with the sheet up to his neck, threshing his feet about and looking up at the ceiling like someone with a fever. There was a small light burning on the table beside the bed which shone directly into his face, so that Miss Goering was able to distinguish many lines which she had not noticed before. She went over to his bed and leaned over him.

"What *is* the matter?" she asked him. "Now it's been a very pleasant evening and we all need some sleep."

He laughed in her face. "You're some lunatic," he said to her, "and you sure don't know anything about people. I'm all right here, though." He pulled the sheet up farther and lay there breathing heavily. "There's a five o'clock ferry that leaves in about a half hour. Will you come back tomorrow evening? I'll be where I was tonight at that bar."

She promised him that she would return on the following evening, and after he had explained to her how to get to the dock, she opened his window for him and left.

Stupidly enough, Miss Goering had forgotten to take her key with her and she was obliged to knock on the door in order to get into her house. She pounded twice, and almost immediately she heard someone running down the steps. She could tell that it was Arnold even before he had opened the door. He was wearing a rose-colored pajama jacket and a pair of trousers. His suspenders were hanging down over his hips. His beard had grown quite a bit for such a short time and he looked sloppier than ever.

"What's the matter with you, Arnold?" said Miss Goering. "You look dreadful."

"Well, I've had a bad night, Christina. I just put Bubbles to sleep a little while ago; she's terribly worried about you. As a matter of fact, I don't think you've shown us much consideration."

"Who is Bubbles?" Miss Goering asked him.

"Bubbles," he said, "is the name I have for Miss Gamelon."

"Well," said Miss Goering, going into the house and seating herself in front of the fireplace, "I took the ferry back across to the mainland and I became very much involved. I might return tomorrow night," she added, "although I don't really want to very much."

"I don't know why you find it so interesting and intellectual to seek out a new city," said Arnold, cupping his chin in his hand and looking at her fixedly.

"Because I believe the hardest thing for me to do is really move from one thing to another, partly," said Miss Goering.

"Spiritually," said Arnold, trying to speak in a more sociable tone, "spiritually I'm constantly making little journeys and changing my entire nature every six months."

"I don't believe it for a minute," said Miss Goering.

"No, no, it is true. Also I can tell you that I think it is absolute nonsense to move physically from one place to another. All places are more or less alike."

Miss Goering did not answer this. She pulled her shawl closer around her shoulders and of a sudden looked quite old and very sad indeed.

Arnold began to doubt the validity of what he had just said, and immediately resolved to make exactly the same excursion from which Miss Goering had just returned, on the following night. He squared his jaw and pulled out a notebook from his pocket.

"Now, will you give me the particulars on how to reach the

mainland?" said Arnold. "The hours when the train leaves, and so forth."

"Why do you ask?" said Miss Goering.

"Because I'm going to go there myself tomorrow night. I should have thought you would have guessed that by this time."

"No, judging by what you just finished saying to me, I would not have guessed it."

"Well, I talk one way," said Arnold, "but I'm really, underneath, the same kind of maniac that you are."

"I would like to see your father," Miss Goering said to him.

"I think he's asleep. I hope he will come to his senses and go home," said Arnold.

"Well, I am hoping the contrary," said Miss Goering. "I'm terribly attached to him. Let's go upstairs and just look into his room."

They went up the stairs together and Miss Gamelon came out to meet them on the landing. Her eyes were all swollen and she was wrapped in a heavy wool bathrobe.

She began speaking to Miss Goering in a voice that was thick with sleep. "Once more, and it will be the last you will see of Lucy Gamelon."

"Now, Bubbles," said Arnold, "remember this is not an ordinary household and you must expect certain eccentricities on the part of the inmates. You see, I have dubbed us all inmates."

"Arnold," said Miss Gamelon, "now don't you begin. You know what I told you this afternoon about talking drivel."

"Please, Lucy," said Arnold.

"Come, come, let's all go and take a peek at Arnold's father," suggested Miss Goering.

Miss Gamelon followed them only in order to continue admonishing Arnold, which she did in a low voice. Miss Goering pulled the door open. The room was very cold and she realized for the first time that it was already bright outdoors. It had all happened very quickly while she was talking to Arnold in the parlor, but there it was nearly always dark because of the thick bushes outside.

Arnold's father was sleeping on his back. His face was still and he breathed regularly without snoring. Miss Goering shook him a few times by the shoulder.

"The procedures in this house," said Miss Gamelon, "are what amount to criminal. Now you're waking up an old man who needs his sleep, at the crack of dawn. It makes me shudder to stand here and see what you've become, Christina."

At last Arnold's father awakened. It took him a little while to realize what had happened, but when he had, he leaned on his elbows and said in a very chipper manner to Miss Goering:

"Good morning, Mrs. Marco Polo. What beautiful treasures have you brought back from the East? I'm glad to see you, and if there's anywhere you want me to go with you, I'm ready." He fell back on his pillow with a thump.

Miss Goering said that she would see him later, that at the moment she was badly in need of some rest. They left the room, and before they had closed the door behind them, Arnold's father was already asleep. On the landing Miss Gamelon began to cry and she buried her face for a moment in Miss Goering's shoulder. Miss Goering held her very tightly and begged her not to cry. Then she kissed both Arnold and Miss Gamelon good-night. When she arrived in her room she was overcome with fright for a few moments, but shortly she fell into a deep sleep.

•

At about five thirty on the following afternoon Miss Goering announced her intention of returning again that evening to the mainland. Miss Gamelon was standing up, sewing one of Arnold's socks. She was dressed more coquettishly than was her habit, with a ruffle around the neck of her dress and a liberal coating of rouge on her cheeks. The old man was in a big chair in the corner reading the poetry of Longfellow, sometimes aloud, sometimes to himself. Arnold was still dressed in the same fashion as the night before, with the exception of a sweater which he had pulled on over his pajama top. There was a big coffee stain on the front of his sweater, and the ashes of his cigarette had spilled over his chest. He was lying on the couch half asleep.

"You will go back there again over my dead body," said Miss Gamelon. "Now, please, Christina, be sane and do let us all have a pleasant evening together."

Miss Goering sighed. "Well, you and Arnold can have a perfectly pleasant evening together without me. I am sorry. I'd love to stay, but I really feel that I must go."

"You drive me wild with your mysterious talk," said Miss Gamelon. "If only some member of your family were here! Why don't we phone for a taxi," she said hopefully, "and go to the city? We might eat some Chinese food and go to the theater afterwards, or a picture show, if you are still in your pinch-penny mood."

"Why don't you and Arnold go to the city and eat some Chinese food and then go to the theater? I will be very glad to have you go as my guests, but I'm afraid I can't accompany you."

Arnold was growing annoyed at the ease with which Miss Goering disposed of him. Her manner also gave him a very bad sense of being inferior to her.

"I'm sorry, Christina," he said from his couch, "but I have no intention of eating Chinese food. I have been planning all along to take a little jaunt to the mainland opposite this end of the island too, and nothing will stop me. I wish you'd come along with me, Lucy; as a matter of fact, I don't see why we can't all go along together. It is quite senseless that Christina should make such a morbid affair out of this little saunter to the mainland. Actually there is nothing to it."

"Arnold!" Miss Gamelon screamed at him. "You're losing your mind too, and if you think I am going on a wild-goose chase aboard a train and a ferry just to wind up in some little rat-trap, you're doubly crazy. Anyway, I've heard that it is a very tough little town, besides being dreary and without any interest whatsoever."

"Nevertheless," said Arnold, sitting up and planting his two feet on the floor, "I'm going this evening."

"In that case," said Arnold's father, "I'm going too."

Secretly Miss Goering was delighted that they were coming and she did not have the courage to deter them, although she felt that it would have been the correct thing for her to do. Her excursions would be more or less devoid of any moral value in her own eyes if they accompanied her, but she was so delighted that she convinced herself that perhaps she might allow it just this time.

"You had better come along, Lucy," said Arnold; "otherwise you are going to be here all alone."

"That's perfectly all right, my dear," said Lucy. "I'll be the only one that comes out whole, in the end. And it might be very delightful to be here without any of you."

Arnold's father made an insulting noise with his mouth, and Miss Gamelon left the room.

This time the little train was filled with people and there were quite a few boys going up and down the aisle selling candy and fruit. It had been a curiously warm day and there had been a shower of short duration, one of those showers that are so frequent in summer but so seldom occur in the fall.

The sun was just setting and the shower had left in its wake quite a beautiful rainbow, which was only visible to those people who were seated on the left side of the train. However, most of the passengers who had been seated on the right side were now leaning over the more fortunate ones and getting quite a fair view of the rainbow too.

Many of the women were naming aloud to their friends the

colors that they were able to distinguish. Everyone on the train seemed to love it except Arnold, who, now that he had asserted himself, felt terribly depressed, partly as a result of having had to move from his couch and consider the prospect of a dull evening and partly also because he doubted very much whether he would be able to make it up with Lucy Gamelon. She was, he felt certain, the type of person who could remain angry for weeks.

"Oh, I think this is terribly, terribly gay," said Miss Goering. "This rainbow and this sunset and all these people jabbering away like magpies. Don't you think it's gay?" Miss Goering was addressing Arnold's father.

"Oh, yes," he said. "It's a real magic carpet."

Miss Goering searched his face because his voice sounded a little sad to her. He did, as a matter of fact, appear to be slightly uneasy. He kept looking around at the passengers and pulling his tie.

They finally left the train and boarded the ferry. They all stood at the prow together as Miss Goering had done on the previous night. This time when the ferry landed, Miss Goering looked up and saw no one coming down the hill.

"Usually," she said to them, forgetting that she herself had only made the trip once before, "this hill is swarming with people. I cannot imagine what has happened to them tonight."

"It's a steep hill," said Arnold's father. "Is there no way of getting into the town without climbing that hill?"

"I don't know," said Miss Goering. She looked at him and noticed that his sleeves were too long for him. As a matter of fact, his overcoat was about a half-size too large.

If there had been no one on the hill going to or from the ferry, the main street was swarming with people. The cinema was all lighted up and there was a long line forming in front of the box office. There had obviously been a fire, because there were three red engines parked on one side of the street, a few blocks up from the cinema. Miss Goering judged that it had been of no consequence since she could see neither traces of smoke nor charred buildings. However, the engines added to the gaiety of the street as there were many young people crowded around them making jokes with the firemen who remained in the trucks. Arnold walked along at a brisk pace, carefully examining everything on the street and pretending to be very much lost in his own impressions of the town.

"I see what you mean," he said to Miss Goering, "it's glorious."

"What is glorious?" Miss Goering asked him.

"All this." Suddenly Arnold stopped dead. "Oh look, Christina, what a beautiful sight!" He had made them stop in front of a large empty lot between two buildings. The empty lot had been converted into a brand-new basket-ball court. The court was very elegantly paved with gray asphalt and brightly lighted by four giant lamps that were focused on the players and on the basket. There was a ticket office at one side of the court where the participants bought their right to play in the game for one hour. Most of the people playing were little boys. There were several men in uniform and Arnold judged that they worked for the court and filled in when an insufficient number of people bought tickets to form two complete teams. Arnold flushed with pleasure.

"Look, Christina," he said, "you run along while I try my hand at this; I'll come and get Pop and you later."

She pointed the bar out to him, but she had the feeling that Arnold was not paying much attention to what she was saying. She stood for a moment with Arnold's father and they watched him rush up to the ticket office and hurriedly push his change through the wicket. He was on the court in no time, running around in his overcoat and jumping up in the air with his arms apart. One of the uniformed men had stepped quickly out of the game in order to cede his place to Arnold. But he was now trying desperately to attract his attention because Arnold had been in such a hurry at the ticket office that the agent

had not had time to give him the colored arm-band by which
the players were able to distinguish the members of their own
team.

"I suppose," said Miss Goering, "that we had better go along.
Arnold, I imagine, will follow us shortly."

They walked down the street. Arnold's father hesitated a
moment before the saloon door.

"What kind of men come in here?" he asked her.

"Oh," said Goering, "all sorts of men, I guess. Rich and
poor, workers and bankers, criminals and dwarfs."

"Dwarfs," Arnold's father repeated uneasily.

The minute they were inside, Miss Goering spotted Andy.
He was drinking at the farther end of the bar with his hat
pulled down over one eye. Miss Goering hastily installed Arnold's father in a booth.

"Take your coat off," she said, "and order yourself a drink
from that man over there behind the bar."

She went over to Andy and stretched her hand out to him.
He was looking very mean and haughty.

"Hello," he said. "Did you decide to come over to the mainland again?"

"Why, certainly," said Miss Goering. "I told you I would."

"Well," said Andy, "I've learned in the course of years that
it doesn't mean a thing."

Miss Goering felt a little embarrassed. They stood side by
side for a little while without saying a word.

"I'm sorry," said Andy, "but I have no suggestions to make
to you for the evening. There is only one picture show in town
and they are showing a very bad movie tonight." He ordered
himself another drink and gulped it down straight. Then he
turned the dial of the radio very slowly until he found a tango.

"Well, may I have this dance?" he asked, appearing to
brighten up a bit.

Miss Goering nodded her head.

He held her very straight and so tightly that she was in an

extremely awkward and uncomfortable position. He danced with her into a far corner of the room.

"Well," he said, "are you going to try and make me happy? Because I have no time to waste." He pushed her away from him and stood up very straight facing her, with his arms hanging down along his sides.

"Step back a little farther, please," he said. "Look carefully at your man and then say whether or not you want him."

Miss Goering did not see how she could possibly answer anything but yes. He was standing now with his head cocked to one side, looking very much as though he were trying to refrain from blinking his eyes, the way people do when they are having snapshots taken.

"Very well," said Miss Goering, "I do want you to be my man." She smiled at him sweetly, but she was not thinking very hard of what she was saying.

He held his arms out to her and they continued to dance. He was looking over her head very proudly and smiling just a little. When they had finished their dance, Miss Goering remembered with a pang that Arnold's father had been sitting in his booth alone all this time. She felt doubly sorry because he seemed to have saddened and aged so much since they had boarded the train that he scarcely resembled at all the chipper, eccentric man he had been for a few days at the island house, or even the fanatical gentleman he had appeared to Miss Goering on the first night that they had met.

"Dear me, I must introduce you to Arnold's father," she said to Andy. "Come over this way with me."

She felt even more remorse when she arrived at the booth because Arnold's father had been sitting there all the while without having ordered himself a drink.

"What's the matter?" asked Miss Goering, her voice rising way up in the air like the voice of an excited mother. "Why on earth didn't you order yourself something to drink?"

Arnold's father looked around him furtively. "I don't know," he said, "I didn't feel any desire to."

She introduced the two men to each other and they all sat down together. Arnold's father asked Andy very politely whether or not he lived in this town and what his business was. During the course of their conversation they both discovered that not only had they been born in the same town, but they had, in spite of difference in age, also lived there once at the same time without ever having met. Andy, unlike most people, did not seem to become more lively when they both happened upon this fact.

"Yes," he answered wearily to the questions of Arnold's father, "I did live there in 1920."

"Then certainly," said Arnold's father sitting up straighter, "then certainly you were well acquainted with the McLean family. They lived up on the hill. They had seven children, five girls and two boys. All of them, as you must remember, were the possessors of a terrific shock of bright red hair."

"I did not know them," said Andy quietly, beginning to get red in the face.

"That's very strange," said Arnold's father. "Then you must have known Vincent Connelly, Peter Jacketson, and Robert Bull."

"No," said Andy, "no, I didn't." His good spirits seemed to have vanished entirely.

"They," said Arnold's father, "controlled the main business interests of the town." He studied Andy's face carefully.

Andy shook his head once more and looked off into space.

"Riddleton?" Arnold's father asked him abruptly.

"What?" said Andy.

"Riddleton, president of the bank."

"Well, not exactly," said Andy.

Arnold's father leaned back against the bench and sighed. "Where did you live?" he asked finally of Andy.

"I lived," said Andy, "at the end of Parliament Street and Byrd Avenue."

"It was terrible around there before they started tearing it up, wasn't it?" Arnold's father said, his eyes filled with memories.

Andy pushed the table roughly aside and walked quickly over to the bar.

"He didn't know anyone decent in the whole blooming town," said Arnold's father. "Parliament and Byrd was the section—"

"Please," said Miss Goering. "Look, you've insulted him. What a shame; because neither one of you cares about this sort of thing at all! What nasty little devil got into you both?"

"I don't think he has very good manners, and he is clearly not the type of man I would expect to find you associating with."

Miss Goering was a little peeved with Arnold's father, but instead of saying anything to him she went over to Andy and consoled him.

"Please don't mind him," she said. "He's really a delightful old thing and quite poetic. It's just that he's been through some radical changes in his life, all in the last few days, and I guess he's feeling the strain now."

"Poetic is he?" Andy snapped at her. "He's a pompous old monkey. That's what he is." Andy was really very angry.

"No," said Miss Goering, "he is not a pompous old monkey."

Andy finished his drink and swaggered over to Arnold's father with his hands in his pockets.

"You're a pompous old monkey!" he said to him. "A pompous old good-for-nothing monkey!"

Arnold's father slid out of his seat with his eyes cast downward and walked towards the door.

Miss Goering, who had overheard Andy's remark, hurried

after him, but she whispered to Andy as she passed him, that she intended to come right back.

When they were outside they leaned together against a lamp post. Miss Goering cold see that Arnold's father was trembling.

"I have never in my life encountered such rudeness," he said. "That man is worse than a gutter puppy."

"Well, I wouldn't worry about it," said Miss Goering. "He was just ill-tempered."

"Ill-tempered?" said Arnold's father. "He's the kind of cheaply dressed brute that is more and more thickly populating the world today."

"Oh, come," said Miss Goering, "that is neither here nor there."

Arnold's father looked at Miss Goering. Her face was very lovely on this particular evening, and he sighed with regret. "I suppose," he said, "that you are deeply disappointed in me in your own particular way, and that you are able to have respect in your heart for him while you are unable to find it within that very same heart for me. Human nature is mysterious and very beautiful, but remember that there are certain infallible signs that I, as an older man, have learned to recognize. I would not trust that man too far. I love you, my dear, with all my heart, you know."

Miss Goering stood in silence.

"You are very close to me," he said after a little while, squeezing her hand.

"Well," she said, "would you care to step back into the saloon or do you feel that you've had enough?"

"It would be literally impossible for me to return to that saloon even should I have the slightest desire to. I think I had better go along. You won't come with me, will you, my dear?"

"I'm very sorry," said Miss Goering, "but unfortunately this was a previous engagement. Would you like me to walk down to the basket-ball court? Perhaps Arnold will have wearied of his game by this time. If not, you can easily sit and watch the players for a little while."

"Yes, that would be very kind of you," said Arnold's father, in such a sad voice that he almost broke Miss Goering's heart.

Very shortly they arrived at the basket-ball court. Things had changed quite a bit. Most of the small boys had dropped out of the game and a great many young men and women had taken the place of both the small boys and the guards. The women were screaming with laughter and quite a large crowd had gathered to watch the players. After Miss Goering and Arnold's father had stood there for a minute they realized that Arnold himself was the cause of most of the merriment. He had removed his coat and his sweater and, to their surprise, they saw that he was still wearing his pajama top. He had pulled it outside of his pants in order to appear more ridiculous. They watched him run across the court with the ball in his arms roaring like a lion. When he arrived at a strategic position, however, instead of passing the ball on to another member of his team he merely dropped it on the court between his feet and proceeded to butt one of his opponents in the stomach like a goat. The crowd roared with laughter. The uniformed guards were particularly delighted because it was a pleasant and unexpected break in the night's routine. They were all standing in a row, smiling very broadly.

"I shall try and see if I can find a chair for you," said Miss Goering. She returned shortly and led Arnold's father to a folding chair that one of the guards had obligingly set up right outside of the ticket office. Arnold's father sat down and yawned.

"Good-by," said Miss Goering. "Good-by, darling, and wait here until Arnold has finished his game."

"But wait a moment," said Arnold's father. "When will you return to the island?"

"I might not return," she said. "I might not return right

away, but I will see that Miss Gamelon receives enough money to manage the house and the food."

"But I must certainly see you. This is not a very human way to make a departure."

"Well, come along a minute," said Miss Goering, taking hold of his hand and pulling him with difficulty through the crowd over to the sidewalk.

Arnold's father remonstrated that he would not return to the saloon for a million dollars.

"I'm not taking you to the saloon. Don't be silly," she said. "Now, do you see that ice-cream parlor across the street?" She pointed to a little white store almost directly opposite them. "If I don't come back, which is very probable, will you meet me there on Sunday morning? That will be in eight days, at eleven o'clock in the morning.

"I will be there in eight days," said Arnold's father.

•

When she returned with Andy to his apartment that night, she noticed that there were three long-stemmed roses on a table next to the couch.

"Why, what lovely flowers!" she exclaimed. "This reminds me that my mother had once the loveliest garden for miles around her. She won many prizes with her roses."

"Well," said Andy, "no one in my family ever won a prize with a rose, but I bought these for you in case you came."

"I'm deeply touched," said Miss Goering.

•

Miss Goering had been living with Andy for eight days. He was still very nervous and tense, but he seemed on the whole to be much more optimistic. To Miss Goering's surprise, he had begun on the second day to talk of the business possibilities in town. He surprised her very much too by knowing the names of the leading families of the community and moreover by being familiar with certain details concerning their private lives. On Saturday night he had announced to Miss Goering his intention of having a business conference the next morning with Mr. Bellamy, Mr. Schlaegel, and Mr. Dockerty. These men controlled most of the real estate not only in the town itself but in several neighboring towns. Besides these interests they also had a good many of the farms of the surrounding country. He was terribly excited when he told her his plans, which were mainly to sell the buildings he owned in the city, for which he had already been offered a small sum, and buy a share in their business.

"They're the three smartest men in town," he said, "but they're not gangsters at all. They come from the finest families here and I think it would be nice for you too."

"That is not the kind of thing that interests me in the least," said Miss Goering.

"Well, naturally, I wouldn't expect it to interest you or me," said Andy, "but you've got to admit we're living in the world, unless we want to behave like crazy kids or escaped lunatics or something like that."

For several days it had been quite clear to Miss Goering that Andy was no longer thinking of himself as a bum. This would have pleased her greatly had she been interested in reforming her friends, but unfortunately she was only interested in the course that she was following in order to attain her own salvation. She was fond of Andy, but during the last two nights she had felt an urge to leave him. This was also very much due to the fact that an unfamiliar person had begun to frequent the bar.

This newcomer was of almost mammoth proportions, and both times that she had seen him he had been wearing a tremendous black overcoat well cut and obviously made of very expensive material. She had seen his face only fleetingly once or twice, but what she had seen of it had so frightened her that she had been able to think of very little else for two days now.

This man, they had noticed, drove up to the saloon in a very beautiful big automobile that resembled more a hearse than a private car. Miss Goering had examined it one day when the man was drinking in the saloon. It appeared to be almost brand-new. She and Andy had looked in through the window and had been a little surprised to see a lot of dirty clothes on the floor. Miss Goering was completely preoccupied now with what course to take should the newcomer be willing to make her his mistress for a little while. She was almost sure that he would, because several times she had caught him looking at her in a certain way which she had learned to recognize. Her only hope was that he would disappear before she had the chance to approach him. If he did, she would be exempt and thus able to fritter away some more time with Andy, who now seemed so devoid of anything sinister that she was beginning to scrap with him about small things the way one does with a younger brother.

On Sunday morning Miss Goering woke up to find Andy in his shirt sleeves, dusting off some small tables in the living-room.

"What is it?" she asked him. "Why are you bustling around like a bride?"

"Don't you remember?" he asked, looking hurt. "Today is the big day—the day of the conference. They are coming here bright and early, all three of them. They live like robins, those business men. Couldn't you," he asked her, "couldn't you do something about making this room prettier? You see, they've all got wives, and even if they probably couldn't tell you what the hell they've got in their living-rooms, their wives have all got plenty of money to spend on little ornaments and their eyes are probably used to a certain amount of fuss."

"Well, this room is so hideous, Andy, I don't see that any-thing would do it any good."

"Yes, I guess it's a pretty bad room. I never used to notice it much." Andy put on a navy-blue suit and combed his hair very neatly, rubbing in a little brilliantine. Then he paced up and down the living-room floor with his hands in his hip pockets. The sun was pouring in through the window, and the radiator was whistling in an annoying manner while it overheated the room as it had done constantly since Miss Goering had arrived.

Mr. Bellamy, Mr. Schlaegel, and Mr. Dockerty had received Andy's note and were on their way up the stairs, having accepted the appointment more out of curiosity and from an old habit of never letting anything slip by than because they actually believed that their visit would prove fruitful. When they smelled the terrible stench of the cheap cooking in the halls, they put their hands over their mouths in order not to laugh too loudly and performed a little mock pantomime of retreating towards the staircase again. They really didn't care very much, however, because it was Sunday and they preferred being together than with their families, so they proceeded to knock on Andy's door. Andy quickly wiped his hands because they were sweaty and ran to open the door. He stood in the doorway and shook hands with each man vigorously before inviting them to come in.

"I'm Andrew McLane," he said to them, "and I'm sorry that we have not met before." He ushered them into the room and all three of them realized at once that it was going to be abominably hot. Mr. Dockerty, the most agressive of the three men, turned to Andy.

"Would you mind opening the window, fellow?" he said in a loud voice. "It's boiling in here."

"Oh," said Andy blushing, "I should have thought of it." He went over and opened the windows.

"How do you stand it, fellow?" said Mr. Dockerty. "You trying to hatch something in here?"

The three men stood in a little group near the couch and pulled out some cigars, which they examined together and discussed for a minute.

"Two of us are going to sit on this couch, fellow," said Mr. Dockerty, "and Mr. Schlaegel can sit here on this little arm-chair. Now where are you going to sit?"

Mr. Dockerty had decided almost immediately that Andy was a complete boob and was taking matters into his own hands. This so disconcerted Andy that he stood and stared at the three men without saying a word.

"Come," said Mr. Dockerty, carrying a chair out of a corner of the room and setting it down near the couch, "come, you sit here."

Andy sat down in silence and played with his fingers.

"Tell me," said Mr. Bellamy, who was a little more soft-spoken and genteel than the other two. "Tell me how long you have been living here."

"I have been living here two years," said Andy listlessly.

The three men thought about this for a little while.

"Well," said Mr. Bellamy, "and tell us what you have done in these three years."

"Two years," said Andy.

Andy had prepared quite a long story to tell them because he had suspected that they might question him a bit about his personal life in order to make certain what kind of man they were dealing with, and he had decided that it would not be wise to admit that he had done absolutely nothing in the past two years. But he had imagined that the meeting was to be conducted on a much more friendly basis. He had supposed that the men would be delighted to have found someone who was willing to put a little money into their business, and would be more than anxious to believe that he was an upright, hard-working citizen. Now, however, he felt that he was being cross-questioned and made a fool of. He could barely control his desire to bolt out of the room.

"Nothing," he said, avoiding their eyes, "nothing."

"It always amazes me," said Mr. Bellamy, "how people are able to have leisure time—that is, if they have more leisure time than they need. Now I mean to say that our business has been running for thirty-two years. There hasn't been a day gone by that I haven't had at least thirteen or fourteen things to attend to. That might seem a little exaggerated to you or maybe even very much exaggerated, but it isn't exaggerated, it's true. In the first place I attend personally to every house on our list. I check the plumbing and the drainage and the what-not. I see whether or not the house is being kept up properly and I also visit it in all kinds of weather to see how it fares during a storm or a blizzard. I know exactly how much coal it takes to heat every house on our list. I talk personally to our clients and I try to influence them on the price they are asking for their house, whether or not they are trying to rent or to sell. For instance, if they are asking a price that I know is too high because I am able to compare it with every price on the market, I try to persuade them to lower their price a little bit so that it will be nearer the norm. If, on the other hand, they are cheating themselves and I know . . ."

The other two men were getting a little bored. One could easily see that Mr. Bellamy was the least important of the three, although he might easily have been the one that accomplished all the tedious work. Mr. Schlaegel interrupted him.

"Well, my man," he said to Andy, "tell us what this is all about. In your letter you stated that you had some suggestions whereby you thought we could profit, as well as yourself, of course."

Andy got up from his chair. It was evident to the men now that he was under a terrific tension, so they were doubly on their guard.

"Why don't you come back some other time?" said Andy very quickly. "Then I will have thought it out more clearly."

"Take your time, take your time, now, fellow," said Mr. Dockerty. "We are all here together and there's no reason why we shouldn't talk it over right away. We don't really live in town, you know. We live twenty minutes out in Fairview. We developed Fairview ourselves, as a matter of fact."

"Well," said Andy, coming back and sitting on the edge of his chair, "I have a little property myself."

"Where's that?" said Mr. Dockerty.

"It's a building, in the city, way down, near the docks." He gave Mr. Dockerty the name of the street and then sat biting his lips. Mr. Dockerty didn't say anything.

"You see," continued Andy, "I thought I might hand my rights to this building over to the corporation in return for an interest in your business—at least a right to work for the firm and get my share out of the selling I do. I wouldn't need to have equal rights with you immediately, naturally, but I thought I'd discuss these details with you later if you were interested."

Mr. Dockerty shut his eyes and then after a little while he addressed himself to Mr. Schlaegel.

"I know the street he is talking about," he said. Mr. Schlaegel shook his head and made a face. Andy looked at his shoes.

"For a long time," said Mr. Dockerty, still addressing Mr. Schlaegel, "for a long time the buildings in that district have been a drag on the market. Even as slums they're pretty bad and the profit from any one of them is just enough to keep body and soul together. That's because, as you remember, Schlaegel, there is no means of transportation at any convenient distance and it's surrounded by fish markets.

"Besides that," went on Mr. Dockerty, turning to Andy, "we have in our charter a clause that prohibits our taking on any more men except on a strict salary basis, and, my friend, there's a list as long as my arm waiting for a job in our offices, if there should be a vacancy. Their tongues are hanging out for any job we can offer them. Fine young men too, the majority of them just out of college, roaring to work, and to put into use every modern trick of selling that they have learned about. I know some of their families personally and I'm sorry I can't help these lads out more than I am able to."

Just then Miss Goering came rushing through the room. "I'm an hour or two late for Arnold's father," she screamed over her shoulder as she went out the door. "I will see you later."

Andy had got up and was facing the window with his back to the three men. His shoulder blades were twitching.

"Was that your wife?" Mr. Dockerty called to him.

Andy did not answer, but in a few seconds Mr. Dockerty repeated his question, mainly because he had a suspicion it had not been Andy's wife and he was anxious to know whether or not he had guessed correctly. He kicked Mr. Schlaegel's foot with his own and they winked at each other.

"No," said Andy, turning around and revealing his flame-red face. "No, she is not my wife. She's my girl friend. She's been living here with me for a week nearly. Is there anything else you men want to know?"

"Now look here, fellow," said Mr. Dockerty, "there's nothing for you to get excited about. She's a very pretty woman, very pretty, and if you're upset about the little business talk we had together, there's no reason for that either. We explained everything to you clearly, like three pals." Andy looked out of the window.

"You know," said Mr. Dockerty, "there are other jobs you can get that will be far more suited to you and your background and that'll make you lots happier in the end. You ask your girl friend if that isn't so." Still Andy did not answer them.

"There are other jobs," Mr. Dockerty ventured to say again, but since there was still no answer from Andy, he shrugged his shoulders, rose with difficulty from the couch, and straightened his vest and his coat. The others did likewise. Then all three of them politely bade good-by to Andy's back and left the room.

•

Arnold's father had been sitting in the ice-cream parlor one
hour and a half when Miss Goering finally came running in.
He looked completely forlorn. It had never occurred to him to
buy a magazine to read and there had been no one to look at
in the ice-cream parlor because it was still morning and people
seldom dropped in before afternoon.

"Oh, I can't tell you, my dear, how sorry I am," said Miss
Goering, taking both his hands in hers and pressing them to
her lips. He was wearing woolen gloves. "I can't tell you how
these gloves remind me of my childhood," Miss Goering continued.

"I've been cold these last few days," said Arnold's father, "so
Miss Gamelon went into town and bought me these."

"Well, and how is everything going?"

"I will tell you all about that in a little while," said Arnold's
father, "but I would like to know if you are all right, my dear
woman, and whether or not you intend to return to the island."

"I—I don't think so," said Miss Goering, "not for a long
time."

"Well, I must tell you of the many changes that have taken
place in our lives, and I hope that you will not think of them
as too drastic or sudden or revolutionary, or whatever you may
call it."

Miss Goering smiled faintly.

"You see," he continued, "it has been growing colder and
colder in the house these last few days. Miss Gamelon has had
the sniffles terribly, I must concede, and also, as you know,
she's been in a wretched test about the old-fashioned cooking
equipment right from the beginning. Now, Arnold doesn't really mind anything if he has enough to eat, but recently Miss
Gamelon has refused to set foot in the kitchen."

"Now what on earth has been the outcome of all this? Do hurry up and tell me," Miss Goering urged him.

"I can't go any faster than I'm going," said Arnold's father. "Now, the other day Adele Wyman, an old school friend of Arnold's, met him in town and they had a cup of coffee together. In the course of the conversation Adele mentioned that she was living in a two-family house on the island and that she liked it but she was terribly worried about who was going to move into the other half."

"Well, then, am I to gather that they have moved into this house and are living there?"

"They have moved into that house until you come back," said Arnold's father. "Fortunately, it seemed that you had no lease on the first little house; therefore, since it was the end of the month, they felt free to move out. Miss Gamelon wonders if you will send the rent checks to the new house. Arnold has volunteered to pay the difference in rent, which is very slight."

"No, no, that is not necessary. Is there anything more that is new?" said Miss Goering.

"Well, it might interest you to know," said Arnold's father, "that I have decided to return to my wife and my original house."

"Why?" Miss Goering asked.

"A combination of circumstances, including the fact that I am old and feel like going home."

"Oh my," said Miss Goering, "it's a shame to see things breaking up this way, isn't it?"

"Yes, my dear, it is a pity, but I have come here to ask you a favor besides having come because I loved you and wanted to say good-by to you."

"I will do anything for you," said Miss Goering, "that I can possibly do."

"Well," said Arnold's father, "I would like you to read over this note that I have written to my wife. I want to send it to her and then I will return on the following day to my house."

"Certainly," said Miss Goering. She noticed there was an envelope on the table in front of Arnold's father. She picked it
up.

> Dear Ethel [*she read*],
>   I hope that you will read this letter with all that indul-
> gence and sympathy which you possess so strongly in your
> heart.
>   I can only say that there is, in every man's life, a strong
> urge to leave his life behind him for a while and seek a new
> one. If he is living near to the sea, a strong urge to take the
> next boat and sail away no matter how happy his home or
> how beloved his wife or mother. It is true also if the man is
> living near a road that he may feel the strong urge to strap
> a knapsack on his back and walk away, again leaving a
> happy home behind him. Very few people follow this urge
> once they have passed their youth without doing so. But it is
> my idea that sometimes age affects us like youth, like strong
> champagne that goes to our heads, and we dare what we
> have never dared before, perhaps also because we feel that
> it is our last chance. However, while as youths we might con-
> tinue in such an adventure, at my age one very quickly finds
> out that it is a mere chimera and that one has not the
> strength. Will you take me back?
>   Your loving husband,
>   Edgar

"It is simple," said Arnold's father, "and it expresses what I
felt."

"Is that really the way you felt?" asked Miss Goering.

"I believe so," said Arnold's father. "It must have been. Of
course I did not mention to her anything concerning my senti-
ments about you, but she will have guessed that, and such
things are better left unsaid. . . ."

He looked down at his woolen gloves and said no more for a
little while. Suddenly he reached in his pocket and pulled out
another letter.

"I'm sorry," he said, "I almost forgot. Here is a letter from
Arnold."

"Now," said Miss Goering opening the letter, "what can this be about?"

"Surely a lot about nothing and about the trollop he is living with, which is worse than nothing." Miss Goering opened the letter and proceeded to read it aloud:

Dear Christina,

I have told Father to explain to you the reasons for our recent change of domicile. I hope he has done so and that you are satisfied that we have not behaved rashly nor in a manner that you might conclude was inconsiderate. Lucy wants you to send her check to this present address. Father was supposed to tell you so but I thought that perhaps he might forget. Lucy, I am afraid, has been very upset by your present escapade. She is constantly in either a surly or melancholic mood. I had hoped that this condition would ameliorate after we had moved, but she is still subject to long silences and often weeps at night, not to mention the fact that she is exceedingly cranky and has twice had a set-to with Adele, although we have only been here two days. I see in all this that Lucy's nature is really one of extreme delicateness and morbidity and I am fascinated to be by her side. Adele on the other hand has a very equable nature, but she is terribly intellectual and very much interested in every branch of art. We are thinking of starting a magazine together when we are more or less settled. She is a pretty blonde girl.

I miss you terribly, my dear, and I want you to please believe that if I could only somehow reach what was inside of me I would break out of this terrible cocoon I am in. I expect to some day really. I will always remember the story you told me when we first met, in which I always felt was buried some strange significance, although I must admit to you now that I could not explain what. I must go and take Bubbles some hot tea to her room now. *Please, please* believe in me.

                                      Love and kisses,
                                              Arnold

"He's a nice man," said Miss Goering. For some reason Arnold's letter made her feel sad, while his father's letter had annoyed and puzzled her.

"Well," said Arnold's father, "I must be leaving now if I want to catch the next ferry."

"Wait," said Miss Goering, "I will accompany you to the dock." She quickly unfastened a rose that she had been wearing on the collar of her coat and pinned it on the old man's lapel.

When they arrived at the dock the gong was being sounded and the ferry was all ready to leave for the island. Miss Goering was relieved to see this, for she had feared a long sentimental scene.

"Well, we made it in the nick of time," said Arnold's father, trying to adopt a casual manner. But Miss Goering could see that his blue eyes were wet with tears. . . . She could barely restrain her own tears and she looked away from the ferry up the hill.

"I wonder," said Arnold's father, "if you could lend me fifty cents. I sent all my money to my wife and I didn't think of borrowing enough from Arnold this morning."

She quickly gave him a dollar and they kissed each other good-by. While the ferry pulled out, Miss Goering stood on the dock and waved; he had asked her to do this as a favor to him.

When she returned to the apartment she found it empty, so that she decided to go to the bar and drink, feeling certain that if Andy was not already there, he would arrive sooner or later.

She had been drinking there a few hours and it was beginning to grow dark. Andy had not yet arrived and Miss Goering felt a little relieved. She looked over her shoulder and saw that the heavy-set man who owned the hearse-like car was coming through the door. She shivered involuntarily and smiled sweetly at Frank, the bartender.

"Frank," she said, "don't you ever get a day off?"

"Don't want one."

"Why not?"

"Because I want to keep my nose to the grindstone and do something worth while later on. I don't get much enjoyment out of anything but thinking my own thoughts, anyway."

"I just hate thinking mine, Frank."

"No, that's silly," said Frank.

The big man in the overcoat had just climbed up on a stool and thrown a fifty-cent piece down on the bar. Frank served him his drink. After he had drunk it he turned to Miss Goering.

"Will you have a drink?" he asked her.

Much as she feared him, Miss Goering felt a peculiar thrill at the fact that he had at last spoken to her. She had been expecting it for a few days now, and felt she could not refrain from telling him so.

"Thank you so much," she said in such an ingratiating manner that Frank, who approved little of ladies who spoke to strangers, frowned darkly and moved over to the other end of the bar, where he began to read a magazine. "Thank you so much, I'd be glad to. It might interest you to know that I have imagined our drinking together like this for some time now and I am not at all surprised that you asked me. I had rather imagined that it would happen at this time of day too, and when there was no one else here." The man nodded his head once or twice.

"Well, what do you want to drink?" he asked her. Miss Goering was very disappointed that he had made no direct answer to her remark.

After Frank had served the drink the man snatched it from in front of her.

"Come on," he said, "let's go and sit in a booth."

Miss Goering clambered down from her stool and followed him to the booth that was farthest from the door.

"Well," he said to her after they had been sitting there for a little while, "do you work here?"

"Where?" said Miss Goering.

"Here, in this town."

"No," said Miss Goering.

"Well, then, do you work in another town?"

"No, I don't work."

"Yes, you do. You don't have to try to fool me, because no one ever has."

"I don't understand."

"You work as a prostitute, after a fashion, don't you?"

Miss Goering laughed. "Heavens!" she said. "I certainly never thought I looked like a prostitute merely because I had red hair; perhaps like a derelict or an escaped lunatic, but never a prostitute!"

"You don't look like no derelict or escaped lunatic to me. You look like a prostitute, and that's what you are. I don't mean a real small-time prostitute. I mean a medium one."

"Well, I don't object to prostitutes, but really I assure you I am no such thing."

"I don't believe you."

"But how are we to form any kind of friendship at all," said Miss Goering, "if you don't believe anything I say?"

The man shook his head once more. "I don't believe you when you say you're not a prostitute because I know you're a prostitute."

"All right," said Miss Goering, "I'm tired of arguing." She had noticed that his face, unlike most other faces, seemed not to take on any added life when he was engaged in conversation and she felt that all her presentiments about him had been justified.

He was now running his foot up her leg. She tried to smile at him but she was unable to.

"Come now," she said, "Frank is very apt to see what you are doing from where he is standing behind the bar and I should feel terribly embarrassed."

He seemed to ignore her remark completely and continued to press on her leg more and more vigorously.

"Would you want to come home with me and have a steak dinner?" he asked her. "I'm having steak and onions and coffee. You could stay a few days if everything worked out, or longer. This other little girl, Dorothy, just went away about a week ago."

"I think that would be nice," said Miss Goering.

"Well," he said, "It's almost an hour's drive there in a car. I have to go now to see someone here in town, but I'll be back in half a hour or so; if you want some steak you better be here too."

"All right, I will," said Miss Goering.

He had not been gone more than a few minutes when Andy arrived. He had both hands in his pockets and his coat collar turned up. He was looking down at his feet.

"Lord God Almighty!" Miss Goering said to herself. "I have to break the news to him right away and I have not seen him so dejected in a week."

"What on earth happened to you?" she asked him.

"I have been to a movie, giving myself a little lesson in self-control."

"What does that mean?"

"I mean that I was upset; my soul was turned inside out this morning and I had but two choices, to drink and continue drinking or to go to a movie. I chose the latter."

"But you still look terribly morose."

"I am less morose. I am just showing the results of the terrific fight that I have waged inside of myself, and you know that the face of victory often resembles the face of defeat."

"Victory fades so quickly that it is scarcely apparent and it is always the face of defeat that we are able to see," said Miss

Goering. She did not want to tell him, in front of Frank, that she was leaving, because she was certain that Frank would know where she was going. "Andy," she said, "would you mind coming across the street with me, to the ice-cream parlor? I have something that I want to talk to you about."

"All right," said Andy rather more casually than Miss Goering had expected. "But I want to come back right away for a drink."

They went across the street to the little ice-cream parlor and sat down at a table opposite each other. There was no one in the store with the exception of themselves and the boy who served the customers. He nodded at them when they came in.

"Back again?" he said to Miss Goering. "That old man sure waited for you a long time this morning."

"Yes," said Miss Goering, "it was dreadful."

"Well, you gave him a flower, anyway, when you left. He must have been tickled about that."

Miss Goering did not answer him as she had very little time to waste.

"Andy," she said, "I'm going in a few minutes to a place that's about an hour away from here and I probably won't be coming back for quite some time."

Andy seemed to understand the situation immediately. Miss Goering sat back and waited while he pressed his palms tighter and tighter to his temples.

Finally he looked up at her. "You," he said, "as a decent human being, cannot do this to me."

"Well, I'm afraid I can, Andy. I have my own star to follow, you know."

"But do you know," said Andy, "how beautiful and delicate a man's heart is when he is happy for the first time? It is like the thin ice that has imprisoned those beautiful young plants that are released when the ice thaws."

"You have read that in some poem," said Miss Goering.

"Does that make it any the less beautiful?"

"No," said Miss Goering, "I admit that it is a very beautiful thought."

"You don't dare tear the plant up now that you have melted the ice."

"Oh, Andy," said Miss Goering, "you make me sound so dreadful! I am merely working out something for myself."

"You have no right to," said Andy. "You're not alone in the world. You've involved yourself with me!" He was growing more excited perhaps because he realized that it was useless saying anything to Miss Goering at all.

"I'll get down on my knees," said Andy, shaking his fist at her. No sooner had he said this than he was down on his knees near her feet. The waiter was terribly shocked and felt that he had better say something.

"Look, Andy," he said in a very small voice, "Why don't you get up off your knees and think things over?"

"Because," said Andy, raising his own voice more and more, "because she daren't refuse a man who is down on his knees. She daren't! It would be sacrilege."

"I don't see why," said Miss Goering.

"If you refuse," said Andy, "I'll disgrace you, I'll crawl out into the street, I'll put you to shame."

"I really have no sense of shame," said Miss Goering, "and I think your own sense of shame is terribly exaggerated, besides being a terrific sap on your energies. Now I must go, Andy. Please get up."

"You're crazy," said Andy. "You're crazy and monstrous— *really*. Monstrous. You are committing a monstrous act."

"Well," said Miss Goering, "perhaps my maneuvers do seem a little strange, but I have thought for a long time now that often, so very often, heroes who believe themselves to be monsters because they are so far removed from other men turn around much later and see really monstrous acts being committed in the name of something mediocre."

"Lunatic!" Andy yelled at her from his knees. "You're not even a Christian."

Miss Goering hurried out of the ice-cream parlor after having kissed Andy lightly on the head, because she realized that if she did not leave him very quickly she would miss her appointment. As a matter of fact, she had judged correctly, because her friend was just coming out of the saloon when she arrived.

"Are you coming out with me?" he said. "I got through a little sooner than I thought and I decided I wasn't going to wait around, because I didn't think you'd come."

"But," said Miss Goering, "I accepted your invitation. Why didn't you think I'd come?"

"Don't get excited," said the man. "Come on, let's get in the car."

As they drove past the ice-cream parlor on their way out of town, Miss Goering looked through the window to see if she could catch a glimpse of Andy. To her surprise, she saw that the store was filled with people, so that they overflowed into the street and quite crowded the sidewalk, and she was unable really to see into the store at all.

The man was sitting in front with the chauffeur, who was not in uniform, and she was sitting alone in the back seat. This arrangement had surprised her at first, but she was pleased. She understood shortly why he had arranged the seating in this manner. Soon after they had left the town behind them he turned around and said to her:

"I'm going to sleep now. I'm more comfortable up here because I don't bounce around so much. You can talk to the chauffeur if you want."

"I don't think I care to talk with anyone," said Miss Goering.

"Well, do whatever the hell you want," he said. "I don't want to be waked up until those steaks are on the grill." He promptly pulled his hat down over his eyes and went to sleep.

As they drove on, Miss Goering felt sadder and lonelier than she had ever felt before in her life. She missed Andy and Arnold and Miss Gamelon and the old man with all her heart and very soon she was weeping silently in the back of the car. It was only with a tremendous exertion of her will that she refrained from opening the door and leaping out into the road.

They passed through several small towns and at last, just at Miss Goering was dozing off, they arrived in a medium-sized city.

"This is the town we were heading for," said the chauffeur, assuming that Miss Goering had been watching the road impatiently. It was a noisy town and there were many tramways all heading in different directions. Miss Goering was astonished that the noise did not awaken her friend in the front seat. They soon left the center of town, although they were still in the city proper when they drove up in front of an apartment building. The chauffeur had quite a difficult time awakening his employer, but at last he succeeded by yelling the man's own address close to his ear.

Miss Goering was waiting on the sidewalk, standing first on one foot and then on the other. She noticed that there was a little garden that ran the length of one side of the apartment house. It was planted with evergreen trees and bushes, all of small dimensions because it was obvious that both the garden and the apartment house were very new. A string of barbed wire surrounded the garden and there was a dog trying to crawl under it. "I'll go put the car away, Ben," said the chauffeur.

Ben got out of the car and pushed Miss Goering ahead of him into the lobby of the apartment.

"Fake Spanish," Miss Goering said more to herself than to Ben.

"This isn't fake Spanish," he said glumly, "this is real Spanish."

Miss Goering laughed a little. "I don't think so," she said. "I have been to Spain."

"I don't believe you," said Ben. "Anyhow, this is real Spanish, every inch of it."

Miss Goering looked around her at the walls, which were made of yellow stucco and ornamented with niches and clusters of tiny columns.

Together they entered a tiny automatic elevator and Miss Goering's heart nearly failed her. Her companion pressed a button, but the elevator remained stationary.

"I could tear the man to pieces who made this gadget," he said, stamping on the floor.

"Oh, please," said Miss Goering, "please let me out."

He paid no attention to her, but stamped even harder than before, and pressed on the button over and over again as though the fear in her voice had excited him. At last the elevator started to rise. Miss Goering hid her face in her hands. They reached the second floor, where the elevator stopped, and they got out. They waited together in front of one of three doors that opened on a narrow hall.

"Jim has the keys with him," said Ben; "he'll be up in a minute. I hope you understand that we won't go dancing or any nonsense. I can't stand what people call fun."

"Oh, I love all that," said Miss Goering. "Fundamentally I am a light-hearted person. That is, I enjoy all the things that light-hearted people enjoy."

Ben yawned.

"He's never going to listen to me," Miss Goering said to herself.

•

Presently the chauffeur returned with the keys and let them into the apartment. The living-room was small and unattractive. Someone had left an enormous bundle in the middle of the floor. Through some rents in the paper Miss Goering could see that the bundle contained a pretty pink quilt. She felt a little heartened at the sight of the quilt and asked Ben whether or not he had chosen it himself. Without answering her question he called to the chauffeur, who had gone into the kitchen adjoining the living-room. The door between the two rooms was open, and Miss Goering could see the chauffeur standing next to the sink in his hat and coat and slowly unwrapping the steaks.

"I told you to see that they called for that damn blanket," Ben shouted to him.

"I forgot."

"Then carry one of those reminder pads with you and pull it out of your pocket once in a while. You can buy one at the corner."

Ben threw himself down on the couch next to Miss Goering, who had seated herself, and put his hand on her knee.

"Why? Don't you want the quilt now that you have bought it?" Miss Goering asked him.

"I didn't buy it. That girl who was here with me last week bought it, to throw over us in bed."

"And you don't like the color?"

"I don't like a lot of extra stuff hanging around."

He sat brooding for a few minutes and Miss Goering, whose heart began to beat much too quickly each time that he lapsed into silence, searched her mind for another question to ask.

"You're not fond of discussions," she said to him.

"You mean talking?"

"Yes."

"No, I'm not."

"Why aren't you?"

"You say too much when you talk," he answered absently.

"Well, aren't you anxious to find out about people?"

He shook his head. "I don't need to find out about people,

and, what's more important, they don't need to find out about me." He looked at her out of the corner of his eye.

"Well," she said a little breathlessly, "there must be something you like."

"I like women a lot and I like to make money if I can make it quickly." Without warning he jumped to his feet and pulled Miss Goering up with him, grabbing hold of her wrist rather roughly. "While he's finishing the steaks let's go inside for a minute."

"Oh, please," Miss Goering pleaded, "I'm so tired. Let's rest here a little before dinner."

"All right," said Ben. "I'm going to my room and stretch out till the steaks are cooked. I like them overdone."

While he was gone, Miss Goering sat on the couch pulling at her sweating fingers. She was torn between an almost overwhelming desire to bolt out of the room and a sickening compulsion to remain where she was.

"I do hope," she said to herself, "that the steaks will be ready before I have a chance to decide."

However, by the time the chauffeur awakened Ben to announce that the steaks were cooked, Miss Goering had decided that it was absolutely necessary for her to stay.

They sat together around a small folding table and ate in silence. They had barely finished their meal when the telephone rang. Ben answered, and when he had finished his conversation he told Miss Goering and Jim that they were all three of them going into the city. The chauffeur looked at him knowingly.

"It doesn't take long from here," said Ben, pulling on his coat. He turned to Miss Goering. "We are going to a restaurant," he said to her. "You'll sit patient at a separate table while I talk business with some friends. If it gets terribly late you and me will spend the night in the city at a hotel where I always go, downtown. Jim will drive the car back out and sleep here. Now is everything understood by everybody?"

"Perfectly," said Miss Goering, who was naturally delighted that they were leaving the apartment.

•

The restaurant was not very gay. It was in a large square room on the first floor of an old house. Ben led her to a table near the wall and told her to sit down.

"Every now and then you can order something," he said, and went over to three men who were standing at a makeshift bar improvised of thin strips of wood and papier-mâché.

The guests were nearly all men, and Miss Goering noticed that there were no distinguished faces among them, although not one of them was shabbily dressed. The three men to whom Ben was talking were ugly and even brutal-looking. Presently she saw Ben make a sign to a woman who was seated not far from her own table. She went and spoke to him and then walked quickly over to Miss Goering's table.

"He wants you to know he's going to be here a long time, maybe over two hours. I am supposed to get you what you want. Would you like some spaghetti or a sandwich? I'll get you whichever you want."

"No, thank you," said Miss Goering. "But won't you sit down and have a drink with me?"

"To tell you the truth, I won't," said the woman, "although I thank you very much." She hesitated a moment before saying good-by. "Of course, I would like to have you come over to our table and join us, but the situation is hard to explain. Most of us here are close friends, and when we see each other we tell each other everything that has happened."

"I understand," said Miss Goering, who was rather sad to see her leave because she did not fancy sitting alone for two or three hours. Although she was not anxious to be in Ben's company, the suspense of waiting all that time with so little to distract her was almost unbearable. It occurred to her that she might possibly telephone to a friend and ask her to come and have a drink at the restaurant. "Certainly," she thought. "Ben can't object to my having a little chat with another woman." Anna and Mrs. Copperfield were the only two people she knew well enough to invite on such short notice. Of the two she preferred Mrs. Copperfield and thought her the most likely to accept such an invitation. But she was not certain that Mrs. Copperfield had returned yet from her trip through Central America. She called the waiter and requested that he take her to the phone. After asking a few questions he showed her into a drafty hall and called the number for her. She was successful in reaching her friend, who was terribly excited the moment she heard Miss Goering's voice.

"I am flying down immediately," she said to Miss Goering. "I can't tell you how terrific it is to hear from you. I have not been back long, you know, and I don't think I'll stay."

Just as Mrs. Copperfield was telling her this, Ben came into the hall and snatched the receiver from Miss Goering's hand. "What's this about, for Christ's sake?" he demanded.

Miss Goering asked Mrs. Copperfield to hold on a moment. "I am calling a woman friend," she said to Ben, "a woman whom I haven't seen in quite some time. She is a lively person and I thought she might like to come down and have a drink with me. I was growing lonely at my table."

"Hello," Ben shouted into the phone, "are you coming down here?"

"By all means and *tout de suite,*" Mrs. Copperfield answered. "I adore her."

Ben seemed satisfied and returned the receiver to Miss Goering without saying a word. Before leaving the hall, however, he announced to Miss Goering that he was not going to take on two women. She nodded and resumed her conversation with Mrs. Copperfield. She told her the address of the restaurant which the waiter had written down for her, and said good-by.

About half an hour later Mrs. Copperfield arrived, accompanied by a woman whom Miss Goering had never seen before.

She was dismayed at the sight of her old friend. She was terribly thin and she appeared to be suffering from a skin eruption. Mrs. Copperfield's friend was fairly attractive, Miss Goering thought, but her hair was far too wiry for her own taste. Both women were dressed expensively and in black.

"There she is," Mrs. Copperfield screamed, grabbing Pacifica by the hand and running over to Miss Goering's table.

"I can't tell you how delighted I am that you called," she said. "You are the one person in the world I wanted to have see me. This is Pacifica. She is with me in my apartment."

Miss Goering asked them to sit down.

"Listen," said Pacifica to Miss Goering, "I have a date with a boy very far uptown. It is wonderful to see you, but he will be very nervous and unhappy. She can talk to you and I'll go and see him now. You are great friends, she told me."

Mrs. Copperfield rose to her feet. "Pacifica," she said, "you must stay here and have drinks first. This is a miracle and you must be in on it."

"It is so late now that I will be in a damned mess if I don't go right away. She would not come here alone," Pacifica said to Miss Goering.

"Remember, you promised to come and get me afterwards," said Mrs. Copperfield. "I will telephone you as soon as Christina is ready to leave."

Pacifica said good-by and hurried out of the room.

"What do you think of her?" Mrs. Copperfield asked Miss Goering, but without waiting for an answer she called for the waiter and ordered two double whiskies. "What do you think of her?" she repeated.

"Where's she from?"

"She is a Spanish girl from Panama, and the most wonderful character that has ever existed. We don't make a move without each other. I am completely satisfied and contented."

"I should say, though, that you are a little run down," said Miss Goering, who was frankly worried about her friend.

"I'll tell you," said Mrs. Copperfield, leaning over the table and suddenly looking very tense. "I am a little worried—not terribly worried, because I shan't allow anything to happen that I don't want to happen—but I am a little worried because Pacifica has met this blond boy who lives way uptown and he has asked her to marry him. He never says anything and he has a very weak character. But I think he has bewitched her because he pays her compliments all the time. I've gone up to his apartment with her, because I won't allow them to be alone, and she has cooked dinner for him twice. He's crazy for Spanish food and eats ravenously of every dish she puts in front of him."

Mrs. Copperfield leaned back and stared intently into Miss Goering's eyes.

"I am taking her back to Panama as soon as I am able to book passage on a boat." She ordered another double whisky. "Well, what do you think of it?" she asked eagerly.

"Perhaps you'd better wait and see whether or not she really wants to marry him."

"Don't be insane," said Mrs. Copperfield. "I can't live without her, not for a minute. I'd go completely to pieces."

"But you have gone to pieces, or do I misjudge you dreadfully?"

"True enough," said Mrs. Copperfield, bringing her fist down on the table and looking very mean. "I *have* gone to pieces, which is a thing I've wanted to do for years. I know I am as guilty as I can be, but I have my happiness, which I guard like a wolf, and I have authority now and a certain amount of daring, which, if you remember correctly, I never had before."

Mrs. Copperfield was getting drunk and looking more disagreeable.

"I remember," said Miss Goering, "that you used to be somewhat shy, but I dare say very courageous. It would take a good deal of courage to live with a man like Mr. Copperfield, whom I gather you are no longer living with. I've admired you very much indeed. I am not sure that I do now."

"That makes no difference to me," said Mrs. Copperfield. "I feel that you have changed anyway and lost your charm. You seem stodgy to me now and less comforting. You used to be so gracious and understanding; everyone thought you were light in the head, but I thought you were extremely instinctive and gifted with magic powers." She ordered another drink and sat brooding for a moment.

"You will contend," she continued in a very clear voice, "that all people are of equal importance, but although I love Pacifica very much, I think it is obvious that I am more important."

Miss Goering did not feel that she had any right to argue this point with Mrs. Copperfield.

"I understand how you feel," she said, "and perhaps you are right."

"Thank God," said Mrs. Copperfield, and she took Miss Goering's hand in her own.

"Christina," she pleaded, "please don't cross me again, I can't bear it."

Miss Goering hoped that Mrs. Copperfield would now question her concerning her own life. She had a great desire to tell someone everything that had happened during the last year. But Mrs. Copperfield sat gulping down her drink, occasionally spilling a little of it over her chin. She was not even looking at Miss Goering and they sat for ten minutes in silence.

"I think," said Mrs. Copperfield at last, "that I will telephone Pacifica and tell her to call for me in three quarters of an hour."

Miss Goering showed her to the phone and returned to the table. She looked up after a moment and noticed that another man had joined Ben and his friends. When her friend returned from the telephone, Miss Goering saw immediately that

something was very much the matter. Mrs. Copperfield fell
into her seat.

"She says that she does not know when she is coming down,
and if she is not here by the time you feel like leaving, I am to
return home with you, or all alone by myself. It's happened to
me now, hasn't it? But the beauty of me is that I am only a step
from desperation all the time and I am one of the few people I
know who could perform an act of violence with the greatest of
ease."

She waved her hand over her head.

"Acts of violence are generally performed with ease," said
Miss Goering. She was at this point completely disgusted with
Mrs. Copperfield, who rose from her seat and walked in a
crooked path over to the bar. There she stood taking drink after
drink without turning her little head which was almost completely hidden by the enormous fur collar on her coat.

Miss Goering went up to Mrs. Copperfield just once, think-
ing that she might persuade her friend to return to the table.
But Mrs. Copperfield showed a furious tear-stained face to
Miss Goering and flung her arm out sideways, striking Miss
Goering in the nose with her forearm. Miss Goering returned
to her seat and sat nursing her nose.

To her great surprise, about twenty minutes later Pacifica
arrived, accompanied by her young man. She introduced him
to Miss Goering and then hurried over to the bar. The young
man stood with his hands in his pockets and looked around
him rather awkwardly.

"Sit down," said Miss Goering. "I thought that Pacifica was
not coming."

"She was not coming," he answered very slowly, "but then
she decided that she would come because she was worried that
her friend would be upset."

"Mrs. Copperfield is a highly strung woman, I am afraid,"
said Miss Goering.

"I don't know her very well," he answered discreetly.

Pacifica returned from the bar with Mrs. Copperfield, who was now terribly gay and wanted to order drinks for everyone. But neither the boy nor Pacifica would accept her offer. The boy looked very sad and soon excused himself, saying that he had only intended to see Pacifica to the restaurant and then return to his home. Mrs. Copperfield decided to accompany him to the door, patting his hand all the way and stumbling so badly that he was obliged to slip his arm around her waist to keep her from falling. Pacifica, meanwhile, leaned over to Miss Goering.

"It is terrible," she said. "What a baby your friend is! I can't leave her for ten minutes because it almost breaks her heart, and she is such a kind and generous woman, with such a beautiful apartment and such beautiful clothes. What can I do with her? She is like a little baby. I tried to explain it to my young man, but I can't explain it really to anyone."

Mrs. Copperfield returned and suggested that they all go elsewhere to get some food.

"I can't," said Miss Goering, lowering her eyes. "I have an appointment with a gentleman." She would have liked to talk to Pacifica a little longer. In some ways Pacifica reminded her of Miss Gamelon although certainly Pacifica was a much nicer person and more attractive physically. At this moment she noticed that Ben and his friends were putting on their coats and getting ready to leave. She hesitated only a second and then hurriedly said good-by to Pacifica and Mrs. Copperfield. She was just drawing her wrap over her shoulders when, to her surprise, she saw the four men walk very rapidly towards the door, right past her table. Ben made no sign to her.

"He must be coming back," she thought, but she decided to go into the hall. They were not in the hall, so she opened the door and stood on the stoop. From there she saw them all get into Ben's black car. Ben was the last one to get in, and just as he stepped on the running board, he turned his head around and saw Miss Goering.

"Hey," he said, "I forgot about you. I've got to go big distances on some important business. I don't know when I'll be back. Good-by."

He slammed the door behind him and they drove off. Miss Goering began to descend the stone steps. The long staircase seemed short to her, like a dream that is remembered long after it has been dreamed.

She stood on the street and waited to be overcome with joy and relief. But soon she was aware of a new sadness within herself. Hope, she felt, had discarded a childish form forever.

"Certainly I am nearer to becoming a saint," reflected Miss Goering, "but is it possible that a part of me hidden from my sight is piling sin upon sin as fast as Mrs. Copperfield?" This latter possibilty Miss Goering thought to be of considerable interest but of no great importance.

❧ In the Summer House

FOR OLIVER SMITH

In the Summer House *was presented at the Playhouse Theatre in New York on December 29, 1953, by Oliver Smith and the Playwrights' Company. It was directed by José Quintero with the following cast:*

GERTRUDE EASTMAN CUEVAS · Judith Anderson
MOLLY, *her daughter* · Elizabeth Ross
MR. SOLARES · Don Mayo
MRS. LOPEZ · Marita Reid
FREDERICA · Miriam Colon
ESPERANZA · Isabel Morel
ALTA GRACIA · Marjorie Eaton
QUINTINA · Phoebe Mackay
LIONEL · Logan Ramsey
A FIGURE BEARER · Paul Bertelsen
ANOTHER FIGURE BEARER · George Spelvin
VIVIAN CONSTABLE · Muriel Berkson
CHAUFFEUR · Daniel Morales
MRS. CONSTABLE · Mildred Dunnock
INEZ · Jean Stapleton

Scenery · Oliver Smith
Costumes · Noel Taylor
Music · Paul Bowles
Lighting · Peggy Clark
Associate Producer · Lyn Austin

SCENES

ACT I

ACT II

Time: the present

· Act One

Scene i

GERTRUDE EASTMAN CUEVAS' *garden somewhere on the coast of Southern California. The garden is a mess, with ragged cactus plants and broken ornaments scattered about. A low hedge at the back of the set separates the garden from a dirt lane which supposedly leads to the main road. Beyond the lane is the beach and the sea. The side of the house and the front door are visible. A low balcony hangs over the garden. In the garden itself there is a round summer house covered with vines.*

GERTRUDE (*A beautiful middle-aged woman with sharply defined features, a good carriage and bright red hair. She is dressed in a tacky provincial fashion. Her voice is tense but resonant. She is seated on the balcony*) Are you in the summer house?

(MOLLY, *a girl of eighteen with straight black hair cut in*

bangs and a somnolent impassive face, does not hear GER-
TRUDE's *question but remains in the summer house.* GER-
TRUDE, *repeating, goes to railing*)

Are you in the summer house?

MOLLY   Yes, I am.

GERTRUDE   If I believed in acts of violence, I would burn
the summer house down. You love to get in there and loll
about hour after hour. You can't even see out because
those vines hide the view. Why don't you find a good flat
rock overlooking the ocean and sit on it?   (MOLLY *fingers
the vine*)   As long as you're so indifferent to the beauties
of nature, I should think you would interest yourself in
political affairs, or in music or painting or at least in the
future. But I've said this to you at least a thousand times
before. You admit you relax too much?

MOLLY   I guess I do.

GERTRUDE   We already have to take in occasional boarders
to help make ends meet. As the years go by the boarders
will increase, and I can barely put up with the few that
come here now; I'm not temperamentally suited to boarders. Nor am I interested in whether this should be considered a character defect or not. I simply hate gossiping
with strangers and I don't want to listen to their business.
I never have and I never will. It disgusts me. Even my
own flesh and blood saps my vitality—particularly you.
You seem to have developed such a slow and gloomy way
of walking lately . . . not at all becoming to a girl. Don't
you think you could correct your walk?

MOLLY   I'm trying. I'm trying to correct it.

GERTRUDE I'm thinking seriously of marrying Mr. Solares,
after all. I would at least have a life free of financial worry
if I did, and I'm sure I could gradually ease his sister,
Mrs. Lopez, out of the house because she certainly gets on
my nerves. He's a manageable man and Spanish men
aren't around the house much, which is a blessing.
They're always out . . . not getting intoxicated or having a wild time . . . just out . . . sitting around with
bunches of other men . . . Spanish men . . . Cubans,
Mexicans . . . I don't know . . . They're all alike,
drinking little cups of coffee and jabbering away to each
other for hours on end. That was your father's life anyway. I minded then. I minded terribly, not so much because he left me alone, but he wasn't in his office for more
than a few hours a day . . . and he wasn't rich enough,
not like Mr. Solares. I lectured him in the beginning. I
lectured him on ambition, on making contacts, on devel-
oping his personality. Often at night I was quite hoarse. I
worked on him steadily, trying to make him worry about
sugar. I warned him he was letting his father's interests
go to pot. Nothing helped. He refused to worry about
sugar; he refused to worry about anything. (*She knits a
moment in silence*) I lost interest finally. I lost interest
in sugar . . . in him. I lost interest in our life together.
I wanted to give it all up . . . start out fresh, but I
couldn't. I was carrying you. I had no choice. All my
hopes were wrapped up in you then, all of them. You
were my reason for going on, my one and only hope . . .
my love. (*She knits furiously. Then, craning her neck to
look in the summer house, she gets up and goes to the
rail*) Are you asleep in there, or are you reading comic
strips?

MOLLY I'm not asleep.

GERTRUDE   Sometimes I have the strangest feeling about you. It frightens me . . . I feel that you are plotting something. Especially when you get inside that summer house. I think your black hair helps me to feel that way. Whenever I think of a woman going wild, I always picture her with black hair, never blond or red. I know that what I'm saying has no connection with a scientific truth. It's very personal. They say red-haired women go wild a lot but I never picture it that way. Do you?

MOLLY   I don't guess I've ever pictured women going wild.

GERTRUDE   And why not? They do all the time. They break the bonds . . . Sometimes I picture little scenes where they turn evil like wolves . . . (*Shuddering*) I don't choose to, but I do all the same.

MOLLY   I've never seen a wild woman.

GERTRUDE   (*Music*)   On the other hand, sometimes I wake up at night with a strange feeling of isolation . . . as if I'd fallen off the cliffs and landed miles away from everything that was close to my heart . . . Even my griefs and my sorrows don't seem to belong to me. Nothing does— as if a shadow had passed over my whole life and made it dark. I try saying my name aloud, over and over again, but it doesn't hook things together. Whenever I feel that way I put my wrapper on and I go down into the kitchen. I open the ice chest and take out some fizzy water. Then I sit at the table with the light switched on and by and by I feel all right again. (*The music fades. Then in a more matter-of-fact tone*)   There is no doubt that each one of us has to put up with a shadow or two as he grows older. But if we occupy ourselves while the shadow passes, it passes swiftly enough and scarcely leaves a trace of our daily lives . . . (*She knits for a moment. Then looks up the road*) The girl who is coming here this afternoon is about seventeen. She should be arriving pretty soon. I also think that Mr. Solares will be arriving shortly and that he'll be bringing one of his hot picnic luncheons with him today. I can feel it in my bones. It's disgraceful of me, really, to allow him to feed us on our own lawn, but then, their mouths count up to six, while ours count up to only two. So actually it's only half a disgrace. I hope Mr. Solares realizes that. Besides, I might be driven to accepting his marriage offer and then the chicken would be in the same pot anyway. Don't you agree?

M O L L Y Yes.

G E R T R U D E You don't seem very interested in what I'm saying.

M O L L Y Well, I . . .

G E R T R U D E I think that you should be more of a conversationalist. You never express an opinion, nor do you seem to have an outlook. What on earth is your outlook?

M O L L Y (*Uncertainly*) Democracy . . .

G E R T R U D E I don't think you feel very strongly about it. You don't listen to the various commentators, nor do you ever glance at the newspapers. It's very easy to say that one is democratic, but that doesn't prevent one from being a slob if one is a slob. I've never permitted myself to become a slob, even though I sit home all the time and avoid the outside world as much as possible. I've never liked going out any more than my father did. He always avoided the outside world. He hated a lot of idle gossip and had no use for people anyway. "Let the world do its dancing and its drinking and its interkilling without me," he always said. "They'll manage perfectly well; I'll stick to myself and my work." *(The music comes up again and she is lost in a dream)* When I was a little girl I made up my mind that I was going to be just like him. He was my model, my ideal. I admired him more than anyone on earth. And he admired me of course. I was so much like him—ambitious, defiant, a fighting cock always. I worshipped him. But I was never meek, not like Ellen my sister. She was very frail and delicate. My father used to put his arms around her, and play with her hair, long golden curls . . . Ellen was the weak one. That's why he spoiled her. He pitied Ellen. *(With wonder, and very delicately, as if afraid to break a spell. The music expresses the sorrow she is hiding from herself)* Once he took her out of school, when she was ten years old. He bought her a little fur hat and they went away together for two whole weeks. I was left behind. I had no reason to leave school. I was healthy and strong. He took her to a big hotel on the edge of a lake. The lake was frozen, and they sat in the sunshine all day long, watching the people skate. When they came back he said, "Look at her, look at Ellen. She has roses in her cheeks." He pitied Ellen, but he was proud of me. I was his true love. He never showed it . . . He was so frightened Ellen would guess. He didn't want her to be jealous, but I knew the truth . . . He didn't have to show it. He didn't have to say anything. *(The music fades and she knits furiously, coming back to the present)* Why don't you go inside and clean up? It might sharpen your wits. Go and change that rumpled dress.

MOLLY (MOLLY *comes out of the summer house and sniffs a blossom*) The honeysuckle's beginning to smell real

good. I can never remember when you planted this vine,
but it's sure getting thick. It makes the summer house so
nice and shady inside.

GERTRUDE (*Stiffening in anger*) I told you never to mention that vine again. You know it was there when we
bought this house. You love to call my attention to that
wretched vine because it's the only thing that grows well
in the garden and you know it was planted by the people
who came here before us and not by me at all. (*She rises
and paces the balcony*) You're mocking me for being
such a failure in the garden and not being able to make
things grow. That's an underhanded Spanish trait of
yours you inherit from your father. You love to mock me.

MOLLY (*Tenderly*) I would never mock you.

GERTRUDE (*Working herself up*) I thought I'd find peace
here . . . with these waving palms and the ocean stretch-
ing as far as the eye can see, but you don't like the ocean
. . . You won't even go in the water. You're afraid to
swim . . . I thought we'd found a paradise at last—the
perfect place—but you don't want paradise . . . You
want hell. Well, go into your little house and rot if you
like . . . I don't care. Go on in while you still can. It
won't be there much longer . . . I'll marry Mr. Solares
and send you to business school. (*The voices of* MR.
SOLARES *and his family arriving with a picnic lunch stop
her. She leans over the railing of the balcony and looks up
the road*) Oh, here they come with their covered pots. I
knew they'd appear with a picnic luncheon today. I could
feel it in my bones. We'll put our own luncheon away for
supper and have our supper tomorrow for lunch . . .
Go and change . . . Quickly . . . Watch that walk.
(MOLLY *exits into the house.* GERTRUDE *settles down in her*

chair to prepare for MR. SOLARES' *arrival*) I wish they weren't coming. I'd rather be here by myself really. *(Enter Spanish people)* Nature's the best company of all. *(She pats her bun and rearranges some hairpins. Then she stands up and waves to her guests, cupping her mouth and yelling at the same time)* Hello there!

> *(In another moment* MR. SOLARES, MRS. LOPEZ *and her daughter,* FREDERICA, *and the three servants enter, walking in single file down the lane. Two of the servants are old hags and the third is a young half caste,* ESPERANZA, *in mulberry-colored satin. The servants all carry pots wrapped with bright bandanas.)*

MR. SOLARES *(He wears a dark dusty suit. Pushing ahead of his sister,* MRS. LOPEZ, *in his haste to greet* GERTRUDE *and thus squeezing his sister's arm rather painfully against the gate post)* Hello, Miss Eastman Cuevas! *(*MRS. LOPEZ *squeals with pain and rubs her arm. She is fat and middle-aged. She wears a black picture hat and black city dress. Her hat is decorated with flowers,* MR. SOLARES *speaks with a trace of an accent, having lived for many years in this country. Grinning and bobbing around)* We brought you a picnic. For you and your daughter. Plenty of everything! You come down into the garden.

> *(The others crowd slowly through the gate and stand awkwardly in a bunch looking up at* GERTRUDE.)

GERTRUDE *(Perfunctorily)* I think I'll stay here on the balcony, thank you. Just spread yourselves on the lawn and we'll talk back and forth this way. It's all the same. *(To the maids)* You can hand me up my food by stepping on that little stump and I'll lean over and get it.

MRS. LOPEZ *(Her accent is much thicker than her brother's, smiling up at* GERTRUDE) You will come down into the garden, Miss Eastman Cuevas?

MR. SOLARES (*Giving his sister a poke*) Acaba de decirte
que se queda arriba. ¿Ya no oyes? (*The next few minutes on the stage have a considerable musical background.
The hags and* ESPERANZA *start spreading bandanas on the
lawn and emptying the baskets. The others settle on the
lawn.* ESPERANZA *and the hags sing a raucous song as they
work, the hags just joining in at the chorus and a bit off
key.* ESPERANZA *brings over a pot wrapped in a Turkish
towel and serves the family group. They all take enormous helpings of spaghetti.* MR. SOLARES *serves himself*)
Italian spaghetti with meat balls! Esperanza, serve a big
plate to Miss Eastman Cuevas up on the porch. You climb
on that.

(*He points to a fake stump with a gnome carved on one side
of it.*)

ESPERANZA (*Disagreeably*) ¡Caramba!

(*She climbs up on the stump after filling a plate with spaghetti and hands it to* GERTRUDE, *releasing her hold on the
plate before* GERTRUDE *has secured her own grip.* ESPERANZA
*jumps out of the way immediately and the plate swings
downward under the weight of the food, dumping the spaghetti on* MRS. LOPEZ' *head.*)

GERTRUDE Oh! (*To* ESPERANZA) You didn't give me a
chance to get a firm hold on it!

MR. SOLARES ¡Silencio!

(ESPERANZA *rushes over to the hags and all three of them become hysterical with laughter. After their hysterics they pull
themselves together and go over to clean up* MRS. LOPEZ *and
to restore* GERTRUDE'S *plate to her filled with fresh spaghetti.
They return to their side of the garden in a far corner and
everyone starts to eat.*)

MR. SOLARES (*To* GERTRUDE) Miss Eastman Cuevas, you like chop suey?

GERTRUDE I have never eaten any.

MRS. LOPEZ (*Eager to get into the conversation and expressing great wonder in her voice*) Chop suey? What is it?

MR. SOLARES (*In a mean voice to* MRS. LOPEZ) You know what it is. (*In Spanish*) Que me dejes hablar con la señora Eastman Cuevas por favor. (*To* GERTRUDE) I'll bring you some chop suey tomorrow in a box, or maybe we better go out to a restaurant, to a dining and dancing. Maybe you would go to try out some chop suey . . . Would you?

GERTRUDE (*Coolly*) That's very nice of you but I've told you before that I don't care for the type of excitement you get when you go out . . . You know what I mean—entertainment, dancing, etc. Why don't you describe chop suey to me and I'll try and imagine it? (MRS. LOPEZ *roars with laughter for no apparent reason.* GERTRUDE *cranes her neck and looks down at her over the balcony with raised eyebrows*) I could die content without ever setting foot in another restaurant. Frankly, I would not care if every single one of them burned to the ground. I really love to sit on my porch and look out over the ocean.

MRS. LOPEZ You like the ocean?

GERTRUDE I love it!

MRS. LOPEZ (*Making a wild gesture with her arm*) I hate it!

GERTRUDE   I love it. It's majestic . . .

MRS. LOPEZ   I hate!

GERTRUDE   (*Freezing up*)   I see that we don't agree.

MR. SOLARES   (*Scowling at* MRS. LOPEZ)   Oh, she loves the
ocean. I don't know what the hell is the matter with her
today.   (GERTRUDE *winces at his language*)   Myself, I like
ocean, land, mountain, all kinds of food, chop suey, chile,
eel, turtle steak . . . Everything. Solares like everything.
(*In hideous French accent*)   Joie de vivre!
    (*He snaps his fingers in the air.*)

GERTRUDE   (*Sucking some long strands of spaghetti into her
mouth*)   What is your attitude toward your business?

MR. SOLARES   (*Happily*)   My business is dandy.

GERTRUDE   (*Irritably*)   Yes, but what is your attitude toward it?

MR. SOLARES   (*With his mouth full*)   O.K.

GERTRUDE   Please try to concentrate on my question, Mr.
Solares. Do you like business or do you really prefer to
stay home and lazy around?

MRS. LOPEZ   (*Effusively*)   He don't like no business—he
likes to stay home and sleep—and eat.   (*Then in a mocking tone intended to impress* MR. SOLARES *himself*)   "Fula,
I got headache . . . I got bellyache . . . I stay home,
no?"   (*She jabs her brother in the ribs with her elbow
several times rolling her eyes in a teasing manner and re-*

peats) "Fula, I got headache . . . I got bellyache . . .
I stay home, no?"

*(She jabs him once again even harder and laughs way down
in her throat.)*

MR. SOLARES ¡Fula! Esta es la última vez que sales con-
migo. Ya, déjame hablar con la señora *Eastman Cuevas!*

MRS. LOPEZ Look, *Miss* Eastman Cuevas?

GERTRUDE *(Looking disagreeably surprised)* Yes?

MRS. LOPEZ You like to talk to me?

GERTRUDE *(As coolly as possible short of sounding rude)*
Yes, I enjoy it.

MRS. LOPEZ *(Triumphantly to* MR. SOLARES*)* Miss Eastman
Cuevas *like* talk to me, so you shut your mouth. He don't
want no one to talk to you, Miss Eastman Cuevas because he think he gonna marry you.

*(*FREDERICA *doubles over and buries her face in her hands.
Her skinny shoulders shake with laughter.)*

MR. SOLARES *(Embarrassed and furious)* Bring the
chicken and rice, Esperanza.

ESPERANZA You ain't finished what you got!

MR. SOLARES Cállate, y tráigame el arroz con pollo.

*(*ESPERANZA *walks across the lawn with the second pot
wrapped in a Turkish towel. She walks deliberately at a
very slow pace, throwing a hip out at each step, and with a
terrible sneer on her face. She serves them all chicken and*

rice, first removing the spaghetti plates and giving them
clean ones. Everyone takes enormous helpings again, with
the exception of GERTRUDE *who refuses to have any.*)

GERTRUDE (*While* ESPERANZA *serves the others*) If Molly
doesn't come out soon she will simply have to miss her
lunch. It's very tiring to have to keep reminding her of
the time and the other realities of life. Molly is a dreamer.

MRS. LOPEZ (*Nodding*) That's right.

GERTRUDE (*Watching* FREDERICA *serve herself*) Do you people always eat such a big midday meal? Molly and I are
in the habit of eating simple salads at noon.

MRS. LOPEZ (*Wiping her mouth roughly with her napkin.*
Then without pausing and with gusto) For breakfast:
chocolate and sugar bread: for lunch: soup, beans, eggs,
rice, roast pork with potatoes and guava paste . . . (*She*
pulls on a different finger for each separate item) Next
day: soup, eggs, beans, rice, chicken with rice and guava
paste—other day: soup, eggs, beans, rice, stew meat,
roasted baby pig and guava paste. Other day: soup, rice,
beans, grilled red snapper, roasted goat meat and guava
paste.

FREDERICA (*Speaking for the first time, rapidly, in a scarcely*
audible voice) Soup, rice, beans, eggs, ground-up meat
and guava paste.

GERTRUDE (*Wearily*) We usually have a simple salad.

MR. SOLARES She's talkin' about the old Spanish custom.
She only come here ten years ago when her old man died.
I don't like a big lunch neither. (*In a sudden burst of*
temerity) Listen, what my sister said was true. I hope I

am gonna marry you some day soon. I've told you so before. You remember?

MRS. LOPEZ (*Laughing and whispering to* FREDERICA, *who goes off into hysterics, and then delving into a shopping bag which lies beside her on the grass. In a very gay voice*) This is what you gonna get if you make a wedding. (*She pulls out a paper bag and hurls it at* GERTRUDE's *head with the gesture of a baseball pitcher. The bag splits and spills rice all over* GERTRUDE. *There is general hilarity and even a bit of singing on the part of* ESPERANZA *and the hags.* MR. LOPEZ *yells above the noise*) Rice!

GERTRUDE (*Standing up and flicking rice from her shoulders*) Stop it! Please! Stop it! I can't stand this racket . . . Really. (*She is genuinely upset. They subside gradually. Bewildered, she looks out over the land toward the road*) Something is coming down the road . . . It must be my boarder . . . No . . . She would be coming in an automobile. (*Pause*) Gracious! It certainly is *no* boarder, but what is it?

MRS. LOPEZ Friend come and see you?

GERTRUDE (*Bewildered, staring hard*) No, it's not a friend. It's . . . (*She stares harder*) It's some sort of king— and others.

MRS. LOPEZ (*To her brother*) ¿Qué?

MR. SOLARES (*Absently absorbed in his food*) King. Un rey y otros más . . .

MRS. LOPEZ (*Nodding*) Un rey y otros más.

(Enter LIONEL, *bearing a cardboard figure larger than himself, representing Neptune, with flowing beard, crown and sceptre, etc. He is followed by two or more other figure bearers, carrying representations of a channel swimmer and a mermaid.* LIONEL *stops at the gate and dangles into the garden a toy lobster which he has tied to the line of a real fishing rod. The music dies down.)*

LIONEL   Advertisement.

(He bobs the lobster up and down.)

GERTRUDE   For what?

LIONEL   For the Lobster Bowl . . . It's opening next week. *(Pointing)*   That figure there represents a mermaid and the other one is Neptune, the sea god. This is a lobster . . . *(He shakes the rod)*   Everything connected with the sea in some capacity. Can we have a glass of water?

GERTRUDE   Yes. *(Calling)*   Molly! Molly!

MOLLY   *(From inside the house)*   What is it?

GERTRUDE   Come out here immediately. *(To* LIONEL)   Excuse me but I think your figures are really awful. I don't like advertising schemes anyway.

LIONEL   I have nothing to do with them. I just have to carry them around a few more days and then after that I'll be working at the Bowl. I'm sorry you don't like them.

GERTRUDE   I've always hated everything that was larger than life size.

*(*LIONEL *opens the gate and enters the garden, followed by the other figure bearers. The garden by now has a very clut-*

tered appearance. The servants, MRS. LOPEZ *and* FREDERICA *have been gaping at the figures in silence since their arrival.)*

MRS. LOPEZ *(Finding her tongue)* ¡Una maravilla!

FREDERICA Ay, sí.

(She is nearly swooning with delight. Enter MOLLY. *She stops short when she sees the figures.)*

MOLLY Oh . . . What are those?

LIONEL Advertisements. This is Neptune, the old god.

*(*MOLLY *approaches the figures slowly and touches Neptune.)*

MOLLY It's beautiful . . .

LIONEL Here's a little lobster.

(He dangles it into MOLLY's *open palm.)*

MOLLY It looks like a real lobster. It even has those long threads sticking out over its eyes.

GERTRUDE Antennae.

MOLLY Antennae.

LIONEL *(Pulling another little lobster from his pocket and handing it to* MOLLY) Here. Take this one. I have a few to give away.

MOLLY Oh, thank you very much.

(There followed a heated argument between FREDERICA *and* MRS. LOPEZ, *who is trying to force* FREDERICA *to ask for a*

lobster too. They almost come to blows and finally MRS.
LOPEZ *gives* FREDERICA *a terrific shove which sends her stum-*
bling over toward LIONEL *and* MOLLY.)

MRS. LOPEZ (*Calling out to* LIONEL) Give my girl a little
fish please!

(LIONEL *digs reluctantly into his pocket and hands* FREDERICA
a little lobster. She takes it and returns to her mother, stub-
bing her toe in her confusion.)

GERTRUDE (*Craning her neck and looking out over the lane*
toward the road) There's a car stopping. This really
must be my boarder. (*She looks down into the garden*
with an expression of consternation on her face) The
garden is a wreck. Mr. Solares, can't your servants organize this mess? Quickly, for heaven's sake. (*She looks*
with disgust at MR. SOLARES, *who is still eating, but holds*
her tongue. Enter VIVIAN, *a young girl of fifteen with wild*
reddish gold hair. She is painfully thin and her eyes ap-
pear to pop out of her head with excitement. She is
dressed in bright colors and wears high heels. She is fol-
lowed by a chauffeur carrying luggage) And get those
figures out of sight!

VIVIAN (*Stopping in the road and staring at the house in-*
tently for a moment) The house is heavenly!

(MOLLY *exits rapidly.*)

GERTRUDE Welcome, Vivian Constable. I'm Gertrude Eastman Cuevas. How was your trip?

VIVIAN Stinky. (*Gazing with admiration into the garden*
packed with people) And your garden is heavenly too.

GERTRUDE The garden is a wreck at the moment.

VIVIAN   Oh, no! It's fascinating.

GERTRUDE   You can't possibly tell yet.

VIVIAN   Oh, but I can. I decide everything the first minute. It's a fascinating garden.

> (*She smiles at everyone.* MR. SOLARES *spits chicken skin out of his mouth onto the grass.*)

MRS. LOPEZ   Do you want some spaghetti?

VIVIAN   Not yet, thank you. I'm too excited.

GERTRUDE   (*To* MR. SOLARES) Will you show Miss Constable and the chauffeur into the house, Mr. Solares? I'll meet you at the top of the stairs.

> (*She exits hurriedly into the house, but* MR. SOLARES *continues gnawing on his bone not having paid the slightest attention to* GERTRUDE'S *request. Enter* MRS. CONSTABLE, VIVIAN'S *mother. She is wearing a distinguished city print, gloves, hat and veil. She is frail like her daughter but her coloring is dull.*)

VIVIAN   (*Spying her mother. Her expression immediately hardens*) Why did you get out of the taxi? You promised at the hotel that you wouldn't get out if I allowed you to ride over with me. You promised me once in the room and then again on the porch. Now you've gotten out. You're dying to spoil the magic. Go back . . . Don't stand there looking at the house. (MRS. CONSTABLE *puts her fingers to her lips entreating silence, shakes her head at* VIVIAN *and scurries off stage after nodding distractedly to the people on the lawn*) She can't keep a promise.

GERTRUDE   (*Coming out onto the balcony again and spotting* MR. SOLARES, *still eating on the grass*) What is the

matter with you, Mr. Solares? I asked you to show Miss
Constable and the chauffeur into the house and you
haven't budged an inch. I've been waiting at the top of
the stairs like an idiot.

(MR. SOLARES *scrambles to his feet and goes into the house
followed by* VIVIAN *and the chauffeur. Enter* MRS. CONSTABLE
again.)

MRS. CONSTABLE (*Coming up to the hedge and leaning
over. To* MRS. LOPEZ)   Forgive me but I would like you to
tell Mrs. Eastman Cuevas that I am at the Herons Hotel.
(MRS. LOPEZ *nods absently.* MRS. CONSTABLE *continues in a
scarcely audible voice*) You see, Mrs. Eastman Cuevas
comes from the same town that I come from and through
mutual friends I heard that she took in boarders these
days, so I wrote her that Vivian my daughter was coming.

MRS. LOPEZ Thank you very much.

MRS. CONSTABLE My daughter likes her freedom, so we
have a little system worked out when we go on vacations.
I stay somewhere nearby but not in the same place. Even
so, I am the nervous type and I would like Mrs. Eastman
Cuevas to know that I'm at the Herons . . . You see my
daughter is unusually high spirited. She feels everything
so strongly that she's apt to tire herself out. I want to be
available just in case she collapses.

MRS. LOPEZ (*Ruffling* FREDERICA's *hair*) Frederica get very
tired too.

MRS. CONSTABLE Yes, I know. I suppose all the young
girls do. Will you tell Mrs. Eastman Cuevas that I'm at
the Herons?

MRS. LOPEZ O.K.

MRS. CONSTABLE Thank you a thousand times. I'll run
along now or Vivian will see me and she'll think that I'm
interfering with her freedom . . . You'll notice right
away what fun she gets out of life. Good-bye.

MRS. LOPEZ Good-bye, Mrs. Vamos; despiértense. Esperanza.
(MRS. CONSTABLE *exits hurriedly. To* MR. SOLARES) Now
we go home.

MR. SOLARES (*Sullenly*) All right. (*Spanish group leaves*)
Esperanza! Esperanza! Frederica!

> (*Enter from the house* VIVIAN, GERTRUDE *and the chauffeur,
> who leaves the garden and exits down the lane.*)

VIVIAN (*To* GERTRUDE, *continuing a conversation*) I'm going to be sky high by dinner time. Then I won't sleep all
night. I know myself.

GERTRUDE Don't you use controls?

VIVIAN No, I never do. When I feel myself going up I just
go on up until I hit the ceiling. I'm like that. The world
is ten times more exciting for me than it is for others.

GERTRUDE Still I believe in using controls. It's a part of the
law of civilization. Otherwise we would be like wild
beasts. (*She sighs*) We're bad enough as it is, controls
and all.

VIVIAN (*Hugging* GERTRUDE *impulsively*) You've got the
prettiest hair I've ever seen, and I'm going to love it here.
(GERTRUDE *backs away a little, embarrassed.* VIVIAN *spots
the summer house*) What a darling little house! It's like
the home of a bird or a poet. (*She approaches the summer house and enters it.* MRS. LOPEZ *motions to the hags*

to start cleaning up. They hobble around one behind the other gathering things and scraping plates very ineffectually. More often than not the hag behind scrapes more garbage onto the plate just cleaned by the hag in front of her. They continue this until the curtain falls. Music begins. Calling to GERTRUDE) I can imagine all sorts of things in here, Miss Eastman Cuevas. I could make plans for hours on end in here. It's so darling and little.

GERTRUDE (*Coldly*) Molly usually sits in there. But I can't say that she plans much. Just dozes or reads trash. Comic strips. It will do no harm if someone else sits in there for a change.

VIVIAN Who is Molly?

GERTRUDE Molly is my daughter.

VIVIAN How wonderful! I want to meet her right away . . . Where is she?

(*The boys start righting the cardboard figures.*)

LIONEL Do you think we could have our water?

GERTRUDE I'm sorry. Yes, of course. (*Calling*) Molly! (*Silence*) Molly! (*More loudly*) Molly! (*Silence*)

LIONEL I think we'll go along to the next place. Don't bother your daughter. I'll come back if I may. I'd like to see you all again . . . and your daughter. She disappeared so quickly.

GERTRUDE You stay right where you are. I'll get her out here in a minute. (*Screaming*) Molly! Come out here immediately! Molly!

VIVIAN   (*In a trilling voice*)   Molly! Come on out! . . . I'm
in your little house . . . Molly!

GERTRUDE   (*Furious*)   Molly!

(*All the players look expectantly at the doorway.* MOLLY
does not appear and the curtain comes down in silence.)

Scene ii

One month later.
A beach and a beautiful backdrop of the water. The SO-
LARES family is again spread out among dirty plates as
though the scenery had changed around them while they
themselves had not stirred since the first act. GERTRUDE is
kneeling and rearranging her hair near the SOLARES family,
VIVIAN at her feet. MOLLY and LIONEL a little apart from the
other people, MOLLY watching VIVIAN. The two old hags are
wearing white slips for swimming.
     The music is sad and disturbing, implying a more serious
mood.

MRS. LOPEZ   (*Poking her daughter who is lying next to her*)
A ver si tú y Esperanza nos cantan algo . . .

FREDERICA   (*From under handkerchief which covers her
face*)   Ay, mamá.

MRS. LOPEZ   (*Calling to* ESPERANZA)   Esperanza, a ver si
nos cantan algo, tú y Frederica.

(*She gives her daughter a few pokes. They argue a bit and*
FREDERICA *gets up and drags herself wearily over to the hags.*
They consult and sing a little song. The hags join in at the
chorus.)

ESPERANZA Bueno—sí . . .

GERTRUDE (*When they have finished*) That was nice. I like sad songs.

VIVIAN (*Still at her feet and looking up at her with adoration*) So do I . . . (MOLLY *is watching* VIVIAN, *a beam of hate in her eye.* VIVIAN *takes* GERTRUDE'S *wrist and plays with her hand just for a moment.* GERTRUDE *pulls it away, instinctively afraid of* MOLLY'S *reaction. To* GERTRUDE) I wish Molly would come swimming with me. I thought maybe she would. (*Then to* MOLLY, *for* GERTRUDE'S *benefit*) Molly, won't you come in, just this once. You'll love it once you do. Everyone loves the water, everyone in the world.

GERTRUDE (*Springing to her feet, and addressing the Spanish people*) I thought we were going for a stroll up the beach after lunch. (*There is apprehension behind her words*) You'll never digest lying on your backs, and besides you're sure to fall asleep if you don't get up right away.

(*She regains her inner composure as she gives her commands.*)

MRS. LOPEZ (*Groaning*) ¡Ay! ¡Caray! Why don't you sleep, Miss Eastman Cuevas?

GERTRUDE It's very bad for you, really. Come on. Come on, everybody! Get up! You too, Alta Gracia and Quintina, get up! Come on, everybody up! (*There is a good deal of protesting while the servants and the* SOLARES *family struggle to their feet*) I promise you you'll feel much better later on if we take just a little walk along the beach.

VIVIAN (*Leaping to* GERTRUDE's *side in one bound*) I *love* to walk on the beach!

(MOLLY *too has come forward to be with her mother.*)

GERTRUDE (*Pause. Again stifling her apprehension with a command*) You children stay here. Or take a walk along the cliffs if you'd like to. But be careful!

FREDERICA I want to be with my mother.

GERTRUDE Well, come along, but we're only going for a short stroll. What a baby you are, Frederica Lopez.

MR. SOLARES I'll run the car up to my house and go and collect that horse I was telling you about. Then I'll catch up with you on the way back.

GERTRUDE You won't get much of a walk.

(FREDERICA *throws her arms around her mother and gives her a big smacking kiss on the cheek.* MRS. LOPEZ *kisses* FREDERICA. *They all exit slowly, leaving* VIVIAN, LIONEL, MOLLY *and the dishes behind.* MOLLY, *sad that she can't walk with her mother, crosses wistfully back to her former place next to* LIONEL, *but* VIVIAN—*eager to cut her out whenever she can—rushes to* LIONEL's *side, and crouches on her heels exactly where* MOLLY *was sitting before.* MOLLY *notices this, and settles in a brooding way a little apart from them, her back to the pair.*)

VIVIAN Lionel, what were you saying before about policies?

LIONEL When?

VIVIAN Today, before lunch. You said, "What are your policies" or something crazy like that?

LIONEL   Oh, yes. It's just . . . I'm mixed up about my own policies, so I like to know how other people's are getting along.

VIVIAN   Well, I'm for freedom and a full exciting life! (*Pointedly to* MOLLY's *back*)   I'm a daredevil. It frightens my mother out of her wits, but I love excitement!

LIONEL   Do you always do what gives you pleasure?

VIVIAN   Whenever I can, I do.

LIONEL   What about conflicts?

VIVIAN   What do you mean?

LIONEL   Being pulled different ways and not knowing which to choose.

VIVIAN   I don't have those. I always know exactly what I want to do. When I have a plan in my head I get so excited I can't sleep.

LIONEL   Maybe it would be a stroke of luck to be like you. I have nothing but conflicts. For instance, one day I think I ought to give up the world and be a religious leader, and the next day I'll turn right around and think I ought to throw myeslf deep into politics.   (VIVIAN, *bored, starts untying her beach shoes*)   There have been ecclesiastics in my family before. I come from a gloomy family. A lot of the men seem to have married crazy wives. Five brothers out of six and a first cousin did. My uncle's first wife boiled a cat alive in the upstairs kitchen.

VIVIAN   What do you mean, the upstairs kitchen?

LIONEL We had the top floor fitted out as an apartment and the kitchen upstairs was called the upstairs kitchen.

VIVIAN (*Hopping to her feet*) Oh, well, let's stop talking dull heavy stuff. I'm going to swim.

LIONEL All right.

VIVIAN (*Archly*) Good-bye, Molly.

> (*She runs off stage in the direction of the cove.* MOLLY *sits on rock.*)

LIONEL (*Goes over and sits next to her*) Doesn't the ocean make you feel gloomy when the sky is gray or when it starts getting dark out?

MOLLY I don't guess it does.

LIONEL Well, in the daytime, if it's sunny out and the ocean's blue it puts you in a lighter mood, doesn't it?

MOLLY When it's blue . . .

LIONEL Yes, when it's blue and dazzling. Don't you feel happier when it's like that?

MOLLY I don't guess I emphasize that kind of thing.

LIONEL I see. (*Thoughtfully*) Well, how do you feel about the future? Are you afraid of the future in the back of your mind?

MOLLY I don't guess I emphasize that much either.

LIONEL Maybe you're one of the lucky ones who looks forward to the future. Have you got some kind of ambition?

MOLLY   Not so far. Have you?

LIONEL   I've got two things I think I should do, like I told Vivian. But they're not exactly ambitions. One's being a religious leader, the other's getting deep into politics. I don't look forward to either one of them.

MOLLY   Then you'd better not do them.

LIONEL   I wish it was that simple. I'm not an easygoing type. I come from a gloomy family . . . I dread being a minister in a way because it brings you so close to death all the time. You would get too deep in to ever forget death and eternity again, as long as you lived—not even for an afternoon. I think that even when you were talking with your friends or eating or joking, it would be there in the back of your mind. Death, I mean . . . and eternity. At the same time I think I might have a message for a parish if I had one.

MOLLY   What would you tell them?

LIONEL   Well, that would only come through divine inspiration, after I made the sacrifice and joined up.

MOLLY   Oh.

LIONEL   I get a feeling of dread in my stomach about being a political leader too . . . That should cheer me up more, but it doesn't. You'd think I really liked working at the Lobster Bowl.

MOLLY   Don't you?

LIONEL   Yes, I do, but of course that isn't life. I have fun too, in between worrying . . . fun, dancing, and eating, and swimming . . . and being with you. I like to be with you because you seem to only half hear me. I think I could say just the opposite and it wouldn't sound any different to you. Now why do I like that? Because it makes me feel very peaceful. Usually if I tell my feelings to a person I don't want to see them any more. That's another peculiar quirk of mine. Also there's something very familiar about you, even though I never met you before two months ago. I don't know what it is quite . . . your face . . . your voice . . . (*Taking her hand*) or maybe just your hand. (*Holds her hand for a moment, deep in thought*) I hope I'm not going to dread it all for too long. Because it doesn't feel right to me, just working at the Lobster Bowl. It's nice though really . . . Inez is always around if you want company. She can set up oyster cocktails faster than anyone on the coast. That's what she claims, anyway. She has some way of checking. You'd like Inez.

M O L L Y   I don't like girls.

L I O N E L   Inez is a grown-up woman. A kind of sturdy rock-of-Gibraltar type but very high strung and nervous too. Every now and then she blows up. (MOLLY *rises suddenly and crosses to the rock*) Well, I guess it really isn't so interesting to be there, but it is outside of the world and gloomy ideas. Maybe it's the decorations. It doesn't always help though, things come creeping in anyway.

M O L L Y   (*Turning to* LIONEL) What?

L I O N E L   Well, like what ministers talk about . . . the valley of the Shadow of Death and all that . . . or the world comes creeping in. I feel like it's a warning that I shouldn't stay too long. That I should go back to St.

Louis. It would be tough though. Now I'm getting too
deep in. I suppose you live mainly from day to day.
That's the way girls live mainly, isn't it?

MOLLY (*Crossing back to* LIONEL) I don't know. I'm all
right as long as I can keep from getting mad. It's hard to
keep from getting mad when you see through people.
Most people can't like I do. I'd emphasize that all right.
The rest of the stuff doesn't bother me much. A lot of
people want to yank you out and get in themselves. Girls
do anyway. I haven't got anything against men. They
don't scheme the way girls do. But I keep to myself as
much as I can.

LIONEL Well, there's that angle too, but my point of view is
different. Have you thought any more about marrying me
if your mother marries Mr. Solares? I know we're both
young, but you don't want to go to business school and
she's sure to send you there if she marries him. She's always talking about it. She'd be in Mexico most of the year
and you'd be in business school. We could live over the
Lobster Bowl and get all the food we wanted free, and it's
good food. Mr. Solares and Mrs. Lopez liked it when they
went to eat there.

MOLLY Yes, I know they did.

LIONEL Well?

MOLLY I won't think of it until it happens. I can't picture
anything being any different than it is. I feel I might just
plain die if everything changes, but I don't imagine it
will.

LIONEL You should look forward to change.

MOLLY   I don't want anything different.

LIONEL   Then you *are* afraid of the future just like me.

MOLLY   (*Stubbornly*)   I don't think much about the future.

(VIVIAN *returns from her swim.*)

LIONEL   (*To* MOLLY)   Well, even if you don't think much about the future you have to admit that . . .

(*He is interrupted by* VIVIAN *who rushes up to them, almost stumbling in her haste.*)

VIVIAN   (*Plopping down next to* LIONEL *and shaking out her wet hair*)   Wait 'til you hear this . . . !   (LIONEL *is startled.* VIVIAN *is almost swooning with delight, to* LIONEL)   It's so wonderful . . . I can hardly talk about it . . . I saw the whole thing in front of my eyes . . . Just now while I was swimming . . .

LIONEL   What?

VIVIAN   Our restaurant.

LIONEL   What restaurant?

VIVIAN   *Our restaurant.* The one we're going to open together, right now, as soon as we can. I'll tell you about it . . . But only on one condition . . . You have to promise you won't put a damper on it, and tell me it's not practical.

(*Shaking him.*)

LIONEL   (*Bored*)   All right.

VIVIAN   Well, this is it. I'm going to sell all the jewelry my grandmother left me and we're going on a trip. We're going to some city I don't know which but some big city that will be as far from here as we can get. Then we'll take jobs and when we have enough money we'll start a restaurant. We could start it on credit with just the barest amount of cash. It's not going to be just an ordinary restaurant but an odd one where everyone sits on cushions instead of on chairs. We could dress the waiters up in those flowing Turkish bloomers and serve very expensive oriental foods, all night long. It will be called Restaurant Midnight. Can you picture it?

LIONEL   (*Very bored*)   Well, yes . . . in a way . . .

VIVIAN   Well, I can see the whole thing . . . very small lamps and perfume in the air, no menus, just silent waiters . . . bringing in elaborate dishes one after the other . . . and music. We could call it "Minuit" . . . as it is in French . . . But either way we must leave soon . . . I can't go on this way with my mother snooping around . . . I can't be tied down . . . I've tried running off before, when I felt desperate . . . But things didn't work out . . . maybe because I never had a real friend before . . . But *now* I have *you*— (*She stops, suddenly aware of* MOLLY—*then with a certain diffidence*)   and Molly, of course, she must come too—we understand each other even if she is still waters run deep. She has to escape from her mother too . . .

(MOLLY *starts at the word "mother." Her face blackens.*)

LIONEL   Molly, you're shivering . . . Why didn't you say something? (*Looking up*) The sun's gone behind a cloud, no wonder you're cold . . . I can go back to the

house and get you a jacket, unless you want to come along and go home now too. (MOLLY *does not move*) I'll go and get it. Sit nearer the rocks you'll be out of the wind. Vivian, do you want something heavier than that?
(*Points to her robe.*)

VIVIAN   No, thanks. I'm much too excited about Restaurant Midnight to notice anything. Besides I'm not very conscious of the physical. (LIONEL *exits*. MOLLY *gets up and walks to the rocks leading to the cliff*) Have you ever eaten Armenian vine leaves with little pine nuts inside of them?

(MOLLY *is climbing the rocks.*)

MOLLY   Don't follow me . . .

VIVIAN   Oh their wonderful flaky desserts with golden honey poured . . .

MOLLY   Don't follow me!

VIVIAN   (*Tapering off*)   . . . all over them . . .

MOLLY   The day you came I was standing on the porch watching you. I heard everything you said. You put your arm around my mother, and you told her she had beautiful hair, then you saw my summer house and you told her how much you loved it. You went and sat in it and you yelled, Come out, Molly. I'm in your little house. You've tried in every way since you came to push me out. She hates you.

VIVIAN   What?

MOLLY   My mother hates you! She hates you!

VIVIAN   (*After recovering from her shock starts out after her in a rage*)   That's a lie, a rotten lie . . . She doesn't hate me . . . She's ashamed of *you* . . . ashamed of you. (*Exits, then repeating several times off stage*)   She's ashamed of you . . . ashamed of you . . .

> (*Her voice is muffled by the entrance of the Mexicans and* GERTRUDE. *The servants head the procession, chattering like magpies and singing.* MR. SOLARES *and* FREDERICA *bring up the rear carrying a tremendous pink rubber horse with purple dots. The hindquarters are supported by* FREDERICA.)

MRS. LOPEZ   (*Signaling to one of the hags who puts a fancy cushion down on the bench, which she sits on, then yelling to* GERTRUDE)   Well, how do you like our gorgeous horse? Pretty big, eh?

MR. SOLARES   It's worth thirty-two dollars.

> (*They all seat themselves.*)

GERTRUDE   Now that you've asked me I'll tell you quite frankly that I would never dream of spending my money on a thing like that.

MRS. LOPEZ   (*Popping a mint into her mouth*)   Pretty big, eh?

GERTRUDE   (*Irritably*)   Yes, yes, it's big all right but I don't see what that has to do with anything.

MRS. LOPEZ   That right. Big, lots of money. Little not so much.

GERTRUDE (*Bitterly*) All the worse.

MRS. LOPEZ (*Merrily*) Maybe next year, bigger. You got one? (GERTRUDE, *bored, does not answer*) You got one?

GERTRUDE What?

MRS. LOPEZ A rubber horse?

GERTRUDE Oh, for heaven's sake! I told you I thought it was silly. I don't believe in toys for grownups. I think they should buy other things, if they have money to spare.

MRS. LOPEZ (*Complacently folding her hands*) What?

GERTRUDE Well, I guess a dresser or a chair or clothing or curtains. I don't know but certainly not a rubber horse. Clothing, of course, one can always buy because the styles change so frequently.

MR. SOLARES Miss Eastman Cuevas, how many dresses you got?

GERTRUDE (*Icily*) I have never counted them.

MRS. LOPEZ (*To her brother*) Cincuenta y nueve, dile.

MR. SOLARES She got fifty-nine back at the house.

GERTRUDE (*In spite of herself*) Fifty-nine!

MR. SOLARES I bought them all for her, since her husband died. He was a no good fellow. No ambition, no brain, no pep.

MRS. LOPEZ (*Smiling, and nodding her head to* GERTRUDE *sweetly*) Fifty-nine dresses. You like to have that many dresses?

(*Enter* MRS. CONSTABLE *carrying a fishing pole and basket, although she is immaculately dressed in a white crocheted summer ensemble. She has on a large hat and black glasses.*)

MRS. CONSTABLE (*Trying to smile and appear at ease*) I hope I'm not interrupting a private discussion.

MR. SOLARES Happy to see you on this beautiful day. Sit down with us. We weren't having no discussion. Just counting up how many dresses the ladies got.

MRS. CONSTABLE (*A little shocked*) Oh! I myself was hunting for a good spot to fish and I passed so near to your house that I dropped in to call, but you weren't there, of course. Then I remembered that you told me about a bathing spot, somewhere in this direction, so I struck out hoping to find you. Where are the children?

GERTRUDE They were here a little while ago . . . They'll be back.

MRS. CONSTABLE I think I might sit down for a few minutes and wait for my bird to come back. I call Vivian my bird. Don't you think it suits her, Mrs. Eastman Cuevas?

GERTRUDE (*Bored*) Yes.

MRS. CONSTABLE (*She sits down on a cushion*) I miss her very badly already. It's partly because she has so much life in her. She finds so many things of interest to do and think about. (*She speaks with wonder in her voice*) I myself can't work up very much interest. I guess that's normal at my age. I can't think of much to do really, not being either a moveiegoer, or a card player or a walker. Don't you think that makes me miss her more?

GERTRUDE (*Icily*) It might.

MRS. CONSTABLE This morning after I was cleaned and dressed I sat on the porch, but I got so tired of sitting there that I went to the front desk and asked them to tell me how to fish. They did and I bought this pole. The clerk gave me a kit with some bait in it. I think it's a worm. I'm not looking forward to opening the kit. I don't like the old hook either. I'll wager I don't fish after all. (*She sighs*) So you see what my days are like.

GERTRUDE Don't you read?

MRS. CONSTABLE I would love to read but I have trouble with concentration.

MR. SOLARES (*Coming over and crouching next to* MRS. CONSTABLE *on his heels*) How are you feeling today, Mrs. Constable? What's new?

MRS. CONSTABLE Not very well, thank you. I'm a little bit blue. That's why I thought I'd get a look at my bird.

MR. SOLARES (*Still to* MRS. CONSTABLE) You're looking real good. (*Studying her crocheted dress*) That's handwork, ain't it?

MRS. CONSTABLE (*Startled*) Why, yes.

MR. SOLARES You like turtle steak?

MRS. CONSTABLE   What?

MR. SOLARES   Turtle steak. You like it, Mrs. Constable?

MRS. CONSTABLE   (*Stammering, bewildered*)   Oh, yes . . .

GERTRUDE   Mr. Solares!

MR. SOLARES   (*Looking up*)   What is it?

GERTRUDE   Perhaps I might try chop suey with you, after all. Did it originate in China or is it actually an American dish?

MR. SOLARES   I don't know, Miss Eastman Cuevas.

(*Quickly turns again to* MRS. CONSTABLE.)

MRS. LOPEZ   (*Loudly to* GERTRUDE)   Now you want to go eat chop suey because he's talkin' to the other lady. You be careful, Señora Eastman Cuevas or you gonna lose him.

(*She chuckles.*)

GERTRUDE   (*Furious but ignoring* MRS. LOPEZ)   I thought we might try some tonight, Mr. Solares—that is, if you'd like to . . .   (*Bitterly*)   Or have you lost your taste for chop suey?

MR. SOLARES   No, it's good.   (*Turning to* MRS. CONSTABLE *again*)   I'll call you up in your hotel and we'll go eat a real good turtle steak with fried potatoes one night. One steak would be too big for you, Mrs. Constable. You look like a dainty eater. Am I right?

GERTRUDE (*Turns and sees* MOLLY *sitting on the rock*) Molly, we met Lionel. He's bringing the coats. (*She sees* MOLLY's *stricken face and questions her*) Molly, what's happened? (MOLLY *doesn't answer*) What is it, Molly? What's happened to you . . . Molly . . . what happened? What is it, Molly? (*Looking around for* VIVIAN) Where's Vivian? (MOLLY *still does not answer*) Molly . . . Where is she? Where's Vivian?

MOLLY (*In a quavering voice*) She's gathering shells . . .

(MRS. CONSTABLE *rises and starts looking vaguely for* VIVIAN. *Then she sits down again.* GERTRUDE *gathers her composure after a moment and speaks to* MR. SOLARES.)

GERTRUDE (*Starts off and meets* LIONEL) Mr. Solares, I'm going home. It's windy and cold . . . The clouds are getting thicker every minute . . . The sun's not coming out again. I'm going back to the house.

LIONEL (*Entering with the coats*) I brought these . . . I brought one for Vivian too. . . . Where's Vivian?

GERTRUDE (*Takes sweater from* LIONEL) She's gathering shells. (*She puts sweater on* MOLLY's *shoulders*) Molly, put this on, you'll freeze. (*She starts off and calls to* MR. SOLARES) I'm going home.

(MOLLY *rises and starts to leave and comes face to face with* MRS. CONSTABLE. *They look at each other a moment.* MOLLY *then rushes off, following her mother.* MRS. CONSTABLE *goes back to the rock.* MR. SOLARES *and the Spanish people start to gather up their stuff and prepare to leave.*)

MR. SOLARES We're coming right away, Miss Eastman Cuevas. (*He gives the servants orders in Spanish. Then to* MRS. CONSTABLE)   Come on back to the house and I'll mix up some drinks.

MRS. CONSTABLE   No, thank you.

MRS. LOPEZ   (*Butting into the conversation*)   You don't come?

MR. SOLARES   (*To* MRS. LOPEZ)   Acaba de decir, no thank you . . . ¿no oyes nunca?

(*The Spanish people all exit noisily.*)

LIONEL   (*As he leaves, sees* MRS. CONSTABLE *alone*)   Aren't you coming Mrs. Constable?

MRS. CONSTABLE   I think I'll sit here and wait for my bird.

LIONEL   But she might climb up the cliffs and go home around the other way. It's getting colder Mrs. Constable . . . I could wait with you . . .

MRS. CONSTABLE   I don't want to talk. No, I'll just sit here and wait a little while.

LIONEL   (*Going off*)   Don't worry, Mrs. Constable. She'll be all right.

MRS. CONSTABLE   (*Left alone on the stage*)   I get so frightened, I never know where she's going to end up.

   The Curtain Falls Slowly

Scene iii

> *Same as Scene i. There is an improvised stand in the upper right-hand corner of the garden (the corner from the house), festooned with crepe paper and laden with a number of hot dogs, as well as part of a wedding cake and other things.* MOLLY *is leaning against the stand wearing a simple wedding dress with a round shirred neck. She has removed her veil and she looks more like a girl graduating from school than like a bride. She is eating a hot dog. The stage is flooded with sunlight.*

GERTRUDE *(Also in bridal costume. She is sitting on a straight-backed chair in the middle of the garden, with her own dress hiked above her ankles, revealing bedroom slippers with pompons. Eyeing* MOLLY*)* Molly! You don't have to stuff yourself just because the others stuffed so much that they had to go and lie down! After all, you and I are brides even if I did take off my shoes. But they pinched so, I couldn't bear it another minute. Don't get mustard spots all over your dress. You'll want to show it to your grandchildren some day.

> *(*MOLLY'S *mouth is so full that she is unable to answer. The hags and* ESPERANZA *are lying with their heads under the stand, for shade, and their legs sticking way out into the garden.* MRS. CONSTABLE *is wandering around in a widow's outfit, with hat and veil. She holds a champagne glass in her hand.)*

MRS. CONSTABLE *(Stopping beside* GERTRUDE'S *chair)* I don't know where to go or what to do next. I can't seem to tear myself away from you or Mr. Solares or Mrs. Lopez or Molly. Isn't that a ridiculous reaction? *(She is obviously tight)* I feel linked to you. That's the only way I can explain it. I don't ever want to have any other friends. It's as if I had been born right here in this garden and had never lived anywhere before in my life. Isn't that funny? I don't want ever to have any other friends. Don't leave me please. (*She throws her arms around* GERTRUDE) I don't know where to go. Don't leave me.

(*She squeezes* GERTRUDE *for a moment in silence.*)

GERTRUDE   Now you must stop brooding. Can't you occupy yourself with something?

MRS. CONSTABLE   (*Firmly*)   I'm not brooding. I can think about it without feeling a thing, because if you must know it's just not real to me. I can't believe it. Now what does seem real is that you and Mr. Solares are going away and deserting me and Mrs. Lopez and Molly and Lionel too. And I don't want to be anywhere except in this garden with all of you. Isn't it funny? Not that I'm enjoying myself, but it's all that I want to do, just hang around in this garden. (*She goes over to the stand rather unsteadily and pours some champagne into her glass out of a bottle. She takes a few sips, then bitterly in a changed tone*)   I want to stay right here, by this stand.

GERTRUDE   (*Looking over her shoulder at* MRS. CONSTABLE) Drinking's not the answer to anything.

MRS. CONSTABLE   Answer? Who said anything about answers? I don't want any answers. It's too late for answers. Not that I ever asked much anyway. (*Angrily*)   I never cared for answers. You can take your answers and flush them down the toilet. I *want* to be able to stay here. Right here where I am, and never, never leave this garden. Why don't you have a drink, or one of these lousy hot dogs? (*She brushes a few hot dogs off the stand, onto the grass.* MOLLY *stoops down and picks them up*)   Let's stay here, Gertrude Eastman Cuevas, please.

GERTRUDE   You're being silly, Mrs. Constable. I know you're upset, but still you realize that I've sold the house and that Molly and I are going on honeymoons.

MRS. CONSTABLE   (*Vaguely*)   What about Mrs. Lopez?

GERTRUDE   Well, now, I guess she has her own affairs to attend to, and Frederica. Mrs. Constable, I think a sanatorium would be the best solution for you until you are ready to face the world again.

MRS. CONSTABLE   (*Thickly*)   What world?

GERTRUDE   Come now, Mrs. Constable, you know what I mean.

MRS. CONSTABLE   I know you're trying to be a bitch!

GERTRUDE   Mrs. Constable . . . I . . . (*She turns to* MOLLY *who has come to her side*)   Molly, go inside. At once . . . (MOLLY *runs into the house*)   Mrs. Constable, you ought to be ashamed. I won't tolerate such . . .

MRS. CONSTABLE   You have no understanding or feeling. Mrs. Lopez is much nicer than you are. You're very coarse. I know that even if I do hate to read. You're coarse, coarse and selfish. Two awful things to be. But I'm stuck here anyway so what difference does it make?

GERTRUDE   (*Refusing to listen to any more of her rambling*)   Mrs. Constable, I'm surprised at you. I'm going in. I won't put up with this. What would Vivian think . . .

MRS. CONSTABLE   Vivian was a bird. How do you know anything about birds? Vivian understood everything I did. Vivian loved me even if she did answer back and act snippy in company. She was much too delicate to show her true feelings all over the place like you do and like I do.

GERTRUDE   (*Crossing to* MRS. CONSTABLE)   I've never in my life shown my feelings. I don't know what you're talking about!

MRS. CONSTABLE   (*Reeling about at the wedding table*)   I don't know what I'm talking about . . . (*She grabs a bottle of champagne and offers it to* GERTRUDE)   Have another drink, Miss Eastman Cuevas.

GERTRUDE   (*In disgust grabs the bottle from her and puts it on the table*)   I don't like to drink!

MRS. CONSTABLE   Then have a hot dog. (*She drops it at* GERTRUDE'S *feet.* GERTRUDE *starts toward the house.* MRS. CONSTABLE *stops her*)   You and I grew up believing this kind of thing would never happen to us or to any of ours.

GERTRUDE   What?

MRS. CONSTABLE   We were kept far away from tragedy, weren't we?

GERTRUDE   No, Mrs. Constable. None of us have been kept from it.

MRS. CONSTABLE   Yes, well, now it's close to me, because Vivian hopped off a cliff—just like a cricket.

GERTRUDE   Life is tragic, Mrs. Constable.

MRS. CONSTABLE I don't want tragic.

GERTRUDE (*Can't put up with it any more*) Why don't you
lie down on the grass and rest? It's dry. (GERTRUDE *starts
toward the door of the house.* MRS. CONSTABLE *takes the
suggestion and falls in a heap behind the stump under the
balcony of the house*) Take your veil off. You'll roast!
(MRS. CONSTABLE *complies and* GERTRUDE *goes into the
house. The two old hags appear from behind the wedding
table and start to take some hot dogs. They are stopped
by* MOLLY *coming out of the house.* MOLLY *looks for a moment at the garden and then runs into her summer house.
A moment later* GERTRUDE *calls to the garden from the balcony*) Molly? Molly, are you in the summer house?

MOLLY Yes, I am.

GERTRUDE They're getting ready. After we've left if Mrs.
Constable is still asleep, will you and Lionel carry her inside and put her to bed in my room? Tomorrow when
you leave for the Lobster Bowl you can take her along
and drop her off at her hotel. Poor thing. Be sure and
clean up this mess in the morning. I have a list of things
here I want you to attend to. I'll leave it on the table
downstairs. Mr. Solares and I will be leaving soon.

MOLLY No!

GERTRUDE Yes.

MOLLY Please don't go away.

GERTRUDE Now, Molly, what kind of nonsense is this? You
know we're leaving, what's the matter with you?

MOLLY   No, I won't let you go!

GERTRUDE   Please, Molly, no mysteries. It's very hard getting everyone started and I'm worn out. And I can't find
my pocketbook. I think I left it in the garden. I'm coming down to look.   (GERTRUDE *leaves the balcony to come
downstairs.* MOLLY *comes out of the summer house and
stands waiting with a small bunch of honeysuckle in her
hands.* GERTRUDE *comes out of the house and crosses to the
wedding table. She looks at* MOLLY *and sees her crying
and goes to her*)   What on earth is wrong, Molly? Why
are you crying? Are you nervous? You've been so contented all day, stuffing yourself right along with the
others. What has happened now?

MOLLY   I didn't picture it.

GERTRUDE   Picture what?

MOLLY   What it would be like when the time came. Your
leaving . . .

GERTRUDE   Why not?

MOLLY   I don't know. I don't know . . . I couldn't picture
it, I guess. I thought so long as we were here we'd go right
on being here. So I just ate right along with the others
like you say.

GERTRUDE   Well, it sounds like nonsense to me. Don't be a
crybaby, and wipe your tears.

(GERTRUDE *starts toward the table when she is stopped by*
MOLLY *who puts the flowers in her hands.*)

MOLLY Stay!

GERTRUDE Molly. Put them back. They belong on your
wedding dress.

MOLLY No, they're from the vine. I picked them for you!

GERTRUDE They're for your wedding. They belong to your
dress. Here, put them back . . .

MOLLY No . . . No . . . They're for you . . . They're
flowers for you! (GERTRUDE *does not know what to make
of this strange and sudden love and moves across the garden*) I love you. I love you. Don't leave me. I love you.
Don't go away!

GERTRUDE (*Shocked and white*) Molly, stop. You can't go
on like this!

MOLLY I love you. You can't go!

GERTRUDE I didn't think you cared this much. If you really
feel this way, why have you tormented me so . . .

MOLLY I never have. I never have.

GERTRUDE You have. You have in a thousand different
ways. What about the summer house?

MOLLY Don't leave me!

GERTRUDE And the vine?

MOLLY I love you!

GERTRUDE   What about the vine, and the ocean, what about that? If you care this much why have you tormented me so about the water . . . when you knew how ashamed I was . . . Crazy, unnatural fear . . . Why didn't you try to overcome it, if you love me so much? Answer that!

(MOLLY, *in a frenzy of despair, starts clawing at her dress, pulling it open.*)

MOLLY   I will. I will. I'll overcome it. I'm sorry. I'll go in the water right away. I'm going now. I'm going . . .

(MOLLY *rips off her veil and throws it on the wedding table and makes a break for the gate to the ocean.* GERTRUDE *in horror grabs* MOLLY'S *arm and drags her back into the garden.*)

GERTRUDE   Stop it! Come back here at once. Are you insane? Button your dress. They'll see you . . . they'll find you this way and think you're insane . . .

MOLLY   I was going in the water . . .

GERTRUDE   Button your dress. Are you insane! This is what I meant. I've always known it was there, this violence. I've told you again and again that I was frightened. I wasn't sure what I meant . . . I didn't want to be sure. But I was right, there's something heavy and dangerous inside you, like some terrible rock that's ready to explode . . . And it's been getting worse all the time. I can't bear it any more. I've got to get away, out of this garden. That's why I married. That's why I'm going away. I'm frightened of staying here with you any more. I can't breathe. Even on bright days the garden seems like a dark place without any air. I'm stifling!

(GERTRUDE *passes below the balcony on her way to the front door,* MRS. LOPEZ *tilts a vessel containing rice and pours it on* GERTRUDE'S *head.*)

MRS. LOPEZ   That's for you, bride number one! Plenty more when you go in the car with Solares. Ha ha! Frederica, ándele, ¡tú también!

(FREDERICA, *terribly embarrassed, tosses a little rice onto* GERTRUDE *and starts to giggle.*)

GERTRUDE   (*Very agitated, ill-humoredly flicking rice from her shoulders*)   Oh, really! Where is Mr. Solares? Is he ready?

MRS. LOPEZ   My brother is coming right away. Where is bride number two?

GERTRUDE   (*Looking around for* MOLLY *who is back in the summer house*)   She's gone back into the summer house.

(*She goes out.*)

MRS. LOPEZ   I got rice for her too! (*Calling down to the servants who are still lying with their heads under the food stand*)   ¡Quinta! ¡Altagracia! ¡Esperanza! ¡Despiértense!

(*The servants wake up and come crawling out from under the food stand.*)

ESPERANZA   (*Scowling*)   ¡Caray!

(*She takes an enormous comb out of her pocket and starts running it through her matted hair. There is a sound of a horn right after* ESPERANZA *begins to comb her hair.*)

FREDERICA (*Beside herself with excitement*) It's Lionel
back with the automobile, mama! It must be time. Tell
the musicians to start playing!

MRS. LOPEZ Yes, querida. ¡Música! (*She kisses her daughter effusively and they both exit from the balcony into
the house talking and laughing.* LIONEL *enters from the
lane, hurries across the lawn and into the house, just
as* FREDERICA *and* MRS. LOPEZ *enter through the front
door onto the lawn.* MRS. LOPEZ *calling to the servants*)
Cuando salga la señora Eastman Cuevas de la casa, em-
pezarán a cantar. (*She sings a few bars herself counting
the time with a swinging finger and facing the servants,
who rise and line up in a row. Calling to* MOLLY) Bride
number two! Bride number two! Molly!

> (*She takes a few steps toward the summer house and throws
> some rice at it. The rice gets stuck in the vines instead of
> reaching* MOLLY *inside. After a few more failures, she goes
> around to the front of the summer house and, standing at
> the entrance, she hurls handful after handful at* MOLLY.
> *Enter from the house* LIONEL, *and* MR. SOLARES. *The men are
> carrying grips.* MRS. CONSTABLE *is still stretched out in a
> corner where she won't interfere with the procession. Some
> very naive music starts back stage (sounding, if possible, like
> a Taxco band), as they proceed across the lawn; then the
> maids begin to sing. While this happens* MRS. LOPEZ *gradu-
> ally ceases to throw her rice and then disappears in the sum-
> mer house where she takes the weeping* MOLLY *into her
> arms.*)

LIONEL Where's Molly?

MRS. LOPEZ (*Over the music, from inside the summer
house*) She don't feel good. She's crying in here. I cried
too when I had my wedding. Many young girls do. I
didn't want to leave my house neither.

(*She steps out of the summer house.*)

LIONEL (*Calling*) I'll be back, Molly, as soon as I load these bags.

> (*Enter* GERTRUDE *as* MRS. LOPEZ *comes out of the summer house. The music swells and the singing is louder.* GERTRUDE *walks rapidly through the garden in a shower of rice and rose petals.* MOLLY *comes out of the summer house and* GER- TRUDE *stops. They confront each other for a second without speaking.* GERTRUDE *continues on her way.* MOLLY *goes back into the summer house.*)

GERTRUDE (*From the road, calling over the music*) Good- bye, Molly!

> (*The wedding party files out, singing,* MRS. LOPEZ *bringing up the rear. She throws a final handful of rice at the sum- mer house, but it does not reach. They exit.* MOLLY *is left alone on the stage. The music gradually fades.*)

LIONEL (*Returning and coming into the garden*) Molly! (*There is no answer. He walks around to the front of the summer house and looks in*) Molly, I'm sorry you feel bad. (*Pause*) Why don't you come out? There's a very pretty sunset. (*He reaches in and pulls her out by the hands. He puts his arm around her shoulder and leads her toward the house*) We can go upstairs on the bal- cony and look at the sunset.

> (*They disappear into the house and reappear on the balcony, where they go to the balustrade and lean over it.*)

MOLLY (*Staring down into the garden, in a very small voice*) It looks different.

LIONEL (*After gazing off into the distance very thoughtfully for a minute*) I've always liked it when something that

I've looked at every day suddenly seems strange and unfamiliar. Maybe not always, but when I was home I used
to like looking out my window after certain storms that
left a special kind of light in the sky.

MOLLY   (*In a whisper*)   It looks different . . .

LIONEL   A very brilliant light that illuminated only the most
distant places, the places nearest to the horizon. Then I
could see little round hills, and clumps of trees, and pas-
tures that I didn't remember ever seeing before, very, very
close to the sky. It always gave me a lift, as if everything
might change around me but in a wonderful way that I
wouldn't have guessed was possible. Do you understand
what I mean?

(MOLLY *shakes her head, negatively. He looks at her for a
moment, a little sadly.*)

MOLLY   (*Anguished, turning away from him*)   I don't know.
I don't know. It looks so different . . .

Curtain

· Act Two

Scene i

The Lobster Bowl, ten months later.
Just before dawn. The oyster-shell door is open and the sound of waves breaking will continue throughout this scene. MOLLY *and* LIONEL *are playing cards at one of the tables, Russian Bank or its equivalent. They are sitting in a circle of light. The rest of the stage is in darkness.* MRS. CONSTABLE *is lying on a bench but can't be seen.*

MOLLY   You just put a king on top of another king.

LIONEL   I was looking for an ace.

MOLLY   (*Smilingly*)   It's right here, silly, under your nose.

LIONEL   It's almost morning.

MOLLY (*Wistful*) Can't we play one more game after this?

LIONEL All right.

> (*They play for a while in silence, then* LIONEL *stops again.*)

MOLLY What is it?

LIONEL Nothing.

MOLLY I don't think you want to play at all. You're thinking about something else.

LIONEL I had a letter from my brother . . . again.

MOLLY (*Tense*) The one who's still in St. Louis?

LIONEL That's right, the popular one, the one who'd like us to come back there.

MOLLY He's big and tall.

LIONEL Yes, he's big and tall, like most boys in this country. I've been thinking a lot about St. Louis, Molly . . .

MOLLY Inez says we've got bigger men here than they have in Europe.

LIONEL Well, Swedes are big and so are Yugoslavians . . .

MOLLY But the French people are little.

LIONEL Well, yes, but they're not as little as all that. They're not midgets. And they're not the way people used to picture them years ago, silly and carefree and saying Oo . . . la . . . la . . . all the time.

MOLLY They're not saying Oo . . . la . . . la?

LIONEL I don't know really, I've never been there. (*Dreaming, neglecting his cards*) Molly, when you close your eyes and picture the world do you see it dark? (MOLLY *doesn't answer right away*) Do you, Molly? Do you see the world dark behind your eyes?

MOLLY I . . . I don't know . . . I see parts of it dark.

LIONEL Like what?

MOLLY Like woods . . . like pine-tree woods.

LIONEL I see it dark, but beautiful like the ocean is right now. And like I saw it once when I was a child . . . just before a total eclipse. Did you ever see a total eclipse?

MOLLY I never saw any kind of eclipse.

LIONEL I saw one with my brother. There was a shadow over the whole earth. I was afraid then, but it stayed in my memory like something that was beautiful. It made me afraid but I knew it was beautiful.

MOLLY It's my game.

(*They start shuffling.*)

LIONEL (*Tentative*) Did you ever worry about running far away from sad things when you were young, and then later getting older and not being able to find your way back to them ever again, even when you wanted to?

MOLLY You would never want to find your way back to sad things.

LIONEL   But you might have lost wonderful things too, mixed in with the sad ones. Suppose in a few years I wanted to remember the way the world looked that day, the day of the eclipse when I saw the shadow.

MOLLY   (*Stops dealing her cards out very slowly, steeped in a dream*)   She had a shadow.

LIONEL   And suppose I couldn't remember it. What Molly?

MOLLY   She had a shadow.

LIONEL   Who?

MOLLY   My mother.

LIONEL   Oh . . .

> (*He deals his cards out more rapidly, becoming deeply absorbed in his game.*)

MOLLY   It used to come and pass over her whole life and make it dark. It didn't come very often, but when it did she used to go downstairs and drink fizzy water. Once I went down I was twelve years old. I waited until she was asleep and I sneaked down into the kitchen very quietly. Then I switched the light on and I opened the ice chest and I took out a bottle of fizzy water just like she did. Then I went over to the table and I sat down.

LIONEL   (*Without looking up from his cards*)   And then . . .

MOLLY   I drank a little water, but I couldn't drink any more. The water was so icy cold. I was going to drink a whole bottleful like she did, but nothing . . . really nothing turned out like I thought it would. (LIONEL *mixes all his cards up together in a sudden gesture.* MOLLY *comes out of her dream*) Why are you messing up the cards? We haven't begun our game . . . (LIONEL *doesn't answer*) What's the matter?

LIONEL Nothing.

MOLLY But you've messed up the cards.

LIONEL I was trying to tell you something . . . It meant a lot to me . . . I wanted you to listen.

MOLLY I was listening.

LIONEL You told me about fizzy water . . . and your mother. (MOLLY *automatically passing her hand over her own cards and messing them up*) I wanted you to listen. I don't want you to half hear me any more. I used to like it but . . .

MOLLY (*Pathetic, bewildered*) I listen to you. We had a nice time yesterday . . . when . . . when we were digging for clams.

LIONEL (*Looking back at her unable to be angry, now with compassion*) Yes, Molly, we did. We had a very good time . . . yesterday. I like digging for clams . . . (*They hold, looking at each other for a moment*) I'm going upstairs. I'm tired. I'm going to bed.

(LIONEL *exits up stairs.* MRS. CONSTABLE *comes out of the darkness, where she has been sleeping on her bench, into the circle of light.*)

MOLLY You woke up.

MRS. CONSTABLE I've been awake . . . for a while. I was
waiting.

MOLLY I won the game, but it wasn't much fun. Lionel
didn't pay attention to the cards.

MRS. CONSTABLE I was waiting because I wanted to tell
you something . . . a secret . . . I always tell you my
secrets . . . But there's one I haven't told you . . . I've
known it all along . . . But I've never said anything to
you . . . never before . . . But now I'm going to . . . I
must.

MOLLY (Wide-eyed, thinking she is referring to VIVIAN) It
wasn't my fault! I didn't mean to . . .

MRS. CONSTABLE My husband never loved me . . . Vivian?

MOLLY Vivian! It wasn't my fault . . . I didn't . . . She
. . . I didn't . . .

(MOLLY starts to sob.)

MRS. CONSTABLE (Clapping her hand over MOLLY's mouth)
Shhhhhh . . . They belonged to each other, my husband
and Vivian. They never belonged to me . . . ever . . .
But I couldn't admit it . . . I hung on hard to the bitter
end. When they died . . . nothing was left . . . no
memories . . . Everything vanished . . . all the panic
. . . and the strain . . . I hardly remember my life.
They never loved me . . . I didn't really love them . . .
My heart had fake roots . . . when the strain was over,

they dried up . . . they shriveled and snapped and my
heart was left empty. There was no blood left in my
heart at all . . . They never loved me! Molly . . . your
mother . . . It's not too late . . . She doesn't . . .

MOLLY (*Interrupting, sensing that* MRS. CONSTABLE *will say
something too awful to hear*) My mother wrote me. I got
the letter today. She *hates* it down in Mexico. She hates it
there.

MRS. CONSTABLE Molly, if you went away from here, I'd
miss you very much. If you went away there wouldn't
be anyone here I loved . . . Molly, go away . . . go
away with Lionel . . . Don't stay here in the Lobster
Bowl . . .

MOLLY (*Commenting on her mother's letter and then reading from it*) She doesn't know how long she can stand
it . . . She says she doesn't feel very well . . . "The climate doesn't suit me . . . I feel sick all the time and I
find it almost impossible to sleep . . . I can't read very
much . . . not at night . . . because the light is too
feeble here in the mountains. Mrs. Lopez has two of her
sisters here at the moment. Things are getting more and
more unbearable. Mrs. Lopez is the least raucous of the
three. I hope that you are occupying yourself with something constructive. Be careful not to dream and be
sure . . ."

MRS. CONSTABLE Why shouldn't you dream?

MOLLY I used to waste a lot of time day-dreaming. I guess I
still do. She didn't want me to dream.

MRS. CONSTABLE Why shouldn't you dream? Why didn't
she want you to?

MOLLY   Because she wanted me to grow up to be wonderful
and strong like she is. Will she come back soon, Mrs. Constable? Will she make them all leave there? Will she?

MRS. CONSTABLE   I don't know dear . . . I don't know
. . . I suppose she will . . . If she needs you, she'll come
back. If she needs you, I'm sure she will.

MOLLY   Are you going to walk home along the edge of the
water?

MRS. CONSTABLE   I like wet sand . . . and I like the
spray.

MOLLY   You'll get the bottom of your dress all soaking wet.
You'll catch cold.

MRS. CONSTABLE   I love the waves breaking in this early
light . . . I run after them. I run after the waves . . . I
scoop up the foam and I rub it on my face. All along the
way I think it's beginning . . .

MOLLY   What?

MRS. CONSTABLE   My life. I think it's beginning, and
then . . .

MOLLY   And then?

MRS. CONSTABLE   I see the hotel.
        (MRS. CONSTABLE *exits through oyster-shell door.*)

MOLLY   (*She reads again part of her mother's letter*)   "Two
day ago, Fula Lopez went into the city and came back
with a hideous white dog. She bought it in the street. The

dog's bark is high and sharp. It hasn't stopped yapping since it came. I haven't slept at all for two nights. Now I'm beginning a cold . . ."

(The lights fade as the curtain falls.)

Scene ii

The Lobster Bowl. Two months later.

INEZ *(She is middle-aged, full bosomed, spirited but a little coarse. She cannot see into* MOLLY's *booth from where she stands behind the bar)* I'd rather hit myself over the head with a club than drag around here the way you do, reading comic books all day long. It's so damp and empty and quiet in here.

(She shakes a whole tray of glasses in the sink, which make a terrific racket.)

MOLLY It's not a comic book. It's a letter from my mother.

INEZ What's new?

MOLLY It came last week.

INEZ What are you doing reading it now?

MOLLY She's coming back today. She's coming back from Mexico.

INEZ Maybe she'll pep things up a little. I hear she's got more personality than you. *(Shifts some oysters)* You didn't model yourself after her, did you?

MOLLY   No.

INEZ   Ever try modeling yourself after anyone?

MOLLY   No.

INEZ   Well, if you don't feel like you've got much personality
yourself, it's an easy way to do. You just pick the right
model and you watch how they act. I never modeled myself after anyone, but there were two or three who modeled after me. And they weren't even relatives—just ordinary girls. It's an easy way to do. (*Shifts some oysters*)
Anyway, I don't see poring over comic books. I'd rather
have someone tell me a good joke any day. What's really
nice is to go out—eight or nine—to an Italian dinner,
and sit around afterwards listening to the different jokes.
You get a better selection that way! Ever try that?

MOLLY   I don't like big bunches of people.

INEZ   You could at least live in a regular home if you don't
like crowds, and do cooking for your husband. You don't
even have a hot plate in your room! (*Crash of stool to
floor, followed by some high giggles*) There goes Mrs.
Constable again. You'd think she'd drink home, at her
hotel, where no one could see her. She's got a whole suite
to herself there. It's been over a year since her daughter's
accident, so I could say her drinking permit had expired.
I think she's just on a plain drunk now. Right? (MOLLY
nods) You sure are a button lip. As long as you're sitting
there you might as well talk. It don't cost extra. (*She
frowns and looks rather mean for a moment. There is
more offstage racket*) I think Mrs. Constable is heading
this way. I hope to God she don't get started on Death.

Not that I blame her for thinking about it after what happened, but I don't like that topic.

(*Enter* MRS. CONSTABLE.)

MRS. CONSTABLE (*She has been drinking*) How is everyone, this afternoon?

MOLLY My mother's coming back today.

INEZ I'm kind of rushing, Mrs. Constable. I've got to have three hundred oyster cocktails ready by tonight and I haven't even prepared the hot sauce yet.

MRS. CONSTABLE Rushing? I didn't know that people still rushed . . .

INEZ Here we go, boys!

MRS. CONSTABLE Then you must be one of the fortunate ones who has not yet stood on the edge of the black pit. There is no rushing after that, only waiting. It seems hardly worthwhile even keeping oneself clean after one has stood on the edge of the black pit.

INEZ If you're clean by nature, you're clean.

MRS. CONSTABLE Oh, really? How very interesting!

INEZ Some people would rather be clean than eat or sleep.

MRS. CONSTABLE How very interesting! How nice that they are all so terribly interested in keeping clean! Cleanliness is so important really, such a *deep deep* thing. Those people who are so interested in keeping clean must have very deep souls. They must think a lot about life and death, that is when they're not too busy *washing,* but I guess washing takes up most of their time. How right they are! Hoorah for them!

(*She flourishes her glass.*)

INEZ   (*With a set face determined to ignore her taunts*)   The tide's pretty far out today. Did you take a look at the . . .

MRS. CONSTABLE   They say that people can't live unless they can fill their lives with petty details. That's people's way of avoiding the black pit. I'm just a weak, ordinary, *very ordinary* woman in her middle years, but I've been able to wipe all the petty details from my life . . . all of them. I never rush or get excited about anything. I've dumped my entire life out the window . . . like that!

(*She tips her whisky glass and pours a little on the floor.*)

INEZ   (*Flaring up*)   Listen here, Mrs. Constable, I haven't got time to go wiping up slops. I've got to prepare three hundred oyster cocktails. That means toothpicks and three hundred little hookers of hot sauce. I haven't got time to talk so I certainly haven't got time to wipe up slops.

MRS. CONSTABLE   I know . . . toothpicks and hot sauce and hookers. Very interesting! How many oysters do you serve to a customer? Please tell me.

INEZ   (*Only half listening to* MRS. CONSTABLE, *automatically*) Five.

MRS. CONSTABLE   (*Smirking as much as she can*)   Five! How fascinating! Really and truly, I can't believe it!

INEZ Balls! Now you get out and don't come back here until I finish my work. Not if you know what's good for you. I can feel myself getting ready to blow up! *(Shifts some more oysters)* I'm going upstairs now and I'm going to put a cold towel on my head. Then, I'm coming down to finish my oyster cocktails, and when I do I want peace and quiet. I've got to have peace and quiet when I'm doing my oyster cocktails. If I don't I just get too nervous. That's all.

MRS. CONSTABLE I'm going . . . whether you're getting ready to blow up or not. *(She walks unsteadily toward exit. Then from the doorway)* I happen to be a very independent woman . . . But you are just plain bossy, Mrs. Oyster Cocktail Sauce.

(Exit MRS. CONSTABLE.*)*

INEZ Independent! I could make her into a slave if I cared to. I could walk all over her if I cared to, but I don't. I don't like to walk all over anyone. Most women do . . . they love it. They like to take some other man or woman and make him or her into a slave, but I don't. I don't like slaves. I like everybody to be going his own independent way. Hello. Good-bye. You go your way and I'll go my way, but no slaves. I'll bet you wouldn't find ten men in this town as democratic as I am. *(Shifts some oysters)* Well, here I go. I guess I'll give myself a fresh apron while I'm up there. Then I'll be ready when they come for their oysters. *(Vaguely touching her head)* I don't like to eat oysters any more. I suppose I've seen too much of them, like everything else in life.

(She pulls the chain on the big light behind the bar so that the scene darkens. There is a little light playing on MOLLY's *booth and on the paper flowers and leaves.* MOLLY *puts her*

book of comics down, sits dreaming for a moment. There is
summer house music to indicate a more lyrical mood. She
pulls a letter out of her pocket and reads it. Enter LIONEL.)

LIONEL   Hey.

MOLLY   Where were you?

LIONEL   I was walking along the beach thinking about something. Molly, listen. I got a wire this morning!

MOLLY   A wire?

LIONEL   Yes, from my brother.

MOLLY   The one in St. Louis? The one who wants us to
come . . .

LIONEL   Yes, Molly. He has a place for me in his business
now. He sells barbecue equipment to people.

MOLLY   To people?

LIONEL   Yes, to people. For their back yards, and he wants
my help.

MOLLY   But . . . but you're going to be a religious leader.

LIONEL   I didn't say I wouldn't be, or I may end up religious
without leading anybody at all. But wherever I end up,
I'm getting out of here. I've made up my mind. This
place is a fake.

MOLLY   These oyster shells are real and so is the turtle. He
just hasn't got his own head and feet. They're wooden.

LIONEL   To me this place is a fake. I chose it for protection,
and it doesn't work out.

MOLLY   It doesn't work out?

LIONEL   Molly, you know that. I've been saying it to you in
a thousand different ways. You know it's not easy for me
to leave. Places that don't work out are ten times tougher
to leave than any other places in the world.

MRS. CONSTABLE   My sisters used to have cherry contests.
They stuffed themselves with cherries all week long and
counted up the pits on Saturday. It made them feel exuberant.

MOLLY   I can't eat cherries.

MRS. CONSTABLE   I couldn't either. I'd eat a few and I'd
feel sick. But that never stopped me. I never missed a
single contest. I despised cherry contests, but I couldn't
stand being left out. Never. Every week I'd sneak off to
the woods with bags full of cherries. I'd sit on a log and
pit each cherry with a knife. Then I'd bury the fruit in a
deep hole and fill it up with dirt. I cheated so hard to be
in them, and I didn't even like them. I was so scared to
be left out.

LIONEL   They are harder to leave, Molly, places that don't
work out. I know it sounds crazy, but they are. Like it's
three times harder for me to leave now than when I first
came here, and in those days I liked the decorations.
Molly, don't look so funny. I can explain it all some other
way. (*Indicates oyster-shell door*) Suppose I kept on
closing that door against the ocean every night because
the ocean made me sad and then one night I went to

open it and I couldn't even find the door. Suppose I couldn't tell it apart from the wall any more. Then it would be too late and we'd be shut in here forever once and for all. It's not going to happen, Molly. I won't let it happen. We're going away—you and me. We're getting out of here. We're not playing cards in this oyster cocktail bar until we're old.

MOLLY (*Turns and looks up the stairs and then back to* LIONEL) If we had a bigger light bulb we could play in the bedroom upstairs.

LIONEL (*Walking away*) You're right Molly, dead right. We could do just that. We could play cards up there in that God-forsaken bedroom upstairs.
    (*Exits.*)

MRS. CONSTABLE (*Gets up and goes to* MOLLY) Molly, call him back.

MOLLY No, I'm going upstairs.

MRS. CONSTABLE It's time . . . Go . . . go with Lionel.

MOLLY My mother's coming. I'm going to her birthday supper.

MRS. CONSTABLE Don't go there . . .

MOLLY I'm late. I must change my dress.
    (*She exits up the stairs.*)

MRS. CONSTABLE (*Stumbling about and crossing to the bar*) You're hanging on just like me. If she brought you her love you wouldn't know her. You wouldn't know who she was. (MRS. CONSTABLE *sinks into a chair below the bar.* GERTRUDE *enters. She is pale, distraught. She does not see* MRS. CONSTABLE) Hello, Gertrude Eastman Cuevas.

GERTRUDE (*Trying to conceal the strain she is under*) Hello, Mrs. Constable. How are you?

MRS. CONSTABLE How are you making out?

GERTRUDE Molly wrote me you were still here. Where is she?

MRS. CONSTABLE You look tired.

GERTRUDE Where is Molly? (LIONEL *enters*) Lionel! How nice to see you! Where's Molly?

LIONEL I . . . I didn't know you were coming.

GERTRUDE Didn't you?

LIONEL I didn't expect to see you. How are you, Mrs. Eastman Cuevas? How was your trip? When did you arrive?

GERTRUDE Well, around two . . . But I *had* to wait . . . They were driving me here . . . Didn't you *know* I was coming?

LIONEL No, I didn't.

GERTRUDE (*Uneasily*) But I wrote Molly. I told her I was coming. I wanted to get here for my birthday. I wrote Molly that. Didn't she tell you about it? I sent her a letter. The paper was very sweet. I was sure that she would show it to you. There's a picture of a little Spanish dancer on the paper with a real lace mantilla pasted round her head. Didn't she show it to you?

LIONEL (*Brooding*) No.

GERTRUDE That's strange. I thought she would. I have others for her too. A toreador with peach satin breeches and a macaw with real feathers.

LIONEL (*Unheeding*) She never said anything about it. She never showed me any letter.

GERTRUDE That's strange. I thought . . . I thought . . . (*She hesitates, feeling the barrier between them. Tentative*) Macaws are called guacamayos down there.

LIONEL Are they?

GERTRUDE Yes, they are. Guacamayos . . .

LIONEL What's the difference between them and parrots?

GERTRUDE They're bigger! Much bigger.

LIONEL Do they talk?

GERTRUDE Yes, they do, but parrots have a better vocabulary. Lionel, my birthday supper's tonight. I suppose you can't come. You work late at night, don't you?

LIONEL I work at night, but not for long . . .

GERTRUDE You'll work in the day then?

LIONEL No.

GERTRUDE   Then when will you work?

LIONEL   I'm quitting.

GERTRUDE   What?

LIONEL   I'm quitting this job. I'm getting out.

GERTRUDE   Getting out. What will you do? Where will you work?

LIONEL   I'm quitting. I'm going.

(*He exits.*)

GERTRUDE   Lionel . . . Wait . . . Where are you going?

MRS. CONSTABLE   Come on over here and talk to me . . . You need a drink.

GERTRUDE   Where is she? Where's Molly?

MRS. CONSTABLE   She's gone down on the rocks, hunting for mussels.

GERTRUDE   Hunting for mussels? But she knew I was coming. Why isn't she here? I don't understand. Didn't she get my letter?

MRS. CONSTABLE   (*Dragging* GERTRUDE *rather roughly to a table*)   Sit down . . . You look sick.

GERTRUDE   I'm not sick . . . I'm just tired, exhausted, that's all. They've worn me out in a thousand different ways. Even today . . . I wanted to see Molly the second we arrived, but I had to wait. I tried to rest. I had a bad dream. It's hanging over me still. But I'll be all right in a little bit. I'll be fine as soon as I see Molly. I'm just tired, that's all.

MRS. CONSTABLE   I'm glad you're well. How is Mrs. Lopez? If I were a man, I'd marry Mrs. Lopez. She'd be my type. We should both have been men. Two Spanish men, married to Mrs. Lopez.

GERTRUDE   She was part of the whole thing! The confusion . . . the racket . . . the pandemonium.

MRS. CONSTABLE   I like Mrs. Lopez, and I'm glad she's fat.

GERTRUDE   There were twelve of us at table every meal.

MRS. CONSTABLE   When?

GERTRUDE   All these months down in Mexico. Twelve of us at least. Old ladies, babies, men, little girls, everyone jabbering, the noise, the screeching never stopped . . . The cooks, the maids, even the birds . . .

MRS. CONSTABLE   Birds?

GERTRUDE   Dirty noisy parrots, trailing around loose. There was a big one called Pepe, with a frightening beak.

MRS. CONSTABLE   (Rather delighted)   Pepe?

GERTRUDE   Their pet, their favorite . . . Crazy undisciplined bird, always climbing up the table leg and plowing through the food.

MRS. CONSTABLE (*Ingenuous*) Didn't you like Pepe?

GERTRUDE (*Dejected, as if in answer to a sad question, not irritated*) No, I didn't like Pepe. I didn't like anything. Where's Molly?
  (*Going to oyster-shell door.*)

MRS. CONSTABLE When are you going back?

GERTRUDE Back? I'm never going back. I've made up my mind. From now on I'm staying in the house up here. It was a terrible mistake. I told him that. I told him that when he had to be there he could go by himself. We had a terrible fight . . . It was disgusting. When he stood there saying that men should never have given us the vote, I slapped him.

MRS. CONSTABLE I never voted. I would vote all right if I could only register.

GERTRUDE He's a barbarian. A subnormal human being. But it doesn't matter. He can stay down there as long as he likes. I'll be up here, where I belong, near Molly. (*Face clouding over*) What was he saying before? What did he mean?

MRS. CONSTABLE Who?

GERTRUDE Lionel. He said he was quitting. He said he was leaving, getting out of here.

MRS. CONSTABLE Lionel's sick of the Lobster Bowl. I'm not. Molly likes it too, more than Lionel.

GERTRUDE Molly. She couldn't like it here, not after our life in the ocean house.

MRS. CONSTABLE Tell me more, Gertrude Eastman Cuevas. Did you enjoy the scenery?

GERTRUDE What?

MRS. CONSTABLE Down in Mexico.

GERTRUDE I didn't enjoy anything. How could I, the way they lived? It wasn't even civilized.

MRS. CONSTABLE (*Merrily*) Great big lunches every day.

GERTRUDE There were three or four beds in every single room.

MRS. CONSTABLE Who was in them?

GERTRUDE Relatives, endless visiting relatives, snapping at each other, jabbering half the night. No wonder I look sick. (*Sadly to herself*) But I'll be fine soon. I know it. I will . . . as soon as I see Molly. If only she'd come back . . . (*To* MRS. CONSTABLE) Which way did she go? Do you think I could find her?

MRS. CONSTABLE She always goes a different way.

GERTRUDE She couldn't like it in this ugly place. It's not true!

MRS. CONSTABLE They take long walks down the beach or go digging for clams. They're very polite. They invite me along. But I never accept. I know they'd rather go off together, all by themselves.

GERTRUDE (*Alarmed*) All by themselves!

MRS. CONSTABLE When they play cards at night, I like to watch them. Sometimes I'm asleep on that bench, but either way I'm around. Inez doesn't know about it. She goes to bed early. She thinks I leave here at a reasonable hour. She's never found out. I take off my shoes and I wade home at dawn.

GERTRUDE I don't know what's happening to the people in this world.

(*Leaves* MRS. CONSTABLE.)

MRS. CONSTABLE Why don't you go back to Mexico, Gertrude Eastman Cuevas, go back to Pepe? (GERTRUDE *looks in disgust at* MRS. CONSTABLE. *More gently*) Then have a drink.

GERTRUDE (*Fighting back a desire to cry*) I don't like to drink.

MRS. CONSTABLE Then what do you like? What's your favorite pleasure?

GERTRUDE I don't know. I don't know. I don't like pleasures. I . . . I like idealism and backbone and ambition. I take after my father. We were both very proud. We had the same standards, the same ideals. We both loved grit and fight.

MRS. CONSTABLE You loved grit and fight.

GERTRUDE We were exactly alike. I was his favorite. He loved me more than anyone in the world!

MRS. CONSTABLE (*Faintly echoing*) More than anyone in the world . . .

GERTRUDE   (*Picking up one of the two boxes she brought with her and brooding over it*)   It was a senseless dream, a nightmare.

MRS. CONSTABLE   What's in the box?

GERTRUDE   Little macaroons. I bought them for Molly on the way up. I thought she'd like them. Some of them are orange and some are bright pink. (*Shakes the box and broods again, troubled, haunted by the dream*)   They were so pretty . . .

MRS. CONSTABLE   Aren't they pretty any more?

GERTRUDE   I had a dream about them just now, before I came. I was running very fast through the night trying to get to Molly, but I couldn't find the way. I kept losing all her presents. Everything I'd bought her I kept scattering on the ground. Then I was in a cold room with my father and she was there too. I asked him for a gift. I said, "I want something to give to my child," and he handed me this box . . . (*Fingering the actual box*)   I opened it up, and took out a macaroon and I gave it to Molly. (*Long pause. She looks haunted, deeply troubled*)   When she began to eat it, I saw that it was hollow, just a shell filled with dust. Molly's lips were gray with dust. Then I heard him . . . I heard my father. (*Excited*)   He was laughing. He was laughing at *me!* (*She goes away from* MRS. CONSTABLE *to collect herself*)   I've loved him so. I don't know what's happening to me. I've never been this way. I've always thrown things off, but now even foolish dreams hang over me. I can't shake anything off. I'm not myself . . . I . . . (*Stiffening against the weakness*)   When I was in the ocean house . . . (*Covering her face with her hands and shaking her head, very softly, almost to herself)* Oh, I miss it so . . . I miss it so.

MRS. CONSTABLE Houses! I hate houses. I like public places. Houses break your heart. Come and be with me in the Lobster Bowl. They gyp you, but it's a great place. They gyp you, but I don't care.

GERTRUDE It was a beautiful house with a wall and a garden and a view of the sea.

MRS. CONSTABLE Don't break your heart, Mrs. Eastman dear, don't . . .

GERTRUDE I was happy in my house. There was nothing wrong. I had a beautiful life. I had Molly. I was busy teaching her. I had a full daily life. Everything was fine. There was nothing wrong. I don't know why I got frightened, why I married again. It must have been . . . it must have been because we had no money. That was it . . . We had so little money, I got frightened for us both . . . I should never have married. Now my life's lost its meaning . . . I have nightmares all the time. I lie awake in the night trying to think of just one standard or one ideal but something foolish pops into my head like Fula Lopez wearing city shoes and stockings to the beach. I've lost my daily life, that's all. I've lost Molly. My life has no meaning now. It's their fault. It's because I'm living their way. But I'm back now with Molly. I'm going to be fine again . . . She's coming with me tonight to my birthday supper . . . It's getting dark out. Where is she? (LIONEL *enters at bar with basket of glasses*) Lionel. Wait . . .

LIONEL What is it?

GERTRUDE   What did you mean just now.

LIONEL   When?

GERTRUDE   Before . . . when I came in. You said you were going, getting out.

LIONEL   I am. I sent a wire just now.

GERTRUDE   Wire?

LIONEL   Yes, to my brother. I'm going to St. Louis. He has a business there.

GERTRUDE   But you can't do that! I've come back. You won't have to live in this stupid Lobster Bowl. You're going to be living in a house with *me*.

LIONEL   We'll never make a life, sticking around here. I've made up my mind. We're going away . . .

GERTRUDE   You talk like a child.

LIONEL   (*Interrupting*)   I'm not staying here.

GERTRUDE   You're running away . . . You're running home to your family . . . to your brother. Don't you have any backbone, any fight?

LIONEL   I don't care what you think about me! It's Molly that . . .

GERTRUDE   What about Molly!

LIONEL   I've got to get Molly out of here, far away from everything she's ever known. It's her only chance.

GERTRUDE You're taking her away from *me*. That's what you're doing.

LIONEL You're like a wall around Molly, some kind of shadow between us. She lives . . .

GERTRUDE (*Interrupting, vehement*) I'm not a shadow any more. I've come back and I'm staying here, where I belong with Molly! (LIONEL *looks at her with an expression of bitterness and revulsion*) What is it? Why do you look at me that way?

LIONEL What way?

GERTRUDE As if I was some terrible witch . . . That's it, some terrible witch!

LIONEL You're using her. You need Molly. You don't love her. You're using her . . .

GERTRUDE You don't know what you're talking about. You don't know anything about me or Molly. You never could. You never will. When she married she was desperate. She cried like a baby and she begged me to stay. But you want to drag her away from me—from her mother. She loves me more than anyone on earth. She needs me. In her heart she's still a child.

LIONEL If you get what you want she'll stay that way. Let her go, if you love her at all, let her go away . . . Don't stop her . . .

GERTRUDE I can't stop her. How can I? She'll do what she likes, but I won't stand here watching while you drag her away. I'll talk to her myself. I'll ask her what she wants, what she'd really like to do. She has a right to choose.

LIONEL   To choose?

GERTRUDE   Between going with you and staying with me!

> (LIONEL *is silent. After a moment he walks away from* GER-
> TRUDE. *Then to himself as if she were no longer there.*)

LIONEL   This morning she was holding her wedding dress
up to the light.

GERTRUDE   (*Proud*)   She's going to wear it to my birthday
supper. It's a party dress, after all.

LIONEL   (*Not really answering*)   She didn't say anything to
me. She just held her dress up to the light.

GERTRUDE   Go and find her. Get her now. Bring her back
. . . tell her I'm here.

LIONEL   If you go half way up those stairs and holler . . .

GERTRUDE   No, Mrs. Constable said she was hunting mussels on the beach.

LIONEL   She's upstairs. (LIONEL *goes up to landing and
calls*)   Molly! Your mother's here. She wants you. Come
on down. Your mother's back.

> (MOLLY *enters down stairs.* LIONEL *backs away and lurks in
> the shadows near the bar.*)

GERTRUDE   (*Tentative, starts forward to embrace her, but
stops*)   Molly, how pretty you look! How lovely . . . and
your wedding dress.

MOLLY (*Spellbound, as if looking at something very beautiful just behind* GERTRUDE) I took it out this morning for your birthday.

GERTRUDE I'm glad, darling. How are you? Are you well, Molly? Are you all right?

MOLLY Yes, I am.

GERTRUDE (*Going to table*) I have something for you. A bracelet! (*She hooks necklace around* MOLLY's *neck*) And a necklace! They're made of real silver. Oh, how sweet you look! How pretty you look in silver! Just like a little girl, just as young as you looked when we were in the ocean house together. The ocean house, Molly! I miss it so. Don't you?

MOLLY I knew you'd come back.

(*They sit down.*)

GERTRUDE I knew it, too, from the beginning. They were strangers—all of them. I couldn't bear it. Nothing, really nothing meant anything to me down there, nothing at all. And you, darling, are you happy? What do you do in this terrible ugly place?

MOLLY In the afternoon we hunt for mussels, sometimes, and at night we play cards . . . Lionel and me.

GERTRUDE (*Uneasily*) I spoke to Lionel just now.

MOLLY Did you?

GERTRUDE Yes, about St. Louis.

MOLLY (*Darkening*) Oh!

LIONEL (*Coming over to them from the bar*) Yes, Molly.
I'm arranging things now for the trip tomorrow. My
mind's made up. If you're not coming with me, I'm going
by myself. I'm coming down in a little while and you've
got to tell me what you're going to do.

(LIONEL *exits upstairs.*)

GERTRUDE You see. With or without you he's determined to
go. Don't look frightened, Molly. I won't allow you to go.
You're coming with me, with your mother, where you belong. I never should have let you marry. I never should
have left you. I'll never leave you again, darling. You're
mine, the only one I have . . . my own blood . . . the
only thing I'm sure of in the world. (*She clasps* MOLLY
greedily to her breast) We're going soon, but we've got
to wait for them, Mrs. Lopez and Frederica. They're calling for us here. You're coming with me and you're never
going back. Tonight, when you go to bed, you can wear
my gown, the one you've always loved with the different
colored tulips stitched around the neck. (*She notices*
MOLLY's *strange expression and the fact that she has re-
coiled just a little*) What is it, dear? Don't you like the
gown with the tulips any more? You used to . . .

MOLLY (*As if from far away*) I like it.

GERTRUDE Tomorrow, after Lionel has gone, I'll come back
to pack you up. (*Fingering the necklace*) Did you like
the paper with the dancing girl on it?

MOLLY I have your letter here.

GERTRUDE There are different ones at home—a toreador
with peach satin breeches and a macaw with real feathers . . . (*It is obvious to her that* MOLLY *is not listening*) You've seen them, dear . . . Those big parrots . . .
(*Anxiously*) Haven't you?

MOLLY What?

GERTRUDE (*Trying to ignore* MOLLY's *coldly remote behavior*) How could you bear it here in this awful public
place after our life together in the ocean house?

MOLLY I used to go back and look into the garden . . . over
the wall. Then the people moved in and I didn't go there
any more. But, after a while . . .

GERTRUDE (*Cutting in*) I'll make it all up to you, darling.
You'll have everything you want.

MOLLY It was all right after a while. I didn't mind so much.
It was like being there . . .

GERTRUDE What, Molly? What was like being there?

MOLLY After a while I could sit in that booth, and if I
wanted to I could imagine I was home in the garden . . .
inside the summer house.

GERTRUDE That's over, Molly. That's over now. All over. I
have a wonderful surprise for you, darling. Can you guess?

MOLLY (*Bewildered*) I don't know. I don't know.

GERTRUDE I ordered the platform built, and the trellis, and
I know where I can get the vines. Fully grown vines,

heavy with leaves . . . just like the ones . . . (*She is stopped again by* MOLLY's *expression. Then, touching her face apologetically*) I know, I know. I don't look well. I look sick. But I'm not . . . I'm not sick.

MOLLY   No, you don't look sick. You look . . . different.

GERTRUDE   It's their fault. It's because I'm living their way. But soon I'll be the same again, my old self.

(*Enter* MRS. LOPEZ *and* FREDERICA *carrying paper bags.*)

MRS. LOPEZ   ¡Inez! ¡Inez! Ya llegamos . . .

GERTRUDE   Here they are.

INEZ   (*Coming downstairs with a heavy tread*) Something tells me I hear Fula Lopez, the girl I love . . .

MRS. LOPEZ   (*Grabbing* INEZ *and whirling her around*) Inez . . . Guapa . . . Inez. Aquí estamos . . . que alegría . . . We are coming back from Mexico, Frederica, Fula . . . (*She spots* GERTRUDE) and Eastman Cuevas. (*Then to* MOLLY, *giving her a big smacking kiss*) Molly . . . Hello, Molly! Inez, guapa, bring us three limonadas, please . . . two for Fula and one for Frederica. Look, look, Eastman Cuevas. We got gorgeous stuff. (*She pulls a chicken out of a bag she is carrying and dangles it for* GERTRUDE) Look and see what a nice one we got . . . Feel him!

GERTRUDE   No, later at home.

MRS. LOPEZ   Pinch him, see how much fat he got on him.

GERTRUDE (*Automatically touching chicken for a second*)
He's very nice . . . (*Then swerving around abruptly
and showing a stern fierce profile to the audience*) Why
is he here?

MRS. LOPEZ (*Looking stupid*) Who?

GERTRUDE The chicken. Why is he here?

MRS. LOPEZ The chicken? He go home. We put him now
with his rice and his peas.

GERTRUDE (*In a fury manifestly about the chicken. But her
rage conceals panic about* MOLLY) But *what* rice and
peas. You know what we're having . . . I ordered it myself . . . It was going to be a light meal . . . something
I liked . . . for once . . . we're having jellied consommé
and little African lobster tails.

MRS. LOPEZ (*Crossing back to center tables and stopping
near* MRS. CONSTABLE) That's right, jelly and Africa and
this one too.

(*She hoists chicken up in the air with a flourish. Enter* MRS.
CONSTABLE.)

MRS. CONSTABLE A chicken. I hate chickens. I'd rather
have a dog.

(FREDERICA *pulls a thin striped horn out of one of the paper
bags and blows on it.*)

GERTRUDE Frederica, stop that. Stop that at once! I told
you I didn't want to hear a single horn on my birthday.
This is a party for adults. Put that away. Come along,
we're leaving. We'll leave here at once.

FREDERICA (*In her pallid voice*) And Umberto? My
uncle . . .

GERTRUDE What about him?

FREDERICA Uncle Umberto say he was calling for us to ride
home all together.

GERTRUDE (*Automatically*) Where *is* he?

FREDERICA He is with Pepe Hernández, Frederica Gómez,
Pacito Sánchez, Pepito Pita Luga . . .

GERTRUDE No more names, Frederica . . . Tell him we're
coming. We'll be right along . . .

MRS. LOPEZ And the limonadas . . .

GERTRUDE Never mind the limonadas. We're leaving here
at once . . . Collect your bundles . . . Go on, go along.

> (*The Mexicans start to collect everything, and there is the
> usual confusion and chatter.* FREDERICA *spills some horns out
> of her bag.* MRS. LOPEZ *screams at her, etc. They reach the
> exit just as* INEZ *arrives with the limonadas.*)

MRS. LOPEZ (*Almost weeping, in a pleading voice to* GER-
TRUDE) Look, Eastman Cuevas, the limonadas!

FREDERICA (*Echoing*) The limonadas . . . ¡Ay!

GERTRUDE No! There isn't time. I said we were leaving.
We're leaving at once . . .

INEZ (*To* MRS. LOPEZ *as they exit, including* MRS. CONSTABLE)
Take them along . . . Drink them in the car, for Christ's
sake.

MRS. LOPEZ (*Off stage*) But the glasses . . .

INEZ (*Off stage*) To hell with the glasses. Toss them down the cliff.

GERTRUDE Molly, it's time to go. (MOLLY *starts for stairway*) Molly, come along. We're going. What is it, Molly? Why are you standing there? You have your silver bracelet on and the necklace to match. We're ready to leave. Why are you waiting? Tonight you'll wear my gown with the tulips on it. I told you that . . . and tomorrow we'll go and I'll show you the vines. When you see how thick the leaves are and the blossoms, you'll know I'm not dreaming. Molly, why do you look at me like that? What is it? What did you forget?

> (LIONEL *comes downstairs.* GERTRUDE *stiffens and pulls* MOLLY *to her side with a strong hand, holding her there as a guard holds his prisoner.*)

GERTRUDE Lionel, we're going. It's all settled. We're leaving at once. Molly's coming with me and she's not coming back.

MOLLY (*Her voice sticking in her throat*) I . . .

LIONEL (*Seeing her stand there, overpowered by her mother, as if by a great tree, accepts the pattern as utterly hopeless once and for all. Then, after a moment*) Good-bye, Molly. Have a nice time at the birthday supper . . . (*Bitterly*) You look very pretty in that dress.

> (*He exits through oyster-shell door.*)

GERTRUDE (*After a moment. Calm and firm, certain of her triumph*) Molly, we're going now. You've said good-bye. There's no point in standing around here any longer.

MOLLY (*Retreating*) Leave me alone . . .

GERTRUDE Molly, what is it? Why are you acting this way?

MOLLY I want to go out.

GERTRUDE Molly!

MOLLY I'm going . . . I'm going out.

GERTRUDE (*Blocking her way*) I'll make it all up to you.
I'll give you everything you wanted, everything you've
dreamed about.

MOLLY You told me not to dream. You're all changed . . .
You're not like you used to be.

GERTRUDE I will be, darling. You'll see . . . when we're together. It's going to be the same, just the way it was. Tomorrow we'll go back and look at the vines, thicker and
more beautiful . . .

MOLLY I'm going . . . Lionel!

GERTRUDE (*Blocking her way, fiendish from now on*) He
did it. He changed you. He turned you against me.

MOLLY Let me go . . . You're all changed.

GERTRUDE You can't go. I won't let you. I can stop you. I
can and I will.

> (*There is a physical struggle between them near the oyster-
shell door.*)

MOLLY (*Straining to get through the door and calling in a voice that seems to come up from the bottom of her heart*) Lionel!

GERTRUDE I know what you did . . . I didn't want to . . . I was frightened, but I knew . . . You hated Vivian. I'm the only one in the world who knows you. (MOLLY *aghast ceases to struggle. They hold for a moment before* GᴇRTRUDE *releases her grip on* MOLLY. *Confident now that she has broken her daughter's will forever*) Molly, we're going . . . We're going home.

MOLLY (*Backing away in horror*) No!

GERTRUDE Molly, we're going! (MOLLY *continues to retreat*) If you don't (MOLLY, *shaking her head still retreats*) If you don't, I'll tell her! I'll call Mrs. Constable.

MOLLY (*Still retreating*) No . . .

GERTRUDE (*Wild, calling like an animal*) Mrs. Constable! Mrs. Constable! (*To* MOLLY, *shaking her*) Do you see what you're doing to me! Do you? (MRS. CONSTABLE *appears in doorway.* GERTRUDE *drags* MOLLY *brutally out of her corner near the staircase and confronts her with* MRS. CONSTABLE) I have something to tell you, Mrs. Constable. It's about Molly. It's about my daughter . . . She hated Vivian. My daughter hated yours and a terrible ugly thing happened . . . an ugly thing happened on the cliffs . . .

MRS. CONSTABLE (*Defiantly*) Nothing happened . . . Nothing!

GERTRUDE (*Hanging on to* MOLLY, *who is straining to go*) It *had* to happen. I know Molly . . . I know her jealousy

. . . I was her whole world, the only one she loved . . .
She wanted me all to herself . . . I know that kind of
jealousy and what it can do to you . . . I know what it
feels like to wish someone dead. When I was a little girl
. . . I . . . *(She stops dead as if a knife had been thrust
in her heart now. The hand holding* MOLLY'S *in its hard
iron grip slowly relaxes. There is a long pause. Then, under her breath)* Go . . . (MOLLY'S *flight is sudden. She
is visible in the blue light beyond the oyster-shell door
only for a second. The Mexican band starts playing the
wedding song from Act One.* GERTRUDE *stands as still as a
statue.* MRS. CONSTABLE *approaches, making a gesture of
compassion)* The band is playing on the beach. They're
playing their music. Go, Mrs. Constable . . . Please.

(MRS. CONSTABLE *exits through oyster-shell door.*)

FREDERICA *(Entering from street, calling, exuberant)*
Eastman Cuevas! Eastman Cuevas! Uncle Umberto is
ready. We are waiting in the car . . . Where's Molly?
(She falters at the sight of GERTRUDE'S *white face. Then,
with awe)* Ay dios . . . ¿Qué pasa? ¿Qué tiene? Miss
Eastman Cuevas, you don't feel happy? *(She unpins a
simple bouquet of red flowers and puts it into* GERTRUDE'S
hand) For your birthday, Miss Eastman Cuevas . . .
your birthday . . .

> *(She backs away into the shadows, not knowing what to do
> next.* GERTRUDE *is standing rigid, the bouquet stuck in her
> hand.)*

GERTRUDE *(Almost in a whisper, as the curtain falls)* When
I was a little girl . . .

Plain Pleasures

· Plain Pleasures

Alva Perry was a dignified and reserved woman of Scotch and Spanish descent, in her early forties. She was still handsome, although her cheeks were too thin. Her eyes particularly were of an extraordinary clarity and beauty. She lived in her uncle's house, which had been converted into apartments, or tenements, as they were still called in her section of the country. The house stood on the side of a steep, wooded hill overlooking the main highway. A long cement staircase climbed halfway up the hill and stopped some distance below the house. It had originally led to a power station, which had since been destroyed. Mrs. Perry had lived alone in her tenement since the death of her husband eleven years ago; however, she found small things to do all day long and she had somehow remained as industrious in her solitude as a woman who lives in the service of her family.

John Drake, an equally reserved person, occupied the tenement below hers. He owned a truck and engaged in free-lance work for lumber companies, as well as in the collection and delivery of milk cans for a dairy.

Mr. Drake and Mrs. Perry had never exchanged more than the simplest greeting in all the years that they had lived here in the hillside house.

One night Mr. Drake, who was standing in the hall, heard Mrs. Perry's heavy footsteps, which he had unconsciously learned to recognize. He looked up and saw her coming downstairs. She was dressed in a brown overcoat that had belonged to her dead husband, and she was hugging a paper bag to her bosom. Mr. Drake offered to help her with the bag and she faltered, undecided, on the landing.

"They are only potatoes," she said to him, "but thank you very much. I am going to bake them out in the back yard. I have been meaning to for a long time."

Mr. Drake took the potatoes and walked with a stiff-jointed gait through the back door and down the hill to a short stretch of level land in back of the house which served as a yard. Here he put the paper bag on the ground. There was a big new incinerator smoking near the back stoop and in the center of the yard Mrs. Perry's uncle had built a roofed-in pigpen faced in vivid artificial brick. Mrs. Perry followed.

She thanked Mr. Drake and began to gather twigs, scuttling rapidly between the edge of the woods and the pigpen, near which she was laying her fire. Mr. Drake, without any further conversation, helped her to gather the twigs, so that when the fire was laid, she quite naturally invited him to wait and share the potatoes with her. He accepted and they sat in front of the fire on an overturned box.

Mr. Drake kept his face averted from the fire and turned in the direction of the woods, hoping in this way to conceal somewhat his flaming-red cheeks from Mrs. Perry. He was a very shy person and though his skin was naturally red all the time it turned to such deep crimson when he was in the presence of a

strange woman that the change was distinctly noticeable. Mrs.
Perry wondered why he kept looking behind him, but she did
not feel she knew him well enough to question him. She waited
in vain for him to speak and then, realizing that he was not
going to, she searched her own mind for something to say.

"Do you like plain ordinary pleasures?" she finally asked
him gravely.

Mr. Drake felt very much relieved that she had spoken and
his color subsided. "You had better first give me a clearer no-
tion of what you mean by ordinary pleasures, and then I'll tell
you how I feel about them," he answered soberly, halting after
every few words, for he was as conscientious as he was shy.

Mrs. Perry hesitated. "Plain pleasures," she began, "like the
ones that come without crowds or fancy food." She searched
her brain for more examples. "Plain pleasures like this potato
bake instead of dancing and whisky and bands. . . . Like a
picnic but not the kind with a thousand extra things that get
thrown out in a ditch because they don't get eaten up. I've
seen grown people throw cakes away because they were too lazy
to wrap them up and take them back home. Have you seen that
go on?"

"No, I don't think so," said Mr. Drake.

"They waste a lot," she remarked.

"Well, I do like plain pleasures," put in Mr. Drake, anxious
that she should not lose the thread of the conversation.

"Don't you think that plain pleasures are closer to the heart
of God?" she asked him.

He was a little embarrassed at her mentioning anything so
solemn and so intimate on such short acquaintance, and he
could not bring himself to answer her. Mrs. Perry, who was
ordinarily shut-mouthed, felt a stream of words swelling in her
throat.

"My sister, Dorothy Alvarez," she began without further introduction, "goes to all gala affairs downtown. She has invited
me to go and raise the dickens with her, but I won't go. She's

the merriest one in her group and separated from her husband.
They take her all the places with them. She can eat dinner in a
restaurant every night if she wants to. She's crazy about fried
fish and all kinds of things. I don't pay much mind to what I
eat unless it's a potato bake like this. We each have only one
single life which is our real life, starting at the cradle and
ending at the grave. I warn Dorothy every time I see her that if
she doesn't watch out her life is going to be left aching and
starving on the side of the road and she's going to get to her
grave without it. The farther a man follows the rainbow, the
harder it is for him to get back to the life which he left starving
like an old dog. Sometimes when a man gets older he has a
revelation and wants awfully bad to get back to the place
where he left his life, but he can't get to that place—not often.
It's always better to stay alongside of your life. I told Dorothy
that life was not a tree with a million different blossoms on it."
She reflected upon this for a moment in silence and then continued. "She has a box that she puts pennies and nickles in
when she thinks she's running around too much and she uses
the money in the box to buy candles with for church. But
that's all she'll do for her spirit, which is not enough for a
grown woman."

Mr. Drake's face was strained because he was trying terribly
hard to follow closely what she was saying, but he was so fearful lest she reveal some intimate secret of her sister's and later
regret it that his mind was almost completely closed to everything else. He was fully prepared to stop her if she went too
far.

The potatoes were done and Mrs. Perry offered him two of
them.

"Have some potatoes?" she said to him. The wind was colder
now than when they had first sat down, and it blew around the
pigpen.

"How do you feel about these cold howling nights that we
have? Do you mind them?" Mrs. Perry asked.

"I surely do," said John Drake.

She looked intently at his face. "He is as red as a cherry," she said to herself.

"I might have preferred to live in a warm climate maybe," Mr. Drake was saying very slowly with a dreamy look in his eye, "if I happened to believe in a lot of unnecessary changing around. A lot of going forth and back, I mean." He blushed because he was approaching a subject that was close to his heart.

"Yes, yes, yes," said Mrs. Perry. "A lot of switching around is no good."

"When I was a younger man I had a chance to go way down south to Florida," he continued. "I had an offer to join forces with an alligator-farm project, but there was no security in the alligators. It might not have been a successful farm; it was not the risk that I minded so much, because I have always yearned to see palm trees and coconuts and the like. But I also believed that a man has to have a pretty good reason for moving around. I think that is what finally stopped me from going down to Florida and raising alligators. It was not the money, because I was not raised to give money first place. It was just that I felt then the way I do now, that if a man leaves home he must leave for some very good reason—like the boys who went to construct the Panama Canal or for any other decent reason. Otherwise I think he ought to stay in his own home town, so that nobody can say about him, 'What does he think he can do here that we can't?' At least that is what I think people in a strange town would say about a man like myself if I landed there with some doutbful venture as my only excuse for leaving home. My brother don't feel that way. He never stays in one place more than three months." He ate his potato with a woeful look in his eye, shaking his head from side to side.

Mrs. Perry's mind was wandering, so that she was very much startled when he suddenly stood up and extended his hand to her.

"I'll leave now," he said, "but in return for the potatoes, will you come and have supper with me at a restaurant tomorrow night?"

She had not received an invitation of this kind in many years, having deliberately withdrawn from life in town, and she did not know how to answer him. "Do you think I should do that?" she asked.

Mr. Drake assured her that she should do it and she accepted his invitation. On the following afternoon, Mrs. Perry waited for the bus at the foot of the short cement bridge below the house. She needed help and advice from her sister about a lavender dress which no longer fitted her. She herself had never been able to sew well and she knew little about altering women's garments. She intended to wear her dress to the restaurant where she was to meet John Drake, and she was carrying it tucked under her arm.

Dorothy Alvarez lived on a side street in one half of a two-family house. She was seated in her parlor entertaining a man when Mrs. Perry rang the bell. The parlor was immaculate but difficult to rest in because of the many bright and complicated patterns of the window curtains and the furniture covers, not the least disquieting of which was an enormous orange and black flowerpot design repeated a dozen times on the linoleum floor covering.

Dorothy pulled the curtain aside and peeked out to see who was ringing her bell. She was a curly-headed little person, with thick, unequal cheeks that were painted bright pink.

She was very much startled when she looked out and saw her sister, as she had not been expecting to see her until the following week.

"Oh!" Dorothy exclaimed.

"Who is it?" her guest asked.

"It's my sister. You better get out of here, because she must have something serious to talk to me about. You better go out the back door. She don't like bumping up against strangers."

The man was vexed, and left without bidding Dorothy good-bye. She ran to the door and let Mrs. Perry in.

"Sit down," she said, pulling her into the parlor. "Sit down and tell me what's new." She poured some hard candy from a paper bag into a glass dish.

"I wish you would alter this dress for me or help me do it," said Mrs. Perry. "I want it for tonight. I'm meeting Mr. Drake, my neighbor, at the restaurant down the street, so I thought I could dress in your house and leave from here. If you did the alteration yourself. I'd pay you for it."

Dorothy's face fell. "Why do you offer to pay me for it when I'm your sister?"

Mrs. Perry looked at her in silence. She did not answer, be-cause she did not know why herself. Dorothy tried the dress on her sister and pinned it here and there. "I'm glad you're going out at last," she said. "Don't you want some beads?"

"I'll take some beads if you've got a spare string."

"Well I hope this is the right guy for you," said Dorothy, with her customary lack of tact. "I would give anything for you to be in love, so you would quit living in that ugly house and come and live on some street nearby. Think how different everything would be for me. You'd be jollier too if you had a husband who was dear to you. Not like the last one. . . . I suppose I'll never stop dreaming and hoping," she added nerv-ously because she realized, but, as always, a little too late, that her sister hated to discuss such matters. "Don't think," she be-gan weakly, "that I'm so happy here all the time. I'm not so serious and solemn as you, of course. . . ."

"I don't know what you've been talking about," said Alva Perry, twisting impatiently. "I'm going out to have a dinner."

"I wish you were closer to me," whined Dorothy. "I get blue in this parlor some nights."

"I don't think you get very blue," Mrs. Perry remarked briefly.

"Well, as long as you're going out, why don't you pep up?"
"I am pepped up," replied Mrs. Perry.

•

Mrs. Perry closed the restaurant door behind her and walked the full length of the room, peering into each booth in search of her escort. He had apparently not yet arrived, so she chose an empty booth and seated herself inside on the wooden bench. After fifteen minutes she decided that he was not coming and, repressing the deep hurt that this caused her, she focused her full attention on the menu and succeeded in shutting Mr. Drake from her mind. While she was reading the menu, she unhooked her string of beads and tucked them away in her purse. She had called the waitress and was ordering pork when Mr. Drake arrived. He greeted her with a timid smile.

"I see that you are ordering your dinner," he said, squeezing into his side of the booth. He looked with admiration at her lavender dress, which exposed her pale chest. He would have preferred that she be bareheaded because he loved women's hair. She had on an ungainly black felt hat which she always wore in every kind of weather. Mr. Drake remembered with intense pleasure the potato bake in front of the fire and he was much more excited than he had imagined he would be to see her once again.

Unfortunately she did not seem to have any impulse to communicate with him and his own tongue was silenced in a very short time. They ate the first half of their meal without saying anything at all to each other. Mr. Drake had ordered a bottle of sweet wine and after Mrs. Perry had finished her second glass she finally spoke. "I think they cheat you in restaurants."

He was pleased she had made any remark at all, even though it was of an ungracious nature.

"Well, it is usually to be among the crowd that we pay large prices for small portions," he said, much to his own surprise, for he had always considered himself a lone wolf, and his behavior had never belied this. He sensed this same quality in Mrs. Perry, but he was moved by a strange desire to mingle with her among the flock.

"Well, don't you think what I say is true?" he asked hesitantly. There appeared on his face a curious, dislocated smile and he held his head in an outlandishly erect position which betrayed his state of tension.

Mrs. Perry wiped her plate clean with a piece of bread. Since she was not in the habit of drinking more than once every few years, the wine was going very quickly to her head.

"What time does the bus go by the door here?" she asked in a voice that was getting remarkably loud.

"I can find out for you if you really want to know. Is there any reason why you want to know now?"

"I've got to get home some time so I can get up tomorrow morning."

"Well, naturally I will take you home in my truck when you want to go, but I hope you won't go yet." He leaned forward and studied her face anxiously.

"I can get home all right," she answered him glumly, "and it's just as good now as later."

"Well, no, it isn't," he said, deeply touched, because there was no longer any mistaking her distinctly inimical attitude. He felt that he must at any cost keep her with him and enlist her sympathies. The wine was contributing to this sudden aggressiveness, for it was not usually in his nature to make any effort to try to get what he wanted. He now began speaking to her earnestly and quickly.

"I want to share a full evening's entertainment with you, or even a week of entertainment," he said, twisting nervously on his bench. "I know where all the roadside restaurants and dance houses are situated all through the county. I am master of my truck, and no one can stop me from taking a vacation if I want to. It's a long time since I took a vacation—not since I was handed out my yearly summer vacation when I went to school. I never spent any real time in any of these roadside houses, but I know the proprietors, nearly all of them, because I have lived here all of my life. There is one dance hall that is built on a lake. I know the proprietor. If we went there, we could stray off and walk around the water, if that was agreeable to you." His face was a brighter red than ever and he appeared to be temporarily stripped of the reserved and cautious demeanor that had so characterized him the evening before. Some quality in Mrs. Perry's nature which he had only dimly perceived at first now sounded like a deep bell within himself because of her anger and he was flung backward into a forgotten and weaker state of being. His yearning for a word of kindness from her increased every minute.

Mrs. Perry sat drinking her wine more and more quickly and her resentment mounted with each new glass.

"I know all the proprietors of dance houses in the county also," she said. "My sister Dorothy Alvarez has them up to her house for beer when they take a holiday. I've got no need to meet anybody new or see any new places. I even know this place we are eating in from a long time ago. I had dinner here with my husband a few times." She looked around her. "I remember *him*," she said, pointing a long arm at the proprietor, who had just stepped out of the kitchen.

"How are you after these many years?" she called to him.

Mr. Drake was hesitant about what to do. He had not realized that Mrs. Perry was getting as drunk as she seemed to be now. Ordinarily he would have felt embarrassed and would have hastened to lead her out of the restaurant, but he thought that she might be more approachable drunk and nothing else mattered to him. "I'll stay with you for as long as you like," he said.

His words spun around in Mrs. Perry's mind. "What are you making a bid for, anyway?" she asked him, leaning back heavily against the bench.

"Nothing dishonorable," he said. "On the contrary, some-

thing extremely honorable if you will accept." Mr. Drake was
so distraught that he did not know exactly what he was saying,
but Mrs. Perry took his words to mean a proposal of marriage,
which was unconsciously what he had hoped she would do.
Mrs. Perry looked at even this exciting offer through the smoke
of her resentment.

"I suppose," she said, smiling joylessly, "that you would like
a lady to mash your potatoes for you three times a day. But I
am not a mashed-potato masher and I never have been. I
would prefer," she added, raising her voice, "I would prefer to
have *him* mash my potatoes for *me* in a big restaurant
kitchen." She nodded in the direction of the proprietor, who
had remained standing in front of the kitchen door so that he
could watch Mrs. Perry. This time he grinned and winked his
eye.

Mrs. Perry fumbled through the contents of her purse in
search of a handkerchief and, coming upon her sister's string of
beads, she pulled them out and laid them in her gravy. "I am
not a mashed-potato masher," she repeated, and then without
warning she clambered out of the booth and lumbered down
the aisle. She disappeared up a dark brown staircase at the back
of the restaurant. Both Mr. Drake and the proprietor assumed
that she was going to the ladies' toilet.

Actually Mrs. Perry was not specifically in search of the toilet, but rather for any place where she could be alone. She
walked down the hall upstairs and jerked open a door on her
left, closing it behind her. She stood in total darkness for a
minute, and then, feeling a chain brush her forehead, she
yanked at it brutally, lighting the room from a naked ceiling
bulb, which she almost pulled down together with its fixtures.

She was standing at the foot of a double bed with a high
Victorian headboard. She looked around her and, noticing a
chair placed underneath a small window, she walked over to it
and pushed the window open, securing it with a short stick;
then she sat down.

"This is perfection," she said aloud, glaring at the ugly little room. "This is surely a gift from the Lord." She squeezed her hands together until her knuckles were white. "Oh, how I love it here! How I love it! How I love it!"

She flung one arm out over the window sill in a gesture of abandon, but she had not noticed that the rain was teeming down, and it soaked her lavender sleeve in a very short time.

"Mercy me!" she remarked, grinning. "It's raining here. The people at the dinner tables don't get the rain, but I do and I like it!" She smiled benignly at the rain. She sat there half awake and half asleep and then slowly she felt a growing certainty that she could reach her own room from where she was sitting without ever returning to the restaurant. "I have kept the pathway open all my life," she muttered in a thick voice, "so that I could get back."

A few moments later she said, "I am sitting there." An expression of malevolent triumph transformed her face and she made a slight effort to stiffen her back. She remained for a long while in the stronghold of this fantasy, but it gradually faded and in the end dissolved. When she drew her cold shaking arm in out of the rain, the tears were streaming down her cheeks. Without ceasing to cry she crept on to the big double bed and fell asleep, face downward, with her hat on.

Meanwhile the proprietor had come quietly upstairs, hoping that he would bump into her as she came out of the ladies' toilet. He had been flattered by her attention and he judged that in her present drunken state it would be easy to sneak a kiss from her and perhaps even more. When he saw the beam of light shining under his own bedroom door, he stuck his tongue out over his lower lip and smiled. Then he tiptoed down the stairs, plotting on the way what he would tell Mr. Drake.

Everyone had left the restaurant, and Mr. Drake was walking up and down the aisle when the proprietor reached the bottom of the staircase.

"I am worried about my lady friend," Mr. Drake said, hurrying up to him. "I am afraid that she may have passed out in
the toilet."

"The truth is," the proprietor answered, "that she has
passed out in an empty bedroom upstairs. Don't worry about
it. My daughter will take care of her if she wakes up feeling
sick. I used to know her husband. You can't do nothing about
her now." He put his hands into his pockets and looked solemnly into Mr. Drake's eyes.

Mr. Drake, not being equal to such a delicate situation, paid
his bill and left. Outside he crawled into his freshly painted
red truck and sat listening desolately to the rain.

•

The next morning Mrs. Perry awakened a little after sunrise.
Thanks to her excellent constitution she did not feel very sick,
but she lay motionless on the bed looking around her at the
walls for a long time. Slowly she remembered that this room
she was lying in was above the restaurant, but she did not
know how she had gotten there. She remembered the dinner
with Mr. Drake, but not much of what she had said to him. It
did not occur to her to blame him for her present circum-
stance. She was not hysterical at finding herself in a strange
bed because, although she was a very tense and nervous
woman, she possessed great depth of emotion and only certain
things concerned her personally.

She felt very happy and she thought of her uncle who had
passed out at a convention fifteen years ago. He had walked
around the town all the morning without knowing where he
was. She smiled.

After resting a little while longer, she got out of bed and
clothed herself. She went into the hall and found the staircase
and she descended with bated breath and a fast-beating heart,
because she was so eager to get back down into the restaurant.

It was flooded with sunshine and still smelled of meat and

sauce. She walked a little unsteadily down the aisle between the rows of wooden booths and tables. The tables were all bare and scrubbed clean. She looked anxiously from one to the other, hoping to select the booth they had sat in, but she was unable to choose among them. The tables were all identical. In a moment this anonymity served only to heighten her tenderness.

"John Drake," she whispered. "My sweet John Drake."

· Everything Is Nice

The highest street in the blue Moslem town skirted the edge of a cliff. She walked over to the thick protecting wall and looked down. The tide was out, and the flat dirty rocks below were swarming with skinny boys. A Moslem woman came up to the blue wall and stood next to her, grazing her hip with the basket she was carrying. She pretended not to notice her, and kept her eyes fixed on a white dog that had just slipped down the side of a rock and plunged into a crater of sea water. The sound of its bark was earsplitting. Then the woman jabbed the basket firmly into her ribs, and she looked up.

"That one is a porcupine," said the woman, pointing a henna-stained finger into the basket.

This was true. A large dead porcupine lay there, with a pair of new yellow socks folded on top of it.

She looked again at the woman. She was dressed in a haik,

and the white cloth covering the lower half of her face was
loose, about to fall down.

"I am Zodelia," she announced in a high voice. "And you
are Betsoul's friend." The loose cloth slipped below her chin
and hung there like a bib. She did not pull it up.

"You sit in her house and you sleep in her house and you eat
in her house," the woman went on, and she nodded in agreement. "Your name is Jeanie and you live in a hotel with other
Nazarenes. How much does the hotel cost you?"

A loaf of bread shaped like a disc flopped on to the ground
from inside the folds of the woman's haik, and she did not
have to answer her question. With some difficulty the woman
picked the loaf up and stuffed it in between the quills of the
porcupine and the basket handle. Then she set the basket
down on the top of the blue wall and turned to her with bright
eyes.

"I am the people in the hotel," she said. "Watch me."

She was pleased because she knew that the woman who
called herself Zodelia was about to present her with a little
skit. It would be delightful to watch, since all the people of the
town spoke and gesticulated as though they had studied at the
Comédie Française.

"The people in the hotel," Zodelia announced, formally beginning her skit. "I am the people in the hotel."

" 'Good-bye, Jeanie, good-bye. Where are you going?'

" 'I am going to a Moslem house to visit my Moslem friends,
Betsoul and her family. I will sit in a Moslem room and eat
Moslem food and sleep on a Moslem bed.'

" 'Jeanie, Jeanie, when will you come back to us in the hotel
and sleep in your own room?'

" 'I will come back to you in three days. I will come back
and sit in a Nazarene room and eat Nazarene food and sleep
on a Nazarene bed. I will spend half the week with Moslem
friends and half with Nazarenes.' "

The woman's voice had a triumphant ring as she finished

her sentence; then, without announcing the end of the sketch, she walked over to the wall and put one arm around her basket.

Down below, just at the edge of the cliff's shadow, a Moslem woman was seated on a rock, washing her legs in one of the holes filled with sea water. Her haik was piled on her lap and she was huddled over it, examining her feet.

"She is looking at the ocean," said Zodelia.

She was not looking at the ocean; with her head down and the mass of cloth in her lap she could not possibly have seen it; she would have had to straighten up and turn around.

"She is *not* looking at the ocean," she said.

"She is looking at the ocean," Zodelia repeated, as if she had not spoken.

She decided to change the subject. "Why do you have a porcupine with you?" she asked her, although she knew that some of the Moslems, particularly the country people, enjoyed eating them.

"It is a present for my aunt. Do you like it?"

"Yes," she said. "I like porcupines. I like big porcupines and little ones, too."

Zodelia seemed bewildered, and then bored, and she decided she had somehow ruined the conversation by mentioning small porcupines.

"Where is your mother?" Zodelia said at length.

"My mother is in her country in her own house," she said automatically; she had answered the question a hundred times.

"Why don't you write her a letter and tell her to come here? You can take her on a promenade and show her the ocean. After that she can go back to her own country and sit in her house." She picked up her basket and adjusted the strip of cloth over her mouth. "Would you like to go to a wedding?" she asked her.

She said she would love to go to a wedding, and they started off down the crooked blue street, heading into the wind. As they passed a small shop Zodelia stopped. "Stand here," she said. "I want to buy something."

After studying the display for a minute or two Zodelia poked her and pointed to some cakes inside a square box with glass sides. "Nice?" she asked her. "Or not nice?"

The cakes were dusty and coated with a thin, ugly-colored icing. They were called *Galletas Ortiz*.

"They are very nice," she replied, and bought her a dozen of them. Zodelia thanked her briefly and they walked on. Presently they turned off the street into a narrow alley and started downhill. Soon Zodelia stopped at a door on the right, and lifted the heavy brass knocker in the form of a fist.

"The wedding is here?" she said to her.

Zodelia shook her head and looked grave. "There is no wedding here," she said.

A child opened the door and quickly hid behind it, covering her face. She followed Zodelia across the black and white tile floor of the closed patio. The walls were washed in blue, and a cold light shone through the broken panes of glass far above their heads. There was a door on each side of the patio. Outside one of them, barring the threshold, was a row of pointed slippers. Zodelia stepped out of her own shoes and set them down near the others.

She stood behind Zodelia and began to take off her own shoes. It took her a long time because there was a knot in one of her laces. When she was ready, Zodelia took her hand and pulled her along with her into a dimly lit room, where she led her over to a mattress which lay against the wall.

"Sit," she told her, and she obeyed. Then, without further comment she walked off, heading for the far end of the room. Because her eyes had not grown used to the dimness, she had the impression of a figure disappearing down a long corridor. Then she began to see the brass bars of a bed, glowing weakly in the darkness.

Only a few feet away, in the middle of the carpet, sat an old lady in a dress made of green and purple curtain fabric. Through the many rents in the material she could see the printed cotton dress and the tan sweater underneath. Across the room several women sat along another mattress, and further along the mattress three babies were sleeping in a row, each one close against the wall with its head resting on a fancy cushion.

"Is it nice here?" It was Zodelia, who had returned without her haik. Her black crepe European dress hung unbelted down to her ankles, almost grazing her bare feet. The hem was lopsided. "Is it nice here?" she asked again, crouching on her haunches in front of her and pointing at the old woman. "That one is Tetum," she said. The old lady plunged both hands into a bowl of raw chopped meat and began shaping the stuff into little balls.

"Tetum," echoed the ladies on the mattress.

"This Nazarene," said Zodelia, gesturing in her direction, "spends half her time in a Moslem house with Moslem friends and the other half in a Nazarene hotel with other Nazarenes."

"That's nice," said the women opposite. "Half with Moslem friends and half with Nazarenes."

The old lady looked very stern. She noticed that her bony cheeks were tattooed with tiny blue crosses.

"Why?" asked the old lady abruptly in a deep voice. "*Why* does she spend half her time with Moslem friends and half with Nazarenes?" She fixed her eye on Zodelia, never ceasing to shape the meat with her swift fingers. Now she saw that her knuckles were also tattooed with blue crosses.

Zodelia stared back at her stupidly. "I don't know why," she said, shrugging one fat shoulder. It was clear that the picture she had been painting for them had suddenly lost all its charm for her.

"Is she crazy?" the old lady asked.

"No," Zodelia answered listlessly. "She is not crazy." There were shrieks of laughter from the mattress.

The old lady fastened her sharp eyes on the visitor, and she saw that they were heavily outlined in black. "Where is your husband?" she demanded.

"He's traveling in the desert."

"Selling things," Zodelia put in. This was the popular explanation for her husband's trips; she did not try to contradict it.

"Where is your mother?" the old lady asked.

"My mother is in our country in her own house."

"Why don't you go and sit with your mother in her own house?" she scolded. "The hotel costs a lot of money."

"In the city where I was born," she began, "there are many, many automobiles and many, many trucks."

The women on the mattress were smiling pleasantly. "Is that true?" remarked the one in the center in a tone of polite interest.

"I hate trucks," she told the woman with feeling.

The old lady lifted the bowl of meat off her lap and set it down on the carpet. "Trucks are nice," she said severely.

"That's true," the women agreed, after only a moment's hesitation. "Trucks are very nice."

"Do *you* like trucks?" she asked Zodelia, thinking that because of their relatively greater intimacy she might perhaps agree with her.

"Yes," she said. "They are nice. Trucks are very nice." She seemed lost in meditation, but only for an instant. "Everything is nice," she announced, with a look of triumph.

"It's the truth," the women said from their mattress. "Everything is nice."

They all looked happy, but the old lady was still frowning. "Aicha!" she yelled, twisting her neck so that her voice could be heard in the patio. "Bring the tea!"

Several little girls came into the room carrying the tea things and a low round table.

"Pass the cakes to the Nazarene," she told the smallest child, who was carrying a cut-glass dish piled with cakes. She saw that they were the ones she had bought for Zodelia; she did not want any of them. She wanted to go home.

"Eat!" the women called out from their mattress. "Eat the cakes."

The child pushed the glass dish forward.

"The dinner at the hotel is ready," she said, standing up.

"Drink tea," said the old woman scornfully. "Later you will sit with the other Nazarenes and eat their food."

"The Nazarenes will be angry if I'm late." She realized that she was lying stupidly, but she could not stop. "They will hit me!" She tried to look wild and frightened.

"Drink tea. They will not hit you," the old woman told her. "Sit down and drink tea."

The child was still offering her the glass dish as she backed away toward the door. Outside she sat down on the black and white tiles to lace her shoes. Only Zodelia followed her into the patio.

"Come back," the others were calling. "Come back into the room."

Then she noticed the porcupine basket standing nearby against the wall. "Is that old lady in the room your aunt? Is she the one you were bringing the porcupine to?" she asked her.

"No. She is not my aunt."

"Where *is* your aunt?"

"My aunt is in her own house."

"When will you take the porcupine to her?" She wanted to keep talking, so that Zodelia would be distracted and forget to fuss about her departure.

"The porcupine sits here," she said firmly. "In my own house."

She decided not to ask her again about the wedding.

When they reached the door Zodelia opened it just enough to let her through. "Good-bye," she said behind her. "I shall see you tomorrow, if Allah wills it."

"When?"

"Four o'clock." It was obvious that she had chosen the first figure that had come into her head. Before closing the door she reached out and pressed two of the dry Spanish cakes into her hand. "Eat them," she said graciously. "Eat them at the hotel with the other Nazarenes."

She started up the steep alley, headed once again for the walk along the cliff. The houses on either side of her were so close that she could smell the dampness of the walls and feel it on her cheeks like a thicker air.

When she reached the place where she had met Zodelia she went over to the wall and leaned on it. Although the sun had sunk behind the houses, the sky was still luminous and the blue of the wall had deepened. She rubbed her fingers along it: the wash was fresh and a little of the powdery stuff came off. And she remembered how once she had reached out to touch the face of a clown because it had awakened some longing. It had happened at a little circus, but not when she was a child.

· A Guatemalan Idyll

When the traveler arrived at the pension the wind was blowing hard. Before going in to have the hot soup he had been thinking about, he left his luggage inside the door and walked a few blocks in order to get an idea of the town. He came to a very large arch through which, in the distance, he could see a plain. He thought he could distinguish figures seated around a far-away fire, but he was not certain because the wind made tears in his eyes.

"How dismal," he thought, letting his mouth drop open. "But never mind. Brace up. It's probably a group of boys and girls sitting around an open fire having a fine time together. The world is the world, after all is said and done, and a patch of grass in one place is green the way it is in any other."

He turned back and walked along quickly, skirting the walls of the low stone houses. He was a little worried that he might not be able to recognize a door of his pension.

"There's not supposed to be any variety in the U.S.A.," he said to himself. "But this Spanish architecture beats everything, it's so monotonous." He knocked on one of the doors, and shortly a child with a shaved head appeared. With a strong American accent he said to her: "Is this the Pension Espinoza?"

"*Sí!*" The child led him inside to a fountain in the center of a square patio. He looked into the basin and the child did too.

"There are four fish inside here," she said to him in Spanish. "Would you like me to try and catch one of them for you?"

The traveler did not understand her. He stood there uncomfortably, longing to go to his room. The little girl was still trying to get hold of a fish when her mother, who owned the pension, came out and joined them. The woman was quite fat, but her face was small and pointed, and she wore glasses attached by a gold chain to her dress. She shook hands with him and asked him in fairly good English if he had had a pleasant journey.

"He wants to see some of the fish," explained the child.

"Certainly," said Señora Espinoza, moving her hands about in the water with dexterity. "Soon now, soon now," she said, laughing as one of the fish slipped between her fingers.

The traveler nodded. "I would like to go to my room," he said.

•

The American was a little dismayed by his room. There were four brass beds in a row, all of them very old and a little crooked.

"God!" he said to himself. "They'll have to remove some of these beds. They give me the willies."

A cord hung down from the ceiling. On the end of it at the height of his nose was a tiny electric bulb. He turned it on and looked at his hands under the light. They were chapped and dirty. A barefoot servant girl came in with a pitcher and a bowl.

In the dining room, calendars decorated the walls, and there was an elaborate cut-glass carafe on every table. Several people had already begun their meal in silence. One little girl was speaking in a high voice.

"I'm not going to the band concert tonight, mamá," she was saying.

"Why not?" asked her mother with her mouth full. She looked seriously at her daughter.

"Because I don't like to hear music. I hate it!"

"Why?" asked her mother absently, taking another large mouthful of her food. She spoke in a deep voice like a man's. Her head, which was set low between her shoulders, was covered with black curls. Her chin was heavy and her skin was dark and coarse; however, she had very beautiful blue eyes. She sat with her legs apart, with one arm lying flat on the table. The child bore no resemblance to her mother. She was frail, with stiff hair of the peculiar light color that is often found in mulattoes. Her eyes were so pale that they seemed almost white.

As the traveler came in, the child turned to look at him.

"Now there are nine people eating in this pension," she said immediately.

"Nine," said her mother. "Many mouths." She pushed her plate aside wearily and looked up at the calendar beside her on the wall. At last she turned around and saw the stranger. Having already finished her own dinner, she followed the progress of his meal with interest. Once she caught his eye.

"Good appetite," she said, nodding gravely, and then she watched his soup until he had finished it.

"My pills," she said to Lilina, holding her hand out without turning her head. To amuse herself, Lilina emptied the whole bottle into her mother's hand.

"Now you have your pills," she said. When Señora Ramirez realized what had happened, she dealt Lilina a terrible blow in the face, using the hand which held the pills, and thus leaving them sticking to the child's moist skin and in her hair. The traveler turned. He was so bored and at the same time disgusted by what he saw that he decided he had better look for another pension that very night.

"Soon," said the waitress, putting his meat in front of him, "the musician will come. For fifty cents he will play you all the songs you want to hear. One night would not be time enough. *She* will be out of the room by then." She looked over at Lilina, who was squealing like a stuck pig.

"Those pills cost me three *quetzales* a bottle," Señora Ramirez complained. One of the young men at a nearby table came over and examined the empty bottle. He shook his head.

"A barbarous thing," he said.

"What a dreadful child you are, Lilina!" said an English lady who was seated at quite a distance from everybody else. All the diners looked up. Her face and neck were quite red with annoyance. She was speaking to them in English.

"Can't you behave like civilized people?" she demanded.

"You be quiet, you!" The young man had finished examining the empty pill bottle. His companions burst out laughing.

"O.K., girl," he continued in English. "Want a piece of chewing gum?" His companions were quite helpless with laughter at his last remark, and all three of them got up and left the room. Their guffaws could be heard from the patio, where they had grouped around the fountain, fairly doubled up.

"It's a disgrace to the adult mind," said the English lady. Lilina's nose had started to bleed, and she rushed out.

"And tell Consuelo to hurry in and eat her dinner," her mother called after her. Just then the musician arrived. He was a small man and he wore a black suit and a dirty shirt.

"Well," said Lilina's mother. "At last you came."

"I was having dinner with my uncle. Time passes, Señora Ramirez! *Gracias a Dios!*"

"*Gracias a Dios* nothing! It's unheard-of, having to eat dinner without music."

The violinist fell into a chair, and, bent over low, he started to play with all his strength.

"Waltzes!" shouted Señora Ramirez above the music. "Waltzes!" She looked petulant and at the same time as though she were about to cry. As a matter of fact, the stranger was quite sure that he saw a tear roll down her cheek.

"Are you going to the band concert tonight?" she asked him; she spoke English rather well.

"I don't know. Are you?"

"Yes, with my daughter Consuelo. If the unfortunate girl ever gets here to eat her supper. She doesn't like food. Only dancing. She dances like a real butterfly. She has French blood from me. She is of a much better type than the little one, Lilina, who is always hurting; hurting me, hurting her sister, hurting her friends. I hope that God will have pity on her." At this she really did shed a tear or two, which she brushed away with her napkin.

"Well, she's young yet," said the stranger. Señora Ramirez agreed heartily.

"Yes, she is young." She smiled at him sweetly and seemed quite content.

Lilina meanwhile was in her room, standing over the white bowl in which they washed their hands, letting the blood drip into it. She was breathing heavily like someone who is trying to simulate anger.

"Stop that breathing! You sound like an old man," said her sister Conseulo, who was lying on the bed with a hot brick on her stomach. Consuelo was small and dark, with a broad flat face and an unusually narrow skull. She had a surly nature, which is often the case when young girls do little else but dream of a lover. Lilina, who was a bully without any curiosity concerning the grown-up world, hated her sister more than anyone else she knew.

"Mamá says that if you don't come in to eat soon she will hit you."

"Is that how *you* got that bloody nose?"

"No," said Lilina. She walked away from the basin and her eye fell on her mother's corset, which was lying on the bed. Quickly she picked it up and went with it into the patio, where she threw it into the fountain. Consuelo, frightened by the appropriation of the corset, got up hastily and arranged her hair.

"Too much upset for a girl of my age," she said to herself patting her stomach. Crossing the patio she saw Señora Córdoba walking along, holding her head very high as she slipped some hairpins more firmly into the bun at the back of her neck. Consuelo felt like a frog or a beetle walking behind her. Together they entered the dining room.

"Why don't you wait for midnight to strike?" said Señora Ramirez to Consuelo. Señorita Córdoba, assuming that this taunt had been addressed to her, bridled and stiffened. Her eyes narrowed and she stood still. Señora Ramirez, a gross coward, gave her a strange idiotic smile.

"How is your health, Señorita Córdoba?" she asked softly, and then feeling confused, she pointed to the stranger and asked him if he knew Señorita Córdoba.

"No, no; he does not know me." She held out her hand stiffly to the stranger and he took it. No names were mentioned.

Consuelo sat down beside her mother and ate voraciously, a sad look in her eye. Señorita Córdoba ordered only fruit. She sat looking out into the dark patio, giving the other diners a view of the nape of her neck. Presently she opened a letter and began to read. The others all watched her closely. The three young men who had laughed so heartily before were now smiling like idiots, waiting for another such occasion to present itself.

The musician was playing a waltz at the request of Señora Ramirez, who was trying her best to attract again the attention of the stranger. "Tra-la-la-la," she sang, and in order better to

convey the beauty of the waltz she folded her arms in front of
her and rocked from side to side.

"Ay, Consuelo! It is for her to waltz," she said to the stranger. "There will be many people in the plaza tonight, and
there is so much wind. I think that you must fetch my shawl,
Consuelo. It is getting very cold."

While awaiting Consuelo's return she shivered and picked
her teeth.

The traveler thought she was crazy and a little disgusting.
He had come here as a buyer for a very important textile concern. Having completed all his work, he had for some reason
decided to stay on another week, perhaps because he had always heard that a vacation in a foreign country was a desirable
thing. Already he regretted his decision, but there was no boat
out before the following Monday. By the end of the meal he
was in such despair that his face wore a peculiarly young and
sensitive look. In order to buoy himself up a bit, he began to
think about what he would get to eat three weeks hence, seated
at his mother's table on Thanksgiving Day. They would be
very glad to hear that he had not enjoyed himself on this trip,
because they had always considered it something in the nature
of a betrayal when anyone in the family expressed a desire to
travel. He thought they led a fine life and was inclined to
agree with them.

Consuelo had returned with her mother's shawl. She was
dreaming again when her mother pinched her arm.

"Well, Consuelo, are you coming to the band concert or are
you going to sit here like a dummy? I daresay the Señor is not
coming with us, but *we* like music, so get up, and we will say
good night to this gentleman and be on our way."

The traveler had not understood this speech. He was therefore very much surprised when Señora Ramirez tapped him on
the shoulder and said to him severely in English: "Good night,
Señor. Consuelo and I are going to the band concert. We will
see you tomorrow at breakfast."

"Oh, but I'm going to the band concert myself," he said, in a panic lest they leave him with a whole evening on his hands.

Señora Ramirez flushed with pleasure. The three walked down the badly lit street together, escorted by a group of skinny yellow dogs.

"These old grilled windows are certainly very beautiful," the traveler said to Señora Ramirez. "Old as the hills themselves, aren't they?"

"You must go to the capital if you want beautiful buildings," said Señora Ramirez. "Very new and clean they are."

"I should think," he said, "that these old buildings were your point of interest here, aside from your Indians and their native costumes."

They walked on for a little while in silence. A small boy came up to them and tried to sell them some lollipops.

"Five *centavos*," said the little boy.

"Absolutely not," said the traveler. He had been warned that the natives would cheat him, and he was acually enraged every time they approached him with their wares.

"Four *centavos* . . . three *centavos*. . . ."

"No, no, no! Go away!" The little boy ran ahead of them.

"I would like a lollipop," said Consuelo to him.

"Well, why didn't you say so, then?" he demanded.

"No," said Consuelo.

"She does not mean no," explained her mother. "She can't learn to speak English. She has clouds in her head."

"I see," said the traveler. Consuelo looked mortified. When they came to the end of the street, Señora Ramirez stood still and lowered her head like a bull.

"Listen," she said to Consuelo. "Listen. You can hear the music from here."

"Yes, mamá. Indeed you can." They stood listening to the faint marimba noise that reached them. The traveler sighed.

"Please, let's get going if we *are* going," he said. "Otherwise there is no point."

The square was already crowded when they arrived. The older people sat on benches under the trees, while the younger ones walked round and round, the girls in one direction and the boys in the other. The musicians played inside a kiosk in the center of the square. Señora Ramirez led both Consuelo and the stranger into the girls' line, and they had not been walking more than a minute before she settled into a comfortable gait, with an expression very much like that of someone relaxing in an armchair.

"We have three hours," she said to Consuelo.

The stranger looked around him. Many of the girls were barefoot and pure Indian. They walked along holding tightly to one another, and were frequently convulsed with laughter.

The musicians were playing a formless but militant-sounding piece which came to many climaxes without ending. The drummer was the man who had just played the violin at Señora Espinoza's pension.

"Look!" said the traveler excitedly. "Isn't that the man who was just playing for us at dinner. He must have run all the way. I'll bet he's sweating some."

"Yes, it is he," said Señora Ramirez. "The nasty little rat. I would like to tear him right off his stand. Remember the one at the Grand Hotel, Consuelo? He stopped at every table, señor, and I have never seen such beautiful teeth in my life. A smile on his face from the moment he came into the room until he went out again. This one looks at his shoes while he is playing, and he would like to kill us all."

Some big boys threw confetti into the traveler's face.

"I wonder," he asked himself. "I wonder what kind of fun they get out of just walking around and around this little park and throwing confetti at each other."

The boys' line was in a constant uproar about something. The broader their smiles became, the more he suspected them of plotting something, probably against him, for apparently he was the only tourist there that evening. Finally he was so upset that he walked along looking up at the stars, or even for short stretches with his eyes shut, because it seemed to him that somehow this rendered him a little less visible. Suddenly he caught sight of Señorita Córdoba. She was across the street buying lollipops from a boy.

"Señorita!" He waved his hand from where he was, and then joyfully bounded out of the line and across the street. He stood panting by her side, while she reddened considerably and did not know what to say to him.

Señora Ramirez and Consuelo came to a standstill and stood like two monuments, staring after him, while the lines brushed past them on either side.

•

Lilina was looking out of her window at some boys who were playing on the corner of the street under the street light. One of them kept pulling a snake out of his pocket; he would then stuff it back in again. Lilina wanted the snake very much. She chose her toys according to the amount of power or responsibility she thought they would give her in the eyes of others. She thought now that if she were able to get the snake, she would perhaps put on a little act called "Lilina and the Viper," and charge admission. She imagined that she would wear a fancy dress and let the snake wriggle under her collar. She left her room and went out of doors. The wind was stronger than it had been, and she could hear the music playing even from where she was. She felt chilly and hurried toward the boys.

"For how much will you sell your snake?" she asked the oldest boy, Ramón.

"You mean Victoria?" said Ramón. His voice was beginning to change and there was a shadow above his upper lip.

"Victoria is too much of a queen for you to have," said one of the smaller boys. "She is a beauty and you are not." They all roared with laughter, including Ramón, who all at once

looked very silly. He giggled like a girl. Lilina's heart sank. She
was determined to have the snake.

"Are you ever going to stop laughing and begin to bargain
with me? If you don't I'll have to go back in, because my
mother and sister will be coming home soon, and they
wouldn't allow me to be talking here like this with you. I'm
from a good family."

This sobered Ramón, and he ordered the boys to be quiet.
He took Victoria from his pocket and played with her in silence. Lilina stared at the snake.

"Come to my house," said Ramón. "My mother will want to
know how much I'm selling her for."

"All right," said Lilina. "But be quick, and I don't want
them with us." She indicated the other boys. Ramón gave them
orders to go back to their houses and meet him later at the
playground near the Cathedral.

"Where do you live?" she asked him.

"Calle de las Delicias number six."

"Does your house belong to you?"

"My house belongs to my Aunt Gudelia."

"Is she richer than your mother?"

"Oh, yes." They said no more to each other.

There were eight rooms opening onto the patio of Ramón's
house, but only one was furnished. In this room the family
cooked and slept. His mother and his aunt were seated opposite one another on two brightly painted chairs. Both were fat
and both were wearing black. The only light came from a
charcoal fire which was burning in a brazier on the floor.

They had bought the chairs that very morning and were
consequently feeling lighthearted and festive. When the children arrived they were singing a little song together.

"Why don't we buy something to drink?" said Gudelia,
when they stopped singing.

"Now you're going to go crazy, I see," said Ramón's mother.
"You're very disagreeable when you're drinking."

"No, I'm not," said Gudelia.

"Mother," said Ramón. "This little girl has come to buy Victoria."

"I have never seen you before," said Ramón's mother to Lilina.

"Nor I," said Gudelia. "I am Ramón's aunt, Gudelia. This is my house."

"My name is Lilina Ramirez. I want to bargain for Ramón's Victoria."

"Victoria," they repeated gravely.

"Ramón is very fond of Victoria and so are Gudelia and I," said his mother. "It's a shame that we sold Alfredo the parrot. We sold him for far too little. He sang and danced. We have taken care of Victoria for a long time, and it has been very expensive. She eats much meat." This was an obvious lie. They all looked at Lilina.

"Where do you live, dear?" Gudelia asked Lilina.

"I live in the capital, but I'm staying now at Señora Espinoza's pension."

"I meet her in the market every day of my life," said Gudelia. "Maria de la Luz Espinoza. She buys a lot. How many people has she staying in her house? Five, six?"

"Nine."

"Nine! Dear God! Does she have many animals?"

"Certainly," said Lilina.

"Come," said Ramón to Lilina. "Let's go outside and bargain."

"He loves that snake," said Ramón's mother, looking fixedly at Lilina.

The aunt sighed. "Victoria . . . Victoria."

Lilina and Ramón climbed through a hole in the wall and sat down together in the midst of some foliage.

"Listen," said Ramón. "If you kiss me, I'll give you Victoria for nothing. You have blue eyes. I saw them when we were in the street."

"I can hear what you are saying," his mother called out from the kitchen.

"Shame, shame," said Gudelia. "Giving Victoria away for nothing. Your mother will be without food. I can buy my own food, but what will your mother do?"

Lilina jumped to her feet impatiently. She saw that they were getting nowhere, and unlike most of her countrymen, she was always eager to get things done quickly.

She stamped back into the kitchen, opened her eyes very wide in order to frighten the two ladies, and shouted as loud as she could: "Sell me that snake right now or I will go away and never put my foot in this house again."

The two women were not used to such a display of rage over the mere settlement of a price. They rose from their chairs and started moving about the room to no purpose, picking up things and putting them down again. They were not quite sure what to do. Gudelia was terribly upset. She stepped here and there with her hand below her breast, peering about cautiously. Finally she slipped out into the patio and disappeared.

Ramón took Victoria out of his pocket. They arranged a price and Lilina left, carrying her in a little box.

•

Meanwhile Señora Ramirez and her daughter were on their way home from the band concert. Both of them were in a bad humor. Consuelo was not disposed to talk at all. She looked angrily at the houses they were passing and sighed at everything her mother had to say. "You have no merriment in your heart," said Señora Ramirez. "Just revenge." As Consuelo refused to answer, she continued. "Sometimes I feel that I am walking along with an assassin."

She stopped still in the street and looked up at the sky. *"Jesu Maria!"* she said. "Don't let me say such things about my own daughter." She clutched at Consuelo's arm.

"Come, come. Let us hurry. My feet ache. What an ugly city this is!"

Consuelo began to whimper. The word "assassin" had affected her painfully. Although she had no very clear idea of an assassin in her mind, she knew it to be a gross insult and contrary to all usage when applied to a young lady of breeding. It so frightened her that her mother had used such a word in connection with her that she actually felt a little sick to her stomach.

"No, mamá, no!" she cried. "Don't say that I am an assassin. Don't!" Her hands were beginning to shake, and already the tears were filling her eyes. Her mother hugged her and they stood for a moment locked in each other's arms.

Maria, the servant, was standing near the fountain looking into it when Consuelo and her mother arrived at the pension. The traveler and Señorita Córdoba were seated together having a chat.

"Doesn't love interest you?" the traveler was asking her.

"No . . . no . . ." answered Señorita Córdoba. "City life, business, the theater. . . ." She sounded somewhat halfhearted about the theater.

"Well, that's funny," said the traveler. "In my country most young girls are interested in love. There are some, of course, who are interested in having a career, either business or the stage. But I've heard tell that even these women deep down in their hearts want a home and everything that goes with it."

"So?" said Señorita Córdoba.

"Well, yes," said the traveler. "Deep down in your heart, don't you always hope the right man will come along some day?"

"No . . . no . . . no. . . . Do you?" she said absent-mindedly.

"Who, me? No."

"No?"

She was the most preoccupied woman he had ever spoken with.

"Look, señoras," said Maria to Consuelo and her mother. "Look what is floating around in the fountain! What is it?"

Consuelo bent over the basin and fished around a bit. Presently she pulled out her mother's pink corset.

"Why, mamá," she said. "It's your corset."

Señora Ramirez examined the wet corset. It was covered with muck from the bottom of the fountain. She went over to a chair and sat down in it, burying her face in her hands. She rocked back and forth and sobbed very softly. Señora Espinoza came out of her room.

"Lilina, my sister, threw it into the fountain," Consuelo announced to all present.

Señora Espinoza looked at the corset.

"It can be fixed. It can be fixed," she said, walking over to Señora Ramirez and putting her arms around her.

"Look, my friend. My dear little friend, why don't you go to bed and get some sleep? Tomorrow you can think about getting it cleaned."

"How can we stand it? Oh, how can we stand it?" Señora Ramirez asked imploringly, her beautiful eyes filled with sorrow. "Sometimes," she said in a trembling voice, "I have no more strength than a sparrow. I would like to send my children to the four winds and sleep and sleep and sleep."

Consuelo, hearing this, said in a gentle tone: "Why don't you do so, mamá?"

"They are like two daggers in my heart, you see?" continued her mother.

"No, they are not," said Señora Espinoza. "They are flowers that brighten your life." She removed her glasses and polished them on her blouse.

"Daggers in my heart," repeated Señora Ramirez.

"Have some hot soup," urged Señora Espinoza. "Maria will

make you some—a gift from me—and then you can go to bed and forget all about this."

"No, I think I will just sit here, thank you."

"Mamá is going to have one of her fits," said Consuelo to the servant. "She does sometimes. She gets just like a child instead of getting angry, and she doesn't worry about what she is eating or when she goes to sleep, but she just sits in a chair or goes walking and her face looks very different from the way it looks at other times." The servant nodded, and Consuelo went in to bed.

"I have French blood," Señora Ramirez was saying to Señora Espinoza. "I am very delicate for that reason—too delicate for my husband."

Señora Espinoza seemed worried by the confession of her friend. She had no interest in gossip or in what people had to say about their lives. To Señora Ramirez she was like a man, and she often had dreams about her in which she became a man.

The traveler was highly amused.

"I'll be damned!" he said. "All this because of an old corset. Some people have nothing to think about in this world. It's funny, though, funny as a barrel of monkeys."

To Señorita Córdoba it was not funny. "It's too bad," she said. "Very much too bad that the corset was spoiled. What are you doing here in this country?"

"I'm buying textiles. At least, I was, and now I'm just taking a little vacation here until the next boat leaves for the United States. I kind of miss my family and I'm anxious to get back. I don't see what you're supposed to get out of traveling."

"Oh, yes, yes. Surely you do," said Señorita Córdoba politely. "Now if you will excuse me I am going inside to do a little drawing. I must not forget how in this peasant land."

"What are you, an artist?" he asked.

"I draw dresses." She disappeared.

"Oh, God!" thought the traveler after she had left. "Here I

am, left alone, and I'm not sleepy yet. This empty patio is so barren and so uninteresting, and as far as Señorita Córdoba is concerned, she's an iceberg. I like her neck though. She has a neck like a swan, so long and white and slender, the kind of neck you dream about girls having. But she's more like a virgin than a swan." He turned around and noticed that Señora Ramirez was still sitting in her chair. He picked up his own chair and carried it over next to hers.

"Do you mind?" he asked. "I see that you've decided to take a little night air. It isn't a bad idea. I don't feel like going to bed much either."

"No," she said. "I don't want to go to bed. I will sit here. I like to sit out at night, if I am warmly enough dressed, and look up at the stars."

"Yes, it's a great source of peace," the traveler said. "People don't do enough of it these days."

"Would you not like very much to go to Italy?" Señora Ramirez asked him. "The fruit trees and the flowers will be wonderful there at night."

"Well, you've got enough fruit and flowers here, I should say. What do you want to go to Italy for? I'll bet there isn't as much variety in the fruit there as here."

"No? Do you have many flowers in your country?"

The traveler was not able to decide.

"I would like really," continued Señora Ramirez, "to be somewhere else—in your country or in Italy. I would like to be somewhere where the life is beautiful. I care very much whether life is beautiful or ugly. People who live here don't care very much. Because they do not think." She touched her finger to her forehead. "I love beautiful things: beautiful houses, beautiful gardens, beautiful songs. When I was a young girl I was truly wild with happiness—doing and thinking and running in and out. I was so happy that my mother was afraid I would fall and break my leg or have some kind of accident. She was a very religious woman, but when I was a young girl I could not remember to think about such a thing. I was up always every morning before anybody except the Indians, and every morning I would go to market with them to buy food for all the houses. For many years I was doing this. Even when I was very little. It was very easy for me to do anything. I loved to learn English. I had a professor and I used to get on my knees in front of my father that the professor would stay longer with me every day. I was walking in the parks when my sisters were sleeping. My eyes were so big." She made a circle with two fingers. "And shiny like two diamonds, I was so excited all the time." She churned the air with her clenched fist. "Like this," she said. "Like a storm. My sisters called me wild Sofía. At the same time they were calling me wild Sofía, I was in love with my uncle, Aldo Torres. He never came much to the house before, but I heard my mother say that he had no more money and we would feed him. We were very rich and getting richer every year. I felt very sorry for him and was thinking about him all the time. We fell in love with each other and were kissing and hugging each other when nobody was there who could see us. I would have lived with him in a grass hut. He married a woman who had a little money, who also loved him very much. When he was married he got fat and started joking a lot with my father. I was glad for him that he was richer but pretty sad for myself. Then my sister Juanita, the oldest, married a very rich man. We were all very happy about her and there was a very big wedding."

"You must have been brokenhearted, though, about your uncle Aldo Torres going off with someone else, when you had befriended him so much when he was poor."

"Oh, I liked him very much," she said. Her memory seemed suddenly to have failed her and she did not appear to be interested in speaking any longer of the past. The traveler felt disturbed.

"I would love to travel," she continued, "very, very much, and I think it would be very nice to have the life of an actress, without children. You know it is my nature to love men and kissing."

"Well," said the traveler, "nobody gets as much kissing as they would like to get. Most people are frustrated. You'd be surprised at the number of people in my country who are frustrated and good-looking at the same time."

She turned her face toward his. The one little light bulb shed just enough light to enable him to see into her beautiful eyes. The tears were still wet on her lashes and they magnified her eyes to such an extent that they appeared to be almost twice their normal size. While she was looking at him she caught her breath.

"Oh, my darling man," she said to him suddenly. "I don't want to be separated from you. Let's go where I can hold you in my arms." The traveler was feeling excited. She had taken hold of his hand and was crushing it very hard.

"Where do you want to go?" he asked stupidly.

"Into your bed." She closed her eyes and waited for him to answer.

"All right. Are you sure?"

She nodded her head vigorously.

"This," he said to himself, "is undoubtedly one of those things that you don't want to remember next morning. I'll want to shake it off like a dog shaking water off its back. But what can I do? It's too far along now. I'll be going home soon and the whole thing will be just a soap bubble among many other soap bubbles."

He was beginning to feel inspired and he could not understand it, because he had not been drinking.

"A soap bubble among many other soap bubbles," he repeated to himself. His inner life was undefined but well controlled as a rule. Together they went into his room.

"Ah," said Señora Ramirez after he had closed the door behind them, "this makes me happy."

She fell onto the bed sideways, like a beaten person. Her feet stuck out into the air, and her heavy breathing filled the room. He realized that he had never before seen a person behave in this manner unless sodden with alcohol, and he did not know what to do. According to all his standards and the standards of his friends she was not a pleasant thing to lie beside.

She was unfastening her dress at the neck. The brooch with which she pinned her collar together she stuck into the pillow behind her.

"So much fat," she said. "So much fat." She was smiling at him very tenderly. This for some reason excited him, and he took off his own clothing and got into bed beside her. He was as cold as a clam and very bony, but being a truly passionate woman she did not notice any of that.

"Do you really want to go through with this?" he said to her, for he was incapable of finding new words for a situation that was certainly unlike any other he had ever experienced. She fell upon him and felt his face and his neck with feverish excitement.

"Dear God!" she said. "Dear God!" They were in the very act of making love. "I have lived twenty years for this moment and I cannot think that heaven itself could be more wonderful."

The traveler hardly listened to this remark. His face was hidden in the pillow and he was feeling the pangs of guilt in the very midst of his pleasure. When it was all over she said to him: "That is all I want to do ever." She patted his hands and smiled at him.

"Are you happy, too?" she asked him.

"Yes, indeed," he said. He got off the bed and went out into the patio.

"She was certainly in a bad way," he thought. "It was almost like death itself." He didn't want to think any further. He stayed outside near the fountain as long as possible. When he returned she was up in front of the bureau trying to arrange her hair.

"I'm ashamed of the way I look," she said. "I don't look the way I feel." She laughed and he told her that she looked perfectly all right. She drew him down onto the bed again. "Don't send me back to my room," she said. "I love to be here with you, my sweetheart."

The dawn was breaking when the traveler awakened next morning. Señora Ramirez was still beside him, sleeping very soundly. Her arm was flung over the pillow behind her head.

"Lordy," said the traveler to himself. "I'd better get her out of here." He shook her as hard as he could.

"Mrs. Ramirez," he said. "Mrs. Ramirez, wake up. Wake up!" When she finally did wake up, she looked frightened to death. She turned and stared at him blankly for a little while. Before he noticed any change in her expression, her hand was already moving over his body.

"Mrs. Ramirez," he said. "I'm worried that perhaps your daughters will get up and raise a hullabaloo. You know, start whining for you, or something like that. Your place is probably in there."

"What?" she asked him. He had pulled away from her to the other side of the bed.

"I say I think you ought to go into your room now the morning's here."

"Yes, my darling, I will go to my room. You are right." She sidled over to him and put her arms around him.

"I will see you later in the dining room, and look at you and look at you, because I love you so much."

"Don't be crazy," he said. "You don't want anything to show in your face. You don't want people to guess about this. We must be cold with one another."

She put her hand over her heart.

"Ay!" she said. "This cannot be."

"Oh, Mrs. Ramirez. Please be sensible. Look, you go to your room and we'll talk about this in the morning . . . or, at least, later in the morning."

"Cold I cannot be." To illustrate this, she looked deep into his eyes.

"I know, I know," he said. "You're a very passionate woman. But my God! Here we are in a crazy Spanish country."

He jumped from the bed and she followed him. After she had put on her shoes, he took her to the door.

"Good-bye," he said.

She couched her cheek on her two hands and looked up at him. He shut the door.

She was too happy to go right to bed, and so she went over to the bureau and took from it a little stale sugar Virgin which she broke into three pieces. She went over to Consuelo and shook her very hard. Consuelo opened her eyes, and after some time asked her mother crossly what she wanted. Señora Ramirez stuffed the candy into her dauther's mouth.

"Eat it, darling," she said. "It's the little Virgin from the bureau."

"Ay, mamá!" Consuelo sighed. "Who knows what you will do next? It is already light out and you are still in your clothes. I am sure there is no other mother who is still in her clothes now, in the whole world. Please don't make me eat any more of the Virgin now. Tomorrow I will eat some more. But it is tomorrow, isn't it? What a mix-up. I don't like it." She shut her eyes and tried to sleep. There was a look of deep disgust on her face. Her mother's spell was a little frightening this time.

Señora Ramirez now went over to Lilina's bed and awakened her. Lilina opened her eyes wide and immediately looked very tense, because she thought she was going to be scolded about the corset and also about having gone out alone after dark.

"Here, little one," said her mother. "Eat some of the Virgin."

Lilina was delighted. She ate the stale sugar candy and patted her stomach to show how pleased she was. The snake was asleep in a box near her bed.

"Now tell me," said her mother. "What did you do today?"
She had completely forgotten about the corset. Lilina was beside herself with joy. She ran her fingers along her mother's lips
and then pushed them into her mouth. Señora Ramirez
snapped at the fingers like a dog. Then she laughed uproari-
ously.

"Mamá, please be quiet," pleaded Consuelo. "I want to go
to sleep."

"Yes, darling. Everything will be quiet so that you can sleep
peacefully."

"I bought a snake, mamá," said Lilina.

"Good!" exclaimed Señora Ramirez. And after musing a little while with her daughter's hand in hers, she went to bed.

·

In her room Señora Ramirez was dressing and talking to her
children.

"I want you to put on your fiesta dresses," she said, "because
I am going to ask the traveler to have lunch with us."

Consuelo was in love with the traveler by now and very jealous of Señorita Córdoba, who she had decided was his sweetheart. "I daresay he has already asked Señorita Córdoba to
lunch," she said. "They have been talking together near the
fountain almost since dawn."

"Santa Catarina!" cried her mother angrily. "You have the
eyes of a madman who sees flowers where there are only cow
turds." She covered her face heavily with a powder that was
distinctly violet in tint, and pulled a green chiffon scarf
around her shoulders, pinning it together with a brooch in the
form of a golf club. Then she and the girls, who were dressed
in pink satin, went out into the patio and sat together just a
little out of the sun. The parrot was swinging back and forth
on his perch and singing. Señora Ramirez sang along with him;
her own voice was a little lower than the parrot's.

Pastores, pastores, vamos a Belén
A ver a María y al niño también.

She conducted the parrot with her hand. The old señora, mother of Señora Espinoza, was walking round and round the patio. She stopped for a moment and played with Señora Ramirez's seashell bracelet.

"Do you want some candy?" she asked Señora Ramirez.

"I can't. My stomach is very bad."

"Do you want some candy?" she repeated. Señora Ramirez smiled and looked up at the sky. The old lady patted her cheek.

"Beautiful," she said. "You are beautiful."

"Mamá!" screamed Señora Espinoza, running out of her room. "Come to bed!"

The old lady clung to the rungs of Señora Ramirez's chair like a tough bird, and her daughter was obliged to pry her hands open before she was able to get her away.

"I'm sorry, Señora Ramirez," she said. "But when you get old, you know how it is."

"Pretty bad," said Señora Ramirez. She was looking at the traveler and Señorita Córdoba. They had their backs turned to her.

"Lilina," she said. "Go and ask him to have lunch with us . . . go. No, I will write it down. Get me a pen and paper."

"Dear," she wrote, when Lilina returned. "Will you come to have lunch at my table this afternoon? The girls will be with me, too. All the three of us send you our deep affection. I tell Consuelo to tell the maid to move the plates all to the same table. Very truly yours, Sofía Piega de Ramirez."

The traveler read the note, acquiesced, and shortly they were all seated together at the dining-room table.

"Now this is really stranger than fiction," he said to himself. "Here I am sitting with these people at their table and feeling as though I had been here all my life, and the truth of the

matter is that I have only been in this pension about fourteen
or fifteen hours altogether—not even one day. Yesterday I felt
that I was on a Zulu island, I was so depressed. The human
animal is the funniest animal of them all."

Señora Ramirez had arranged to sit close beside the stranger,
and she pressed her thigh to his all during the time that she
was eating her soup. The traveler's appetite was not very good.
He was excited and felt like talking.

After lunch Señora Ramirez decided to go for a walk instead
of taking a siesta with her daughters. She put on her gloves and
took with her an umbrella to shield her from the sun. After she
had walked a little while she came to a long road, completely
desolate save for a few ruins and some beautiful tall trees
along the way. She looked about her and shook her head at the
thought of the terrible earthquake that had thrown to the
ground this city, reputed to have been once the most beautiful
city in all the Western Hemisphere. She could see ahead of her,
way at the road's end, the volcano named Fire. She crossed
herself and bit her lips. She had come walking with the intention of dreaming of her lover, but the thought of this volcano
which had erupted many centuries ago chased all dreams of
love from her mind. She saw in her mind the walls of the
houses caving in, and the roofs falling on the heads of the babies . . . and the mothers, their skirts covered with mud, running through the streets in despair.

"The innocents," she said to herself. "I am sure that God
had a perfect reason for this, but what could it have been?
Santa María, but what could it have been! If such a disorder
should happen again on this earth, I would turn completely to
jelly like a helpless idiot."

She looked again at the volcano ahead of her, and although
nothing had changed, to her it seemed that a cloud had passed
across the face of the sun.

"You are crazy," she went on, "to think that an earthquake
will again shake this city to the earth. You will not be going

through such a trial as these other mothers went through, because everything now is different. God doesn't send such big trials any more, like floods over the whole world, and plagues."

She thanked her stars that she was living now and not before. It made her feel quite weak to think of the women who had been forced to live before she was born. The future too, she had heard, was to be very stormy because of wars.

"Ay!" she said to herself. "Precipices on all sides of me!" It had not been such a good idea to take a walk, after all. She thought again of the traveler, shutting her eyes for a moment.

"*Mi amante! Amante querido!*" she whispered; and she remembered the little books with their covers lettered in gold, books about love, which she had read when she was a young girl, and without the burden of a family. These little books had made the ability to read seem like the most worthwhile and delightful talent to her. They had never, of course, touched on the coarser aspects of love, but in later years she did not find it strange that it was for such physical ends that the heroes and heroines had been pining. Never had she found any difficulty in associating nosegays and couplets with the more gross manifestations of love.

She turned off into another road in order to avoid facing the volcano, constantly ahead of her. She thought of the traveler without really thinking of him at all. Her eyes glowed with the pleasure of being in love and she decided that she had been very stupid to think of an earthquake on the very day that God was making a bed of roses for her.

"Thank you, thank you," she whispered to Him, "from the bottom of my heart. Ah!" She smoothed her dress over her bosom. She was suddenly very pleased with everything. Ahead she noticed that there was a very long convent, somewhat ruined, in front of which some boys were playing. There was also a little pavilion standing not far away. It was difficult to understand why it was so situated, where there was no formal park, nor any trees or grass—just some dirt and a few bushes.

It had the strange static look of a ship that has been grounded. Señora Ramirez looked at it distastefully; it was a small kiosk anyway and badly in need of a coat of paint. But feeling tired, she was soon climbing up the flimsy steps, red in the face with fear lest she fall through to the ground. Inside the kiosk she spread a newspaper over the bench and sat down. Soon all her dreams of her lover faded from her mind, and she felt hot and fretful. She moved her feet around on the floor impatiently at the thought of having to walk all the way home. The dust rose up into the air and she was obliged to cover her mouth with her handkerchief.

"I wish to heaven," she said to herself, "that he would come and carry me out of this kiosk." She sat idly watching the boys playing in the dirt in front of the convent. One of them was a good deal taller than the others. As she watched their games, her head slumped forward and she fell asleep.

No tourists came, so the smaller boys decided to go over to the main square and meet the buses, to sell their lollipops and picture postcards. The oldest boy announced that he would stay behind.

"You're crazy," they said to him. "Completely crazy."

He looked at them haughtily and did not answer. They ran down the road, screaming that they were going to earn a thousand *quetzales.*

He had remained behind because for some time he had noticed that there was someone in the kiosk. He knew even from where he stood that it was a woman because he could see that her dress was brightly colored like a flower garden. She had been sitting there for a long time and he wondered if she were not dead.

"If she is dead," he thought, "I will carry her body all the way into town." The idea excited him and he approached the pavilion with bated breath. He went inside and stood over Señora Ramirez, but when he saw that she was quite old and fat and obviously the mother of a good rich family he was frightened and all his imagination failed him. He thought he would go away, but then he decided differently, and he shook her foot. There was no change. Her mouth, which had been open, remained so, and she went on sleeping. The boy took a good piece of the flesh on her upper arm between his thumb and forefinger and twisted it very hard. She awakened with a shudder and looked up at the boy, perplexed.

His eyes were soft.

"I awakened you," he said, "because I have to go home to my house, and you are not safe here. Before, there was a man here in the bandstand trying to look under your skirt. When you are asleep, you know, people just go wild. There were some drunks here too, singing an obscene song, standing on the ground, right under you. You would have had red ears if you had heard it. I can tell you that." He shrugged his shoulders and spat on the floor. He looked completely disgusted.

"What is the matter?" Señora Ramirez asked him.

"Bah! This city makes me sick. I want to be a carpenter in the capital, but I can't. My mother gets lonesome. All my brothers and sisters are dead."

"Ay!" said Señora Ramirez. "How sad for you! I have a beautiful house in the capital. Maybe my husband would let you be a carpenter there, if you did not have to stay with your mother."

The boy's eyes were shining.

"I'm coming back with you," he said. "My uncle is with my mother."

"Yes," said Señora Ramirez. "Maybe it will happen."

"My sweetheart is there in the city," he continued. "She was living here before."

Señora Ramirez took the boy's long hand in her own. The word sweetheart had recalled many things to her.

"Sit down, sit down," she said to him. "Sit down here beside me. I too have a sweetheart. He's in his room now."

"Where does he work?"

"In the United States."

"What luck for you! My sweetheart wouldn't love him better than she loves me, though. She wants me or simply death.
She says so any time I ask her. She would tell the same thing to
you if you asked her about me. It's the truth."

Señora Ramirez pulled him down onto the bench next to
her. He was confused and looked out over his shoulder at the
road. She tickled the back of his hand and smiled up at him in
a coquettish manner. The boy looked at her and his face
seemed to weaken.

"You have blue eyes," he said.

Señora Ramirez could not wait another minute. She took his
head in her two hands and kissed him several times full on the
mouth.

"Oh, God!" she said. The boy was delighted with her fine
clothes, her blue eyes, and her womanly ways. He took Señora
Ramirez in his arms with real tenderness.

"I love you," he said. Tears filled his eyes, and because he
was so full of a feeling of gratitude and kindness, he added: "I
love my sweetheart and I love you too."

He helped her down the steps of the kiosk, and with his arm
around her waist he led her to a sequestered spot belonging to
the convent grounds.

•

The traveler was lying on his bed, consumed by a feeling of
guilt. He had again spent the night with Señora Ramirez, and
he was wondering whether or not his mother would read this
in his eyes when he returned. He had never done anything like
this before. His behavior until now had never been without
precedent, and he felt like a two-headed monster, as though he
had somehow slipped from the real world into the other world,
the world that he had always imagined as a little boy to be
inhabited by assassins and orphans, and children whose mothers went to work. He put his head in his hands and won-

dered if he could ever forget Señora Ramirez. He remembered having read that the careers of many men had been ruined by women who because they had a certain physical stranglehold over them made it impossible for them to get away. These women, he knew, were always bad, and they were never Americans. Nor, he was certain, did they resemble Señora Ramirez. It was terrible to have done something he was certain none of his friends had ever done before him, nor would do after him. This experience, he knew, would have to remain a secret, and nothing made him feel more ill than having a secret. He liked to imagine that he and the group of men whom he considered to be his friends, discoursed freely on all things that were in their hearts and in their souls. He was beginning to talk to women in this free way, too—he talked to them a good deal, and he urged his friends to do likewise. He realized that he and Señora Ramirez never spoke, and this horrified him. He shuddered and said to himself: "We are like two gorillas."

He had been, it is true, with one or two prostitutes, but he had never taken them to his own bed, nor had he stayed with them longer than an hour. Also, they had been curly-headed blond American girls recommended to him by his friends.

"Well," he told himself, "there is no use making myself into a nervous wreck. What is done is done, and anyway, I think I might be excused on the grounds that: one, I am in a foreign country, which has sort of put me off my balance; two, I have been eating strange foods that I am not used to, and living at an unusually high altitude for me; and, three, I haven't had my own kind to talk to for three solid weeks."

He felt quite a good deal happier after having enumerated these extenuating conditions, and he added: "When I get onto my boat I shall wave goodby to the dock, and say good riddance to bad rubbish, and if the boss ever tries to send me out of the country, I'll tell him: 'not for a million dollars!'" He wished that it were possible to change pensions, but he had

already paid for the remainder of the week. He was very
thrifty, as, indeed, it was necessary for him to be. Now he lay
down again on his bed, quite satisfied with himself, but soon
he began to feel guilty again, and like an old truck horse, la-
boriously he went once more through the entire process of reassuring himself.

•

Lilina had put Victoria into a box and was walking in the
town with her. Not far from the central square there was a dry-
goods shop owned by a Jewish woman. Lilina had been there
several times with her mother to buy wool. She knew the son
of the proprietress, with whom she often stopped to talk. He
was very quiet, but Lilina liked him. She decided to drop in at
the shop now with Victoria.

When she arrived, the boy's mother was behind the counter
stamping some old bolts of material with purple ink. She saw
Lilina and smiled brightly.

"Enrique is in the patio. How nice of you to come and see
him. Why don't you come more often?" She was very eager to
please Lilina, because she knew the extent of Señora Ramirez's
wealth and was proud to have her as a customer.

Lilina went over to the little door that led into the patio
behind the shop, and opened it. Enrique was crouching in the
dirt beside the washtubs. She was surprised to see that his head
was wrapped in bandages. From a distance the dirty bandages
gave the effect of a white turban.

She went a little nearer, and saw that he was arranging some
marbles in a row.

"Good morning, Enrique," she said to him.

Enrique recognized her voice, and without turning his head,
he started slowly to pick up the marbles one at a time and put
them into his pocket.

His mother had followed Lilina into the patio. When she

saw that Enrique, instead of rising to his feet and greeting Lilina, remained absorbed in his marbles, she walked over to him and gave his arm a sharp twist.

"Leave those damned marbles alone and speak to Lilina," she said to him. Enrique got up and went over to Lilina, while his mother, bending over with difficulty, finished picking up the marbles he had left behind on the ground.

Lilina looked at the big, dark red stain on Enrique's bandage. They both walked back into the store. Enrique did not enjoy being with Lilina. In fact, he was a little afraid of her. Whenever she came to the shop he could hardly wait for her to leave.

He went over now to a bolt of printed material which he started to unwind. When he had unwound a few yards, he began to follow the convolutions of the pattern with his index finger. Lilina, not realizing that his gesture was a carefully disguised insult to her, watched him with a certain amount of interest.

"I have something with me inside this box," she said after a while.

Enrique, hearing his mother's footsteps approaching, turned and smiled at her sadly.

"Please show it to me," he said.

She lifted the lid from the snake's box and took it over to Enrique.

"This is Victoria," she said.

Enrique thought she was beautiful. He lifted her from her box and held her just below the head very firmly. Then he raised his arm until the snake's eyes were on a level with his own.

"Good morning, Victoria," he said to her. "Do you like it here in the store?"

This remark annoyed his mother. She had slipped down to the other end of the counter because she was terrified of the snake.

"You speak as though you were drunk," she said to Enrique. "That snake can't understand a word you're saying."

"She's really beautiful," said Enrique.

"Let's put her back in the box and take her to the square," said Lilina. But Enrique did not hear her, he was so enchanted with the sensation of holding Victoria.

His mother again spoke up. "Do you hear Lilina talking to you?" she shouted. "Or is that bandage covering your ears as well as your head?"

She had meant this remark to be stinging and witty, but she realized herself that there had been no point to it.

"Well, go with the little girl," she added.

Lilina and Enrique set off toward the square together. Lilina had put Victoria back into her box.

"Why are we going to the square?" Enrique asked Lilina.

"Because we are going there with Victoria."

Six or seven buses had converged in one of the streets that skirted the square. They had come from the capital and from other smaller cities in the region. The passengers who were not going any farther had already got out and were standing in a bunch talking together and buying food from the vendors. One lady had brought with her a cardboard fan intended as an advertisement for beer. She was fanning not only herself, but anyone who happened to come near her.

The bus drivers were racing their motors, and some were trying to move into positions more advantageous for departing. Lilina was excited by the noise and the crowd. Enrique, however, had sought a quiet spot, and was now standing underneath a tree. After a while she ran over to him and told him that she was going to let Victoria out of her box.

"Then we'll see what happens," she said.

"No, no!" insisted Enrique. "She'll only crawl under the buses and be squashed to death. Snakes live in the woods or in the rocks."

Lilina paid little attention to him. Soon she was crouching

on the edge of the curbstone, busily unfastening the string around Victoria's box.

Enrique's head had begun to pain him and he felt a little ill. He wondered if he could leave the square, but he decided he did not have the courage. Although the wind had risen, the sun was very hot, and the tree afforded him little shade. He watched Lilina for a little while, but soon he looked away from her, and began to think instead about his own death. He was certain that his head hurt more today than usual. This caused him to sink into the blackest gloom, as he did whenever he remembered the day he had fallen and pierced his skull on a rusty nail. His life had always been precious to him, as far back as he could recall, and it seemed perhaps even more so now that he realized it could be violently interrupted. He disliked Lilina; probably because he suspected intuitively that she was a person who could fall over and over again into the same pile of broken glass and scream just as loudly the last time as the first.

By now Victoria had wriggled under the buses and been crushed flat. The buses cleared away, and Enrique was able to see what had happened. Only the snake's head, which had been severed from its body, remained intact.

Enrique came up and stood beside Lilina. "Now are you going home?" he asked her, biting his lip.

"Look how small her head is. She must have been a very small snake," said Lilina.

"Are you going home to your house?" he asked her again.

"No. I'm going over by the cathedral and play on the swings. Do you want to come? I'm going to run there."

"I can't run," said Enrique, touching his fingers to the bandages. "And I'm not sure that I want to go over to the playground."

"Well," said Lilina. "I'll run ahead of you and I'll be there if you decide to come."

Enrique was very tired and a little dizzy, but he decided to follow her to the playground in order to ask her why she had allowed Victoria to escape under the buses.

When he arrived, Lilina was already swinging back and forth. He sat on a bench near the swings and looked up at her. Each time her feet grazed the ground, he tried to ask her about Victoria, but the question stuck in his throat. At last he stood up, thrust his hands into his pockets, and shouted at her.

"Are you going to get another snake?" he asked. It was not what he had intended to say. Lilina did not answer, but she did stare at him from the swing. It was impossible for him to tell whether or not she had heard his question.

At last she dug her heel into the ground and brought the swing to a standstill. "I must go home," she said, "or my mother will be angry with me."

"No," said Enrique, catching hold of her dress. "Come with me and let me buy you an ice."

"I will," said Lilina. "I love them."

They sat together in a little store, and Enrique bought two ices.

"I'd like to have a swing hanging from the roof of my house," said Lilina. "And I'd have my dinner and my breakfast served while I was swinging." This idea amused her and she began to laugh so hard that her ice ran out of her mouth and over her chin.

"Breakfast, lunch, and dinner and take a bath in the swing," she continued. "And make *pipi* on Consuelo's head from the swing."

Enrique was growing more and more nervous because it was getting late, and still they were not talking about Victoria.

"Could I swing with you in your house?" he asked Lilina.

"Yes. We'll have two swings and you can make *pipi* on Consuelo's head, too."

"I'd love to," he said.

His question seemed more and more difficult to present. By now it seemed to him that it resembled more a declaration of love than a simple question.

Finally he tried again. "Are you going to buy another snake?" But he still could not ask her why she had been so careless.

"No," said Lilina. "I'm going to buy a rabbit."

"A rabbit?" he said. "But rabbits aren't as intelligent or as beautiful as snakes. You had better buy another snake like Victoria."

"Rabbits have lots of children," said Lilina. "Why don't we buy a rabbit together?"

Enrique thought about this for a while. He began to feel almost lighthearted, and even a little wicked.

"All right," he said. "Let's buy two rabbits, a man and a woman." They finished their ices and talked together more and more excitedly about the rabbits.

On the way home, Lilina squeezed Enrique's hand and kissed him all over his cheeks. He was red with pleasure.

At the square they parted, after promising to meet again that afternoon.

•

It was a cloudy day, rather colder than usual, and Señora Ramirez decided to dress in her mourning clothes, which she always carried with her. She hung several strands of black beads around her neck and powdered her face heavily. She and Consuelo began to walk slowly around the patio.

Consuelo blew her nose. "Ay, mamá," she said. "Isn't it true that there is a greater amount of sadness in the world than happiness?"

"I don't know why you are thinking about this," said her mother.

"Because I have been counting my happy days and my sad days. There are many more sad days, and I am living now at the best age for a girl. There is nothing but fighting, even at balls. I would not believe any man if he told me he liked dancing better than fighting."

"This is true," said her mother. "But not all men are really like this. There are some men who are as gentle as little lambs. But not so many."

"I feel like an old lady. I think that maybe I will feel better when I'm married." They walked slowly past the traveler's door.

"I'm going inside," said Consuelo suddenly.

"Aren't you going to sit in the patio?" her mother asked her.

"No, with all those children screaming and the chickens and the parrot talking and the white dog. And it's such a terrible day. Why?"

Señora Ramirez could not think of any reason why Consuelo should stay in the patio. In any case she preferred to be there alone if the stranger should decide to talk to her.

"What white dog?" she said.

"Señora Espinoza has bought a little white dog for the children."

The wind was blowing and the children were chasing each other around the back patio. Señora Ramirez sat down on one of the little straight-backed chairs with her hands folded in her lap. The thought came into her mind that most days were likely to be cold and windy rather than otherwise, and that there would be many days to come exactly like this one. Unconsciously she had always felt that these were the days preferred by God, although they had never been much to her own liking.

The traveler was packing with the vivacity of one who is in the habit of making little excursions away from the charmed fold to return almost immediately.

"Wow!" he said joyfully to himself. "I sure have been giddy in this place, but the bad dream is over now." It was nearly bus time. He carried his bags out to the patio, and was confused to find Señora Ramirez sitting there. He prompted himself to be pleasant.

"Señora," he said, walking over to her. "It's goodby now till we meet again."

"What do you say?" she asked.

"I'm taking the twelve o'clock bus. I'm going home."

"Ah! You must be very happy to go home." She did not think of looking away from his face. "Do you take a boat?" she asked, staring harder.

"Yes. Five days on the boat."

"How wonderful that must be. Or maybe it makes you sick." She put her hand over her stomach.

"I have never been seasick in my life."

She said nothing to this.

He backed against the parrot swinging on its perch, and stepped forward again quickly as it leaned to bite him.

"Is there anyone you would like me to look up in the United States?"

"No. You will be coming back in not such a long time?"

"No. I don't think I will come back here again. Well. . . ." He put out his hand and she stood up. She was fairly impressive in her black clothes. He looked at the beads that covered her chest.

"Well, good-bye, señora. I was very happy to have met you."

"*Adios,* señor, and may God protect you on your trip. You will be coming back maybe. You don't know."

He shook his head and walked over to the Indian boy standing by his luggage. They went out into the street and the heavy door closed with a bang. Señora Ramirez looked around the patio. She saw Señorita Córdoba move away from the half-open bedroom door where she had been standing.

· Camp Cataract

Beryl knocked on Harriet's cabin door and was given permission to enter. She found her friend seated near the window, an open letter in her hand.

"Good evening, Beryl," said Harriet. "I was just reading a letter from my sister." Her fragile, spinsterish face wore a canny yet slightly hysterical expression.

Beryl, a stocky blond waitress with stubborn eyes, had developed a dogged attachment to Harriet and sat in her cabin whenever she had a moment to spare. She rarely spoke in Harriet's presence, nor was she an attentive listener.

"I'll read you what she says; have a seat." Harriet indicated a straight chair and Beryl dragged it into a dark corner where she sat down. It creaked dangerously under the weight of her husky body.

"Hope I don't bust the chair," said Beryl, and she blushed furiously, digging her hands deep into the pockets of the checked plus-fours she habitually wore when she was not on duty.

" 'Dear Sister,' " Harriet read. " 'You are still at Camp Cataract visiting the falls and enjoying them. I always want you to have a good time. This is your fifth week away. I suppose you go on standing behind the falls with much enjoyment like you told me all the guests did. I think you said only the people who don't stay overnight have to pay to stand behind the waterfall . . . you stay ten weeks . . . have a nice time, dear. Here everything is exactly the same as when you left. The apartment doesn't change. I have something I want to tell you, but first let me say that if you get nervous, why don't you come home instead of waiting until you are no good for the train trip? Such a thing could happen. I wonder of course how you feel about the apartment once you are by the waterfall. Also, I want to put this to you. Knowing that you have an apartment and a loving family must make Camp Cataract quite a different place than it would be if it were all the home and loving you had. There must be wretches like that up there. If you see them, be sure to give them loving because they are the lost souls of the earth. I fear nomads. I am afraid of them and afraid for them too. I don't know what I would do if any of my dear ones were seized with the wanderlust. We are meant to cherish those who through God's will are given into our hands. First of all come the members of the family, and for this it is better to live as close as possible. Maybe you would say, "Sadie is old-fashioned; she doesn't want people to live on their own." I am not old-fashioned, but I don't want any of us to turn into nomads. You don't grow rich in spirit by widening your circle but by tending your own. When you are gone, I get afraid about you. I think that you might be seized with the wanderlust and that you are not remembering the apartment very much. Particularly this trip . . . but then I know this cannot be true and that only my nerves make me think such things. It's so hot out. This is a record-breaking summer. Remember, the apartment is not just a row of rooms. It is the material proof that our spirits are so wedded that we have but one blessed roof over our heads. There are only three of us in the apartment related by blood, but Bert Hoffer has joined the three through the normal channels of marriage, also sacred. I know that you feel this way too about it and that just nerves makes me think Camp Cataract can change anything. May I remind you also that if this family is a garland, you are the middle flower; for me you are anyway. Maybe Evy's love is now flowing more to Bert Hoffer because he's her husband, which is natural. I wish they didn't think you needed to go to Camp Cataract because of your spells. Haven't I always tended you when you had them? Bert's always taken Evy to the Hoffers and we've stayed together, just the two of us, with the door safely locked so you wouldn't in your excitement run to a neighbor's house at all hours of the morning. Evy liked going to the Hoffers because they always gave her chicken with dumplings or else goose with red cabbage. I hope you haven't got it in your head that just because you are an old maid you have to go somewhere and be by yourself. Remember, I am also an old maid. I must close now, but I am not satisfied with my letter because I have so much more to say. I know you love the apartment and feel the way I feel. You are simply getting a tourist's thrill out of being there in a cabin like all of us do. I count the days until your sweet return. Your loving sister, Sadie.' "

Harriet folded the letter. "Sister Sadie," she said to Beryl, "is a great lover of security."

"She sounds swell," said Beryl, as if Harriet were mentioning her for the first time, which was certainly not the case.

"I have no regard for it whatsoever," Harriet announced in a positive voice. "*None.* In fact, I am a great admirer of the nomad, vagabonds, gypsies, seafaring men. I tip my hat to them; the old prophets roamed the world for that matter too, and most of the visionaries." She folded her hands in her lap with an air of satisfaction. Then, clearing her throat as if for a public address, she continued. "I don't give a tinker's damn about feeling part of a community, I can assure you. . . . That's not why I stay on at the apartment . . . not for a minute, but it's a good reason why she does . . . I mean Sadie; she loves a community spirit and she loves us all to be in the apartment because the apartment is in the community. She can get an actual thrill out of knowing that. But of course I can't . . . I never could, never in a thousand years."

She tilted her head back and half-closed her eyes. In the true style of a person given to interminable monologues, she was barely conscious of her audience. "Now," she said, "we can come to whether I, on the other hand, get a thrill out of Camp Cataract." She paused for a moment as if to consider this. "Actually, I don't," she pronounced sententiously, "but if you like, I will clarify my statement by calling Camp Cataract my *tree house*. You remember tree houses from your younger days. . . . You climb into them when you're a child and plan to run away from home once you are safely hidden among the leaves. They're popular with children. Suppose I tell you point-blank that I'm an extremely original woman, but also a very shallow one . . . in a sense, a *very* shallow one. I am afraid of scandal." Harriet assumed a more erect position. "I despise anything that smacks of a bohemian dash for freedom; I know that this has nothing to do with the more serious things in life . . . I'm sure there are hundreds of serious people who kick over their traces and jump into the gutter; but I'm too shallow for anything like that . . . I know it and I enjoy knowing it. Sadie on the other hand cooks and cleans all day long and yet takes her life as seriously as she would a religion . . . myself and the apartment and the Hoffers. By the Hoffers, I mean my sister Evy and her big pig of a husband Bert." She made a wry face. "I'm the only one with taste in the family but I've never even suggested a lamp for the apartment. I wouldn't lower myself by becoming involved. I do however refuse to make an unseemly dash for freedom. I refuse to be

known as 'Sadie's wild sister Harriet.' There is something in-
tensively repulsive to me about unmarried women setting out
on their own . . . also a very shallow attitude. You may wonder
how a woman can be shallow and know it at the same time,
but then, this is precisely the tragedy of any person, if he al-
lows himself to be griped." She paused for a moment and
looked into the darkness with a fierce light in her eyes. "Now
let's get back to Camp Cataract," she said with renewed vigor.
"The pine groves, the canoes, the sparkling purity of the brook
water and cascade . . . the cabins . . . the marshmallows,
the respectable clientele."

"Did you ever think of working in a garage?" Beryl suddenly
blurted out, and then she blushed again at the sound of her
own voice.

"No," Harriet answered sharply. "Why should I?"

Beryl shifted her position in her chair. "Well," she said, "I
think I'd like that kind of work better than waiting on tables.
Especially if I could be boss and own my garage. It's hard,
though, for a woman."

Harriet stared at her in silence. "Do you think Camp Cataract smacks of the gutter?" she asked a minute later.

"No, sir. . . ." Beryl shook her head with a woeful air.

"Well then, there you have it. It is, of course, the farthest
point from the gutter that one could reach. Any blockhead can
see that. My plan is extremely complicated and from my point
of view rather brilliant. First I will come here for several years
. . . I don't know yet exactly how many, but long enough to
imitate roots . . . I mean to imitate the natural family roots
of childhood . . . long enough so that I myself will feel:
"Camp Cataract is *habit*, Camp Cataract is life, Camp Cataract
is not escape." Escape is unladylike, habit isn't. As I remove
myself gradually from within my family circle and establish
myself more and more solidly into Camp Cataract, then from
here at some later date I can start making my sallies into the
outside world almost unnoticed. None of it will seem to the

onlooker like an ugly impetuous escape. I intend to rent the same cabin every year and to stay a little longer each time. Meanwhile I'm learning a great deal about trees and flowers and bushes . . . I am interested in nature." She was quiet for a moment. "It's rather lucky too," she added, "that the doctor has approved of my separating from the family for several months out of every year. He's a blockhead and doesn't remotely suspect the extent of my scheme nor how perfectly he fits into it . . . in fact, he has even sanctioned my request that no one visit me here at the camp. I'm afraid if Sadie did, and she's the only one who would dream of it, I wouldn't be able to avoid a wrangle and then I might have a fit. The fits are unpleasant; I get much more nervous than I usually am and there's a blank moment or two." Harriet glanced sideways at Beryl to see how she was reacting to this last bit of information, but Beryl's face was impassive.

"So you see my plan," she went on, in a relaxed, offhand manner, "complicated, a bit dotty and completely original . . . but then, I *am* original . . . not like my sisters . . . oddly enough I don't even seem to belong socially to the same class as my sisters do. I am somehow"—she hesitated for a second—"more fashionable."

Harriet glanced out of the window. Night had fallen during the course of her monologue and she could see a light burning in the next cabin. "Do you think I'm a coward?" she asked Beryl.

The waitress was startled out of her torpor. Fortunately her brain registered Harriet's question as well. "No, sir," she answered. "If you were, you wouldn't go out paddling canoes solo, with all the scary shoots you run into up and down these rivers. . . ."

Harriet twisted her body impatiently. She had a sudden and uncontrollable desire to be alone. "Good-bye," she said rudely. "I'm not coming to supper."

Beryl rose from her chair. "I'll save something for you in

case you get hungry after the dining room's closed. I'll be hanging around the lodge like I always am till bedtime." Harriet nodded and the waitress stepped out of the cabin, shutting the door carefully behind her so that it would not make any noise.

•

Harriet's sister Sadie was a dark woman with loose features and sad eyes. She was turning slightly to fat in her middle years, and did not in any way resemble Harriet, who was only a few years her senior. Ever since she had written her last letter to Harriet about Camp Cataract and the nomads Sadie had suffered from a feeling of steadily mounting suspense—the suspense itself a curious mingling of apprehension and thrilling anticipation. Her appetite grew smaller each day and it was becoming increasingly difficult for her to accomplish her domestic tasks.

She was standing in the parlor gazing with blank eyes at her new furniture set—two enormous easy chairs with bulging arms and a sofa in the same style—when she said aloud: "I can talk to her better than I can put it in a letter." Her voice had been automatic and when she heard her own words a rush of unbounded joy flooded her heart. Thus she realized that she was going on a little journey to Camp Cataract. She often made important decisions this way, as if some prearranged plot were being suddenly revealed to her, a plot which had immediately to be concealed from the eyes of others, because for Sadie, if there was any problem implicit in making a decision, it lay, not in the difficulty of choosing, but in the concealment of her choice. To her, secrecy was the real absolution from guilt, so automatically she protected all of her deepest feelings and compulsions from the eyes of Evy, Bert Hoffer and the other members of the family, although she had no interest in understanding or examining these herself.

The floor shook; recognizing Bert Hoffer's footsteps, she

made a violent effort to control the flux of her blood so that the power of her emotion would not be reflected in her cheeks. A moment later her brother-in-law walked across the room and settled in one of the easy chairs. He sat frowning at her for quite a little while without uttering a word in greeting, but Sadie had long ago grown accustomed to his unfriendly manner; even in the beginning it had not upset her too much because she was such an obsessive that she was not very concerned with outside details.

"God-damned velours," he said finally. "It's the hottest stuff I ever sat on."

"Next summer we'll get covers," Sadie reassured him, "with a flower pattern if you like. What's your favorite flower?" she asked, just to make conversation and to distract him from looking at her face.

Bert Hoffer stared at her as if she'd quite taken leave of her senses. He was a fat man with a red face and wavy hair. Instead of answering this question, which he considered idiotic, he mopped his brow with his handkerchief.

"I'll fix you a canned pineapple salad for supper," she said to him with glowing eyes. "It will taste better than heavy meat on a night like this."

"If you're going to dish up pineapple salad for supper," Bert Hoffer answered with a dark scowl, "you can telephone some other guy to come and eat it. You'll find me over at Martie's Tavern eating meat and potatoes, if there's any messages to deliver."

"I thought because you were hot," said Sadie.

"I was talking about the velvet, wasn't I? I didn't say anything about the meat."

He was a very trying man indeed, particularly in a small apartment, but Sadie never dwelled upon this fact at all. She was delighted to cook and clean for him and for her sister Evelyn so long as they consented to live under the same roof with her and Harriet.

Just then Evelyn walked briskly into the parlor. Like Sadie she was dark, but here the resemblance ceased, for she had a small and wiry build, with a flat chest, and her hair was as straight as an Indian's. She stared at her husband's shirt sleeves and at Sadie's apron with distaste. She was wearing a crisp summer dress with a very low neckline, an unfortunate selection for one as bony and fierce-looking as she.

"You both look ready for the dump heap, not for the dining room," she said to them. "Why do we bother to have a dining room . . . is it just a farce?"

"How was the office today?" Sadie asked her sister.

Evelyn looked at Sadie and narrowed her eyes in closer scrutiny. The muscles in her face tightened. There was a moment of dead silence, and Bert Hoffer, cocking a wary eye in his wife's direction, recognized the dangerous flush on her cheeks. Secretly he was pleased. He loved to look on when Evelyn blew up at Sadie, but he tried to conceal his enjoyment because he did not consider it a very masculine one.

"What's the matter with you?" Evelyn asked finally, drawing closer to Sadie. "There's something wrong besides your dirty apron."

Sadie colored slightly but said nothing.

"You look crazy," Evelyn yelled. "What's the matter with you? You look so crazy I'd be almost afraid to ask you to go to the store for something. Tell me what's happened!" Evelyn was very excitable; nonetheless hers was a strong and sane nature.

"I'm not crazy," Sadie mumbled. "I'll go get the dinner." She pushed slowly past Evelyn and with her heavy step she left the parlor.

The mahogany dining table was much too wide for the small oblong-shaped room, clearing the walls comfortably only at the two ends. When many guests were present some were seated first on one side of the room and were then obliged to draw the table toward themselves, until its edge pressed painfully into their diaphragms, before the remaining guests could slide into their seats on the opposite side.

Sadie served the food, but only Bert Hoffer ate with any appetite. Evelyn jabbed at her meat once or twice, tasted it, and dropped her fork, which fell with a clatter on to her plate.

Had the food been more savory she might not have pursued her attack on Sadie until later, or very likely she would have forgotten it altogether. Unfortunately, however, Sadie, although she insisted on fulfilling the role of housewife, and never allowed the others to acquit themselves of even the smallest domestic task, was a poor cook and a careless cleaner as well. Her lumpy gravies were tasteless, and she had once or twice boiled a good cut of steak out of indifference. She was lavish, too, in spite of being indifferent, and kept her cupboards so loaded with food that a certain quantity spoiled each week and there was often an unpleasant odor about the house. Harriet, in fact, was totally unaware of Sadie's true nature and had fallen into the trap her sister had instinctively prepared for her, because beyond wearing an apron and simulating the airs of other housewives, Sadie did not possess a community spirit at all, as Harriet had stated to Beryl the waitress. Sadie certainly yearned to live in the grown-up world that her parents had established for them when they were children, but in spite of the fact that she had wanted to live in that world with Harriet, and because of Harriet, she did not understand it properly. It remained mysterious to her even though she did all the housekeeping and managed the apartment entirely alone. She couldn't ever admit to herself that she lived in constant fear that Harriet would go away, but she brooded a great deal on outside dangers, and had she tried, she could not have remembered a time when this fear had not been her strongest emotion.

Sometimes an ecstatic and voracious look would come into her eyes, as if she would devour her very existence because she loved it so much. Such passionate moments of appreciation were perhaps her only reward for living a life which she knew in her heart was one of perpetual narrow escape. Although Sadie was neither sly nor tricky, but on the contrary profoundly sincere and ingenuous, she schemed unconsciously to keep the Hoffers in the apartment with them, because she did not want to reveal the true singleness of her interest either to Harriet or to herself. She sensed as well that Harriet would find it more difficult to break away from all three of them (because as a group they suggested a little society, which impressed her sister) than she would to escape from her alone. In spite of her mortal dread that Harriet might strike out on her own, she had never brooded on the possibility of her sister's marrying. Here, too, her instinct was correct: she knew that she was safe and referred often to the "normal channels of marriage," conscious all the while that such an intimate relationship with a man would be as uninteresting to Harriet as it would to herself.

From a financial point of view this communal living worked out more than satisfactorily. Each sister had inherited some real estate which yielded her a small monthly stipend; these stipends, combined with the extra money that the Hoffers contributed out of their salaries, covered their common living expenses. In return for the extra sum the Hoffers gave toward the household expenses, Sadie contributed her work, thus saving them the money they would have spent hiring a servant, had they lived alone. A fourth sister, whose marriage had proved financially more successful than Evy's, contributed generously toward Harriet's support at Camp Cataract, since Harriet's stipend certainly did not yield enough to cover her share of their living expenses at the apartment and pay for a long vacation as well.

Neither Sadie nor Bert Hoffer had looked up when Evy's fork clattered onto her plate. Sadie was truly absorbed in her own thoughts, whereas Bert Hoffer was merely pretending to be, while secretly he rejoiced at the unmistakable signal that his wife was about to blow up.

"When I find out why Sadie looks like that if she isn't going to be crazy, then I'll eat," Evelyn announced flatly, and she folded her arms across her chest.

"I'm not crazy," Sadie said indistinctly, glancing toward Bert Hoffer, not in order to enlist his sympathies, but to avoid her younger sister's sharp scrutiny.

"There's a big danger of your going crazy because of Grandma and Harriet," said Evelyn crossly. "That's why I get so nervous the minute you look a little out of the way, like you do tonight. It's not that you get Harriet's expression . . . but then you might be getting a different kind of craziness . . . maybe worse. She's all right if she can go away and there's not too much excitement . . . it's only in spells anyway. But you —you might get a worse kind. Maybe it would be steadier."

"I'm not going to be crazy," Sadie murmured apologetically.

Evelyn glowered in silence and picked up her fork, but then immediately she let it fall again and turned on her sister with renewed exasperation. "Why don't you ask me why *I'm* not going to be crazy?" she demanded. "Harriet's my sister and Grandma's my grandma just as much as she is yours, isn't she?"

Sadie's eyes had a faraway look.

"If you were normal," Evelyn pursued, "you'd give me an intelligent argument instead of not paying any attention. Do you agree, Hoffer?"

"Yes, I do," he answered soberly.

Evelyn stiffened her back. "I'm too much like everybody else to be crazy," she announced with pride. "At a picture show, I feel like the norm."

The technical difficulty of disappearing without announcing her plan to Evelyn suddenly occurred to Sadie, who glanced up quite by accident at her sister. She knew, of course, that Harriet was supposed to avoid contact with her family during these vacation months at the doctor's request and even at Harriet's own; but like some herd animal, who though threatened with the stick continues grazing, Sadie pursued her thoughts imperturbably. She did not really believe in Harriet's craziness nor in the necessity of her visits to Camp Cataract, but she was never in conscious opposition to the opinions of her sisters. Her attitude was rather like that of a child who is bored by the tedium of grown-up problems and listens to them with a vacant ear. As usual she was passionately concerned only with successfully dissimulating what she really felt, and had she been forced to admit openly that there existed such a remarkable split between her own opinions and those of her sisters, she would have suffered unbelievable torment. She was able to live among them, listening to their conferences with her dead outside ear (the more affluent sister was also present at these sessions, and her husband as well), and even to contribute a pittance toward Harriet's support at the camp, without questioning the validity either of their decisions or of her own totally divergent attitude. By a self-imposed taboo, awareness of this split was denied her, and she had never reflected upon it.

Harriet had gone to Camp Cataract for the first time a year ago, after a bad attack of nerves combined with a return of her pleurisy. It had been suggested by the doctor himself that she go with his own wife and child instead of traveling with one of her sisters. Harriet had been delighted with the suggestion and Sadie had accepted it without a murmur. It was never her habit to argue, and in fact she had thought nothing of Harriet's leaving at the time. It was only gradually that she had begun writing the letters to Harriet about Camp Cataract, the nomads and the wanderlust—for she had written others similar to her latest one, but never so eloquent or full of conviction. Previous letters had contained a hint or two here and there, but had been for the main part factual reports about her summer life in the apartment. Since writing this last letter she had not been able to forget her own wonderful and solemn words (for she was rarely eloquent), and even now at the dinner table they rose continually in her throat so that she was thrilled over and over again and could not bother her head about announcing her departure to Evelyn. "It will be easier to write a note," she said to herself. "I'll pack my valise and walk out tomorrow afternoon, while they're at business. They can get their own dinners for a few days. Maybe I'll leave a great big meat loaf." Her eyes were shining like stars.

"Take my plate and put it in the warmer, Hoffer," Evelyn was saying. "I won't eat another mouthful until Sadie tells us what we can expect. If she feels she's going off, she can at least warn us about it. I deserve to know how she feels . . . I tell every single thing I feel to her and Harriet . . . I don't sneak around the house like a thief. In the first place I don't have any time for sneaking, I'm at the office all day! Is this the latest vogue, this sneaking around and hiding everything you can from your sister? Is it?" She stared at Bert Hoffer, widening her eyes in fake astonishment. He shrugged his shoulders.

"I'm no sneak or hypocrite and neither are you, Hoffer, you're no hypocrite. You're just sore at the world, but you don't pretend you love the world, do you?"

Sadie was lightheaded with embarrassment. She had blanched at Evy's allusion to her going, which she mistook naturally for a reference to her intention of leaving for Camp Cataract.

"Only for a few days . . ." she mumbled in confusion, "and then I'll be right back here at the table."

Evelyn looked at her in consternation. "What do you mean by announcing calmly how many days it's going to be?" she shouted at her sister. "That's really sacrilegious! Did you ever hear of such a crusty sacrilegious remark in your life before?" She turned to Bert Hoffer, with a horror-stricken expression on her face. "How can I go to the office and look neat and clean and happy when this is what I hear at home . . . when my sister sits here and says she'll only go crazy for a few days? How *can* I go to the office after that? How can I look right?"

"I'm not going to be crazy," Sadie assured her again in a sorrowful tone, because although she felt relieved that Evelyn had not, after all, guessed the truth, hers was not a nature to indulge itself in trivial glee at having put someone off her track.

"You just said you were going to be crazy," Evelyn exclaimed heatedly. "Didn't she, Bert?"

"Yes," he answered, "she did say something like that. . . ."

The tendons of Evelyn's neck were stretched tight as she darted her eyes from her sister's face to her husband's. "Now, tell me this much," she demanded, "do I go to the office every day looking neat and clean or do I go looking like a bum?"

"You look O.K.," Bert said.

"Then why do my sisters spit in my eye? Why do they hide everything from me if I'm so decent? I'm wide open, I'm frank, there's nothing on my mind besides what I say. Why can't they be like other sisters all over the world? One of them is so crazy that she must live in a cabin for her nerves at *my* expense, and the other one is planning to go crazy deliberately and behind my back." She commenced to struggle out of her chair, which as usual proved to be a slow and laborious task. Exasperated, she shoved the table vehemently away from her toward the opposite wall. "Why don't we leave the space all on one side when there's no company?" she screamed at both of them, for she was now annoyed with Bert Hoffer as well as with Sadie. Fortunately they were seated at either end of the table and so did not suffer as a result of her violent gesture, but the table jammed into four chairs ranged on the opposite side, pinning three of them backward against the wall and knocking the fourth onto the floor.

"Leave it there," Evelyn shouted dramatically above the racket. "Leave it there till doomsday," and she rushed headlong out of the room.

They listened to her gallop down the hall.

"What about the dessert?" Bert Hoffer asked Sadie with a frown. He was displeased because Evelyn had spoken to him sharply.

"Leftover bread pudding without raisins." She had just gotten up to fetch the pudding when Evelyn summoned them from the parlor.

"Come in here, both of you," she hollered. "I have something to say."

They found Evelyn seated on the couch, her head tilted way back on a cushion, staring fixedly at the ceiling. They settled into easy chairs opposite her.

"I could be normal and light in any other family," she said, "I'm normally a gay light girl . . . not a morose one. I like all the material things."

"What do you want to do tonight?" Bert Hoffer interrupted, speaking with authority. "Do you want to be excited or do you want to go to the movies?" He was always bored by these self-appraising monologues which succeeded her explosions.

Evy looked as though she had not heard him, but after a moment or two of sitting with her eyes shut she got up and walked briskly out of the room; her husband followed her.

Neither of them had said good-bye to Sadie, who went over to the window as soon as they'd gone and looked down on the huge unsightly square below her. It was crisscrossed by trolley tracks going in every possible direction. Five pharmacies and seven cigar stores were visible from where she stood. She knew that modern industrial cities were considered ugly, but she liked them. "I'm glad Evy and Bert have gone to a picture show," Sadie remarked to herself after a while. "Evy gets high-strung from being at the office all day."

A little later she turned her back on the window and went to the dining room.

"Looks like the train went through here," she murmured, gazing quietly at the chairs tilted back against the wall and the

table's unsightly angle; but the tumult in her breast had not
subsided, even though she knew she was leaving for Camp Cataract. Beyond the first rush of joy she had experienced when
her plan had revealed itself to her earlier, in the parlor, the
feeling of suspense remained identical, a curious admixture of
anxiety and anticipation, difficult to bear. Concerning the me-
chanics of the trip itself she was neither nervous nor foolishly
excited. "I'll call up tomorrow," she said to herself, "and find
out when the buses go, or maybe I'll take the train. In the
morning I'll buy three different meats for the loaf, if I don't
forget. It won't go rotten for a few days, and even if it does
they can eat at Martie's or else Evy will make bologna and
eggs . . . she knows how, and so does Bert." She was not really
concentrating on these latter projects any more than she usually did on domestic details.

The lamp over the table was suspended on a heavy iron
chain. She reached for the beaded string to extinguish the
light. When she released it the massive lamp swung from side
to side in the darkness.

"Would you like it so much by the waterfall if you didn't
know the apartment was here?" she whispered into the dark,
and she was thrilled again by the beauty of her own words.
"How much more I'll be able to say when I'm sitting right
next to her," she murmured almost with reverence. ". . . And
then we'll come back here," she added simply, not in the least
startled to discover that the idea of returning with Harriet had
been at the root of her plan all along.

Without bothering to clear the plates from the table, she
went into the kitchen and extinguished the light there. She was
suddenly overcome with fatigue.

•

When Sadie arrived at Camp Cataract it was raining hard.

"This shingled building is the main lodge," the hack driver
said to her. "The ceiling in there is three times higher than

average, if you like that style. Go up on the porch and just walk in. You'll get a kick out of it."

Sadie reached into her pocketbook for some money.

"My wife and I come here to drink beer when we're in the mood," he continued, getting out his change. "If there's nobody much inside, don't get panicky; the whole camp goes to the movies on Thursday nights. The wagon takes them and brings them back. They'll be along soon."

After thanking him she got out of the cab and climbed the wooden steps on to the porch. Without hesitating she opened the door. The driver had not exaggerated; the room was indeed so enormous that it suggested a gymnasium. Wicker chairs and settees were scattered from one end of the floor to the other and numberless sawed-off tree stumps had been set down to serve as little tables.

Sadie glanced around her and then headed automatically for a giant fireplace, difficult to reach because of the accumulation of chairs and settees that surrounded it. She threaded her way between these and stepped across the hearth into the cold vault of the chimney, high enough to shelter a person of average stature. The andirons, which reached to her waist, had been wrought in the shape of witches. She fingered their pointed iron hats. "Novelties," she murmured to herself without enthusiasm. "They must have been especially made." Then, peering out of the fireplace, she noticed for the first time that she was not alone. Some fifty feet away a fat woman sat reading by the light of an electric bulb.

"She doesn't even know I'm in the fireplace," she said to herself. "Because the rain's so loud, she probably didn't hear me come in." She waited patiently for a while and then, suspecting that the woman might remain oblivious to her presence indefinitely, she called over to her. "Do you have anything to do with managing Camp Cataract?" she asked, speaking loudly so that she could be heard above the rain.

The woman ceased reading and switched her big light off at

once, since the strong glare prevented her seeing beyond the radius of the bulb.

"No, I don't," she answered in a booming voice. "Why?"

Sadie, finding no answer to this question, remained silent.

"Do you think I look like a manager?" the woman pursued, and since Sadie had obviously no intention of answering, she continued the conversation by herself.

"I suppose you might think I was manager here, because I'm stout, and stout people have that look; also I'm about the right age for it. But I'm not the manager . . . I don't manage anything, anywhere. I have a domineering cranium all right, but I'm more the French type. I'd rather enjoy myself than give orders."

"French . . ." Sadie repeated hesitantly.

"Not French," the woman corrected her. "French *type*, with a little of the actual blood." Her voice was cold and severe.

For a while neither of them spoke, and Sadie hoped the conversation had drawn to a definite close.

"Individuality is my god," the woman announced abruptly, much to Sadie's disappointment. "That's partly why I didn't go to the picture show tonight. I don't like doing what the groups do, and I've seen the film." She dragged her chair forward so as to be heard more clearly. "The steadies here—we call the ones who stay more than a fortnight steadies—are all crazy to get into birds-of-a-feather-flock-together arrangements. If you look around, you can see for yourself how clubby the furniture is fixed. Well, they can go in for it, if they want, but I won't. I keep my chair out in the open here, and when I feel like it I take myself over to one circle or another . . . there's about ten or twelve circles. Don't you object to the confinement of a group?"

"We haven't got a group back home," Sadie answered briefly.

"I don't go in for group worship either," the woman continued, "any more than I do for the heavy social mixing. I don't even go in for individual worship, for that matter. Most likely I was born to such a vigorous happy nature I don't feel the need to worry about what's up there over my head. I get the full flavor out of all my days whether anyone's up there or not. The groups don't allow for that kind of zip . . . never. You know what rotten apples in a barrel can do to the healthy ones."

Sadie, who had never before met an agnostic, was profoundly shocked by the woman's blasphemous attitude. "I'll bet she slept with a lot of men she wasn't married to when she was younger," she said to herself.

"Most of the humanity you bump into is unhealthy and nervous," the woman concluded, looking at Sadie with a cold eye, and then without further remarks she struggled out of her chair and began to walk toward a side door at the other end of the room. Just as she approached it the door was flung open from the other side by Beryl, whom the woman immediately warned of the new arrival. Beryl, without ceasing to spoon some beans out of a can she was holding, walked over to Sadie and offered to be of some assistance. "I can show you rooms," she suggested. "Unless you'd rather wait till the manager comes back from the movies."

When she realized, however, after a short conversation with Sadie, that she was speaking to Harriet's sister, a malevolent scowl darkened her countenance, and she spooned her beans more slowly.

"Harriet didn't tell me you were coming," she said at length; her tone was unmistakably disagreeable.

Sadie's heart commenced to beat very fast as she in turn realized that this woman in plus-fours was the waitress, Beryl, of whom Harriet had often spoken in her letters and at home.

"It's a surprise," Sadie told her. "I meant to come here before. I've been promising Harriet I'd visit her in camp for a long time now, but I couldn't come until I got a neighbor in

to cook for Evy and Bert. They're a husband and wife . . . my
sister Evy and her husband Bert."

"I know about those two," Beryl remarked sullenly. "Harriet's told me all about them."

"Will you please take me to my sister's cabin?" Sadie asked,
picking up her valise and stepping forward.

Beryl continued to stir her beans around without moving.

"I thought you folks had some kind of arrangement," she
said. She had recorded in her mind entire passages of Harriet's
monologues out of love for her friend, although she felt no curiosity concerning the material she had gathered. "I thought
you folks were supposed to stay in the apartment while she was
away at camp."

"Bert Hoffer and Evy have never visited Camp Cataract,"
Sadie answered in a tone that was innocent of any subterfuge.

"You bet they haven't," Beryl pronounced triumphantly.
"That's part of the arrangement. They're supposed to stay in
the apartment while she's here at camp; the doctor said so."

"They're not coming up," Sadie repeated, and she still wore,
not the foxy look that Beryl expected would betray itself at
any moment, but the look of a person who is attentive though
being addressed in a foreign language. The waitress sensed
that all her attempts at starting a scrap had been successfully
blocked for the present and she whistled carefully, dragging
some chairs into line with a rough hand. "I'll tell you what,"
she said, ceasing her activities as suddenly as she had begun
them. "Instead of taking you down there to the Pine Cones—
that's the name of the grove where her cabin is—I'll go myself
and tell her to come up here to the lodge. She's got some nifty
rain equipment so she won't get wet coming through the
groves like you would . . . lots of pine trees out there."

Sadie nodded in silence and walked over to a fantasy chair,
where she sat down.

"They get a lot of fun out of that chair. When they're

drunk," said Beryl pointing to its back, made of a giant straw disc. "Well . . . so long. . . ." She strode away. "Dear Valley . . ." Sadie heard her sing as she went out the door.

Sadie lifted the top off the chair's left arm and pulled two books out of its woven hamper. The larger volume was entitled *The Growth and Development of the Texas Oil Companies,* and the smaller, *Stories from Other Climes.* Hastily she replaced them and closed the lid.

•

Harriet opened the door for Beryl and quickly shut it again, but even in that instant the wooden flooring of the threshold was thoroughly soaked with rain. She was wearing a lavender kimono with a deep ruffle at the neckline; above it her face shone pale with dismay at Beryl's late and unexpected visit. She feared that perhaps the waitress was drunk. "I'm certainly not hacking out a free place for myself in this world just in order to cope with drunks," she said to herself with bitter verve. Her loose hair was hanging to her shoulders and Beryl looked at it for a moment in mute admiration before making her announcement.

"Your sister Sadie's up at the lodge," she said, recovering herself; then, feeling embarrassed, she shuffled over to her usual seat in the darkest corner of the room.

"What are you saying?" Harriet questioned her sharply.

"Your sister Sadie's up at the lodge," she repeated, not daring to look at her. "Your sister Sadie who wrote you the letter about the apartment."

"But she can't be!" Harriet screeched. "She can't be! It was all arranged that no one was to visit me here."

"That's what I told her," Beryl put in.

Harriet began pacing up and down the floor. Her pupils were dilated and she looked as if she were about to lose all control of herself. Abruptly she flopped down on the edge of the bed and began gulping in great draughts of air. She was actu-

ally practicing a system which she believed had often saved her
from complete hysteria, but Beryl, who knew nothing about
her method, was horrified and utterly bewildered. "Take it
easy," she implored Harriet. "Take it easy!"

"Dash some water in my face," said Harriet in a strange
voice, but horror and astonishment anchored Beryl securely to
her chair, so that Harriet was forced to stagger over to the
basin and manage by herself. After five minutes of steady dous-
ing she wiped her face and chest with a towel and resumed her
pacing. At each instant the expression on her face was more
indignant and a trifle less distraught. "It's the boorishness of it
that I find so appalling," she complained, a suggestion of the-
atricality in her tone which a moment before had not been
present. "If she's determined to wreck my schemes, why doesn't
she do it with some style, a little slight bit of cunning? I can't
picture anything more boorish than hauling oneself onto a
train and simply chugging straight up here. She has no sense of
scheming, of intrigue in the grand manner . . . none whatever. Anyone meeting only Sadie would think the family raised
potatoes for a living. Evy doesn't make a much better impression, I must say. If they met her they'd decide we were all
clerks! But at least she goes to business. . . . She doesn't sit
around thinking about how to mess my life up all day. She
thinks about Bert Hoffer. Ugh!" She made a wry face.

"When did you and Sadie start fighting?" Beryl asked her.

"I don't fight with Sadie," Harriet answered, lifting her
head proudly. "I wouldn't dream of fighting like a common
fishwife. Everything that goes on between us goes on under-
cover. It's always been that way. I've always hidden everything
from her ever since I was a little girl. She's perfectly aware that
I know she's trying to hold me a prisoner in the apartment out
of plain jealousy and she knows too that I'm afraid of being
considered a bum, and that makes matters simpler for her. She
pretends to be worried that I might forget myself if I left the
apartment and commit a folly with some man I wasn't married

to, but actually she knows perfectly well that I'm as cold as ice. I haven't the slightest interest in men . . . nor in women either for that matter; still if I stormed out of the apartment dramatically the way some do, they might think I was a bum on my way to a man . . . and I won't give Sadie that satisfaction, ever. As for marriage, of course I admit I'm peculiar and there's a bit wrong with me, but even so I shouldn't want to marry: I think the whole system of going through life with a partner is repulsive in every way." She paused, but only for a second. "Don't you imagine, however," she added severely, looking directly at Beryl, "don't you imagine that just because I'm a bit peculiar and different from the others, that I'm not fussy about my life. I *am* fussy about it, and I *hate* a scandal."

"To hell with sisters!" Beryl exclaimed happily. "Give 'em all a good swift kick in the pants." She had regained her own composure watching the color return to Harriet's cheeks and she was just beginning to think with pleasure that perhaps Sadie's arrival would serve to strengthen the bond of intimacy between herself and Harriet, when this latter buried her head in her lap and burst into tears. Beryl's face fell and she blushed at her own frivolousness.

"I can't any more," Harriet sobbed in anguished tones. "I can't . . . I'm old . . . I'm much too old." Here she collapsed and sobbed so pitifully that Beryl, wringing her hands in grief, sprang to her side, for she was a most tenderhearted person toward those whom she loved. "You are not old . . . you are beautiful," she said, blushing again, and in her heart she was thankful that Providence had granted her the occasion to console her friend in a grief-stricken moment, and to compliment her at the same time.

After a bit, Harriet's sobbing subsided, and jumping up from the bed, she grabbed the waitress. "Beryl," she gasped, "you must run back to the lodge right away." There was a beam of cunning in her tear-filled eyes.

"Sure will," Beryl answered.

"Go back to the lodge and see if there's a room left up there, and if there is, take her grip into it so that there will be no question of her staying in my cabin. I can't have her staying in my cabin. It's the only place I have in the whole wide world." The beam of cunning disappeared again and she looked at Beryl with wide, frightened eyes. ". . . And if there's no room?" she asked.

"Then I'll put her in my place," Beryl reassured her. "I've got a neat little cabin all to myself that she can have and I'll go bunk in with some dopey waitress."

"Well, then," said Harriet, "go, and hurry! Take her grip to a room in the upper lodge annex or to your own cabin before she has a chance to say anything, and then come straight back here for me. I can't get through these pine groves alone . . . now . . . I know I can't." It did not occur to her to thank Beryl for the kind offer she had made.

"All right," said the waitress, "I'll be back in a jiffy and don't you worry about a thing." A second later she was lumbering through the drenched pine groves with shining eyes.

•

When Beryl came into the lodge and snatched Sadie's grip up without a word of explanation, Sadie did not protest. Opposite her there was an open staircase which led to a narrow gallery hanging halfway between the ceiling and the floor. She watched the waitress climbing the stairs, but once she had passed the landing Sadie did not trouble to look up and follow her progress around the wooden balcony overhead.

A deep chill had settled into her bones, and she was like a person benumbed. Exactly when this present state had succeeded the earlier one Sadie could not tell, nor did she think to ask herself such a question, but a feeling of dread now lay like a stone in her breast where before there had been stirring such powerful sensations of excitement and suspense. "I'm so low," she said to herself. "I feel like I was sitting at my own funeral."

She did not say this in the spirit of hyperbolic gloom which some people nurture to work themselves out of a bad mood, but in all seriousness and with her customary attitude of passivity; in fact, she wore the humble look so often visible on the faces of sufferers who are being treated in a free clinic. It did not occur to her that a connection might exist between her present dismal state and the mission she had come to fulfill at Camp Cataract, nor did she take any notice of the fact that the words which were to enchant Harriet and accomplish her return were no longer welling up in her throat as they had done all the past week. She feared that something dreadful might happen, but whatever it was, this disaster was as remotely connected with her as a possible train wreck. "I hope nothing bad happens . . ." she thought, but she didn't have much hope in her.

Harriet slammed the front door and Sadie looked up. For the first second or two she did not recognize the woman who stood on the threshold in her dripping rubber coat and hood. Beryl was beside her; puddles were forming around the feet of the two women. Harriet had rouged her cheeks rather more highly than usual in order to hide all traces of her crying spell. Her eyes were bright and she wore a smile that was fixed and hard.

"Not a night fit for man or beast," she shouted across to Sadie, using a voice that she thought sounded hearty and yet fashionable at the same time; she did this, not in order to impress her sister, but to keep her at a safe distance.

Sadie, instead of rushing to the door, stared at her with an air of perplexity. To her Harriet appeared more robust and coarse-featured than she had five weeks ago at the apartment, and yet she knew that such a rapid change of physiognomy was scarcely possible. Recovering, she rose and went to embrace her sister. The embrace failed to reassure her because of Harriet's wet rubber coat, and her feeling of estrangement became more defined. She backed away.

Upon hearing her own voice ring out in such hearty and
fashionable tones, Harriet had felt crazily confident that she
might, by continuing to affect this manner, hold her sister at
bay for the duration of her visit. To increase her chances of
success she had determined right then not to ask Sadie why she
had come, but to treat the visit in the most casual and natural
way possible.

"Have you put on fat?" Sadie asked, at a loss for anything
else to say.

"I'll never be fat," Harriet replied quickly. "I'm a fruit
lover, not a lover of starches."

"Yes, you love fruit," Sadie said nervously. "Do you want
some? I have an apple left from my lunch."

Harriet looked aghast. "Now!" she exclaimed. "Beryl can
tell you that I never eat at night; in fact I never come up to the
lodge at night, *never*. I stay in my cabin. I've written you all
about how early I get up . . . I don't know anything about
the lodge at night," she added almost angrily, as though her
sister had accused her of being festive.

"You don't?" Sadie looked at her stupidly.

"No, I don't. Are you hungry, by the way?"

"If she's hungry," put in Beryl, "we can go into the Grotto
Room and I'll bring her the food there. The tables in the main
dining room are all set up for tomorrow morning's breakfast."

"I despise the Grotto," said Harriet with surprising bitterness. Her voice was getting quite an edge to it, and although it
still sounded fashionable it was no longer hearty.

"I'm not hungry," Sadie assured them both. "I'm sleepy."

"Well, then," Harriet replied quickly, jumping at the opportunity, "we'll sit here for a few minutes and then you must
go to bed."

The three of them settled in wicker chairs close to the cold
hearth. Sadie was seated opposite the other two, who both remained in their rubber coats.

"I really do despise the Grotto," Harriet went on. "Actually

I don't hang around the lodge at all. This is not the part of Camp Cataract that interests me. I'm interested in the pine groves, my cabin, the rocks, the streams, the bridge, and all the surrounding natural beauty . . . the sky also."

Although the rain still continued its drumming on the roof above them, to Sadie, Harriet's voice sounded intolerably loud, and she could not rid herself of the impression that her sister's face had grown fatter. "Now," she heard Harriet saying in her loud voice, "tell me about the apartment. . . . What's new, how are the dinners coming along, how are Evy and Bert?"

Fortunately, while Sadie was struggling to answer these questions, which unaccountably she found it difficult to do, the stout agnostic reappeared, and Harriet was immediately distracted.

"Rover," she called gaily across the room, "come and sit with us. My sister Sadie's here."

The woman joined them, seating herself beside Beryl, so that Sadie was now facing all three.

"It's a surprise to see you up at the lodge at night, Hermit," she remarked to Harriet without a spark of mischief in her voice.

"You see!" Harriet nodded at Sadie with immense satisfaction. "I was not fibbing, was I? How are Evy and Bert?" she asked again, her face twitching a bit. "Is the apartment hot?"

Sadie nodded.

"I don't know how long you plan to stay," Harriet rattled on, feeling increasingly powerful and therefore reckless, "but I'm going on a canoe trip the day after tomorrow for five days. We're going up the river to Pocahontas Falls. . . . I leave at four in the morning, too, which rather ruins tomorrow as well. I've been looking forward to this trip ever since last spring when I applied for my seat, back at the apartment. The canoes are limited, and the guides. . . . I'm devoted to canoe trips, as you know, and can fancy myself a red-skin all the way to the Falls and back, easily."

Sadie did not answer.

"There's nothing weird about it," Harriet argued. "It's in keeping with my hatred of industrialization. In any case, you can see what a chopped-up day tomorrow's going to be. I have to make my pack in the morning and I must be in bed by eight-thirty at night, the latest, so that I can get up at four. I'll have only one real meal, at two in the afternoon. I suggest we meet at two behind the souvenir booth; you'll notice it tomorrow." Harriet waited expectantly for Sadie to answer in agreement to this suggestion, but her sister remained silent.

"Speaking of the booth," said Rover, "I'm not taking home a single souvenir this year. They're expensive and they don't last."

"You can buy salt-water taffy at Gerald's Store in town," Beryl told her. "I saw some there last week. It's a little stale but very cheap."

"Why would they sell salt-water taffy in the mountains?" Rover asked irritably.

Sadie was half listening to the conversation; as she sat watching them, all three women were suddenly unrecognizable; it was as if she had flung open the door to some dentist's office and seen three strangers seated there. She sprang to her feet in terror.

Harriet was horrified. "What is it?" she yelled at her sister. "Why do you look like that? Are you mad?"

Sadie was pale and beads of sweat were forming under her felt hat, but the women opposite her had already regained their correct relation to herself and the present moment. Her face relaxed, and although her legs were trembling as a result of her brief but shocking experience, she felt immensely relieved that it was all over.

"Why did you jump up?" Harriet screeched at her. "Is it because you are at Camp Cataract and not at the apartment?"

"It must have been the long train trip and no food . . ." Sadie told herself, "only one sandwich."

"Is it because you are at Camp Cataract and not at the apartment?" Harriet insisted. She was really very frightened and wished to establish Sadie's fit as a purposeful one and not as an involuntary seizure similar to one of hers.

"It was a long and dirty train trip," Sadie said in a weary voice. "I had only one sandwich all day long, with no mustard or butter . . . just the processed meat. I didn't even eat my fruit."

"Beryl offered to serve you food in the Grotto!" Harriet ranted. "Do you want some now or not? For heaven's sake, speak up!"

"No . . . no." Sadie shook her head sorrowfully. "I think I'd best go to bed. Take me to your cabin . . . I've got my slippers and my kimono and my nightgown in my satchel," she added, looking around her vaguely, for the fact that Beryl had carried her grip off had never really impressed itself upon her consciousness.

Harriet glanced at Beryl with an air of complicity and managed to give her a quick pinch. "Beryl's got you fixed up in one of the upper lodge annex rooms," she told Sadie in a false, chatterbox voice. "You'll be much more comfortable up here than you would be down in my cabin. We all use oil lamps in the grove and you know how dependent you are on electricity."

Sadie didn't know whether she was dependent on electricity or not since she had never really lived without it, but she was so tired that she said nothing.

"I get up terribly early and my cabin's drafty, besides," Harriet went on. "You'll be much more comfortable here. You'd hate the Boulder Dam wigwams as well. Anyway, the wigwams are really for boys and they're always full. There's a covered bridge leading from this building to the annex on the upper floor, so that's an advantage."

"O.K., folks," Beryl cut in, judging that she could best help Harriet by spurring them on to action. "Let's get going."

"Yes," Harriet agreed, "if we don't get out of the lodge soon the crowd will come back from the movies and we certainly want to avoid them."

They bade good night to Rover and started up the stairs.

"This balustrade is made of young birch limbs," Harriet told Sadie as they walked along the narrow gallery overhead. "I think it's very much in keeping with the lodge, don't you?"

"Yes, I do," Sadie answered.

Beryl opened the door leading from the balcony onto a covered bridge and stepped through it, motioning to the others. "Here we go onto the bridge," she said, looking over her shoulder. "You've never visited the annex, have you?" she asked Harriet.

"I've never had any reason to," Harriet answered in a huffy tone. "You know how I feel about my cabin."

They walked along the imperfectly fitted boards in the darkness. Gusts of wind blew about their ankles and they were constantly spattered with rain in spite of the wooden roofing. They reached the door at the other end very quickly, however, where they descended two steps leading into a short, brightly lit hall. Beryl closed the door to the bridge behind them. The smell of fresh plaster and cement thickened the damp air.

"This is the annex," said Beryl. "We put old ladies here mostly, because they can get back and forth to the dining room without going outdoors . . . and they've got the toilet right here, too." She flung open the door and showed it to them. "Then also," she added, "we don't like the old ladies dealing with oil lamps and here they've got electricity." She led them into a little room just at their left and switched on the light. "Pretty smart, isn't it?" she remarked, looking around her with evident satisfaction, as if she herself had designed the room; then, sauntering over to a modernistic wardrobe-bureau combination, she polished a corner of it with her pocket handkerchief. This piece was made of shiny brown wood and fitted with a rimless circular mirror. "Strong and good-looking,"

Beryl said, rapping on the wood with her knuckles. "Every room's got one."

Sadie sank down on the edge of the bed without removing her outer garments. Here, too, the smell of plaster and cement permeated the air, and the wind still blew about their ankles, this time from under the badly constructed doorsill.

"The cabins are much draftier than this," Harriet assured Sadie once again. "You'll be more comfortable here in the annex." She felt confident that establishing her sister in the annex would facilitate her plan, which was still to prevent her from saying whatever she had come to say.

Sadie was terribly tired. Her hat, dampened by the rain, pressed uncomfortably against her temples, but she did not attempt to remove it. "I think I've got to go to sleep," she muttered. "I can't stay awake any more."

"All right," said Harriet, "but don't forget tomorrow at two by the souvenir booth . . . you can't miss it. I don't want to see anyone in the morning because I can make my canoe pack better by myself . . . it's frightfully complicated. . . . But if I hurried I could meet you at one-thirty; would you prefer that?"

Sadie nodded.

"Then I'll do my best. . . . You see, in the morning I always practice imagination for an hour or two. It does me lots of good, but tomorrow I'll cut it short." She kissed Sadie lightly on the crown of her felt hat. "Good night," she said. "Is there anything I forgot to ask you about the apartment?"

"No," Sadie assured her. "You asked everything."

"Well, good night," said Harriet once again, and followed by Beryl, she left the room.

•

When Sadie awakened the next morning a feeling of dread still rested like a leaden weight on her chest. No sooner had she left the room than panic, like a small wing, started to beat

under her heart. She was inordinately fearful that if she
strayed any distance from the main lodge she would lose her
way and so arrive late for her meeting with Harriet. This fear
drove her to stand next to the souvenir booth fully an hour
ahead of time. Fortunately the booth, situated on a small
knoll, commanded an excellent view of the cataract, which
spilled down from some high rock ledges above a deep chasm.
A fancy bridge spanned this chasm only a few feet below her,
so that she was able to watch the people crossing it as they
walked back and forth between the camp site and the waterfall. An Indian chief in full war regalia was seated at the
bridge entrance on a kitchen chair. His magnificent feather
headdress curved gracefully in the breeze as he busied himself
collecting the small toll that all the tourists paid on returning
from the waterfall; he supplied them with change from a
nickel-plated conductor's belt which he wore over his deer-hide
jacket, embroidered with minute beads. He was an Irishman
employed by the management, which supplied his costume.
Lately he had grown careless, and often neglected to stain his
freckled hands the deep brick color of his face. He divided his
time between the bridge and the souvenir booth, clambering
up the knoll whenever he sighted a customer.

A series of wooden arches, Gothic in conception, succeeded
each other all the way across the bridge; bright banners flut-
tered from their rims, each one stamped with the initials of the
camp, and some of them edged with a glossy fringe. Only a few
feet away lay the dining terrace, a huge flagstone pavilion
whose entire length skirted the chasm's edge.

Unfortunately, neither the holiday crowds, nor the festooned bridge, nor even the white waters of the cataract across
the way could distract Sadie from her misery. She constantly
glanced behind her at the dark pine groves wherein Harriet's
cabin was concealed. She dreaded to see Harriet's shape define
itself between the trees, but at the same time she feared that if
her sister did not arrive shortly some terrible catastrophe

would befall them both before she'd had a chance to speak. In truth all desire to convince her sister that she should leave Camp Cataract and return to the apartment had miraculously shriveled away, and with the desire, the words to express it had vanished too. This did not in any way alter her intention of accomplishing her mission; on the contrary, it seemed to her all the more desperately important now that she was almost certain, in her innermost heart, that her trip was already a failure. Her attitude was not an astonishing one, since like many others she conceived of her life as separate from herself; the road was laid out always a little ahead of her by sacred hands, and she walked down it without a question. This road, which was her life, would go on existing after her death, even as her death existed now while she still lived.

There were close to a hundred people dining on the terrace, and the water's roar so falsified the clamor of voices that one minute the guests seemed to be speaking from a great distance and the next right at her elbow. Every now and then she thought she heard someone pronounce her name in a dismal tone, and however much she told herself that this was merely the waterfall playing its tricks on her ears she shuddered each time at the sound of her name. Her very position next to the booth began to embarrass her. She tucked her hands into her coat sleeves so that they would not show, and tried to keep her eyes fixed on the foaming waters across the way, but she had noticed a disapproving look in the eyes of the diners nearest her, and she could not resist glancing back at the terrace every few minutes in the hope that she had been mistaken. Each time, however, she was more convinced that she had read their expressions correctly, and that these people believed, not only that she was standing there for no good reason, but that she was a genuine vagrant who could not afford the price of a dinner. She was therefore immensely relieved when she caught sight of Harriet advancing between the tables from the far end of the dining pavilion. As she drew nearer, Sadie noticed that she was wearing her black winter coat trimmed with red fur, and that her marceled hair remained neatly arranged in spite of the strong wind. Much to her relief Harriet had omitted to rouge her cheeks and her face therefore had regained its natural proportions. She saw Harriet wave at the sight of her and quicken her step. Sadie was pleased that the diners were to witness the impending meeting. "When they see us together," she thought, "they'll realize that I'm no vagrant, but a decent woman visiting her sister." She herself started down the knoll to hasten the meeting. "I thought you'd come out of the pine grove," she called out, as soon as they were within a few feet of one another. "I kept looking that way."

"I would have ordinarily," Harriet answered, reaching her side and kissing her lightly on the cheek, "but I went to the other end of the terrace first, to reserve a table for us from the waiter in charge there. That end is quieter, so it will be more suitable for a long talk."

"Good," thought Sadie as they climbed up the knoll together. "Her night's sleep has done her a world of good." She studied Harriet's face anxiously as they paused next to the souvenir booth, and discovered a sweet light reflected in her eyes. All at once she remembered their childhood together and the great tenderness Harriet had often shown towards her then.

"They have Turkish pilaff on the menu," said Harriet, "so I told the waiter to save some for you. It's such a favorite that it usually runs out at the very beginning. I know how much you love it."

Sadie, realizing that Harriet was actually eager for this dinner, the only one they would eat together at Camp Cataract, to be a success, felt the terrible leaden weight lifted from her heart; it disappeared so suddenly that for a moment or two she was like a balloon without its ballast; she could barely refrain from dancing about in delight. Harriet tugged on her arm.

"I think we'd better go now," she urged Sadie, "then after lunch we can come back here if you want to buy some souvenirs for Evy and Bert . . . and maybe for Flo and Carl and Bobby too. . . ."

Sadie bent down to adjust her cotton stockings, which were wrinkling badly at the ankles, and when she straightened up again her eyes lighted on three men dining very near the edge of the terrace; she had not noticed them before. They were all eating corn on the cob and big round hamburger sandwiches in absolute silence. To protect their clothing from spattering kernels, they had converted their napkins into bibs.

"Bert Hoffer's careful of his clothes too," Sadie reflected, and then she turned to her sister. "Don't you think men look different sitting all by themselves without women?" she asked her. She felt an extraordinary urge to chat—an urge which she could not remember ever having experienced before.

"I think," Harriet replied, as though she had not heard Sadie's comment, "that we'd better go to our table before the waiter gives it to someone else."

"I don't like men," Sadie announced without venom, and she was about to follow Harriet when her attention was arrested by the eyes of the man nearest her. Slowly lowering his corn cob to his plate, he stared across at her, his mouth twisted into a bitter smile. She stood as if rooted to the ground, and under his steady gaze all her newborn joy rapidly drained away. With desperation she realized that Harriet, darting in and out between the crowded tables, would soon be out of sight. After making what seemed to her a superhuman effort she tore herself away from the spot where she stood and lunged after Harriet shouting her name.

Harriet was at her side again almost instantly, looking up at her with a startled expression. Together they returned to the souvenir booth, where Sadie stopped and assumed a slightly bent position as if she were suffering from an abdominal pain.

"What's the trouble?" she heard Harriet asking with concern. "Are you feeling ill?"

Instead of answering Sadie laid her hand heavily on her sister's arm and stared at her with a hunted expression in her eyes.

"Please try not to look so much like a gorilla," said Harriet in a kind voice, but Sadie, although she recognized the accuracy of this observation (for she could feel very well that she was looking like a gorilla), was powerless to change her expression, at least for a moment or two. "Come with me," she said finally, grabbing Harriet's hand and pulling her along with almost brutal force. "I've got something to tell you."

She headed down a narrow path leading into a thickly planted section of the grove, where she thought they were less likely to be disturbed. Harriet followed with such a quick, light step that Sadie felt no pull behind her at all and her sister's hand, folded in her own thick palm, seemed as delicate as the body of a bird. Finally they entered a small clearing where they stopped. Harriet untied a handkerchief from around her neck and mopped her brow. "Gracious!" she said. "It's frightfully hot in here." She offered the kerchief to Sadie. "I suppose it's because we walked so fast and because the pine trees shut out all the wind. . . . First I'll sit down and then you must tell me what's wrong." She stepped over to a felled tree whose length blocked the clearing. Its torn roots were shockingly exposed, whereas the upper trunk and branches lay hidden in the surrounding grove. Harriet sat down; Sadie was about to sit next to her when she noticed a dense swarm of flies near the roots. Automatically she stepped toward them. "Why are they here?" she asked herself—then immediately she spotted the cause, an open can of beans some careless person had deposited inside a small hollow at the base of the trunk. She turned away in disgust and looked at Harriet. Her sister was seated on the fallen tree, her back gracefully erect and her head tilted in a listening attitude. The filtered light imparted to her face an incredibly fragile and youthful look, and Sadie gazed at her with tenderness and wonder. No sound reached them in the clearing, and she realized with a pounding heart that she could no longer postpone telling Harriet why she had come. She could not have wished for a moment more favorable to the accomplishment of her purpose. The stillness in the air, their isolation, the expectant and gentle light in Harriet's eye, all these elements should have combined to give her back her faith—faith in her own powers to persuade Harriet to come home with her and live among them once again, winter and summer alike, as she had always done before. She opened her mouth to speak and doubled over, clutching at her stomach as though an animal were devouring her. Sweat beaded her fore-head and she planted her feet wide apart on the ground as if this animal would be born. Though her vision was barred with pain, she saw Harriet's tear-filled eyes, searching hers.

"Let's not go back to the apartment," Sadie said, hearing her own words as if they issued not from her mouth but from a pit in the ground. "Let's not go back there . . . let's you and me go out in the world . . . just the two of us." A second before covering her face to hide her shame Sadie glimpsed Harriet's eyes, impossibly close to her own, their pupils pointed with a hatred such as she had never seen before.

It seemed to Sadie that it was taking an eternity for her sister to leave. "Go away . . . go away . . . or I'll suffocate." She was moaning the words over and over again, her face buried deep in her hands. "Go away . . . please go away . . . I'll suffocate. . . ." She could not tell, however, whether she was thinking these words or speaking them aloud.

At last she heard Harriet's footstep on the dry branches, as she started out of the clearing. Sadie listened, but although one step followed another, the cracking sound of the dry branches did not grow any fainter as Harriet penetrated far-ther into the grove. Sadie knew then that this agony she was suffering was itself the dreaded voyage into the world—the very voyage she had always feared Harriet would make. That she herself was making it instead of Harriet did not affect her certainty that this was it.

•

Sadie stood at the souvenir booth looking at some birchbark canoes. The wind was blowing colder and stronger than it had a while ago, or perhaps it only seemed this way to her, so recently returned from the airless clearing. She did not recall her trip back through the grove; she was conscious only of her haste to buy some souvenirs and to leave. Some chains of paper tacked to the side of the booth as decoration kept flying into her face. The Indian chief was smiling at her from behind the counter of souvenirs.

"What can I do for you?" he asked.

"I'm leaving," said Sadie, "so I want souvenirs. . . ."

"Take your choice; you've got birchbark canoes with or without mailing cards attached, Mexican sombrero ashtrays, exhilarating therapeutic pine cushions filled with the regional needles . . . and banners for a boy's room."

"There's no boy home," Sadie said, having caught only these last words.

"How about cushions . . . or canoes?"

She nodded.

"Which do you want?"

"Both," she answered quickly.

"How many?"

Sadie closed her eyes. Try as she would she could not count up the members of the family. She could not even reach an approximate figure. "Eleven," she blurted out finally, in desperation.

"Eleven of each?" he asked raising his eyebrows.

"Yes . . . yes," she answered quickly, batting the paper chains out of her face, "eleven of each."

"You sure don't forget the old folks at home, do you?" he said, beginning to collect the canoes. He made an individual package of each souvenir and then wrapped them all together in coarse brown paper which he bound with thick twine.

Sadie had given him a note and he was punching his money belt for the correct change when her eyes fell on his light, freckled hand. Startled, she shifted her glance from his hand punching the nickel belt to his brick-colored face streaked with purple and vermilion paint. For the first time she noticed his Irish blue eyes. Slowly the hot flush of shame crept along the nape of her neck. It was the same unbearable mortification that she had experienced in the clearing; it spread upward from her neck to the roots of her hair, coloring her face a dark red. That she was ashamed for the Indian this time, and not of her own words, failed to lessen the intensity of her suffering; the boundaries of her pride had never been firmly fixed inside herself. She stared intently at his Irish blue eyes, so oddly light in his brick-colored face. What was it? She was tormented by the sight of an incongruity she couldn't name. All at once she remembered the pavilion and the people dining there; her heart started to pound. "They'll see it," she said to herself in a panic. "They'll see it and they'll know that I've seen it too." Somehow this latter possibility was the most perilous of all.

"They must never know I've seen it," she said, grinding her teeth, and she leaned over the counter, crushing some canoes under her chest. "Quickly," she whispered. "Go out your little door and meet me back of the booth. . . ."

A second later she found him there. "Listen!" She clutched his hand. "We must hurry . . . I didn't mean to see you . . . I'm sorry . . . I've been trying not to look at you for years . . . for years and years and years. . . ." She gaped at him in horror. "Why are you standing there? We've got to hurry. . . . They haven't caught me looking at you yet, but we've got to hurry." She headed for the bridge, leading the Indian behind her. He followed quickly without saying a word.

The water's roar increased in volume as they approached the opposite bank of the chasm, and Sadie found relief in the sound. Once off the bridge she ran as fast as she could along the path leading to the waterfall. The Indian followed close on her heels, his hand resting lightly in her own, as Harriet's had earlier when they'd sped together through the grove. Reaching the waterfall, she edged along the wall of rock until she stood directly behind the water's cascade. With a cry of delight she leaned back in the curve of the wall, insensible to its icy dampness, which penetrated even through the thickness of her woollen coat. She listened to the cataract's deafening roar and her heart almost burst for joy, because she had hidden the Indian safely behind the cascade where he could be neither seen nor heard. She turned around and smiled at him kindly. He too smiled, and she no longer saw in his face any trace of the incongruity that had shocked her so before.

The foaming waters were beautiful to see. Sadie stepped forward, holding her hand out to the Indian.

●

When Harriet awakened that morning all traces of her earlier victorious mood had vanished. She felt certain that disaster would overtake her before she could start out for Pocahontas Falls. Heavyhearted and with fumbling hands, she set about making her pack. Luncheon with Sadie was an impossible cliff which she did not have the necessary strength to scale. When she came to three round cushions that had to be snapped into their rainproof casings she gave up with a groan and rushed headlong out of her cabin in search of Beryl.

Fortunately Beryl waited table on the second shift and so she found her reading a magazine, with one leg flung over the arm of her chair.

"I can't make my pack," Harriet said hysterically, bursting into Beryl's cabin without even knocking at the door.

Beryl swung her leg around and got out of her chair, "I'll make your pack," she said in a calm voice, knocking some tobacco out of her pipe. "I would have come around this morning, but you said last night you wanted to make it alone."

"It's Sadie," Harriet complained. "It's that cursed lunch

with Sadie. I can't go through with it. I know I can't. I shouldn't have to in the first place. She's not even supposed to be here. . . . I'm an ass. . . ."

"To hell with sisters," said Beryl. "Give 'em all a good swift kick in the pants."

"She's going to stop me from going on my canoe trip . . . I know she is. . . ." Harriet had adopted the whining tone of a little girl.

"No, she isn't," said Beryl, speaking with authority.

"Why not?" Harriet asked. She looked at Beryl almost wistfully.

"She'd better not try anything . . ." said Beryl. "Ever hear of jujitsu?" She grunted with satisfaction. "Come on, we'll go make your pack." She was so pleased with Harriet's new state of dependency that she was rapidly overcoming her original shyness. An hour later she had completed the pack, and Harriet was dressed and ready.

"Will you go with me to the souvenir booth?" she begged the waitress. "I don't want to meet her alone." She was in a worse state of nerves than ever.

"I'll go with you," said Beryl, "but let's stop at my cabin on the way so I can change into my uniform. I'm on duty soon."

They were nearly twenty minutes late arriving at the booth, and Harriet was therefore rather surprised not to see Sadie standing there. "Perhaps she's been here and gone back to the lodge for a minute," she said to Beryl. "I'll find out." She walked up to the souvenir counter and questioned the Indian, with whom she was slightly familiar. "Was there a woman waiting here a while ago, Timothy?" she asked.

"A dark middle-aged woman?"

"That's right."

"She was here for an hour or more," he said, "never budged from this stall until about fifteen minutes ago."

"She couldn't have been here an hour!" Harriet argued. "Not my sister. . . . I told her one-thirty and it's not yet two."

"Then it wasn't your sister. The woman who was here stayed more than an hour, without moving. I noticed her because it was such a queer-looking thing. I noticed her first from my chair at the bridge and then when I came up here she was still standing by the booth. She must have stood here over an hour."

"Then it was a different middle-aged woman."

"That may be," he agreed, "but anyway, this one left about fifteen minutes ago. After standing all that time she turned around all of a sudden and bought a whole bunch of souvenirs from me . . . then just when I was punching my belt for the change she said something I couldn't understand—it sounded like Polish—and then she lit out for the bridge before I could give her a penny. That woman's got impulses," he added with a broad grin. "If she's your sister, I'll give you her change, in case she don't stop here on her way back. . . . But she sounded to me like a Polak."

"Beryl," said Harriet, "run across the bridge and see if Sadie's behind the waterfall. I'm sure this Polish woman wasn't Sadie, but they might both be back there. . . . If she's not there, we'll look in the lodge."

•

When Beryl returned her face was dead white; she stared at Harriet in silence, and even when Harriet finally grabbed hold of her shoulders and shook her hard, she would not say anything.

· A Day in the Open

In the outskirts of the capital there was a low white house, very much like the other houses around it. The street on which it stood was not paved, as this was a poor section of the city. The door of this particular house, very new and studded with nails, was bolted inside and out. A large room, furnished with some modern chromium chairs, a bar, and an electric record machine, opened onto the empty patio. A fat little Indian boy was seated in one of the chairs, listening to the tune *Good Night, Sweetheart,* which he had just chosen. It was playing at full volume and the little boy was staring very seriously ahead of him at the machine. This was one of the houses owned and run by Señor Kurten, who was half Spanish and half German.

It was a gray afternoon. In one of the bedrooms Julia and Inez had just awakened. Julia was small and monkey-like. She was appealing only because of her extraordinarily large and luminous eyes. Inez was tall and high-breasted. Her head was a bit too small for her body and her eyes were too close together. She wore her hair in stiff waves.

Julia was moaning on her bed.

"My stomach is worse today," she said to Inez. "Come over and feel it. The lump on the right side is bigger." She twisted her head on the pillow and sighed. Inez was staring sternly into space.

"No," she said to Julia. "I cannot bear to feel that lump. *Santa María!* With something like that inside me I should go wild." She made a wry face and shuddered.

"You must not feel it if you do not want to," said Julia drowsily. Inez poured herself some *guaro*. She was a heavy drinker but her vitality remained unimpaired, although her skin often broke out in pimples. She ate violet lozenges to cover the smell of liquor on her breath and often popped six or seven of them into her mouth at once. Being full of enterprise she often made more money outside the whorehouse than she did at her regular job.

Julia was Mexican and a great favorite with the men, who enjoyed feeling that they were endangering her very life by going to bed with her.

"Well," said Inez, "I think that this afternoon I will go to the movies, if you will lend me a pair of your stockings. You had better lie here in your bed. I would sit here with you but it makes me feel very strange now to stay in this room. It is peculiar because, you know, I am a very calm woman and have suffered a great deal since I was born. You should go to a doctor," she added.

"I cannot bear to be out in the street," said Julia. "The sun is too hot and the wind is too cold. The smell of the market makes me feel sick, although I have known it all my life. No sooner have I walked a few blocks than I must find some park to sit in, I am so tired. Then somebody comes and tries to sell me orchids and I buy them. I have been out three times this week and each time I have bought some flowers. Now you know I can't afford to do this, but I am so weak and ill that I am becoming more like my grandmother every day. She had a feeling that she was not wanted here on this earth, either by God or by other people, so she never felt that she could refuse anyone anything."

"Well, if you are going to become like your grandmother," said Inez, "it will be a sad mistake. I should forget this sort of thing. You'll get to the doctor. Meanwhile, sit in the sun more. I don't want to be unkind. . . ."

"No, no. You are not unkind," Julia protested.

"You sit in this dark room all day long even when there is sun and you do not feel so sick."

Julia was feeling more desperately lonely than she had ever felt before in her life. She patted her heart. Suddenly the door pushed open and Señor Kurten came into the room. He was a slight man with a low forehead and a long nose.

"Julia and Inez," he said. "Señor Ramirez just telephoned that he is coming over this afternoon with a friend. He is going to take you both out to the country on a picnic and you are to hurry up and be ready. Try to bring them back to the bar in the evening."

"Hans," said Julia. "I am sick. I can't see Señor Ramirez or anyone else."

"Well, you know I can't do anything if he wants to see you. If he was angry he could make too much trouble. I am sorry." Señor Kurten left the room, closing the door slowly behind him.

"He is so important," said Inez, rubbing some eau de cologne over Julia's forehead. "So important, poor child. You must go." Her hand was hard and dry.

"Inez—" Julia clutched at Inez's kimono just as she was walking away. She struggled out of bed and threw herself into the arms of her friend. Inez was obliged to brace herself against the foot of the bed to keep from being knocked over.

"Don't make yourself crazy," said Inez to Julia, but then

Inez began to cry; the sound was high like the squeal of a pig.

"Inez," said Julia. "Get dressed and don't cry. I feel better, my little baby."

They went into the bar and sat down to await the arrival of Señor Ramirez and his friend. Julia's arm was flung over the side of the chair, and her purse was swinging from her hand on an unusually long strap. She had put a little red dot in the corner of each eye, and rouged her cheeks very highly.

"You don't look very good," said Inez. "I'm afraid in my heart for you."

Julia opened her eyes wide and stared fixedly ahead of her at the wall. The Indian boy was polishing a very large alarm clock with care.

Soon Señor Ramirez stuck his head through the doorway. He had a German face but there was something very Spanish in the angle of his slouched fedora hat. His mustaches were blond and abundant. He had just shaved, and the talcum powder was visible on his chin and on his cheeks. He wore a pink shirt and a light tweed jacket, and on the fourth finger of each hand a heavy gold ring studded with a jewel.

"Come on, daughters," he said. "The car is waiting outside, with my friend. Move along."

Señor Ramirez drove very quickly. Julia and Inez sat uncomfortably on the edge of the back seat, hanging onto the straps at the side.

"We are going on a picnic," shouted Señor Ramirez. "I've brought with me five bottles of champagne. They are in the back of the car and they were all packed in ice by my cook. There is no reason why we should not have everything we want with us. They are inside a basket in the back. She wrapped the ice in a towel. That way it doesn't melt so quickly, but still we have to get there in a pretty short time. I drink nothing but American whiskey, so I brought along a quart of it for myself. What do you think of that?"

"Oh, how nice," said Julia.

"I think we shall have a wonderful time," said Inez.

Señor Ramirez's friend Alfredo looked ill and disgruntled. He did not say anything himself, nor did the angle of his head indicate that he was listening to a word that anyone else was saying.

It was a cold day and the parasols under which the policemen stood were flapping in the wind. They passed a new yellow brick building, high at the top of six or seven flights of yellow brick steps.

"That is going to be a new museum," said Señor Ramirez. "When it opens we are all going to have a big dinner there together. Everyone there will be an old friend of mine. That's nothing. I can have dinner with fifty people every night of my life."

"A life of fiesta," put in Inez.

"Even more than that. They are more than just fiestas," he said, without quite knowing what he meant himself.

The sun was shining into Julia's lap. She felt lightheaded and feverish. Señor Ramirez turned the radio on as loud as he could. They were broadcasting *Madame Butterfly* as the car reached the outskirts of the city.

"I have three radios at home," said Señor Ramirez.

"Ah," said Inez. "One for the morning, one for the night and one for the afternoon." Julia listened to Inez with interest and wonder. They were on the edge of a deep ravine, going round a curve in the road. The mountainside across the ravine was in the shade, and some Indians were climbing toward the summit.

"Walk, walk, walk . . ." said Julia mournfully. "Oh, how tired it makes me feel to watch them."

Inez pinched her friend's arm. "Listen," she whispered to her. "You are not in your room. You daren't say things like that. You must not speak of being tired. It's no fun for them. They wouldn't like it."

"We'll be coming to that picnic spot in a minute," said

Señor Ramirez. "Nobody knows where it is but me. I like to
have a spot, you know, where all my friends won't come and
disturb me. Alfredo," he added, "are you hungry?"

"I don't think this Alfredo is very nice, do you?" Inez asked
very softly of Julia.

"Oh, yes," said Julia, for she was not quick to detect a mean
nature in anybody, being altogether kind and charitable herself. At last, after driving through a path wide enough for only
one car, they arrived at the picnic spot. It was a fair-sized clearing in a little forest. Not far from it, at the bottom of a hill,
was a little river and a waterfall. They got out and listened to
the noise of the water. Both of the women were delighted with
the sound.

"Since it is so sunny out, ladies," said Señor Ramirez, "I am
going to walk around in my underpants. I hope that my friend
will do the same if he wants to."

"What a lucky thing for us," said Inez in a strident voice.
"The day begins right." Señor Ramirez undressed and slipped
on a pair of tennis shoes. His legs were very white and freckled.

"Now I will give you some champagne right away," he said
to them, a little out of breath because he had struggled so
quickly out of his clothes. He went over to where he had laid
the basket and took from it a champagne bottle. On his way
back he stumbled over a rock; the bottle fell from his hand and
was smashed in many pieces. For a moment his face clouded
over and he looked as though he were about to lose his temper;
instead, seizing another bottle from the basket, he flung it high
into the air, almost over the tops of the trees. He returned
elated to his friends.

"A gentleman," he said, "always knows how to make fun. I
am one of the richest businessmen in this country. I am also
the craziest. Like an American. When I am out I always have a
wonderful time, and so does everyone who is with me, because
they know that while I am around there is always plenty.
Plenty to eat, plenty to drink, and plenty of beautiful women

to make love to. Once you have been out with me," he pointed his finger at Julia and Inez, "any other man will seem to you like an old-lady schoolteacher."

He turned to Alfredo. "Tell me, my friend, have you not had the time of your life with me?"

"Yes, I have," said Alfredo. He was thinking very noticeably of other things.

"His mind is always on business," Señor Ramirez explained to Julia. "He is also very clever. I have gotten him this job with a German concern. They are manufacturing planes." Alfredo said something to Señor Ramirez in German, and they spoke no longer on the subject. They spread out their picnic lunch and sat down to eat.

Señor Ramirez insisted on feeding Julia with his own fingers. This rather vexed Inez, so she devoted herself to eating copiously. Señor Ramirez drank quantities of whiskey out of a tin folding cup. At the end of fifteen or twenty minutes he was already quite drunk.

"Now, isn't it wonderful to be all together like this, friends? Alfredo, aren't these two women the finest, sweetest women in the world? I do not understand why in the eyes of God they should be condemned to the fires of hell for what they are. Do you?"

Julia moaned and rose to her feet.

"No, no!" she said, looking up helplessly at the branches overhead.

"Come on," said Señor Ramirez. "We're not going to worry about this today, are we?" He took hold of her wrist and pulled her down to the ground beside him. Julia hid her face in her hands and leaned her head against his shoulder. Soon she was smiling up at him and stroking his face.

"You won't leave me alone?" she asked, laughing a little in an effort to bring him to terms with her. If anyone were to be pitted successfully against the Divine, she thought, it would certainly be someone like Señor Ramirez. The presence of such

men is often enough to dispel fear from the hearts of certain
people for whom God is more of an enemy than a friend. Señor
Ramirez's principal struggle in life was one of pride rather
than of conscience; and because his successes were numerous
each day, replenishing his energy and his taste for life, his
strength was easily felt by those around him. Now that he was
near her, Julia felt that she was safe from hell, and she was
quite happy even though her side still hurt her very badly.

"Now," said Inez, "I think that we should all play a game, to
chase gloomy thoughts out of this girl's head."

She rose to her feet and snatched Señor Ramirez's hat from
where it lay beside him on the ground, placing it a few feet
away upside down on the grass. Then she gathered some acorns
in the picnic basket.

"Now," she said. "We will see who can throw these acorns
into the hat. He will win."

"I think," said Señor Ramirez, "that the two women should
be naked while we are playing this; otherwise it will be just a
foolish children's game."

"And we are not children at all," said Inez, winking at him.
The two women turned and looked at Alfredo questioningly.

"Oh, don't mind him," said Señor Ramirez. "He sees nothing but numbers in his head."

The two girls went behind some bushes and undressed.
When they returned, Alfredo was bending over a ledger and
trying to explain something to Señor Ramirez, who looked up,
delighted that they had returned so quickly, so that he would
not be obliged to listen.

"Ah," he said. "Now this looks much more like friends together, doesn't it, Alfredo?"

"Come on," said Inez. "We will all get into line here with
this basket and each one will try to throw the acorn into the
hat."

Señor Ramirez grew quite excited playing the game; then he
began to get angry because he never managed to get the acorn

into the hat. Inez screeched with laughter and threw her acorn wider and wider of the mark, each time purposely, in order to soothe, if possible, the hurt pride of Señor Ramirez. Alfredo refused to play at all.

"Games don't interest me," said Señor Ramirez suddenly. "I'd like to play longer with you, daughters, but I can't honestly keep my mind on the game."

"It is of no importance at all, really," said Inez, busily trying to think up something to do next.

"How are your wife and children?" Julia asked him.

Inez bit her lip and shook her head.

"They are well taken care of. I have sent them to a little town where they are staying in a pension. Quiet women—all three of them—the little girls and the mother. I am going to sleep." He stretched out under a tree and put his hat over his face. Alfredo was absorbed in his ledger. Inez and Julia sat side by side and waited.

"You have the brain of a baby chicken," Inez said to Julia. "I must think for both of us. If I had not had a great deal of practice when I had to keep count of all the hundreds of tortillas that I sold for my mother, I don't know where we would be."

"Dead, probably," said Julia. They began to feel cold.

"Come," said Inez. "Sing with me." They sang a song about leaving and never returning, four or five times through. When Señor Ramirez awakened he suggested to Julia that they go for a walk. She accepted sweetly, and so they started off through the woods. Soon they reached a good-sized field where Señor Ramirez suggested that they sit for a while.

"The first time I went to bed with a woman," he said, "it was in the country like this. The land belonged to my father. Three or four times a day we would come out into the fields and make love. She loved it, and would have come more often if I had asked her to. Some years later I went to her wedding and I had a terrible fight there. I don't even remember who the man was, but in the end he was badly hurt. I can tell you that."

"If you put your arms around me," said Julia, "I will feel less cold. You don't mind my asking you to do this, but I love you very much and I feel very contented with you."

"That's good," said Señor Ramirez, looking off at the mountains and shielding his eyes from the sun. He was listening to the sound of the waterfall, which was louder here. Julia was laughing and touching various parts of his body.

"Ah," she said. "I don't mind my side hurting me so badly if I can only be happy the way I am now with you. You are so sweet and so wonderful."

He gave her a quick loud kiss on the mouth and rose to his feet.

"Listen," he said. "Wouldn't you like to come into the water with me?"

"I am too sick a woman to go into the water, and I am a little bit afraid."

"In my arms you don't have to be afraid. I will carry you. The current would be too strong for you to manage anyway." Señor Ramirez was now as gay as a lark, although he had been bored but a moment before. He liked nothing better than performing little feats that were assured of success from the beginning. He carried her down to the river, singing at the top of his voice.

The noise of the falls was very loud here, and Julia clung tightly to her escort.

"Don't let go, now," she said. But her voice seemed to fly away behind her like a ribbon caught in the wind. They were in the water and Señor Ramirez began to walk in the direction of the falls.

"I will hold tight, all right," he said. "Because the water runs pretty swiftly near the falls." He seemed to enjoy stepping precariously from one stone to another with Julia in his arms.

"This is not so easy, you know. This is damned hard. The

stones are slippery." Julia tightened her grip around his neck
and kissed him quickly all over his face.

"If I let you go," he said, "the current would carry you along
like a leaf over the falls, and then one of those big rocks would
make a hole in your head. That would be the end, of course."
Julia's eyes widened with horror, and she yelled with the sud-
denness of an animal just wounded.

"But why do you scream like that, Julia? I love you, sweetheart." He had had enough of struggling through the water,
and so he turned around and started back.

"Are we going away from the waterfall?"

"Yes. It was wonderful, wasn't it?"

"Very nice," she said.

He grew increasingly careless as the current slackened, with
the result that he miscalculated and his foot slipped between
two stones. This threw him off his balance and he fell. He was
unhurt, but the back of Julia's head had hit a stone. It started
to bleed profusely. He struggled to his feet and carried her to
the riverbank. She was not sure that she was not dying, and
hugged him all the more closely. Pulling her along, he walked
quickly up the hill and back through the woods to where Inez
and Alfredo were still sitting.

"It will be all right, won't it?" she asked him a bit weakly.

"Those damn rocks were slippery," he growled. He was
sulky, and eager to be on his way home.

"Oh, God of mine!" lamented Inez, when she saw what had
happened. "What a sad ending for a walk! Terrible things always happen to Julia. She is a daughter of misfortune. It's a
lucky thing that I am just the contrary."

Señor Ramirez was in such a hurry to leave the picnic spot
that he did not even want to bother to collect the various baskets and plates he had brought with him. They dressed, and he
yelled for them all to get into the car. Julia wrapped a shawl
around her bleeding head. Inez went around snatching up all
the things, like an enraged person.

"Can I have these things?" she asked her host. He nodded his head impatiently. Julia was by now crying rhythmically like a baby that has almost fallen asleep.

The two women sat huddled together in the back of the car. Inez explained to Julia that she was going to make presents of the plates and baskets to her family. She shed a tear or two herself. When they arrived at the house, Señor Ramirez handed some banknotes to Inez from where he was sitting.

"*Adios,*" he said. The two women got out of the car and stood in the street.

"Will you come back again?" Julia asked him tenderly, ceasing to cry for a moment.

"Yes, I'm coming back again," he said. "*Adios.*" He pressed his foot on the accelerator and drove off.

The bar was packed with men. Inez led Julia around through the patio to their room. When she had shut the door, she slipped the banknotes into her pocket and put the baskets on the floor.

"Do you want any of these baskets?" she asked.

Julia was sitting on the edge of her bed, looking into space. "No, thank you," she said. Inez looked at her, and saw that she was far away.

"Señor Ramirez gave me four drinking cups made out of plastic," said Inez. "Do you want one of them for yourself?"

Julia did not answer right away. Then she said: "Will he come back?"

"I don't know," Inez said. "I'm going to the movies. I'll come and see you afterwards, before I go into the bar."

"All right," said Julia. But Inez knew that she did not care. She shrugged her shoulders and went out through the door, closing it behind her.

· A Quarreling Pair

The two puppets are sisters in their early fifties. The puppet stage should have a rod or string dividing it down the middle to indicate two rooms. One puppet is seated on each side of the dividing line. If it is not possible to seat them they will have to stand. Harriet, the older puppet, is stronger-looking and wears brighter colors.

HARRIET (*The stronger puppet*)   I hope you are beginning to think about our milk.

RHODA (*After a pause*)   Well, I'm not.

HARRIET   Now what's the matter with you? You're not going to have a visitation from our dead, are you?

RHODA   I don't have visitations this winter because I'm too
tired to love even our dead. Anyway, I'm disgusted with
the world.

HARRIET   Just mind your business. I mind mine and I *am*
thinking about our milk.

RHODA   I'm so tired of being sad. I'd like to change.

HARRIET   You don't get enough enjoyment out of your
room. Why don't you?

RHODA   Oh, because the world and its sufferers are always on
my mind.

HARRIET   That's not normal. You're not smart enough to be
of any use to the outside, anyway.

RHODA   If I were young I'd succor the sick. I wouldn't care
about culture, even, if I were young.

HARRIET   You don't have any knack for making a home.
There's blessed satisfaction in that, at any rate.

RHODA   My heart's too big to make a home.

HARRIET   No. It's because you have no self-sufficiency. If I
wasn't around, you wouldn't have the leisure to worry.
You're a lost soul, when I'm not around. You don't even
have the pep to worry about the outside when I'm not
around. Not that the outside loses by that! (*She sniffs
with scorn.*)

RHODA   You're right. But I swear that my heart is big.

HARRIET I've come to believe that what is inside of people is not so very interesting. You can breed considerable discontent around you with a big heart, and considerable harmony with a small one. Compare your living quarters to mine. And my heart is small like Papa's was.

RHODA You chill me to the marrow when you tell me that your heart is small. You do love me, though, don't you?

HARRIET You're my sister, aren't you?

RHODA Sisterly love is one of the few boons in this life.

HARRIET Now, that's enough exaggerating. I could enumerate other things.

RHODA I suppose it's wicked to squeeze love from a small heart. I suppose it's a sin. I suppose God meant for small hearts to be busy with other things.

HARRIET Possibly. Let's have our milk in my room. It's so much more agreeable to sit in here. Partly because I'm a neater woman than you are.

RHODA Even though you have a small heart, I wish there were no one but you and me in the world. Then I would never feel that I had to go among the others.

HARRIET Well, I wish I could hand you my gift for contentment in a box. It would be so lovely if you were like me. Then we could have our milk in *either* room. One day in your room and the next day in mine.

RHODA I'm sure that's the sort of thing that never happens.

HARRIET   It happens in a million homes, seven days a week. I'm the type that's in the majority.

RHODA   Never, never, never . . .

HARRIET   (*Very firmly*)   It happens in a million homes.

RHODA   *Never, never, never!*

HARRIET   (*Rising*)   Are you going to listen to me when I tell you that it happens in a million homes, or must I lose my temper?

RHODA   You have already lost it.   (HARRIET *exits rapidly in a rage.* RHODA *goes to the chimes and sings*)

> My horse was frozen like a stone
> A long, long time ago.
> Frozen near the flower bed
> In the wintry sun.
> Or maybe in the night time
> Or maybe not at all.
>
> My horse runs across the fields
> On many afternoons.
> Black as dirt and filled with blood
> I glimpse him fleeing toward the woods
> And then not at all.

HARRIET   (*Offstage*)   I'm coming with your milk, and I hope the excitement is over for today.   (*Enters, carrying two small white glasses*)   Oh, why do I bring milk to a person who is dead-set on making my life a real hell?

RHODA   (*Clasping her hands with feeling*)   Yes, Why? Why? Why? Why? Oh, what a hideous riddle!

HARRIET You love to pretend that everything is a riddle. You think that's the way to be intellectual. There is no riddle. I am simply keeping up my end of the bargain.

RHODA Oh, bargains, bargains, bargains!

HARRIET Will you let me finish, you excitable thing? I'm trying to explain that I'm behaving the way I was molded to behave. I happen to be appreciative of the mold I was cast in, and neither heaven, nor earth is going to make me damage it. Your high-strung emotions are not going to affect me. Here's your milk.

> (*She enters* RHODA'S *side of the stage and hands her the milk, but* RHODA *punches the bottom of the glass with her closed fist and sends it flying out of* HARRIET'S *hand.* HARRIET *deals* RHODA *a terrific blow on the face and scurries back to her own room. There is silence for a moment. Then* HARRIET *buries her face in her hands and weeps.* RHODA *exits and* HARRIET *goes to the chimes and sings.*)

HARRIET (*Singing*)

> I dreamed I climbed upon a cliff,
> My sister's hand in mine.
> Then searched the valley for my house
> But only sunny fields could see
> And the church spire shining.
> I searched until my heart was cold
> But only sunny fields could see
> And the church spire shining.
> A girl ran down the mountainside
> With bluebells in her hat.
> I asked the valley for her name
> But only wind and rain could hear
> And the church bell tolling.
> I asked until my lips were cold
> But wakened not yet knowing
> If the name she bore was my sister's name
> Or if it was my own.

HARRIET   Rhoda?

RHODA   What do you want?

HARRIET   Go away if you like.

RHODA   The moment hasn't come yet, and it won't come to-day because the day is finished and the evening is here. Thank God!

HARRIET   I know I should get some terrible disease and die if I thought I did not live in the right. It would break my heart.

RHODA   You do live in the right, sweetie, so don't think about it. (*Pause*)   I'll go and get your milk.

HARRIET   I'll go too. But let's drink it in here because it really *is* much pleasanter in here, isn't it? (*They rise*) Oh, I'm so glad the evening has come! I'm nervously exhausted. (*They exit*)

· A Stick of Green Candy

The clay pit had been dug in the side of a long hill. By leaning back against the lower part of its wall, Mary could see the
curved highway above her and the cars speeding past. On the
other side of the highway the hill continued rising, but at a
steeper angle. If she tilted her head farther back, she could
glimpse the square house on the hill's summit, with its flight of
stone steps that led from the front door down to the curb, dividing the steep lawn in two.

She had been playing in the pit for a long time. Like many
other children, she fancied herself at the head of a regiment; at
the same time, she did not join in any neighborhood games,
preferring to play all alone in the pit, which lay about a mile
beyond the edge of town. She was a scrupulously clean child
with a strong, immobile face and long, well-arranged curls.
Sometimes when she went home toward evening there were

traces of clay on her dark coat, even though she had worked diligently with the brush she carried along every afternoon. She despised untidiness, and she feared that the clay might betray her headquarters, which she suspected the other children of planning to invade.

One afternoon she stumbled and fell on the clay when it was still slippery and wet from a recent rainfall. She never failed to leave the pit before twilight, but this time she decided to wait until it was dark so that her sullied coat would attract less attention. Wisely she refrained from using her brush on the wet clay.

Having always left the pit at an earlier hour, she felt that an explanation was due to her soldiers; to announce simply that she had fallen down was out of the question. She knew that her men trusted her and would therefore accept in good faith any reason she chose to give them for this abrupt change in her day's routine, but convincing herself was a more difficult task. She never told them anything until she really believed what she was going to say. After concentrating a few minutes, she summoned them with a bugle call.

"Men," she began, once they were lined up at attention, "I'm staying an hour longer today than usual, so I can work on the mountain goat maneuvers. I explained mountain-goat fighting last week, but I'll tell you what it is again. It's a special technique used in the mountains around big cliffs. No machine can do mountain-goat fighting. We're going to specialize." She paused. "Even though I'm staying, I want you to go right ahead and have your recreation hour as usual, like you always do the minute I leave. I have total respect for your recreation, and I know you fight as hard as you play."

She dismissed them and walked up to her own headquarters in the deepest part of the pit. At the end of the day the color of the red pit deepened; then, after the sun had sunk behind the hill, the clay lost its color. She began to feel cold and a little uneasy. She was so accustomed to leaving her men each day at the same hour, just before they thronged into the gymnasium, that now lingering on made her feel like an intruder.

It was almost night when she climbed out of the pit. She glanced up at the hilltop house and then started down toward the deserted lower road. When she reached the outskirts of town she chose the darkest streets so that the coat would be less noticeable. She hated the thick pats of clay that were embedded in its wool; moreover she was suffering from a sense of inner untidiness as a result of the unexpected change in her daily routine. She walked along slowly, scuffing her heels, her face wearing the expression of a person surfeited with food. Far underneath her increasingly lethargic mood lurked a feeling of apprehension; she knew she would be reprimanded for returning home after dark, but she never would admit either the possibility of punishment or the fear of it. At this period she was rapidly perfecting a psychological mechanism which enabled her to forget, for long stretches of time, that her parents existed.

She found her father in the vestibule hanging his coat up on a peg. Her heart sank as he turned around to greet her. Without seeming to, he took in the pats of clay at a glance, but his shifting eyes never alighted candidly on any object.

"You've been playing in that pit below the Speed house again," he said to her. "From now on, I want you to play at the Kinsey Memorial Grounds." Since he appeared to have nothing to say, she started away, but immediately he continued. "Some day you may have to live in a town where the administration doesn't make any provision for children at all. Or it may provide you with a small plot of land and a couple of dinky swings. There's a very decent sum goes each year to the grounds here. They provide you with swings, seesaws and chin bars." He glanced furtively at her coat. "Tomorrow," he said, "I drive past that pit on my way out to Sam's. I'll draw up to

the edge of the road and look down. See that you're over at the
Memorial Grounds with the other children."

Mary never passed the playgrounds without quickening her
step. This site, where the screams of several dozen children
mingled with the high, grinding sound of the moving swings,
she had always automatically hated. It was the antithesis of her
clay pit and the well-ordered barracks inside it.

When she went to bed, she was in such a state of wild excitement that she was unable to sleep. It was the first time that her
father's observations had not made her feel either humiliated
or ill. The following day after school she set out for the pit. As
she was climbing the long hill (she always approached her barracks from the lower road), she slackened her pace and stood
still. All at once she had had the fear that by looking into her
eyes the soldiers might divine her father's existence. To each
one of them she was like himself—a man without a family.
After a minute she resumed her climb. When she reached the
edge of the pit, she put both feet together and jumped inside.

"Men," she said, once she had blown the bugle and made a
few routine announcements, "I know you have hard muscles in
your legs. But how would you like to have even harder ones?"
It was a rhetorical question to which she did not expect an
answer. "We're going to have hurdle races and plain running
every day now for two hours."

Though in her mind she knew dimly that this intensified
track training was preparatory to an imminent battle on the
Memorial playgrounds, she did not dare discuss it with her
men, or even think about it too precisely herself. She had to
avoid coming face to face with an impossibility.

"As we all know," she continued, "we don't like to have
teams because we've been through too much on the battlefield
all together. Every day I'll divide you up fresh before the racing, so that the ones who are against each other today, for instance, will be running on the same side tomorrow. The men

in our outfit are funny about taking sides against each other, even just in play and athletics. The other outfits in this country don't feel the same as we do."

She dug her hands into her pockets and hung her head sheepishly. She was fine now, and certain of victory. She could feel the men's hearts bursting with love for her and with pride in their regiment. She looked up—a car was rounding the bend, and as it came nearer she recognized it as her father's.

"Men," she said in a clear voice, "you can do what you want for thirty minutes while I make out the racing schedule and the team lists." She stared unflinchingly at the dark blue sedan and waited with perfect outward calm for her father to slow down; she was still waiting after the car had curved out of sight. When she realized that he was gone, she held her breath. She expected her heart to leap for joy, but it did not.

•

"Now I'll go to my headquarters," she announced in a flat voice. "I'll be back with the team lists in twenty-five minutes." She glanced up at the highway; she felt oddly disappointed and uneasy. A small figure was descending the stone steps on the other side of the highway. It was a boy. She watched in amazement; she had never seen anyone come down these steps before. Since the highway had replaced the old country road, the family living in the hilltop house came and went through the back door.

Watching the boy, she felt increasingly certain that he was on his way down to the pit. He stepped off the curb after looking prudently for cars in each direction; then he crossed the highway and clambered down the hill. Just as she had expected him to, when he reached the edge of the pit he seated himself on the ground and slid into it, smearing his coat—dark like her own—with clay.

"It's a big clay pit," he said, looking up at her. He was

younger than she, but he looked straight into her eyes without a trace of shyness. She knew he was a stranger in town; she had never seen him before. This made him less detestable, nonetheless she had to be rid of him shortly because the men were expecting her back with the team lists.

"Where do you come from?" she asked him.

"From inside that house." He pointed at the hilltop.

"Where do you live when you're not visiting?"

"I live inside that house," he repeated, and he sat down on the floor of the pit.

"Sit on the orange crate," she ordered him severely. "You don't pay any attention to your coat."

He shook his head. She was exasperated with him because he was untidy, and he had lied to her. She knew perfectly well that he was merely a visitor in the hilltop house.

"Why did you come out this door?" she asked, looking at him sharply. "The people in that house go out the back. It's level there and they've got a drive."

"I don't know why," he answered simply.

"Where do you come from?" she asked again.

"That's my house." He pointed to it as if she were asking him for the first time. "The driveway in back's got gravel in it. I've got a whole box of it in my room. I can bring it down."

"No gravel's coming in here that belongs to a liar," she interrupted him. "Tell me where you come from and then you can go get it."

He stood up. "I live in that big house up there," he said calmly. "From my room I can see the river, the road down there and the road up here, and this pit and you."

"It's not your room!" she shouted angrily. "You're a visitor there. I was a visitor last year at my aunt's."

"Good-bye."

He was climbing out of the pit. Once outside he turned around and looked down at her. There was an expression of fulfillment on his face.

"I'll bring the gravel some time soon," he said.

She watched him crossing the highway. Then automatically she climbed out of the pit.

She was mounting the tedious stone steps behind him. Her jaw was clamped shut, and her face had gone white with anger. He had not turned around once to look at her. As they were nearing the top it occurred to her that he would rush into the house and slam the door in her face. Hurriedly she climbed three steps at once so as to be directly behind him. When he opened the door, she pushed across the threshold with him; he did not seem to notice her at all. Inside the dimly lit vestibule the smell of fresh paint was very strong. After a few seconds her eyes became more accustomed to the light, and she saw that the square room was packed solid with furniture. The boy was already pushing his way between two identical bureaus which stood back to back. The space between them was so narrow that she feared she would not be able to follow him. She looked around frantically for a wider artery, but seeing that there was none, she squeezed between the bureaus, pinching her flesh painfully, until she reached a free space at the other end. Here the furniture was less densely packed—in fact, three armchairs had been shoved together around an uncluttered area, wide enough to provide leg room for three people, providing they did not mind a tight squeeze. To her left a door opened on to total darkness. She expected him to rush headlong out of the room into the dark in a final attempt to escape her, but to her astonishment he threaded his way carefully in the opposite direction until he reached the circle of chairs. He entered it and sat down in one of them. After a second's hesitation, she followed his example.

The chair was deeper and softer than any she had ever sat in before. She tickled the thick velvet arms with her fingertips. Here and there, they grazed a stiff area where the nap had worn thin. The paint fumes were making her eyes smart, and she was beginning to feel apprehensive. She had forgotten to consider that grown people would probably be in the house, but now she gazed uneasily into the dark space through the open door opposite her. It was cold in the vestibule, and despite her woollen coat she began to shiver.

"If he would tell me now where he comes from," she said to herself, "then I could go away before anybody else came." Her anger had vanished, but she could not bring herself to speak aloud, or even to turn around and look at him. He sat so still that it was hard for her to believe he was actually beside her in his chair.

Without warning, the dark space opposite her was lighted up. Her heart sank as she stared at a green wall, still shiny with wet paint. It hurt her eyes. A woman stepped into the visible area, her heels sounding on the floorboards. She was wearing a print dress and over it a long brown sweater which obviously belonged to a man.

"Are you there, Franklin?" she called out, and she walked into the vestibule and switched on a second light. She stood still and looked at him.

"I thought I heard you come in," she said. Her voice was flat, and her posture at that moment did not inspire Mary with respect. "Come to visit Franklin?" she asked, as if suddenly aware that her son was not alone. "I think I'll visit for a while." She advanced toward them. When she reached the circle she squeezed in and sat opposite Mary.

"I hoped we'd get a visitor or two while we were here," she said to her. "That's why I arranged this little sitting place. All the rest of the rooms are being painted, or else they're still too smelly for visiting. Last time we were here we didn't see anyone for the whole two weeks. But he was a baby then. I thought maybe this time he'd contact when he went out. He goes out a lot of the day." She glanced at her son. "You've got some dirt on that chair," she remarked in a tone which did not express the slightest disapproval. She turned back to Mary. "I'd rather have a girl than a boy," she said. "There's nothing much I can discuss with a boy. A grown woman isn't interested in the same things a boy is interested in." She scratched a place below her shoulder blades. "My preference is discussing furnishings. Always has been. I like that better than I like discussing styles. I'll discuss styles if the company wants to, but I don't enjoy it nearly so well. The only thing about furnishings that leaves me cold is curtains. I never was interested in curtains, even when I was young. I like lamps about the best. Do you?"

Mary was huddling as far back into her chair as she could, but even so, without drawing her legs up and sitting on her feet, it was impossible to avoid physical contact with the woman, whose knees lightly touched hers every time she shifted a little in her chair. Inwardly, too, Mary shrank from her. She had never before been addressed so intimately by a grown person. She closed her eyes, seeking the dark gulf that always had separated her from the adult world. And she clutched the seat cushion hard, as if she were afraid of being wrenched from the chair.

"We came here six years ago," the woman continued, "when the Speeds had their house painted, and now they're having it painted again, so we're here again. They can't be in the house until it's good and dry because they've both got nose trouble— both the old man and the old lady—but we're not related. Only by marriage. I'm a kind of relative to them, but not enough to be really classed as a relative. Just enough so that they'd rather have me come and look after the house than a stranger. They gave me a present of money last time, but this time it'll be clothes for the boy. There's nothing to boys' clothes really. They don't mean anything."

She sighed and looked around her.

"Well," she said, "we would like them to ask us over here more often than they do. Our town is way smaller than this, way smaller, but you can get all the same stuff there that you can here, if you've got the money to pay. I mean groceries and clothing and appliances. We've got all that. As soon as the walls are dry we go back. Franklin doesn't want to. He don't like his home because he lives in an apartment; it's in the business section. He sits in a lot and don't go out and contact at all."

The light shone through Mary's tightly closed lids. In the chair next to her there was no sound of a body stirring. She opened her eyes and looked down. His ankles were crossed and his feet were absolutely still.

"Franklin," the woman said, "get some candy for me and the girl."

When he had gone she turned to Mary. "He's not a rough boy like the others," she said. "I don't know what I'd do if he was one of the real ones with all the trimmings. He's got some girl in him, thank the Lord. I couldn't handle one of the real ones."

He came out of the freshly painted room carrying a box.

"We keep our candy in tea boxes. We have for years," the woman said. "They're good conservers." She shrugged her shoulders. "What more can you expect? Such is life." She turned to her son. "Open it and pass it to the girl first. Then me."

The orange box was decorated with seated women and temples. Mary recognized it; her mother used the same tea at home. He slipped off the two rubber bands that held the cover on, and offered her the open box. With stiff fingers she took a stick of green candy from the top; she did not raise her eyes.

A few minutes later she was running alone down the stone steps. It was almost night, but the sky was faintly green near the horizon. She crossed the highway and stood on the hill only a few feet away from the pit. Far below her, lights were twinkling in the Polish section. Down there the shacks were stacked one against the other in a narrow strip of land between the lower road and the river.

After gazing down at the sparkling lights for a while, she

began to breathe more easily. She had never experienced the need to look at things from a distance before, nor had she felt the relief that it can bring. All at once, the air stirring around her head seemed delightful; she drank in great draughts of it, her eyes fixed on the lights below.

"This isn't the regular air from up here that I'm breathing," she said to herself. "It's the air from down there. It's a trick I can do."

She felt her blood tingle as it always did whenever she scored a victory, and she needed to score several of them in the course of each day. This time she was defeating the older woman.

The following afternoon, even though it was raining hard, her mother could not stop her from going out, but she had promised to keep her hood buttoned and not to sit on the ground.

The stone steps were running with water. She sat down and looked into the enveloping mist, a fierce light in her eyes. Her fingers twitched nervously, deep in the recess of her rubber pockets. It was unbelievable that they should not at any moment encounter something wonderful and new, unbelievable, too, that he should be ignorant of her love for him. Surely he knew that all the while his mother was talking, she in secret had been claiming him for her own. He would come out soon to join her on the steps, and they would go away together.

Hours later, stiff with cold, she stood up. Even had he remained all day at the window he could never have sighted her through the heavy mist. She knew this, but she could never climb the steps to fetch him; that was impossible. She ran headlong down the stone steps and across the highway. When she reached the pit she stopped dead and stood with her feet in the soft clay mud, panting for breath.

"Men," she said after a minute, "men, I told you we were going to specialize." She stopped abruptly, but it was too late. She had, for the first time in her life, spoken to her men before summoning them to order with a bugle call. She was shocked, and her heart beat hard against her ribs, but she went on. "We're going to be the only outfit in the world that can do real mountain-goat fighting." She closed her eyes, seeking the dark gulf again; this time she needed to hear the men's hearts beating, more clearly than her own. A car was sounding its horn on the highway. She looked up.

"We can't climb those stone steps up there." She was shouting and pointing at the house. "No outfit can, no outfit ever will. . . ." She was desperate. "It's not for outfits. It's a flight of steps that's not for outfits . . . because it's . . . because. . . ." The reason was not going to come to her. She had begun to cheat now, and she knew it would never come.

She turned her cold face away from the pit, and without dismissing her men, crept down the hill.

❧ Other Stories

The fictional pieces collected here are fragments of longer, unfinished works, taken from the author's notebooks. They date from the 1940s and 1950s.

· Andrew

Andrew's mother looked at her son's face. "He wants to get away from us," she thought, "and he will." She felt overcome by a mortal fatigue. "He simply wants to spring out of his box into the world." With a flippant and worldly gesture she described a flight through the air. Then abruptly she burst into tears and buried her face in her hands.

Andrew watched her thin shoulders shaking inside her woollen dress. When his mother cried he felt as though his face were made of marble. He could not accept the weeping as a part of her personality. It did not appear to be the natural climax of a mood. Instead it seemed to descend upon her from somewhere far away, as if she were giving voice to the crying of a child in some distant place. For it was the crying of a creature many years younger than she,

a disgrace for which he felt responsible, since it was usually
because of him that she cried.

There was nothing he could say to console her because
she was right. He wanted to go away, and there was nothing else he wanted at all. "It's natural when you're young
to want to go away," he would say to himself, but it did not
help; he always felt that his own desire to escape was different from that of others. When he was in a good humor he
would go about feeling that he and many others too were
all going away. On such days his face was smooth and he
enjoyed his life, although even then he was not commu-
nicative. More than anything he wanted all days to be like
those rare free ones when he went about whistling and
enjoying every simple thing he did. But he had to work
hard to get such days, because of his inner conviction that
his own going away was like no other going away in the
world, a certainty he found it impossible to dislodge. He
was right, of course, but from a very early age his life had
been devoted to his struggle to rid himself of his feeling of
uniqueness. With the years he was becoming more expert
at travesty, so that now his mother's crying was more de-
structive. Watching her cry now, he was more convinced
than ever that he was not like other boys who wanted to go
away. The truth bit into him harder, for seeing her he
could not believe even faintly that he shared his sin with
other young men. He and his mother were isolated, sharing the same disgrace, and because of this sharing, separated from one another. His life was truly miserable compared to the lives of other boys, and he knew it.

When his mother's sobs had quieted down somewhat,
his father called the waitress and asked for the check.
"That's good tomato soup," he told her. "And ham with
Hawaiian pineapple is one of my favorites, as you know."
The waitress did not answer, and the engaging expression
on his face slowly faded.

They pushed their chairs back and headed for the cloak-room. When they were outside Andrew's father suggested that they walk to the summit of the sloping lawn where some cannonballs were piled in the shape of a pyramid. "We'll go over to the cannonballs," he said. "Then we'll come back."

They struggled up the hill in the teeth of a bitterly cold wind, holding on to their hats. "This is the north, folks!" his father shouted into the gale. "It's hard going at times, but in a hot climate no one develops."

Andrew put his foot against one of the cannonballs. He could feel the cold iron through the sole of his shoe.

•

He had applied for a job in a garage, but he was inducted into the Army before he knew whether or not they had accepted his application. He loved being in the Army, and even took pleasure in the nickname which his hutmates had given him the second day after his arrival. He was called Buttonlip; because of this name he talked even less than usual. In general he hated to talk and could not imagine talking as being a natural expression of a man's thoughts. This was not shyness, but secretiveness.

One day in the Fall he set out on a walk through the pine grove surrounding the camp. Soon he sniffed smoke and stopped walking. "Someone's making a fire," he said to himself. Then he continued on his way. It was dusk in the grove, but beyond, outside, the daylight was still bright. Very shortly he reached a clearing. A young soldier sat there, crouched over a fire which he was feeding with long twigs. Andrew thought he recognized him—he too was undoubtedly a recent arrival—and so his face was not altogether unfamiliar.

The boy greeted Andrew with a smile and pointed to a tree trunk that lay on the ground nearby. "Sit down," he

said. "I'm going to cook dinner. The mess sergeant gives
me my stuff uncooked when I want it that way so I can
come out here and make a campfire."

Andrew had an urge to bolt from the clearing, but he
seated himself stiffly on the end of the tree trunk. The boy
was beautiful, with an Irish-American face and thick curly
brown hair. His cheeks were blood red from the heat of the
flames. Andrew looked at his face and fell in love with him.
Then he could not look away.

A mess kit and a brown paper package lay on the ground.
"My food is there in that brown bag," the boy said. "I'll
give you a little piece of meat so you can see how good it
tastes when it's cooked here, out in the air. Did you go in
for bonfires when you were a kid?"

"No," said Andrew. "Too much wind," he added, some
vague memory stirring in his mind.

"There's lots of wind," he agreed, and Andrew was un-
reasonably delighted that the boy considered his remark a
sensible one. "Lots of wind, but that never need stop you."
He looked up at Andrew with a bright smile. "Not if you
like a fire and the outdoors. Where I worked they used to
call me Outdoor Tommy. Nobody got sore."

Andrew was so disarmed by his charm that he did not
find the boy's last statement odd until he had heard the
sentence repeated several times inside his head.

"Sore?"

"Yes, sore." He untied the string that bound his food
package and set the meat on a little wire grate. "They
never got sore at me," he repeated, measuring his words.
"They were a right nice bunch. Sometimes guys don't take
to it if you like something real well. They get sore. These
guys didn't get sore. Never. They saw me going off to the
woods with my supper every evening, and sometimes even,
one or two of them would come along. And sometimes
twenty-five of us would go out with steaks. But mostly I
just went by myself and they stayed back playing games in

the cottages or going into town. If it had been winter I'd
have stayed in the cottages more. I was never there in
winter. If I had been, I might have gone out anyway. I like
to make a fire in the snow."

"Where were you?" asked Andrew.

"In a factory by a stream." The meat was cooked, and he
cut off a tiny piece for Andrew. "This is all you're going to
get. Otherwise I won't have enough in me."

"I've eaten. With the others," said Andrew shortly.

"You've got to try this," the boy insisted. "And see if you
like eating it this way, cooked on the coals outdoors. Then
maybe you can get on the good side of the mess sergeant
and bring your food out here, too. They're all right here.
I could stay in this outfit. Just as good as I could stay back
home in the hotel."

"You live in a hotel?"

"I lived in a hotel except the summer I was in the factory."

"Well, I'll see you," Andrew mumbled, walking away.

One night after he had eaten his supper he found himself wandering among the huts on the other side of the
mess hall. It was Saturday night and most of the huts were
dark. He was dejected, and thought of going into town and
drinking beer by himself. Andrew drank only beer because
he considered other forms of alcohol too expensive, although most of the other soldiers, who had less money
than he, drank whiskey. As he walked along thinking of
the beer he heard a voice calling to him. He looked up and
saw Tommy standing in the doorway of a hut only a few
feet away. They greeted each other, and Tommy motioned
to him to wait. Then he went inside to get something.

Andrew leaned against a tree with his hands in his
pockets. When Tommy came out he held a flat box in his
hand. "Sparklers," he said. "I bought them after the
Fourth, cut-rate. It's the best time to buy them."

"That's good to know," said Andrew. He had never

touched fireworks except on the day of the Fourth. He had a brief memory of alleys on summer nights, where boys were grinding red devils under their heels in the dark. Compared to him they were poor, and he was therefore, like all well-off children, both revolted by them and envious of them. The fact that they played with fireworks after the Fourth of July was disgusting in a way. It had a foreign flavor, and made him feel a little sick, just as the Irish did, and the Jews, and circus people. But he was also excited by them. The sick feeling was part of the excitement.

Andrew had never dressed as a ragamuffin on Thanksgiving, and he had once almost fainted when two boys disguised as hags had come begging at the door. His father's rage had contributed greatly to the nightmarish quality of the memory. It was usually his mother, and not his father, who was angry. But he remembered that his father had seemed to attach great importance to the custom of masquerading on Thanksgiving. "He should be dressed up himself and out there with the others!" he had cried. "He has no right to be lying there, white as a sheet. There's no earthly reason for it. This is a holiday. It's time for *fun*. My God, doesn't anyone in the house ever have any fun? I was a ragamuffin every year until I was grown. Why doesn't he tear up an old pair of pants and go out? I'll take the crown out of my straw hat if he wants to wear it. But he should go out!"

Quite naturally Andrew had thought of running away. This was one of his worst memories. He hated to hear his father speak about the poor. His own romantic conception of them made his father's democratic viewpoint unacceptable. It was as incongruous as if he had come into the parlor and found his father offering one of his cigarettes to a pirate or a gypsy. He preferred his mother's disdain for the poor. In fact, she liked nothing but the smell of her intimates. Of course, she made him feel sick, too, but sick in a different way.

"Come on. Take one," Tommy was saying, and he lighted a sparkler. Andrew stared at the needle-like sparks. The hissing sound of the sparkler awakened old sick feelings, and he longed to pull the little stick from between Tommy's fingers and bury the bright sparks in the earth. Instead, he looked gloomy and said nothing. He liked the fact that Tommy was poor, but he did not want him to be so poor that he seemed foreign. Then he realized that others might not see a connection between being a foreigner and playing with sparklers after the Fourth of July, and he was aware that there was really no logical connection. Yet he himself felt that there was one. Sometimes he wondered whether or not other people went about pretending to be logical while actually they felt as he did inside, but this was not very often, since he usually took it for granted that everyone was more honest than he. The fact that it was impossible to say anything of all this to Tommy both depressed and irritated him.

"I saved a whole box of sparklers for you," Tommy said. "I thought you'd be coming to the clearing."

Andrew could not believe he was hearing the words. At the same time his heart had begun to beat faster. He told himself that he must retain a natural expression.

"I don't know if you like to fool around with stuff they make for kids," Tommy went on. "Maybe you think it's not worth your while. But you don't have to pay much attention to these. You light 'em and they burn themselves out. You can swing 'em around and talk at the same time. Or you don't even have to swing 'em. You can stick 'em in the ground and they go on all by themselves, like little pinwheels. There's not much point to 'em, but I get 'em anyway, every summer after the Fourth of July is over with. This isn't the box I saved for you. That one I gave to someone else who had a nephew." He handed the box to Andrew.

Andrew's face was like stone and his mouth was drawn.

"Here." Tommy tapped the back of Andrew's hand with the flat box. "Here are your sparklers."

"No," said Andrew. "I don't want any sparklers." He was not going to offer any explanation for refusing them. Tommy did not seem to want one in any case. He went on tracing designs in the night with his sparkler. "I'll just stash this box away if you don't want 'em. I can use 'em up. It's better to have one of these going than nothing, and sometimes there's no time for me to build a bonfire."

"You take things easy, don't you?" Andrew said.

· Emmy Moore's Journal

On certain days I forget why I'm here. Today once again
I wrote my husband all my reasons for coming. He encouraged me to come each time I was in doubt. He said
that the worst danger for me was a state of vagueness, so
I wrote telling him why I had come to the Hotel Henry—
my eighth letter on this subject—but with each new letter
I strengthen my position. I am reproducing the letter here.
Let there be no mistake. My journal is intended for publication. I want to publish for glory, but also in order to
aid other women. This is the letter to my husband, Paul
Moore, to whom I have been married sixteen years. (I
am childless.) He is of North Irish descent, and a very
serious lawyer. Also a solitary and lover of the country.
He knows all mushrooms, bushes and trees, and he is interested in geology. But these interests do not exclude me.

He is sympathetic towards me, and kindly. He wants very much for me to be happy, and worries because I am not. He knows everything about me, including how much I deplore being the feminine kind of woman that I am. In fact, I am unusually feminine for an American of Anglo stock. (Born in Boston.) I am almost a "Turkish" type. Not physically, at least not entirely, because though fat I have ruddy Scotch cheeks and my eyes are round and not slanted or almond-shaped. But sometimes I feel certain that I exude an atmosphere very similar to theirs (the Turkish women's) and then I despise myself. I find the women in my country so extraordinarily manly and independent, capable of leading regiments, or of fending for themselves on desert islands if necessary. (These are poor examples, but I am getting my point across.) For me it is an experience simply to have come here alone to the Hotel Henry and to eat my dinner and lunch by myself. If possible before I die, I should like to become a little more independent, and a little less Turkish than I am now. Before I go any further, I had better say immediately that I mean no offense to Turkish women. They are probably busy combating the very same Turkish quality in themselves that I am controlling in me. I understand, too (though this is irrelevant), that many Turkish women are beautiful, and I think that they have discarded their veils. Any other American woman would be sure of this. She would know one way or the other whether the veils had been discarded, whereas I am afraid to come out with a definite statement. I have a feeling that they really have got rid of their veils, but I won't swear to it. Also, if they have done so, I have no idea when they did. Was it many years ago or recently?

Here is my letter to Paul Moore, my husband, in which there is more about Turkish women. Since I am writing this journal with a view to publication, I do not want to

ramble on as though I had all the space in the world. No
publisher will attempt printing an *enormous* journal
written by an unknown woman. It would be too much of
a financial risk. Even I, with my ignorance of all matters
pertaining to business, know this much. But they may
print a small one.

My letter (written yesterday, the morrow of my drunken
evening in the Blue Bonnet Room when I accosted the
society salesman):

Dearest Paul:

I cannot simply live out my experiment here at the
Hotel Henry without trying to justify or at least explain
in letters my reasons for being here, and with fair regular-
ity. You encouraged me to write whenever I felt I needed
to clarify my thoughts. But you did tell me that I must not
feel the need to *justify* my actions. However, I *do* feel the
need to justify my actions, and I am certain that until the
prayed-for metamorphosis has occurred I shall go on feeling just this need. Oh, how well I know that you would
interrupt me at this point and warn me against expecting
too much. So I shall say in lieu of metamorphosis, the
prayed-for *improvement*. But until then I must justify
myself every day. Perhaps you will get a letter every day.
On some days the need to write lodges itself in my throat
like a cry that must be uttered.

As for the Turkish problem, I am coming to it. You must
understand that I am an admirer of Western civilization;
that is, of the women who are members of this group. I
feel myself that I fall short of being a member, that by
some curious accident I was not born in Turkey but should
have been. Because of my usual imprecision I cannot even
tell how many countries belong to what we call Western
Civilization, but I believe Turkey is the place where East
meets West, isn't it? I can just about imagine the women

there, from what I have heard about the country and the pictures I have seen of it. As for being troubled or obsessed by real Oriental women, I am not. (I refer to the Chinese, Japanese, Hindus, and so on.) Naturally I am less concerned with the Far Eastern women because there is no danger of my being like them. (The Turkish women are just near enough.) The Far Eastern ones are so very far away, at the opposite end of the earth, that they could easily be just as independent and masculine as the women of the Western world. The ones living in-between the two masculine areas would be soft and feminine. Naturally I don't believe this for a minute, but still, the real Orientals are so far away and such a mystery to me that it might as well be true. Whatever they are, it couldn't affect me. They look too different from the way I look. Whereas Turkish women don't. (Their figures are exactly like mine, alas!)

Now I shall come to the point. I know full well that you will consider the above discourse a kind of joke. Or if you don't, you will be irritated with me for making statements of such a sweeping and inaccurate nature. For surely you will consider the picture of the world that I present as inaccurate. I myself know that this concept of the women (all three sets—Western, Middle and Eastern) is a puerile one. It could even be called downright idiotic. Yet I assure you that I see things this way, if I relax even a little and look through my own eyes into what is really inside my head. (Though because of my talent for mimicry I am able to simulate looking through the eyes of an educated person when I wish to.) Since I am giving you such a frank picture of myself, I may as well go the whole hog and admit to you that my secret picture of the world is grossly inaccurate. I have completely forgotten to include in it any of the Latin countries. (France, Italy, Spain.) For instance, I have jumped from the Anglo world to the semi-Oriental as if there were no countries in between at all. I know that

these exist. (I have even lived in two of them.) But they do
not fit into my scheme. I just don't think about the Latins
very much, and this is less understandable than my not
thinking about the Chinese or Javanese or Japanese wom-
en. You can see why without my having to explain it to
you. I do know that the French women are more interested
in sports than they used to be, and for all I know they may
be indistinguishable from Anglo women by now. I haven't
been to France recently so I can't be sure. But in any case
the women of those countries don't enter into my picture
of the world. Or shall I say that the fact of having forgotten
utterly to consider them has not altered the way I visualize
the division of the world's women? Incredible though it
may seem to you, it hasn't altered anything. (My having
forgotten all Latin countries, South America included.) I
want you to know the whole truth about me. But don't
imagine that I wouldn't be capable of concealing my ignorance from you if I wanted to. I am so wily and feminine
that I could live by your side for a lifetime and deceive you
afresh each day. But I will have no truck with feminine
wiles. I know how they can absorb the hours of the day.
Many women are delighted to sit around spinning their
webs. It is an absorbing occupation, and the women feel
they are getting somewhere. And so they are, but only for
as long as the man is there to be deceived. And a wily
woman alone is a pitiful sight to behold. Naturally.

I shall try to be honest with you so that I can live with
you and yet won't be pitiful. Even if tossing my feminine
tricks out the window means being left no better than an
illiterate backwoodsman, or the bottom fish scraping along
the ocean bed, I prefer to have it this way. Now I am too
tired to write more. Though I don't feel that I have clarified enough or justified enough.

I shall write you soon about the effect the war has had
upon me. I have spoken to you about it, but you have

never seemed to take it very seriously. Perhaps seeing in black and white what I feel will affect your opinion of me. Perhaps you will leave me. I accept the challenge. My Hotel Henry experience includes this risk. I got drunk two nights ago. It's hard to believe that I am forty-seven, isn't it?

My love,
Emmy

Now that I have copied this letter into my journal (I had forgotten to make a carbon), I shall take my walk. My scheme included a few weeks of solitude at the Hotel Henry before attempting anything. I did not even intend to write in my journal as soon as I started to, but simply to sit about collecting my thoughts, waiting for the knots of habit to undo themselves. But after only a week here—two nights ago—I felt amazingly alone and disconnected from my past life, so I began my journal.

My first interesting contact was the salesman in the Blue Bonnet Room. I had heard about this eccentric through my in-laws, the Moores, before I ever came up here. My husband's cousin Laurence Moore told me about him when he heard I was coming. He said: "Take a walk through Grey and Bottle's Department Store, and you'll see a man with a lean red face and reddish hair selling materials by the bolt. That man has an income and is related to Hewitt Molain. He doesn't need to work. He was in my fraternity. Then he disappeared. The next I heard of him he was working there at Grey and Bottle's. I stopped by and said hello to him. For a nut he seemed like a very decent chap. You might even have a drink with him. I think he's quite up to general conversation."

I did not mention Laurence Moore to the society salesman because I thought it might irritate him. I lied and

pretended to have been here for months, when actually
this is still only my second week at the Hotel Henry. I
want everyone to think I have been here a long time.
Surely it is not to impress them. Is there anything impressive about a lengthy stay at the Hotel Henry? Any sane
person would be alarmed that I should even ask such a
question. I ask it because deep in my heart I *do* think a
lengthy stay at the Hotel Henry is impressive. Very easy to
see that I would, and even sane of me to think it impressive, but not sane of me to expect anyone else to think so,
particularly a stranger. Perhaps I simply like to hear myself
telling it. I hope so. I shall write some more tomorrow,
but now I must go out. I am going to buy a supply of
cocoa. When I'm not drunk I like to have a cup of cocoa
before going to sleep. My husband likes it too.

•

She could not stand the overheated room a second longer.
With some difficulty she raised the window, and the cold
wind blew in. Some loose sheets of paper went skimming
off the top of the desk and flattened themselves against the
bookcase. She shut the window and they fell to the floor.
The cold air had changed her mood. She looked down at
the sheets of paper. They were part of the letter she had
just copied. She picked them up: *"I don't feel that I have
clarified enough or justified enough,"* she read. She closed
her eyes and shook her head. She had been so happy copy-
ing this letter into her journal, but now her heart was
faint as she scanned its scattered pages. "I have said nothing," she muttered to herself in alarm. "I have said nothing
at all. I have not clarified my reasons for being at the Hotel
Henry. I have not justified myself."

Automatically she looked around the room. A bottle of
whiskey stood on the floor beside one of the legs of the
bureau. She stepped forward, picked it up by the neck, and
settled with it into her favorite wicker chair.

· Going to Massachusetts

Bozoe rubbed away some tears with a closed fist.

"Come on, Bozoe," said Janet. "You're not going to the North Pole."

Bozoe tugged at the woolly fur, and pulled a little of it out.

"Leave your coat alone," said Janet.

"I don't remember why I'm going to Massachusetts," Bozoe moaned. "I knew it would be like this, once I got to the station."

"If you don't want to go to Massachusetts," said Janet, "then come on back to the apartment. We'll stop at Fanny's on the way. I want to buy those tumblers made out of knobby glass. I want brown ones."

Bozoe started to cry in earnest. This caused Janet considerable embarrassment. She was conscious of herself as a public figure because the fact that she owned and ran a garage had given her a good deal of publicity not only in East Clinton but in the neighboring counties. This scene, she said to herself, makes us look like two Italians saying goodbye. Everybody'll think we're Italians. She did not feel true sympathy for Bozoe. Her sense of responsibility was overdeveloped, but she was totally lacking in real tenderness.

"There's no reason for you to cry over a set of whiskey tumblers," said Janet. "I told you ten days ago that I was going to buy them."

"Passengers boarding Bus Number Twenty-seven, northbound. . . ."

"I'm not crying about whiskey tumblers." Bozoe managed with difficulty to get the words out. "I'm crying about Massachusetts. I can't remember my reasons."

"Rockport, Rayville, Muriel. . . ."

"Why don't you listen to the loudspeaker, Bozoe? It's giving you information. If you paid attention to what's going on around you you'd be a lot better off. You concentrate too much on your own private affairs. Try more to be a part of the world."

•

". . . The truth is that I am only twenty-five miles away from the apartment, as you have probably guessed. In fact, you could not help but guess it, since you are perfectly familiar with Larry's Bar and Grill. I could not go to Massachusetts. I cried the whole way up to Muriel and it was as if someone else were getting off the bus, not myself. But someone who was in a desperate hurry to reach the next stop. I was in mortal terror that the bus would not stop at Muriel but continue on to some further destination where I would not know any familiar face. My terror was so great that I actually stopped crying. I kept from crying

all the way. That is a lie. Not an actual lie because I never lie as you know. Small solace to either one of us, isn't it? I am sure that you would prefer me to lie, rather than be so intent on explaining my dilemma to you night and day. I am convinced that you would prefer me to lie. It would give you more time for the garage."

"So?" queried Sis McEvoy, an unkind note in her voice. To Janet she did not sound noticeably unkind, since Sis McEvoy was habitually sharp-sounding, and like her had very little sympathy for other human beings. She was sure that Sis McEvoy was bad, and she was determined to save her. She was going to save her quietly without letting Sis suspect her determination. Janet did everything secretly; in fact, secrecy was the essence of her nature, and from it she derived her pleasure and her sense of being an important member of society.

"What's it all about?" Sis asked irritably. "Why doesn't she raise kids or else go to a psychologist or a psychoanalyst or whatever? My ovaries are crooked or I'd raise kids myself. That's what God's after, isnt' it? Space ships or no space ships. What's the problem, anyway? How are her ovaries and the rest of the mess?"

Janet smiled mysteriously. "Bozoe has never wanted a child," she said. "She told me she was too scared."

"Don't you despise cowards?" said Sis. "Jesus Christ, they turn my stomach."

Janet frowned. "Bozoe says she despises cowards, too. She worries herself sick about it. She's got it all linked up together with Heaven and Hell. She thinks so much about Heaven and Hell that she's useless. I've told her for years to occupy herself. I've told her that God would like her better if she was occupied. But she says God isn't interested. That's a kind of slam at me, I suppose. At me and the garage. She's got it in for the garage. It doesn't bother me, but it makes me a little sore when she tries to convince me that I wouldn't be interested in the garage unless she talked to me day and night about her troubles. As if I was interested in the garage just out of spite. I'm a normal woman and I'm interested in my work, like all women are in modern times. I'm a little stockier than most, I guess, and not fussy or feminine. That's because my father was my ideal and my mother was an alcoholic. I'm stocky and I don't like pretty dresses and I'm interested in my work. My work is like God to me. I don't mean I put it above Him, but the next thing to Him. I have a feeling that he approves of my working. That he approves of my working in a garage. Maybe that's cheeky of me, but I can't help it. I've made a name for myself in the garage and I'm decent. I'm normal." She paused for a moment to fill the two whiskey tumblers.

"Do you like my whiskey tumblers?" She was being unusually spry and talkative. "I don't usually have much time to buy stuff. But I had to, of course. Bozoe never bought anything in her life. She's what you'd call a dead weight. She's getting fatter, too, all the time."

"They're good tumblers," said Sis McEvoy. "They hold a lot of whiskey."

Janet flushed slightly at the compliment. She attributed the unaccustomed excitement she felt to her freedom from the presence of Bozoe Flanner.

"Bozoe was very thin when I first knew her," she told Sis. "And she didn't show any signs that she was going to sit night and day making up problems and worrying about God and asking me questions. There wasn't any of that in the beginning. Mainly she was meek, I guess, and she had soft-looking eyes, like a doe or a calf. Maybe she had the problems the whole time and was just planning to spring them on me later. I don't know. I never thought she was going to get so tied up in knots, or so fat either. Naturally if she were heavy and happy too it would be better."

"I have no flesh on my bones at all," said Sis McEvoy, as if she had not even heard the rest of the conversation. "The whole family's thin, and every last one of us has a rotten lousy temper inherited from both sides. My father and my mother had rotten tempers."

"I don't mind if you have a temper display in my apartment," said Janet. "Go to it. I believe in people expressing themselves. If you've inherited a temper there isn't much you can do about it except express it. I think it's much better for you to break this crockery pumpkin, for instance, than to hold your temper in and become unnatural. For instance, I could buy another pumpkin and you'd feel relieved. I'd gather that, at any rate. I don't know much about people, really. I never dabbled in people. They were never my specialty. But surely if you've inherited a temper from both sides it would seem to me that you would have to express it. It isn't your fault, is it, after all?" Janet seemed determined to show admiration for Sis McEvoy.

"I'm having fun," she continued unexpectedly. "It's a long time since I've had any fun. I've been too busy getting the garage into shape. Then there's Bozoe trouble. I've kept to the routine. Late Sunday breakfast with popovers and home-made jam. She eats maybe six of them, but with the same solemn expression on her face. I'm husky but a small eater. We have record players and television. But nothing takes her mind off herself. There's no point in my getting any more machines. I've got the cash and the good will, but there's absolutely no point."

"You seem to be very well set up," said Sis McEvoy, narrowing her eyes. "Here's to you." She tipped her glass and drained it.

Janet filled Sister's glass at once. "I'm having a whale of a good time," she said. "I hope you are. Of course I don't want to butt into your business. Bozoe always thought I pored over my account books for such a long time on purpose. She thought I was purposely trying to get away from her. What do you think, Sis McEvoy?" She asked this almost in a playful tone that bordered on a yet unexpressed flirtatiousness.

"I'm not interested in women's arguments with each other," said Sis at once. "I'm interested in women's arguments with men. What else is there? The rest doesn't amount to a row of monkeys."

"Oh, I agree," Janet said, as if she were delighted by this statement which might supply her with the stimulus she was after. "I agree one thousand percent. Remember I spend more time in the garage with the men than I do with Bozoe Flanner."

"I'm not actually living with my husband because of my temper," said Sis. "I don't like long-standing relationships. They disagree with me. I get the blues. I don't want anyone staying in my life for a long time. It gives me the creeps. Men are crazy about me. I like the cocktails and the compliments. Then after a while they turn my stomach."

"You're a very interesting woman," Janet Murphy announced, throwing caution to the winds and finding it pleasant.

"I know I'm interesting," said Sis. "But I'm not so sure life is interesting."

"Are you interested in money?" Janet asked her. "I don't mean money for the sake of money, but for buying things."

Sis did not answer, and Janet feared that she had been rude. "I didn't mean to hurt your feelings," she said. "After all, money comes up in everybody's life. Even duchesses have to talk about money. But I won't, any more. Come on. Let's shake." She held out her hand to Sis McEvoy, but Sis allowed it to stay there foolishly, without accepting the warm grip Janet had intended for her.

"I'm really sorry," she went on, "if you think I was

trying to be insulting and personal. I honestly was not. The fact is that I have been so busy building up a reputation for the garage that I behave like a savage. I'll never mention money again." In her heart she felt that Sis was somehow pleased that the subject had been brought up, but was not yet ready to admit it. Sis's tedious work at the combination tearoom and soda fountain where they had met could scarcely make her feel secure.

Bozoe doesn't play one single feminine trick, she told herself, and after all, after struggling nearly ten years to build up a successful and unusual business I'm entitled to some returns. I'm in a rut with Bozoe and this Sis is going to get me out of it. (By now she was actually furious with Bozoe.) I'm entitled to some fun. The men working for me have more fun than I have.

"I feel grateful to you, Sis," she said without explaining her remark. "You've done me a service. May I tell you that I admire your frankness, without offending you?"

Sis McEvoy was beginning to wonder if Janet were another nut like Bozoe Flanner. This worried her a little, but she was too drunk by now for clear thinking. She was enjoying the compliments, although it was disturbing that they should be coming from a woman. She was very proud of never having been depraved or abnormal, and pleased to be merely mean and discontented to the extent of not having been able to stay with any man for longer than the three months she had spent with her husband.

"I'll read you more of Bozoe's letter," Janet suggested.

"I can't wait," said Sis. "I can't wait to hear a lunatic's mind at work first-hand. Her letter's so cheerful and elevating. And so constructive. Go to it. But fill my glass first so I can concentrate. I'd hate to miss a word. It would kill me."

Janet realized that it was unkind of her to be reading her friend's letter to someone who so obviously had only contempt for it. But she felt no loyalty—only eagerness to make Sis see how hard her life had been. She felt that in this way the bond between them might be strengthened.

"Well, here it comes," she said. "Stop me when you can't stand it any more. *I know that you expected me to come back. You did not feel I had the courage to carry out my scheme. I still expect to work it out. But not yet. I am more than ever convinced that my salvation lies in solitude, and coming back to the garage before I have even reached Massachusetts would be a major defeat for me, as I'm sure you must realize, even though you pretend not to know what I'm talking about most of the time. I am convinced that you do know what I'm talking about and if you pretend ignorance of my dilemma so you can increase efficiency at the garage you are going to defeat yourself. I can't actually save you, but I can point little things out to you constantly. I refer to your soul, naturally, and not to any success you've had or to your determination. In any case it came to me on the bus that it was not time for me to leave you, and that although going to Massachusetts required more courage and strength than I seemed able to muster, I was at the same time being very selfish in going. Selfish because I was thinking in terms of my salvation and not yours. I'm glad I thought of this. It is why I stopped crying and got off the bus. Naturally you would disapprove, because I had paid for my ticket which is now wasted, if for no other reason. That's the kind of thing you like me to think about, isn't it? It makes you feel that I'm more human. I have never admired being human, I must say. I want to be like God. But I haven't begun yet. First I have to go to Massachusetts and be alone. But I got off the bus. And I've wasted the fare. I can hear you stressing that above all else, as I say. But I want you to understand that it was not cowardice alone that stopped me from going to Massachusetts. I don't feel that I can allow you to sink into the mire of contentment and happy ambitious enterprise. It is my duty to prevent you from it as much as I do for myself. It is not fair of me to go away until you completely understand how I feel about God and my destiny. Surely we have been brought together for some purpose, even if that purpose ends by our being separate again. But not until the time is ripe. Naturally, the psychiatrists would at once declare that I was laboring under a compulsion. I am violently against psychiatry, and, in fact, against happiness. Though of course I love it. I love happiness, I mean. Of course you would not believe this. Naturally darling I love you, and I'm afraid that if you don't start suffering soon God will take some terrible vengeance. It is better for you to offer yourself. Don't accept social or financial security as your final aim. Or fame in the garage. Fame is unworthy of you; that is, the desire for it. Janet, my beloved, I do not expect you to be gloomy or fanatical as I am. I do not believe that God intended you for quite as harrowing a destiny as He did for me. I don't mean this as an insult. I believe you should actually thank your stars. I would really like to be fulfilling humble daily chores myself and listening to a concert at night or television or playing a card game. But I can find no rest, and I don't think you should either. At least not until you have fully understood my dilemma on earth. That means that you must no longer turn a deaf ear to me and pretend that your preoccupation with the garage is in a sense a holier absorption than trying to understand and fully realize the importance and meaning of my dilemma. I think that you hear more than you admit, too. There is a stubborn streak in your nature working against you, most likely unknown to yourself. An insistence on being shallow rather than profound. I repeat: I do not expect you to be as profound as I am. But to insist on exploiting the most shallow side of one's nature, out of stubbornness and merely because it is more pleasant*

*to be shallow, is certainly a sin. Sis McEvoy will help you
to express the shallow side of your nature, by the way. Like
a toboggan slide."*

Janet stopped abruptly, appalled at having read this last
part aloud. She had not expected Bozoe to mention Sis at
all. "Gee," she said. "Gosh! She's messing everything up
together. I'm awfully sorry."

Sis McEvoy stood up and walked unsteadily to the television set. Some of her drink slopped onto the rug as she
went. She faced Janet with fierce eyes. "There's nobody in
the world who can talk to me like that, and there's not
going to be. Never!" She was leaning on the set and steady-
ing herself against it with both hands. "I'll keep on building double-decker sandwiches all my life first. It's five
flights to the top of the building where I live. It's an insurance building, life insurance, and I'm the only woman who
lives there. I have boy friends come when they want to.
I don't have to worry, either. I'm crooked so I don't have
to bother with abortions or any other kind of mess. The
hell with television anyway."

She likes the set, Janet said to herself. She felt more
secure. "Bozoe and I don't have the same opinions at all,"
she said. "We don't agree on anything."

"Who cares? You live in the same apartment, don't you?
You've lived in the same apartment for ten years. Isn't that
all anybody's got to know?" She rapped with her fist on the
wood panelling of the television set. "Whose is it, anyhow?" She was growing increasingly aggressive.

"It's mine," Janet said. "It's my television set." She
spoke loud so that Sis would be sure to catch her words.

"What the hell do I care?" cried Sis. "I live on top of a
life-insurance building and I work in a combination soda-
fountain lunch-room. Now read me the rest of the letter."

"I don't think you really want to hear any more of
Bozoe's nonsense," Janet said smoothly. "She's spoiling our

evening together. There's no reason for us to put up with it all. Why should we? Why don't I make something to eat? Not a sandwich. You must be sick of sandwiches."

"What I eat is my own business," Sis snapped.

"Naturally," said Janet. "I thought you might like something hot like bacon and eggs. Nice crisp bacon and eggs." She hoped to persuade her so that she might forget about the letter.

"I don't like food," said Sis. "I don't even like million-aires' food, so don't waste your time."

"I'm a small eater myself." She had to put off reading Bozoe's letter until Sis had forgotten about it. "My work at the garage requires some sustenance, of course. But it's brainwork now more than manual labor. Being a man-ager's hard on the brain."

Sis looked at Janet and said: "Your brain doesn't impress me. Or that garage. I like newspaper men. Men who are champions. Like champion boxers. I've known lots of champions. They take to me. Champions all fall for me, but I'd never want any of them to find out that I knew someone like your Bozoe. They'd lose their respect."

"I wouldn't introduce Bozoe to a boxer either, or any-body else who was interested in sports. I know they'd be bored. I know." She waited. "You're very nice. Very intel-ligent. You *know* people. That's an asset."

"Stay with Bozoe and her television set," Sis growled.

"It's not her television set. It's mine, Sis. Why don't you sit down? Sit on the couch over there."

"The apartment belongs to both of you, and so does the set. I know what kind of a couple you are. The whole world knows it. I could put you in jail if I wanted to. I could put you and Bozoe both in jail."

In spite of these words she stumbled over to the couch and sat down. "Whiskey," she demanded. "The world loves drunks but it despises perverts. Athletes and boxers drink when they're not in training. All the time."

Janet went over to her and served her a glass of whiskey with very little ice. Let's hope she'll pass out, she said to herself. She couldn't see Sis managing the steps up to her room in the insurance building, and in any case she didn't want her to leave. She's such a relief after Bozoe, she thought. Alive and full of fighting spirit. She's much more my type, coming down to facts. She thought it unwise to go near Sis, and was careful to pour the fresh drink quickly and return to her own seat. She would have preferred to sit next to Sis, in spite of her mention of jail, but she did not relish being punched or smacked in the face. It's all Bozoe's fault, she said to herself. That's what she gets for thinking she's God. Her holy words can fill a happy peaceful room with poison from twenty-five miles away.

"I love my country," said Sis, for no apparent reason. "I love it to death!"

"Sure you do, Hon," said Janet. "I could murder Bozoe for upsetting you with her loony talk. You were so peaceful until she came in."

"Read that letter," said Sister. After a moment she repeated, as if from a distance: "Read the letter."

Janet was perplexed. Obviously food was not going to distract Sis, and she had nothing left to suggest, in any case, but some Gorton's Codfish made into cakes, and she did not dare to offer her these.

What a rumpus that would raise, she said to herself. And if I suggest turning on the television she'll raise the roof. Stay off television and codfish cakes until she's normal again. Working at a lunch counter is no joke.

There was nothing she could do but do as Sis told her and hope that she might fall asleep while she was reading her the letter. "Damn Bozoe anyway," she muttered audibly.

"Don't put on any acts," said Sis, clearly awake. "I hate liars and I always smell an act. Even though I didn't go to college. I have no respect for college."

"I didn't go to college," Janet began, hoping Sis might be led on to a new discussion. "I went to commercial school."

"Shut up, God damn you! Nobody ever tried to make a commercial school sound like an interesting topic except you. Nobody! You're out of your mind. Read the letter."

"Just a second," said Janet, knowing there was no hope for her. "Let me put my glasses on and find my place. Doing accounts at the garage year in and year out has ruined my eyes. My eyes used to be perfect." She added this last weakly, without hope of arousing either sympathy or interest.

Sis did not deign to answer.

"Well, here it is again," she began apologetically. "Here it is in all its glory." She poured a neat drink to give herself courage. *"As I believe I just wrote you, I have been down to the bar and brought a drink back with me. (One more defeat for me, a defeat which is of course a daily occurrence, and I daresay I should not bother to mention it in this letter.) In any case I could certainly not face being without one after the strain of actually boarding the bus, even if I did get off without having the courage to stick on it until I got where I was going. However, please keep in mind the second reason I had for stopping short of my destination. Please read it over carefully so that you will not have only contempt for me. The part about the responsibility I feel toward you. The room here over Larry's Bar and Grill is dismal. It is one of several rented out by Larry's sister whom we met a year ago when we stopped here for a meal. You remember. It was the day we took Stretch for a ride and let him out of the car to run in the woods, that scanty patch of woods you found just as the sun was setting, and you kept picking up branches that were stuck together with wet leaves and dirt. . . ."*

❧ From the Notebooks

· The Iron Table

They sat in the sun, looking out over a big new boulevard. The waiter had dragged an old iron table around from the other side of the hotel and set it down on the cement near a half-empty flower bed. A string stretched between stakes separated the hotel grounds from the sidewalk. Few of the guests staying at the hotel sat in the sun. The town was not a tourist center, and not many Anglo-Saxons came. Most of the guests were Spanish.

"The whole civilization is going to pieces," he said.

Her voice was sorrowful. "I know it." Her answers to his ceaseless complaining about the West's contamination of Moslem culture had become increasingly unpredictable. Today, because she felt that he was in a very irritable mood and in need of an argument, she automatically agreed with him. "It's going to pieces so quickly, too," she said, and her tone was sepulchral.

He looked at her without any light in his blue eyes. "There are places where the culture has remained untouched," he announced as if for the first time. "If we went into the desert you wouldn't have to face all this. Wouldn't you love that?" He was punishing her for her swift agreement with him a moment earlier. He knew she had no desire to go to the desert, and that she believed it was not possible to continue trying to escape from the Industrial Revolution. Without realizing he was doing it he had provoked the argument he wanted.

"Why do you ask me if I wouldn't love to go into the desert, when you know as well as I do I wouldn't. We've talked about it over and over. Every few days we talk about it." Although the sun was beating down on her chest, making it feel on fire, deep inside she could still feel the cold current that seemed to run near her heart.

"Well," he said. "You change. Sometimes you say you *would* like to go."

It was true. She did change. Sometimes she would run to him with bright eyes. "Let's go," she would say. "Let's go into the desert." But she never did this if she was sober.

There was something wistful in his voice, and she had to remind herself that she wanted to feel cranky rather than heartbroken. In order to go on talking she said: "Sometimes I feel like going, but it's always when I've had something to drink. When I've had nothing to drink I'm afraid." She turned to face him, and he saw that she was beginning to have her hunted expression.

"Do you think I *ought* to go?" she asked him.

"Go where?"

"To the desert. To live in an oasis." She was pronouncing her words slowly. "Maybe that's what I should do, since I'm your wife."

"You must do what you really want to do," he said. He had been trying to teach her this for twelve years.

"What I really want. . . . Well, if you'd be happy in an oasis, maybe I'd really want to do that." She spoke hesitantly, and there was a note of doubt in her voice.

"What?" He shook his head as if he had run into a spiderweb. "What is it?"

"I meant that maybe if you were happy in an oasis I would be, too. Wives get pleasure out of making their husbands happy. They really do, quite aside from its being moral."

He did not smile. He was in too bad a humor. "You'd go to an oasis because you wanted to escape from Western civilization."

"My friends and I don't feel there's any *way* of escaping it. It's not interesting to sit around talking about industrialization."

"What friends?" He liked her to feel isolated.

"Our friends." Most of them she had not seen in many years. She turned to him with a certain violence. "I think you come to these countries so you can complain. I'm tired of hearing the word *civilization*. It has no meaning. Or I've forgotten what it meant, anyway."

The moment when they might have felt tenderness had passed, and secretly they both rejoiced. Since he did not answer her, she went on. "I think it's uninteresting. To sit and watch costumes disappear, one by one. It's uninteresting even to mention it."

"They are not costumes," he said distinctly. "They're simply the clothes people wear."

She was as bitter as he about the changes, but she felt it would be indelicate for them both to reflect the same sorrow. It would happen some day, surely. A serious grief would silence their argument. They would share it and not be able to look into each other's eyes. But as long as she could she would hold off that moment.

· Lila and Frank

Frank pulled hard on the front door and opened it with a jerk, so that the pane of glass shook in its frame. It was his sister's custom never to go to the door and open it for him. She had an instinctive respect for his secretive nature.

He hung his coat on a hook in the hall and walked into the parlor, where he was certain he would find his sister. She was seated as usual in her armchair. Next to her was a heavy round table of an awkward height which made it useful for neither eating nor writing, although it was large enough for either purpose. Even in the morning Lila always wore a silk dress, stockings, and well-shined shoes. In fact, at all times of the day she was fully dressed to go into the town, although she seldom ventured from the house. Her hair was not very neat, but she took the trouble to rouge her lips.

"How were the men at the Coffee Pot tonight?" she asked when her brother entered the room. There was no variety in the inflection of her voice. It was apparent that, like him, she had never tried, either by emphasis or coloring of tone, to influence or charm a listener.

Frank sat down and rested for a while without speaking.

"How were the men at the Coffee Pot?" she said again with no change of expression.

"The same as they always are."

"You mean by that, hungry and noisy." For an outsider it would have been hard to say whether she was being critical of the men at the Coffee Pot or sincerely asking for information. This was a question she had asked him many times, and he had various ways of answering, depending upon his mood. On this particular night he was uncommunicative. "They go to the Coffee Pot for a bite to eat," he said.

She looked at him. The depths of her dark eyes held neither warmth nor comfort. "Was it crowded?" she asked.

He considered this for a moment while she watched him attentively. He was near the lamp and his face was raspberry-colored, an even deeper red than it would have been otherwise.

"It was."

"Then it must have been noisy." The dropping of her voice at the end of a sentence gave her listener, if he was a stranger, the impression that she did not intend to continue with the conversation. Her brother of course knew this was not the case, and he was not surprised at all when a minute later she went on. "Did you speak with anyone?"

"No, I didn't." He jumped up from his chair and went over to a glass bookcase in the corner. "I don't usually, do I?"

"That doesn't mean that you won't, does it?" she said calmly.

"I wouldn't change my habits from one night to the next," he said. "Not sitting at the Coffee Pot."

"Why not?"

"It's not human nature to do that, is it?"

"I know nothing about human nature at all," she said. "Nor do you, for that matter. I don't know why you'd refer to it. I do suspect, though, that I at least might change very suddenly." Her voice remained indifferent, as though the subject were not one which was close to her. "It's a feeling that's always present with me . . . here." She touched her breast.

Although he wandered around the room for a moment feigning to have lost interest in the conversation, she knew this was not so. Since they lied to each other in different ways, the excitement they felt in conversing together was very great.

"Tell me," she said. "If you don't expect to experience anything new at the Coffee Pot, why do you continue to go there?" This too she had often asked him in the past weeks, but the repetition of things added to rather than detracting from the excitement.

"I don't like to talk to anybody. But I like to go out," he said. "I may not like other men, but I like the world."

"I should think you'd go and hike in the woods, instead of sitting at the Coffee Pot. Men who don't like other men usually take to nature, I've heard."

"I'm not interested in nature, beyond the ordinary amount."

They settled into silence for a while. Then she began to question him again. "Don't you feel uneasy, knowing that most likely you're the only man at the Coffee Pot who feels so estranged from his fellows?"

He seated himself near the window and half smiled. "No," he said. "I think I like it."

"Why do you like it?"

"Because I'm aware of the estrangement, as you call it, and they aren't." This too he had answered many times before. But such was the faith they had in the depth of the mood they created between them that there were no dead sentences, no matter how often repeated.

"We don't feel the same about secrets," she told him. "I don't consider a secret such a great pleasure. In fact, I should hesitate to name what my pleasure is. I simply know that I don't feel the lack of it."

"Good night," said Frank. He wanted to be by himself. Since he very seldom talked for more than ten or fifteen minutes at a time, she was not at all surprised.

She herself was far too excited for sleep at that moment. The excitement that stirred in her breast was familiar, and could be likened to what a traveler feels on the eve of his departure. All her life she had enjoyed it or suffered from it, for it was a sensation that lay between suffering and enjoyment, and it had a direct connection with her brother's lies. For the past weeks they had concerned the Coffee Pot, but this was of little importance, since he lied to her consistently and had done so since early childhood. Her excitement had its roots in the simultaneous rejection and acceptance of these lies, a state which might be compared to that of the dreamer when he is near to waking, and who knows then that he is moving in a dream country which at any second will vanish forever, and yet is unable to recall the existence of his own room. So Lila moved about in the vivid world of her brother's lies, with the full awareness always that just beyond them lay the amorphous and hidden world of reality. These lies which thrilled her heart seemed to cull their exciting quality from her never-failing consciousness of the true events they concealed. She had not changed at all since childhood, when to expose a statement of her brother's as a lie was as unthinkable to her as the denial of God's existence is to most children. This treatment of her brother, unbalanced though it was, contained within it both dignity and merit, and these were reflected faithfully in her voice and manner.

· Friday

He sat at a little table in the Green Mountain Luncheonette apathetically studying the menu. Faithful to the established tradition of his rich New England family, he
habitually chose the cheapest dish listed on the menu
whenever it was not something he definitely abhorred.
Today was Friday, and there were two cheap dishes listed,
both of which he hated. One was haddock and the other
fried New England smelts. The cheaper meat dishes had
been omitted. Finally, with compressed lips, he decided on
a steak. The waitress was barely able to hear his order.

"Did you say steak?" she asked him.

"Yes. There isn't anything else. Who eats haddock?"

"Nine tenths of the population." She spoke without
venom. "Look at Agnes." She pointed to the table next to
his.

Andrew looked up. He had noticed the girl before. She had a long freckled face with large, rather roughly sketched features. Her hair, almost the color of her skin, hung down to her shoulders. It was evident that her mustard-colored wool dress was homemade. It was decorated at the throat with a number of dark brown woollen balls. Over the dress she wore a man's lumber jacket. She was a large-boned girl. The lower half of her face was long and solid and insensitive-looking, but her eyes, Andrew noted, were luminous and starry.

Although it was bitterly cold outside, the lunch room was steaming hot and the front window had clouded over.

"Don't you like fish?" the girl said.

He shook his head. Out of the corner of his eye he had noticed that she was not eating her haddock. However, he had quickly looked away, in order not to be drawn into a conversation. The arrival of his steak obliged him to look up, and their eyes met. She was gazing at him with a rapt expression. It made him feel uncomfortable.

"My name is Agnes Leather," she said in a hushed voice, as if she were sharing a delightful secret. "I've seen you eating in here before."

He realized that there was no polite way of remaining silent, and so he said in an expressionless voice, "I ate here yesterday and the day before yesterday."

"That's right." She nodded. "I saw you both times. At noon yesterday, and then the day before a little later than that. At night I don't come here. I have a family. I eat home with them like everybody else in a small town." Her smile was warm and intimate, as if she would like to include him in her good fortune.

He did not know what to say to this, and asked himself idly if she was going to eat her haddock.

"You're wondering why I don't touch my fish?" she said, catching his eye.

"You haven't eaten much of it, have you?" He coughed discreetly and cut into his little steak, hoping that she would soon occupy herself with her meal.

"I almost never feel like eating," she said. "Even though I do live in a small town."

"That's too bad."

"Do you think it's too bad?"

She fixed her luminous eyes upon him intently, as if his face held the true meaning of his words, which might only have seemed banal.

He looked at the long horselike lower half of her face, and decided that she was unsubtle and strong-minded despite her crazy eyes. It occurred to him that women were getting entirely too big and bony. "Do I think what's too bad?" he asked her.

"That I don't care about eating."

"Well, yes," he said with a certain irritation. "It's always better to have an appetite. At least, that's what I thought."

She did not answer this, but looked pensive, as if she were considering seriously whether or not to agree with him. Then she shook her head from side to side, indicating that the problem was insoluble.

"You'd understand if I could give you the whole picture," she said. "This is just a glimpse. But I can't give you the whole picture in a lunchroom. I know it's a good thing to eat. I know." And as if to prove this, she fell upon her haddock and finished it off with three stabs of her fork. It was a very small portion. But the serious look in her eye remained.

"I'm sorry if I startled you," she said gently, wetting her lips. "I try not to do that. You can blame it on my being from a small town if you want, but it has nothing to do with that. It really hasn't. But it's just impossible for me to explain it all to you, so I might as well say I'm from a small town as to say my name is Agnes Leather."

She began an odd nervous motion of pulling at her wrist, and to his surprise shouted for some hotcakes with maple syrup.

At that moment a waitress opened the door leading into the street, and put down a cast-iron cat to hold it back. The wind blew through the restaurant and the diners set up a clamor.

"Orders from the boss!" the waitress screamed. "Just hold your horses. We're clearing the air." This airing occurred every day, and the shrieks of the customers were only in jest. As soon as the clouded glass shone clear, so that the words GREEN MOUNTAIN LUNCHEONETTE in reverse were once again visible, the waitress removed the iron cat and shut the door.